The King's Prerogative

Iain Colvin

Clink Street

Published by Clink Street Publishing 2019

Copyright © 2019

First edition.

The author asserts the moral right under the Copyright, Designs and Patents Act 1988 to be identified as the author of this work.

All rights reserved. No part of this publication may be reproduced, stored in a retrieval system or transmitted, in any form or by any means without the prior consent of the author, nor be otherwise circulated in any form of binding or cover other than that with which it is published and without a similar condition being imposed on the subsequent purchaser.

ISBNs:
978-1-913136-24-6 paperback
978-1-913136-25-3 Ebook

For my dad, who instilled in me from an early age a love of reading and a fascination for the events of the Second World War.

And mum, I miss you every day.

Author's Note

This is a work of fiction, however the vast majority of the events from 1941–42 described in this book are real and in the public domain. I have invented a very few additional elements to aid the telling of the story.

Prologue

Saturday 10th May, 1941

The Messerschmitt Bf 110 night fighter continued to fly westward, no more than a few hundred feet off the ground. The pilot had flown over Alnwick Castle more than half an hour before and he knew he had to be close to his destination by now. He became more anxious with each minute that passed, straining to see through the darkness, willing the landing lights to come into view.

Finally he saw them. He climbed to ensure he cleared a group of hills he had memorised from his map, and as the plane levelled out he could see the landing strip in the distance. A faint double line of lights marked the RAF emergency landing ground, and the pilot breathed out again. Almost there. The plan was for him to approach from the west to provide a safer landing for the twin-engined aeroplane. He overflew Dungavel House and headed towards the coast. A few minutes later he crossed the Clyde coast over West Kilbride. The plane circled above the wide estuary and released its two 900-litre drop-in fuel tanks which had provided the extra capacity needed for the flight from Bavaria. The pilot then turned east once more, flying over the southern outskirts of Glasgow on the approach to the landing strip.

Except the landing strip had gone. He couldn't see the lights. Were they obscured by trees? He strained every sinew as he willed them to come back into view. He had to think fast. Should he abort the mission? It was too late for that, he had already gone beyond the point of no return. With the drop tanks gone there was no guarantee he'd have enough fuel to reach Aldergrove. There was nothing else to do, he had to continue as planned. The lights had definitely been there before, perhaps there was a fault in the electrics? He had to take the gamble that they were still waiting for him. But he couldn't risk a landing in pitch dark. Not only would it be impossible to gauge the height from the ground on approach, there was every chance of hitting a tree.

The pilot came to a grim decision. He pulled the column back and climbed into the night sky. Once the plane levelled out again, he opened the cockpit canopy. He undid his harness and tried to pull himself out of his seat but the air pressure prevented him from doing so. He realised that there was no alternative but to turn the plane upside down and literally fall out of the plane.

He rolled the plane onto its back and this time gravity overcame the air pressure and he fell out of the cockpit. As he cleared the fuselage, his ankle caught the tail of the Messerschmitt and a searing pain shot through his foot. He pulled his parachute cord and briefly lost consciousness. The cold night air quickly caused him to regain his senses and he heard the explosion as his plane crashed into the countryside below. He could make out the dark outline of the ground rushing to meet him and several seconds later he hit the earth hard and tumbled over and over.

It was shortly before midnight and Rudolf Hess, deputy leader of Germany's Nazi party, had arrived in Scotland.

Chapter 1

Saturday 15th January, 1983.

It was one of those bright, brisk Scottish winter mornings that made everything seem possible. The sky was as crisp and clear as ice. The sun had barely managed to heave itself over the horizon, the effort in doing so draining it of any prospect of warming the air this side of April. Craig Dunlop stood looking out to sea as his dog busily sniffed a lamp post, making the most of its Saturday excursion. In the far distance, the ferry rounded the point that guarded the western approach to Loch Ryan and turned towards Craig. He looked at his watch. 9:10. Bang on time.

He breathed in deeply and the sea air stung his lungs. The cobwebs from the night before slowly began to blow away into the cold breeze. It had been a good party. One of those impromptu nights where he'd invited his friends back for a few beers and before he knew it the stereo was on and there had been dancing and more drinking and more laughing. The only thing missing had been his girlfriend, Fiona. His ex-girlfriend, Fiona.

It had been Craig who'd broken it off and there had barely been a day since that he hadn't regretted his stupidity. They'd had a row about something and nothing. No, that wasn't correct. Craig knew exactly why they rowed. He'd seen her talking to another student. Laughing with him. A good-looking student. Better looking than Craig anyway, or so he thought. He couldn't control the overwhelming jealousy that clouded his judgement in the minutes afterwards. He accused Fiona of two-timing him, even though he didn't actually believe that she was. It was just him getting his retaliation in first. He knew she was out of his league, and he'd convinced himself that sooner or later she'd get fed up with him and move on. Even though the fear was without a shred of foundation, Craig was convinced that sooner or later he'd be dumped and he couldn't bear the thought of that. So he contrived the argument. She told him not to be so immature. That only made Craig more aware of his shortcomings as a boyfriend. He'd stormed off in a strop, and didn't look back. And that was that. Fiona had phoned and written but by that time Craig had wrapped himself in the security blanket of his blind obstinacy. And then one day the phone didn't ring any more, and too late he realised with every fibre in his body that he wanted it to. All this happened over a year ago and he hadn't seen her since. But today, like most days, in the quiet moments he found himself thinking about her.

Craig continued to stare at the loch. It may have been the hangover, or his regrets about Fiona, or a combination of the two, but today he felt more than ever that the love-hate relationship he had with his home town was becoming a hate-hate relationship. He looked across at the ferry terminal and smiled ruefully at Stranraer's crest above the entrance. The town's Latin motto read 'Tutissima Statio'. It translated as 'safest of harbours'. The irony wasn't lost on him. The hills that provided a finger and thumb of green landscape on either side of Loch Ryan provided shelter from the vagaries of the North Channel beyond. Most people only passed through on their way to and from Northern Ireland. Not Craig though. He wasn't passing through. What was he doing with his life? He was twenty-five, reasonably good looking, doing reasonably well at work, he lived reasonably comfortably, was reasonably happy. Hmmmmm, maybe that was the problem. Maybe in another twenty years he'd still be going to the same parties and he'd still be reasonably comfortable, reasonably successful, reasonably happy. Safe, living his risk-free life in his little risk-free town. He wondered if Stranraer's motto could be more accurately translated as 'most comfortable of dormitories'.

He took a last breath of sea air. 'Come on Guinness, let's go.' He tugged at the lead and the Doberman obediently fell into step beside Craig. They crossed the road and headed towards the centre of town where the promise of freshly baked rolls prompted Craig to quicken his step just a little.

Fifteen minutes later Craig reached his parents' house and called a greeting as he opened the back door, allowing Guinness to run past him and straight into his basket at the other side of the kitchen. Although the dog was officially Craig's it had always lived at his parents'. When Craig moved out to his own place shortly after starting in the bank, his mum and dad agreed that it made sense not to make Guinness move out too.

The portable television was showing Saturday Superstore but no one was in the kitchen watching Keith Chegwin. Craig deposited the bag of rolls on the worktop and picked up the newspaper sitting there. As usual, he immediately turned to the back page and started to read about the latest crisis affecting Scottish football. From the corner of his eye he was aware of his dad making his way through the hall and as he came into the kitchen, Craig looked up and said, 'I don't know why you still buy this paper, Dad. You should invest in something proper like the Glasgow Herald.'

Peter Dunlop stood in the doorway, holding the wooden handle. Friends used to comment on how much Craig resembled his father. In his old Navy pictures, the tall, dark-haired young man with warm eyes and a cheeky grin looked like he could have been Craig's brother. Not at that moment though. His dad looked all of his sixty-two years.

Craig crossed the room towards him. 'What's wrong, Dad?'

'The hospital just phoned. There's been some bad news. It's your grandad, he passed away during the night.'

The news wasn't unexpected but it still came as a shock to Craig. A flood of childhood memories momentarily flicked through his mind, as if he'd just summoned up then fanned through a hundred old photographs.

'Where's Mum?'

'In the front room.'

Craig went through to the living room where he found his mother sitting with a cup of tea. Marion Dunlop was fifty-five years old, with dark hair, piercing eyes and the energy of a woman half her age. But today the energy had drained from her and to Craig she looked smaller than usual. Craig's older sister Helen sat next to her on the sofa with her arm round her, her head nestled against her mother's shoulder.

'Hi Mum. I'm so sorry.' He knelt down and gave her a hug.

'I know son. It's for the best though. He's in a better place'. His mum tried to smile, and Craig could see that she'd been crying.

And that was all that was said on the subject. His family wasn't one for overt shows of emotion to be fair. It's probably what they'd call a good Presbyterian upbringing, thought Craig. His grandad, his maternal grandfather that is, had been ill for some time. He'd been in the hospital near where he lived in Bellshill for months and months. They all knew that it was unlikely that he'd ever get back out, but they lived in hope that he'd recover sufficiently to spend his last days with his family. But it wasn't to be. They had gone through to visit as often as they could. His mum made the trip every other week which was a bit of a trek all the way from Stranraer considering she didn't drive. He'd held on like the stubborn old goat he could be, until just a week shy of his eighty-fifth birthday. A good innings in anyone's book considering he'd smoked like a chimney since he was fourteen. The cigarettes killed him in the end, like so many others who had lived through the Second World War.

The funeral was held the following Thursday, at Daldowie Crematorium in the east side of Glasgow, followed by a small gathering at the Golden Gates hotel in Mount Vernon. It was good to see the family all together again, thought Craig. Good for his mum, anyway. On occasions like these; weddings, christenings, funerals, he was always reminded that he had a very small family. His parents were both only children, so he only had a handful of distant cousins and a few close friends of the family whom he'd always called aunt or uncle. At least they'd had the presence of mind to book the smaller of the function rooms in the hotel. Craig made sure he got round to talk to everyone and hear their news and he promised to come and visit them soon. His dad came over and touched him on the arm. Craig took the hint and followed him over to a quiet corner where the remnants of the buffet lay on a table against the wall.

'How are you doing?'

'I'm okay Dad, Mum's being strong as usual.'

'Yes, she is. I'm glad we're staying in Glasgow tonight, it'll give her a chance to relax this evening hopefully.' Peter looked over at his wife, who was listening to two grey-haired aunts chatting in hushed tones. A smile broke across her face and she glanced across at Peter.

'Your mum asked me to get her another cup of tea. I just wanted to check that you're still okay to go into town with me tomorrow?'

Craig remembered that his father had made an appointment with the solicitor to sort out his grandad's affairs. He couldn't work out if Peter wanted the company or if his father thought that Craig might appreciate escaping the clutches of Marion's relatives, aunts and all, for an hour or two.

'I'll come with you Dad, no problem.'

The King's Prerogative

The next morning was spent visiting old neighbours and drinking cups of tea before going back to the hotel for lunch. By the time Peter and Craig left in a taxi to travel the few minutes into Glasgow city centre they were ready for a change of scenery. Peter was quite talkative in the taxi. Craig wasn't sure if it was because they'd escaped or because his father felt good to be back in Glasgow. He suspected it was a bit of both. Glaswegians always felt good to be back in their home town. They'd moved to Stranraer when Craig was a young teenager, his father having secured a better job down there. At first Craig really liked it, especially the novelty of living beside the water. He'd learned to sail GP14s and pull twenty-seven-foot whalers, and he even sailed across to Ulster or the Isle of Man, or up to Campbeltown on occasion when a friend had invited him to crew his racing yacht. He had lots of friends. He had a good job too, straight from school into the bank. But then one by one his friends started to leave, to go to university or to start exciting careers in the Central Belt or in England. And one day Craig realised that he was in the minority, left behind as the majority of his friends moved away to kick start their lives elsewhere.

He was shaken out of this morbid re-examination of his life by the taxi pulling up outside a row of impressive looking Victorian offices in Blythswood Street.

'That'll be two pound ten gents, when you're ready.'

'I'll get this, you can buy me a pint later,' said Craig. He handed over two notes and a fifty pence piece to the driver. 'Keep the change, pal.'

'Cheers.'

Father and son got out of the taxi and looked up. It had begun to drizzle. They walked up the few steps to the main door of what looked like a suite of offices. An information board told them that the office they were looking for was on the first floor. They climbed a wide staircase that doubled back on itself and arrived at a door with 'Beveridge &

Clark, solicitors and notaries public' written on the frosted glass panel that formed the top half. Craig and Peter entered and closed the door behind them. They could see a small row of seats and opposite them, behind a large oak desk, sat an attractive young secretary who was dwarfed by a typewriter twice her size and probably twice her age. She greeted them with a small smile.

'Good afternoon, gentlemen. How may I help you?'

'We have an appointment with Mr. Rodgers at two-thirty. Sorry, we're a bit early'.

'Not at all, you must be Mr Dunlop. Please take a seat, I'll tell Mr Rodgers you're here.'

She stood up and walked over to a door sandwiched between two identical doors on the far wall of the office. She knocked briefly and entered. Craig looked around as they waited for her to return. The walls were tastefully decorated in a light green regency striped wallpaper. On each wall hung a print of what could be described as a typical Highland Scottish scene, with a brass lamp above it to draw attention to the dreariness of the landscape depicted. Each painting was different, and yet the same, mused Craig. Probably by the same artist. He couldn't help thinking that the office probably hadn't changed much in thirty years.

'Mr Rodgers will see you now.'

'Thank you.'

The secretary showed them in to a small office. Craig noted the same wallpaper but this time there were no landscape paintings, only several large filing cabinets, three leather chairs, a desk and a large sash and case window facing on to Blythswood Street.

'Mr Dunlop, so nice to see you again.' A tall, grey-haired man dressed in a double-breasted grey suit came out from behind the desk and shook Peter's hand. He couldn't be much younger than eighty-five himself, thought Craig drily, thinking of his grandad.

'And you must be Craig.' More handshaking. 'I'm Thomas Rodgers, pleased to meet you. Please, take a seat.'

They sat down in the leather chairs while Thomas Rodgers took his seat across the other side of the desk.

'Firstly, let me say how sorry I was to hear about your father-in-law's passing. Please give my sincere regards to Mrs Dunlop, I assume she's with her family this afternoon?'

'Yes, the funeral was yesterday and we drive back to Stranraer this evening.'

'Yes, yes, I understand. Well, this shouldn't take too long. These things usually take longer to bring to a conclusion but as you've had power of attorney for your father-in-law's affairs these last five years, and the estate is small, I saw no reason for you to have to make another long journey in the coming weeks.' He gave a weak smile. So, thought Craig, no hidden millions then. He knew his grandfather had worked hard his whole life, first on farms and then as a delivery man for a local butcher, but he had lived modestly. Craig didn't even think he'd been abroad in his life. And he included England in that definition.

'Mr McLean's flat was rented as you know, although the furnishings were his. I believe they're in storage?'

'Yes, that's correct. We put them into storage when he had to move out of the flat and into hospital.'

'Quite. I have his will in front of me here.' Thomas Rodgers fished out a pair of wire-framed glasses from his breast pocket and put them on. 'You can of course take this with you for Mrs Dunlop, but in essence everything passes to her. That includes the savings in Mr McLean's bank account, in the region of seven hundred pounds as you know, and his personal effects. In addition, he has stipulated that the following items be given to family members as follows. To you, his silver pocket watch and chain, as a token of his deep affection. To Master Craig Dunlop – I do apologise, Mr McLean's will was written some time ago – a brown leather document wallet which I believe you are already aware of.

And finally to Miss Helen Dunlop, a necklace and a pair of earrings from J. Macintyre & Son, jewellers, which belonged to the late Mrs McLean. Now, I just need your signature here Mr Dunlop, and that concludes our business for today.'

Thomas Rodgers handed over a form to Craig's father and it was duly signed and handed back. A copy of the will was put in an envelope for Craig's mother's attention then the three men stood up, shook hands again and Thomas Rodgers showed them out, offering his commiserations once more.

'That was short and sweet.'

'Yes, I suppose there wasn't much more to be said or done.'

'What do you think Mum will do with the money?'

'Oh you know your mother, she'll probably splash out and buy the dog a new collar or something.'

They allowed themselves a brief laugh as they stepped out into the fresh air again. The rain was getting heavier. The grey streets reflected the mood of the low, brooding clouds. The two men hurried the few yards to the nearest taxi rank. Luckily no one else was queuing so they jumped in the first cab and told the driver where they were going.

'I can't believe Grandad remembered that I was fascinated with that old wallet when I was younger.'

'Remember? How could he forget? Every time you came with us to visit him you made a bee line for it. Do you remember how you used to open it up, take out all the old cigarette cards, line them up, and put them back together again? You used to play with that wallet for hours.'

'Yeah, not exactly the best example to set a young boy growing up was it – dozens of old cigarette cards. They were great though. All those old footballers. And the German cards too, from before the war so Grandad said. Pictures of ships and planes and generals with big moustaches. I can still see them all. Was it true what he said about who the wallet belonged to?'

'Definitely. He could prove it too – it was in all the papers at the time. For a brief time your grandad was world famous. He liked to tell his mates down the pub that he was at any rate.'

'Well I don't expect it's everyone who could say they own a wallet given to them by Rudolf Hess himself.'

Chapter 2

Marion and Helen Dunlop had packed and were ready to go when Peter and Craig arrived back at the hotel. They thanked the staff for looking after them so well and went out to the car park.

'What would you rather do? Go straight home?'

'What time is it?' asked Marion.

'Just after half three.'

'It would make sense to swing by the storage place first before we head home. Is that okay?'

'Of course.'

'Mrs Simpson said she would take the dog out and feed him, so we don't need to get back in a hurry.'

Peter Dunlop smiled as he recognised the hidden meaning in his wife's words. 'It's okay, I won't drive too fast.'

Craig's mum smiled. She'd smiled a lot that day, in between the tears. Before long they arrived at the storage facility, which was really only a series of lock-ups in a secured building supplies yard.

'You stay here, I won't be long, they shut at four-thirty,' said Marion, and she climbed out the car and disappeared into the office to speak to the man in charge.

'She wants some time to herself,' said Helen.

'She's allowed, I suppose,' said Craig.

Ten minutes later Marion arrived back, carrying a smallish cardboard box. She settled herself in the front seat then turned round to face her children.

The King's Prerogative

'This is for you, Helen,' she said, handing her daughter a blue velvet jewellery case about the size of a dinner plate.

'Oh!' said Helen as she carefully took the case from her mum. She undid the small metal catch and opened the case to reveal a necklace and earrings. Clearly old but timelessly, beautifully elegant. 'I don't know what to say'.

'You don't need to say a word'. Marion smiled at her then turned to her son. 'This is for you, Craig.' She fished out a large leather wallet from the box on her lap and gave it to Craig. Craig recognised it immediately even though it must have been ten years since he'd last seen it. He suddenly felt a pang of guilt. He hadn't seen his grandad often enough in the past few years and now it was too late. He hadn't known his paternal grandfather. He had died in the war when Peter was just a bit younger than Craig was now. His world was shrinking even smaller, or so it felt to him in that moment.

He turned the wallet over. It felt warm and familiar in his hands. It was ten inches long but right now it seemed smaller than he remembered. He decided that most things from childhood tend to be smaller when revisited in adulthood. His grandad had kept it for years in the old shoe box, with newspaper cuttings kept from the time when Davy McLean had his moment in the glare of the world's press. Craig ran his hands across the small gold monogrammed letters embossed in one corner. A.H. His grandfather had told him that the airman he found that morning identified himself as Alfred Horn.

'It used to be in a shoe box, remember?'

'It's still here.' She reached across and gave the battered old shoe box to Craig, who rested it on his lap and started leafing through the old clippings inside. Marion then turned to her husband. 'And this is for you, from my dad.' She held out her hand and offered her husband a beautiful old pocket watch on a long silver chain.

'Thanks, love, it's a lovely keepsake,' said Peter Dunlop, taking the watch and opening it carefully to look at the intricate face. 'It was good of your dad to want me to have it.' He looked up. 'But hang on, how did you know? You haven't even read what it says in the will.'

Marion looked over her shoulder at her two children in the back seat, and she beamed. 'For a clever man your dad can be a bit slow at times, can't he?' She squeezed his hand. 'You might have had the power of attorney, but he was my father, of course I knew that he wanted you to have it.'

With the funeral over, Craig took advantage of a quiet weekend. He phoned his mate Kenny to find out where the guys were going to be on Saturday night and he joined them for a couple of pints before saying goodnight as the rest set off to whatever party was happening that weekend. It wasn't that Craig didn't fancy going, in fact he'd been specifically invited by the hostess who pleaded with him a fortnight before. 'Please come Craig, it'll be great, I've booked the Downshire and Bobby's going to deejay.' But he felt tired and he fancied a quiet one, so he left them to it and headed home after stopping off at the Sun Kai to pick up a char sui curry with fried rice. Craig lived about a hundred yards along the street from his parents' house. Not by design, but the landlord was a friend of Kenny's dad and Craig was given first refusal on renting it when it became available. Craig loved it, it was on two floors with a huge living room downstairs and two bedrooms, a bathroom and a kitchen/dining room upstairs. Great for parties even if his neighbours didn't always agree with him on that point. Still, it was freedom of sorts.

The Sunday dawned grey, wet and cold. Craig couldn't be bothered going for the papers but in the end he dragged himself along to the newsagent-stroke-mini market and came out with an armful, a forest of Sunday supplements and a packet of dog treats for Guinness. He sauntered up the street and popped in to see his parents. His mum was in the kitchen and waved as she saw Craig come round the back of the house. He kissed her and she put the kettle on. She asked him if he'd been out the previous evening. Craig thought about telling a white lie but he guessed she had probably already been told the truth by Mrs Jamieson next door who seemed to have spies everywhere. His dad heard their voices and came in to check that the kettle was on, said hello to Craig, thanked him for getting the papers and disappeared through to the front room with the *Sunday Mail* and the *Sunday Post*. Helen breezed down the stair, through the kitchen and out the back door, pausing only to pinch Craig's waist and tell him that he was getting fat. Craig grabbed a tea towel and flicked it at her as she dodged out the door which was Guinness's cue to jump up from his basket and bolt out the door into the garden.

And life goes on, thought Craig.

He stayed for dinner mainly because his mum had forced him to. It never ceased to amaze Craig that his mother never stopped feeding people. If it wasn't breakfast, dinner or tea it was a snack around ten o'clock, or a wee sandwich to keep him going about half past three, or oatcakes and cheese after *Coronation Street*. It was her west of Scotland way of telling you that she loved you. Craig had decided that today was not the day to refuse the offer of Sunday dinner so he helped his mum peel the veg and they chatted about what the week ahead had in store and don't forget that it's so-and-so's birthday. Craig finally took his leave after roast chicken, roast potatoes, carrots, gravy, lemon meringue pie with ice cream, coffee and the obligatory oatcakes and cheese. It was only just gone five o'clock when he got home so he rescued a handful of clean shirts from the tumble dryer and ironed them. Good, he thought, they wouldn't nag him from the corner of the kitchen for the rest of the evening.

He was just about to go downstairs with a coffee to watch some television when his eye fell on the shoe box sitting on the bottom shelf of his kitchen unit. He picked it up, sat down at his dining table and took out the contents. He opened out the newspaper cuttings and read through them. They were all dated from May 1941, and some featured photographs of his grandfather as a younger man, standing next to the wreck of an aeroplane which bore the distinctive markings of a World War Two German cross. The headlines were variations of 'Scots farmer captures downed German pilot' and some, printed a few days later, stated that the farmer had in fact captured Rudolf Hess, deputy leader of the Nazi party and third in the chain of command of Nazi Germany, with nothing more than a pitchfork. Craig took the wallet out and felt its warm leather again. It was bound by a thin leather lace. Craig loosened it and unfolded the wallet. Opened, it had three compartments, and Craig put his hand in the middle compartment and brought out the cigarette cards that were so familiar to him.

He took a sip of coffee then carefully laid out the cards on the table. They were all there, just as he'd remembered. He reached over to pick one up when his elbow caught the handle of his coffee mug, spun it round and tipped it on its side, spilling the hot liquid all over the table. 'Shit, shit, shit, shit!' Craig made a grab for the mug but only succeeded in scattering cards, wallet and mug across the table and on to the floor. He grabbed a tea towel from the kitchen and mopped the coffee up, trying to be as delicate as possible. Two towels later he had just about succeeded in mopping up the damage made on the table. He retrieved the wet cards and laid them out on the worktop, which he'd lined with kitchen roll. Thankfully they didn't look too bad. A couple were completely ruined but the rest looked salvageable. He picked up the wallet from the floor and examined it. It had escaped the worst of the mess, thank God. Craig opened each of the flaps to check if the compartments inside were wet. The first one was fine, as was the second one. The third one, the right-hand flap, was a bit damp, and Craig saw that the lining at the bottom of the right hand flap had ripped and there was a tear roughly three inches long at the bottom.

Did I do that? he wondered. Christ, the thing has survived for forty-odd years and I've had it two days and practically destroyed it, thought Craig, cursing to himself. It was then that he saw a creamy yellow *something* in the space made between the torn pieces of lining. He examined the gap more closely and realised whatever was inside was made of paper. He stopped for a moment, in two minds about what to do. He didn't want to ruin the wallet completely but at the same time the itch of his curiosity had to be scratched. Craig went to the kitchen drawer and selected the sharpest knife he had. He sat down, adjusted the lamp beside him so it provided the best light possible, and slowly cut away at the tear in the lining. At first he was scared to use too much force, but he quickly realised he had to be quite firm and after a minute or so he managed to increase the tear from three inches long to five inches. He reached inside with a finger. It was definitely a piece of paper. He managed to grab the edge with his index finger and middle finger but whatever it was was too big to fit through the hole. He picked up the knife and cut the lining again. This time he reached in and was able to pull the piece of paper out. He placed it on the table in front of him and dried his hands on the knees of his jeans before picking it up once more. It was four inches wide by six inches long, folded twice. Craig delicately unfolded the paper and laid it down flat. It read:

Iain Colvin

> Sandringham,
> Norfolk.
>
> 25th April 1941

The German airman who carries this letter of safe conduct is using it as a sign of his genuine wish to give himself up to the appropriate authorities. He is unarmed and will identify himself as Hauptmann Alfred Horn. He is to be well looked after, to receive food and medical supplies as required, and to be removed from any danger zone as soon as possible.

On behalf of His Gracious Majesty, King George,

Lieutenant-Colonel William Spelman Pilcher, DSO
3rd Battalion Grenadier Guards (Ret).

Chapter 3

Monday 14th February, 1983.

Claire Marshall walked towards the staff room in Stranraer Academy. The twenty-seven-year-old teacher had just come from a double period of 3rd year English and she needed a coffee. This particular 3rd year class hadn't grasped the reality that playtime was over and it was time for the serious business of knuckling down and getting ready for their 'O' grades the following year. The really annoying thing was that even though she knew this was now her second full year in the job she still felt that she was on probation. And she also hated the fact that part of the reason she felt like that was because the department head had taught her when she herself was a spotty eighteen-year-old pupil at the school nine years ago. It didn't help that at five foot four most eighteen-year-olds were taller than her. She still had to catch herself before she called Mr Ross 'sir' instead of Mr Ross. Worse still, he'd told her to call him Patrick, which gave her the creeps. Especially when he stood too close in the staff room and his breath smelled of onion.

'Miss Marshall. Phone call for you.'

Grace, one of the school secretaries, had seen Claire walk past the office and stuck her head out of the door to call after her. 'Second time he's called this morning, I think you've got an admirer.'

'Shut up, Grace. I told you, I'm saving myself for Harrison Ford,' said Claire as she picked up the receiver that was sitting on the secretary's desk. She put her hand over the mouthpiece. 'Anyway, I don't see many Valentine cards on your desk either,' she said, sticking her tongue out at the secretary. They shared a giggle before Claire composed herself again.

'Hello, Claire Marshall speaking.'

'Hi Claire, it's Craig Dunlop. How are things with you?'

'Oh, hi, Craig. Fine, fine. Busy, busy, you know. What's up?' The surprise of hearing his voice out of the blue caused her face to burn with a sudden embarrassment she couldn't control. She hoped to God that he didn't pick up on the fact that she was having a minor panic.

'Em, I wondered if you'd have some time free one night this week, I wanted to ask your advice on something.'

'Of course, what can I do?' She was delighted that he'd phoned her and was only too eager to meet up. A spark of excitement tingled through her fingers and toes.

'I'd value your professional opinion on something. There's a drink in it for you.'

'Sounds very mysterious,' laughed Claire. 'Ok, count me in. It'll cost you more than one drink though.'

'Great. When's the best time for you?'

Claire pushed her hair behind an ear.

'No time like the present. Say eight o'clock tonight?'

'Perfect. In the Ruddicot?'

'The Ruddicot's dead on a Monday, why don't we meet in L'Aperitif?'

'Sounds good. Okay, see you at eight.'

'Great. Just remember it's a school night though, don't go trying to get me drunk on Millisle Mindbenders.'

'Em, okay, I'll be on my best behaviour.'

Claire put the receiver down and winced. Why had she said that? Bloody hell, Craig was her best friend's wee brother. Plus she was a respectable English teacher at the town's respectable secondary school. There was a line to be drawn on any number of levels. Oh, bugger it, she thought on reflection. He was tall, good-looking and funny, and she had a massive crush on him. What else mattered? She thanked Grace and headed out towards the staff room. Grace gave her a look that said 'I knew it' and went back to her paperwork.

There was no shortage of drinking establishments in Stranraer and each had its own clientele. Some, the ones situated next to the bookmakers, were usually filled from opening to closing time with cigarette smoke and hardy regulars. Others were the haunts of local residents, local meaning those who lived within two blocks of said hostelry. For Craig and his friends, there was a circuit of half a dozen pubs they frequented on a regular or semi-regular basis. These were the Ruddicot Hotel (Friday night), the Royal Hotel (live band on a Saturday), and as the mood took them, the Stag's Head, the Downshire, the Grapes, the Burns, and the Coachman's, depending on who was out, what entertainment was lined up, and which pubs happened to be flavour of the month. For those evenings requiring an added element of sophistication, the place to go was L'Aperitif. Run by the same Italian family since just after the war, the restaurant served fabulous food and their small cocktail bar was famed for the delicious liquid concoctions dreamt up and served by Massimo, the maitre d' and host. Craig walked into the bar and looked around. The room was just about big enough to cope with customers who arrived early and fancied a pre-dinner drink, or those who wanted to take their time over postprandial coffees, ports or brandies. Craig was inwardly pleased to see that only two of the six tables were occupied, by the look of things by couples waiting to be shown through to the restaurant. There was no one propping up the bar or sitting on the four barstools lined up to his left. Massimo came through from the restaurant, saw Craig and shook his hand.

'Hello Craig, nice to see you my friend. I'll be with you in just one second.'

He escorted one of the couples through to their table then returned to the other side of the bar.

'Now then, I didn't see your name on the bookings for tonight. Just in for a drink?'

'Yes Massi, just catching up with a friend. Can I have a pint please. Lager.'

'Coming up.' Massimo selected the ideal glass from a shelf behind him and poured Craig's drink.

'Sixty-five pence please, Craig.'

Craig handed over the cash, picked up his glass and walked over to a seat as far away from the bar as he could, which took all of eight strides. He took the letter from the zip pocket of his jacket, unfolded it and read the contents for the hundredth time. It had been Helen who suggested asking Claire for help but Craig wasn't sure if she was being sarcastic at the time. After all, just because Craig had developed a bee in his bonnet didn't mean that someone coming to it cold would share his enthusiasm. He'd hummed and hawed for two weeks and eventually decided to do something about it even though he still wasn't sure if he'd look like an idiot. He looked up as Claire walked in. It must have started to rain again because she carried a small brolly and was shaking it as she made her way to the table. Craig noticed that under her coat she wore a red satin dress with a high collar, in a Chinese-style print. Maybe she's going on somewhere else after meeting me, he thought. He looked down at his jeans and jumper and felt decidedly scruffy. He smiled as she approached the table.

'Hi Claire, what can I get you?'.

'Gin and bitter lemon please.'

Craig bought the drink and returned to the table.

'Thanks for coming out on such an awful night.'

'It was either this or marking so believe me this was the better option. Anyway, you sounded very cloak and dagger on the phone earlier, what did you want to ask?'

Craig considered his words for a moment.

'I don't know if Helen ever told you much about our grandad, about what he did during the war?'

Claire had built herself up to expect a totally different conversation and was somewhat taken aback at this non sequitur, but to her credit she didn't show a trace of her disappointment. She now wished she hadn't worn her glad rags on a wet Monday night though.

'I can't remember if she did or not to be honest. Is that what you wanted to ask me about?'.

'Yes. Maybe it'll be easier if I gave you the potted family history.'

'Okay.' This was becoming weird, thought Claire.

Craig moved forward in his seat.

'Well, my grandfather used to be a farmer. A ploughman to be exact. During the war he lived and worked at a place called Floors Farm near Eaglesham. He was in his forties at the time so he wasn't called up. Anyway, one night in 1941, a plane crashed near the farm and my grandad was the first on the scene. To cut a long story short it turned out to be a big deal and... well, actually, maybe it would be quicker to let you see these.' Craig produced the newspaper cuttings and passed them across the table. Claire was by this time convinced that she had been transported into a parallel universe but she reasoned that she was here now and she enjoyed Craig's company even though he seemed oblivious to her charms, so she took the cuttings and dutifully read through each. After a few minutes of silence she looked up and met Craig's stare.

'Okay, I get the picture about your grandfather. It is a pretty remarkable story I agree. I assume you want to tell your grandad's story and get it published? Well, I'm flattered, but I don't think I'm the right person to do it justice, but if you like–'

'Oh no, no, sorry Claire, I haven't finished. My grandad left me a memento from that night, it was a wallet that was given to him by Hess himself, for his hospitality.'

'His hospitality?'

'Yes. Hess hurt his ankle in the crash, or rather, when he baled out before the crash. My grandfather helped him to his cottage and sat him down by the fire until the Home Guard came along and took Hess into custody. Hess gave him the wallet as a thank you.'

'And you now have the wallet?'

'Correct. He used to show it to me when I was a wee boy and tell me the story that went with it. He always made it into a big performance for my benefit. Anyway, when I took the wallet home after my grandad's funeral, I found this hidden in the lining. No one realised it had been there all these years.' He gave Claire the letter and waited till she read it before continuing. 'If that letter is what it appears to be, then it throws the whole story upside down. These press cuttings...' Craig picked up two in particular which were dated three weeks after Hess's arrival. 'These press cuttings say that Hess came to Scotland on a crazy whim, that Hitler disowned him saying he'd had some kind of brainstorm. That he just up and left on some mad scheme to try to convince Britain to make peace. But...'

'But this letter not only suggests that he was expected, but that he was expected by the Royal Family.'

'Exactly.'

'Jesus.'

'My thoughts precisely.'

They studied each other's faces for a long moment. 'I'll get us another drink,' said Craig and he went back up to the bar.

Claire found herself caught up in the moment, the gears in her head turning furiously as she tried to process a dozen thoughts at once. Craig came back with their drinks.

'But hold on,' said Claire. 'This has to be a prank.'

'Why?'

'There's no way the Royal Family would expose themselves like that. Britain was at war for heaven's sake'.

'I've been thinking about that for the past fortnight.

What if it had been a genuine peace offer? Maybe the only way Hess would make such a journey was if he was given a guarantee in advance that he would be received as the peace envoy he claimed to be. Maybe a letter of safe conduct was that guarantee.'

Claire caught his thread.

'That might explain why it was hidden. Maybe Hess didn't actually intend to use it because it would cause embarrassment to the King. The fact that it had been written and given to Hess at all was sufficient proof that his flight wouldn't be in vain.'

'That's what I think.'

'Wait a minute though. Why did Hess have it on him if he didn't intend to use it?'

'Pass. I don't know. I can't work that out.'

'Which brings us back to the question of whether it's genuine or an elaborate practical joke.'

'It does.'

'Are you sure this is *the* wallet Hess had with him?'

'What do you mean?'

'I mean, could your grandfather have bought the wallet and created the story around it because it was such a good story? You said yourself that he liked to make it into a performance.'

'Why would he go to those lengths? And even if he did, why would he conceal the letter inside? That particular letter. And who is, or was Lieutenant-Colonel William Spelman Pilcher?'

'Do you know what would be useful?' asked Claire.

'What?'

'If we could find someone who could authenticate the letter.'

Chapter 4

Tuesday 15th February, 1983.

It was twenty past three when Craig looked at the clock on the wall above the Ledger Desk. It was ten minutes until the branch was due to shut its doors and then with luck only another ninety minutes or so before they'd be finished for another working day. That was one of the things he liked about working at the bank; the hours were pretty good. Normally he'd be out by half past five, apart from the late sessions on a Thursday when the branch reopened at four-thirty and stayed open till six. It hadn't been all that busy today so Craig had cleared a backlog of filing and was now finishing off some letters.

'I will therefore be grateful if you would sign and return the attached bridging loan application form at your earliest convenience. Yours sincerely, etc., etc.'

He clicked the Dictaphone off, took out the small tape cassette, and went through to the secretaries in the back room. Jacqui and Jeanette were busily typing away, plugged in to their own bigger versions of the handheld recording machines. The combination of the earphones and typewriters had the effect of making them look like a pair of piano-playing doctors complete with stethoscopes. Jacqui saw Craig come in and took off her earphones. She was the same age as Craig and, having just returned from her honeymoon, she still had the flush of the newlywed about her.

'Uh oh. Here's trouble.'

Craig smiled. 'Me? Never.' He produced the microcassette with a flourish as if he was a conjurer producing the ten of hearts from thin air. He dropped it in Jacqui's in-tray. 'Ta-da!'.

'Wow, wonders shall never cease,' she said, for Jeanette's benefit.

Jeannette stopped typing and took off her earphones too. She was the senior of the two secretaries and this was her domain. She was in her late fifties, with short, stylish grey hair, and Craig thought of her as his second mum. She looked at her wristwatch with an equally theatrical wave of her hand.

'Well Jacqueline, would you look at that? Mr Dunlop has honoured us with his correspondence before five o'clock this evening. I do declare I might have to go and lie down.'

'You two are hysterical, do you know that? Did no one tell you that sarcasm is the lowest form of wit…'

'And is not appreciated in the best of circles,' chimed the ladies in unison. They all laughed.

Craig walked backed through to his desk. One of his colleagues pointed at a telephone lying off the hook. 'Phone call for you, Craig.'

'Thanks Sheena.' He picked up the receiver. 'Craig Dunlop speaking'.

'Craig, it's Claire.'

'Oh hi, Claire, how's things? Had any more thoughts since last night?'

'I have funnily enough, yes. I've just phoned a lecturer I used to have at Strathclyde Uni. Brian Irving his name is. I had him for a couple of terms when I was there. I phoned him on the off-chance because he teaches political science and I thought that he could point us in the right direction. Well it looks like we've aroused his curiosity and he said he'd help us. He's keen to speak to us and to find out more about the letter.'

'Fantastic! How did you leave it with him?'

'I assumed you'd want to speak to him sooner rather than later so I took the liberty of saying we'll phone him again tonight. I don't know what your plans are?'

'I've got absolutely no plans tonight. That sounds brilliant. Do you want to come round to mine later?'

'Tell you what, I'm using up the remains of a curry tonight, why don't you come round to mine once you finish, we can demolish it and then phone Brian.'

'Excellent. Helen's told me about your famous Ruby Murrays, I'm honoured.'

'You haven't tasted it yet. Okay, see you about six. Don't forget to bring the letter. You know where, don't you? Bayview Crescent. Number fourteen.'

'No problem, see you then. Oh and Claire?'

'Yes?'

'Thanks.'

'My pleasure.'

Craig put the phone down, got up from the desk and went over to the office photocopier. He'd brought the Hess letter with him to work because he thought it might be useful to make some copies of it to save wear and tear on the original, and it meant he could also give Claire a copy of her own. As he started up the machine and waited for it to produce the Photostats, he thought about the conversation with Claire and decided that he liked her. Maybe one day he might pluck up the courage to ask her out properly. But on reflection he knew he probably wouldn't. Not in the foreseeable future at least. Maybe eventually, after he'd got Fiona out of his system.

Jacqui brought through the letters for Craig to sign at a quarter to five. Craig did so, made sure the correct attachments were clipped to the correct letters, stuffed them in window envelopes and gave them to David, the office junior, to frank and post. He fetched his coat from the staff room, said goodnight to the few members of staff still finishing up and made his way round to the front office just as the manager, Mr Grant, opened the main door on his way in.

The King's Prerogative

'You getting off, Craig?'
'Yes Mr Grant, unless you need me for anything?'
'No, no, not at all. Football tonight?'
'Not till Thursday.'
'Jolly good. Have a good night then.'
'You too, sir.'

Craig stopped at the Coopers Fine Fare on the way home for some beer and wine to take along, and went home to pick up the wallet. He was about to go back out when he saw that the rain had started so he phoned a taxi and went to freshen up in the bathroom. Five minutes later he saw the mini cab pull up outside. He locked up and jumped in the back seat.

Just over a mile away Claire had learned her lesson from the night before and had decided that a pair of jeans and a baggy top were appropriate attire. When she opened the door to let Craig in, she remembered that he'd come straight from work and now she was the one who was underdressed. Well done hen, she thought.

'Come in, don't stand there getting wet.' She stood back and ushered him in.

'Hi, sorry I'm late', said Craig and gratefully stepped inside.

'Your timing's fine. Here, give me your coat.'

'Thanks. I brought something to drink.'

'You're a saviour, well done. Come through to the kitchen and talk to me, the curry's nearly ready.'

Craig followed her through a narrow L-shaped corridor to a kitchen at the far end. It was small but had enough room for a small table and two chairs. On the cooker, two pots were simmering away, and Claire opened the oven to check on some naan bread that was warming up.

'Take a seat,' said Claire and handed him a corkscrew-cum-bottle opener. 'And you're in charge of the drinks.'

'What do you fancy?'

'A glass of wine, please.'

Craig opened the bottle of wine and chose a beer for himself. He poured a glass for Claire and handed it to her as she stirred the curry.

'So what's this Brian like?'

'He's very clever, as you'd expect. I always felt a bit in awe of him. But the reason he sprang to mind is that he always encouraged you to challenge him and ask questions.

Craig took a sip of beer. 'That and the fact that he teaches political science. Not much use if he taught home economics,' he offered.

Claire laughed. 'Well yes, obviously. Grub's up.' She dished out a bed of rice on two plates, and ladled two scoops of steaming hot curry on top of each. She fetched the bread from the oven and they sat down.

'What did he say when you called him?' said Craig in between mouthfuls. 'This is delicious by the way.'

'Thanks, it's my *piece de resistance* from my uni days. Well after the usual pleasantries and chit-chat I asked him if he had a special interest in World War Two mysteries. When I mentioned Rudolf Hess, I heard him audibly groan on the line. Apparently there are more conspiracy theories swimming around Hess than there are for JFK, the moon landings and Jack the Ripper put together. I told him the story about your grandad and he made polite noises but I got the feeling that he'd heard it all before.'

'But the letter changed his mind?'

'Not at first. When I told him you had a wallet and there was a letter in it, I almost thought I could hear him scoff at how gullible I could be. But when I said that the letter was hidden in the lining, and I gave him the gist of what it said, he went quiet for ages. I thought I'd got cut off, but then he asked me to repeat what I'd said. I did, and he asked if I had the letter in front of me. I said I didn't but suggested I could get together with you and we'd phone him back.'

'That sounds encouraging. The first step has to be him taking us seriously, without that we're wasting our time.'

The King's Prerogative

Claire smiled. She liked the thought of there being an 'us'.
'What time did you say you'd ring him?'
'Seven o'clock.' She looked at her watch. 'It's gone seven, I'll bring the phone through, you put the dishes in the sink.'

Chapter 5

Brian Irving hadn't stopped since he'd received the telephone call from his former student earlier in the day. He had intended to finish some prep for a lecture he was due to give the following afternoon, but the phone call had knocked him off his stride. The forty-five-year-old had been studying, and then teaching, political history for most of his life. He always made a point of telling every new crop of students that it was healthy to regularly re-examine and reappraise historical events in the light of new facts or new insights. That said, he maintained a profound scepticism when it came to historical mysteries and associated conspiracy theories. Whether it was unexplained events like the finding of the *Marie Celeste*, the disappearances of Glenn Miller, Jimmy Hoffa or Lord Lucan, or convenient 'magical mystery' theories like the Bermuda Triangle, Brian Irving treated them all with a similar bored sense of doubt. But he didn't mock anyone else for wanting to believe in something that wasn't there. It was human nature to an extent. It was comforting to be able to offer an explanation for the puzzling or the confusing or the disconcerting, no matter how far-fetched or irrational the explanation might be. He didn't blame people for choosing to believe in UFOs, the Loch Ness monster or spontaneous human combustion, any more than he would deride anyone who believed in this religion or that religion or that the world was supported on the back of a giant turtle floating in the cosmos. He didn't believe in them himself because, as he said to his students, where's the evidence? If he was to apportion blame to anyone for the modern fascination with conspiracy theories it would be to controversial authors, like Erich von Däniken, who made a lot of money from advocating bizarre theories, and who in Brian's opinion were responsible for popularising the recent trait towards 'pseudohistory'. As he frequently told his students, 'If you're going to join the dots, join them with facts, not lazy speculation masking half-formed research.'

When Claire Marshall phoned that afternoon, he was first of all surprised to get her call, then pleased to hear from her again, then slightly disappointed in the fact that she'd been taken in by such an implausible story. But then she described how the letter came to be found and what it contained, and Brian had to admit that his interest was piqued despite his better judgement. The odds of course were stacked in favour of the story being completely fabricated and the letter a forgery, but the question that he had to ask himself was, why would someone go to the effort of creating such an opaque hoax? He didn't know this Craig Dunlop from Adam, and this letter was likely to turn out to be a 'Piltdown Man', and yet Claire was prepared to vouch for him and his story. Something in her voice had made the hairs on the back of his neck stand up. He decided that it was at least worth a look, and if it turned out to be a practical joke or a deliberate fraud, he should be able to expose it without too much effort. Since the phone call he'd spent a few hours in the university library and had already made several pages of notes as well as a list of questions to ask this Dunlop bloke. The telephone on his desk rang.

'Brian Irving.'
   'Hello, Brian. It's Claire Marshall again. Are you okay to speak?'
   'Hi Claire, yes, it's fine. Is your friend with you?'
   'Yes, he's here, hold on a second.' She passed the receiver to Craig.

'Hello, Doctor Irving, it's Craig Dunlop. Thank you for agreeing to help us.'

'Hello Craig, Claire's no doubt filled you in on our earlier conversation.' Brian took a breath before continuing. 'I have to be up front with you before we start. I explained to Claire that I must approach this from the standpoint that your wallet and letter are *not* genuine.' He paused briefly. 'I am sorry for your recent bereavement, and I'm not in any way casting aspersions on your late grandfather's character or his intentions, but you do understand that the chances are that the items are... well, not to put too fine a point on it, fake?'

Craig felt irked, but swallowed his indignation.

'I understand that you need to deal in facts, sir, and I can assure you that's how I'm approaching it too,' he said.

'Good. Now, first of all, can you read out exactly what the letter says?'

Craig read out the letter, slowly. Brian asked him to hold on a couple of times while his note-taking caught up with Craig's speech. Then he asked Craig to describe how the wallet came to be in his grandfather's possession. After Craig related the whole story, Brian asked some follow-up questions then paused for a long moment while he read through the notes he had taken down. Finally he spoke again.

'How much do you know about Hess's flight to Scotland?'

Craig told him he knew the timeline and the broad outline of events and the official explanation that Hess had come up with this self-imposed peace mission because he felt sidelined from Hitler's inner circle and thought that a grand gesture would restore him to the Fuhrer's good graces.

'Yes, that's the story that's been handed down over the years,' agreed Brian Irving.

'But the letter's existence would imply that there was a genuine peace offer after all,' added Craig. 'And that Hess's flight had been prearranged with the involvement of people from within the British establishment.'

'Quite so, *if* the letter is genuine. It's a big "if". You see, the biggest problem is that there are so many conspiracy theories around the whole mystery. And that lends itself to people seeing what they want to see, or inventing things that back up their pet theory.'

Craig was about to interrupt but Brian continued.

'I've visited the Hess affair during my studies over the years and I'm familiar with all the claims and counter claims. For instance, *was* it prearranged? Why did he risk the flight at all? Who could have been involved on the British side? Was it carried out under Hitler's orders or at the very least, with his knowledge? Did British Intelligence lure Hess to fly to Scotland through diplomatic back channels?'

'Did they?'

'Well if they did, they didn't capitalise on such an astounding propaganda coup. In fact they did their best to cover up the whole affair. Goebbels himself commented on the British missing such a gift-wrapped open goal. It's not something he would have passed up if the situation had been reversed. But the trouble with all these conflicting theories is that they're all based on circumstantial evidence. There's no smoking gun, as it were.'

'Do you think this letter might be the smoking gun?'

'It's far too early to say, and on its own I'd have to say that it's unlikely.'

Craig thought for a moment then asked the question that had been bothering him. 'Doctor Irving, why would Hess have the letter on him and yet conceal it the way he did?'

Brian Irving paused. 'Now that is the $64,000 question. And I confess that's what has me intrigued. Let's for a moment assume that the letter is genuine. There are two key questions to ask. One: why was the letter written? Two: why did Hess have it and not use it? Claire told me about your discussion last night and I tend to agree with your assessment that the letter would have been written as a token of good faith. Without it Hess wouldn't have committed to such a potentially dangerous journey.'

'But why risk flying to Scotland at all? Wouldn't it have been safer to meet whoever he was due to meet in neutral territory?'

'The obvious answer to that is perhaps he came to Scotland because the person he intended to meet couldn't leave the country. There's been all kinds of speculation about who that could have been. And there's another reason why he could have risked the flight – you also have to remember the timing. Germany wanted Britain out of the war before June 1941.'

'Why, what happened in June 19–?' Craig pulled up short. '– Hitler invaded the Soviet Union.'

'Indeed. That was the main reason Hess made the flight at that time. The stakes were huge and the clock was ticking.'

Craig mulled this over. Brian continued. 'Moving on to the second part of the $64,000 question, we can have a pretty good guess as to why Hess would have had the letter on his person. A letter of safe conduct performs two functions. Firstly, it provides an element of security for the bearer. He knows that if necessary he can use it to ensure fair treatment. Secondly, it provides proof that the bearer is who he says he is.'

'But Rudolf Hess was extremely well known. He was the deputy leader of the Nazi Party.'

'He was. But let's say the plan went wrong and Hess was captured. Let's say he fell into the wrong hands. If you were him, what would you do?'

Craig turned this over in his mind. 'I'd ask to be taken to whoever was expecting me.'

'And Hess did exactly that. His first words on landing are reported as being 'Am I on the estate of the Duke of Hamilton? My name is Alfred Horn. Please tell the Duke I have arrived.' Let's say a message was relayed to the person – or people – expecting him. How would they know that a lone German airman captured in the middle of the night was who he claimed to be?'

'Because he would have been in possession of the letter,' said Craig.

'Exactly,' said Brian Irving.

'Of course. But he gave the wallet to my grandfather and said nothing about the letter hidden in the lining. Why would he do that?'

'We can't possibly know for sure forty years after the event. The details of his capture are extremely vague. But in contrast to the picture painted of him since, Hess was a careful man who planned meticulously and was very considered in his words and actions.'

'My grandfather said that when the Home Guard arrived at his cottage that night, there was pandemonium all around and yet Hess was the calmest man in the room.'

'That doesn't surprise me. So I think it would have been a deliberate decision by Hess. He didn't want the letter to be found. He may have given the wallet to your grandfather to hide it from his captors.'

'Why? To save the King from embarrassment?'

'Not as such. It wasn't signed by King George himself, only by, one presumes, an equerry. No, it's more likely that Hess decided not to expose the people who were expecting him. Any plans for peace discussions would have been guarded by those involved with the utmost secrecy, for obvious reasons. Anyone collaborating to undermine the war effort could have been hanged for treason. In the first hours of Hess's capture, the outcome of his mission must have been perched on a knife edge. Hess didn't know who to trust and presentation of the letter to the wrong people could have exposed those involved on the British side before the plan, whatever it was, had been put into effect. So the fact that the letter was hidden is what aroused my interest when Claire called me. Particularly when taken with another often overlooked fact from that night in May 1941. Hess announced himself as Captain Alfred Horn and that was who your grandfather and the Home Guard thought they had captured. But at some point in the course of the night Alfred Horn did something strange.'

Craig felt a chill run through him. 'Which was what?'

'He handed over his Iron Cross to his captors. He presumably wanted it delivered to whoever was expecting him as proof of his arrival. His Iron Cross would have been inscribed with Hess's own name, not that of Alfred Horn. That apparent inconsistency from a man as meticulous as Hess has always puzzled me. But it makes sense if his story was true and he had been expected by a welcoming committee. He needed to get an urgent message to the people waiting for him. The plan had gone awry and Hess was no doubt becoming increasingly concerned as time passed that no one had come to collect him. He was in the dark about what was happening and wanted to alert his guests that he had arrived, but he didn't want to use the letter of safe conduct. So he blew his own cover without wanting to blow theirs, as it were.'

Craig absorbed this. So far he'd heard nothing that didn't corroborate the authenticity of the letter and he could feel his excitement growing.

Brian Irving continued. 'But as I said, this is all speculation. To leave the theories aside for the moment, I thought you'd be interested to hear about some initial research I did this afternoon. I tried to find out who this Lieutenant-Colonel William Spelman Pilcher was.'

Craig looked at Claire and mouthed the word 'Pilcher'. 'What did you manage to find out?'

'Well he was born in 1888, served in the Grenadier Guards as the letter suggests, was involved in the British Military Mission to Poland in 1920 to 1921. He retired in 1936. He was a governor of the Royal Bank of Scotland...'

'How strange that he should be a governor of that bank,' interjected Craig.

'Why?'

'It's just that I work there. Sorry, I interrupted you, please go on.'

'Our Colonel Pilcher was then re-engaged by the army in 1939. And then nothing.'

'You mean you ran out of time today?'

'No, it means that all trace of him disappears from official records, or at least the ones I was able to reference.'

'Really?' Craig thought for a second. 'But it was during the war. Is that so unusual?'

'It is unusual if you're in *Who's Who* one minute and then suddenly you're not. Not even an obituary.'

'Could it have been an oversight?'

'I don't think it was. To all intents and purposes he was erased.'

Craig looked up at Claire again. She mouthed 'what?' at him, clearly frustrated that she couldn't follow the thread of the conversation without hearing both ends.

'Erased? What does that mean?' asked Craig.

'When someone has an entry in *Who's Who*, they continue to be included in each year's edition while they remain in office or continue to be prominent in their field. Even when they die, there's an obituary and then their biography is moved into *Who Was Who*, the companion publication. If they fall into obscurity, the same thing happens, they move to *Who Was Who*. The last entry for Pilcher was in 1943. Then nothing. Absolutely no record exists. No obituary, no entry in *Who Was Who*. His name is even missing from the general index of anyone who has ever appeared in *Who's Who* at any time in its history. And from what I can tell, there are no other official documents from either the army or the civil service records that would indicate what happened to him. It's as if he vanished after 1943.'

Craig processed this for a moment. 'What do you think it means?'

'I don't know. It's unheard of. I need to do more research before I can reach any conclusions. I have a feeling there could be more to Lieutenant-Colonel Pilcher than meets the eye. Is there any chance you can send me your letter, registered post, to my office here at the university? I'd like to study it and delve into this some more.'

'Of course, I'd be happy to do that. Would it be useful to meet up in person?'

'Yes it would, but let me do a bit more digging first. I've got Claire's number, shall I ring her when I've got more to tell you? I can't promise I won't hit a blind alley but I'll take it as far as I can.'

'That's all I can ask, Doctor Irving, thank you.'

'No, thank *you*, and please, call me Brian.'

Craig said goodbye and handed the receiver to Claire who confirmed the address and then said goodbye too. She put the receiver down and looked at Craig. 'What are you grinning at?' she asked.

'I think he's starting to take us seriously,' said Craig.

Chapter 6

Wednesday 2nd March, 1983.

In the two weeks since the telephone call with Brian Irving, Claire had sent off the letter as requested and Brian had rung her to confirm that he'd received it. Craig spent most of his spare time at the library, in the evenings and on the Saturday mornings before playing football in the local pub league. He'd devoured every book he could find on Hess, on how Germany conducted the war and about events in Britain during those early war years. It struck him that, with the benefit of what he now knew (or at least, what he believed to be true), a number of facts about those war days slotted into place. First of all, and most pertinently, in May 1941 it was clear that Britain was losing the war. Rommel was winning in North Africa, Greece had fallen, and German U-boats were sinking British shipping at an alarming rate. In addition to that, British cities were suffering a horrendous amount of damage and loss of life from the nightly bombing raids inflicted by the Luftwaffe. The received wisdom since the war was that in 1941 the British bulldog was at its most defiant as the country stood alone against the tyranny of the Nazi war machine. And Churchill with his cigar and his V for victory sign was the living embodiment of the Dunkirk spirit during those dark days.

The more Craig read, the more he came to believe that it wasn't quite as black and white as that. From a personal point of view, Churchill's own position wasn't as secure as post-war legend would have people believe. He had endured a confidence vote in the House of Commons on 7th May 1941, only a few days before Hess's flight. Even as late as 1942, every parliamentary byelection candidate who had the Prime Minister's backing was routed at the polls. There were a number of prominent politicians and establishment figures who favoured peace, including David Lloyd George, Lord Halifax, Lord Beaverbrook and Sir Samuel Hoare. Craig had come to the conclusion that the existence of a peace group in Britain in 1941 wasn't a strange idea after all.

More than anything, Craig kept himself busy at the library to keep his frustration at bay. It had been two weeks, and no word from Brian Irving. He had phoned Claire twice, she had popped into the bank once and Helen had brought her round to his parents' house a couple of times. 'Be patient' was what she told him. These things take time. He knew she was right but it didn't make him feel any calmer. In the end, she agreed to phone Brian during that week to ask how things were progressing. That made Craig feel a bit better, but only just.

He had only been home for a few minutes when there was a knock on the door. He looked at his watch. Ten past nine. He went downstairs, opened the door and was slightly thrown off guard to see a uniformed policeman and another man in a blue raincoat. The man in the blue raincoat spoke.

'Mr Dunlop?'

'Yes.'

The man in the blue raincoat held an identity card up for Craig to read. 'Detective Constable Jarvis. This is Constable McMillan. May we come in?'

Craig showed the policemen through to the living room and asked them to sit down. The phone rang. Craig looked at it. 'Do you need to answer that?' asked DC Jarvis.

Craig picked up the receiver. 'Hello, 2462?'

'Hello Craig? It's me.' His mum's voice was shaking.

'Mum, I'm sorry, I'll have to call you back,' and he put the receiver down.

'We've just been speaking to your parents, and your sister.'

'What's wrong? What's happened?'

'I'm afraid I have some bad news. I believe you know Miss Claire Marshall?'

'Yes, she's a friend.'

'I'm very sorry to have to tell you that she was found dead this evening.'

Craig looked from DC Jarvis to PC McMillan and back to the detective. He could feel the colour run from his face.

'What?' Craig looked blankly at the policeman, not comprehending. 'Dead?'

'Yes.'

'Are you sure? She can't be. Are you sure it's Claire?'

'Yes, it's Miss Marshall. She was found in her flat by a work colleague about four hours ago. She didn't show up at work today.'

'But how? How did it happen?'

'She was murdered, Mr Dunlop.'

'What?' Craig heard the words but they refused to register. It's not possible, it can't be possible.

'We'd like to ask you a few questions if you don't mind.'

Craig felt faint for an instant.

'Mr Dunlop, are you feeling alright? Can we get you a drink of water?'

'I just spoke to her on Monday.'

'Mr Dunlop, can we get you a glass of water?' He nodded at PC McMillan, who left the room and came back a minute later with a glass of water. He handed it to Craig, who drank half of it and then cradled the glass in both hands.

'Do you mind if we ask you a few questions?'

Craig heard the detective's words in the distance. He nodded without really hearing the question.

DC Jarvis took out a small notebook and pen. 'What was your relationship with Miss Marshall?'

'My relationship? She's a friend. Well, she's a friend of my sister's. Helen.'

'Have you ever been to her flat?'

'Yes, a few times.'

'When was the last time?'

'A couple of weeks ago.'

'Why was that?'

'She cooked me dinner. She was helping me with some research I'm doing.'

'You work in the Royal Bank here in Stranraer?'

'Yes, that's right. How did–'

'Your mother told us earlier. Were you and Miss Marshall seeing each other as a couple?'

'You mean, is she my girlfriend? No. We're friends. I've known her for years.'

'Do you know if she was seeing anyone?'

Craig frowned. 'No, I mean, I don't know. I don't think so. Helen would know better than me.'

'Do you have any money worries, Mr Dunlop?'

Craig was confused. 'Money worries? No. Like most people I live from pay day to pay day but I'm not in debt if that's what you mean. What's that got to do with Claire?'

DC Jarvis ignored the question and made some notes.

'Just one more question if I may. Do you know of any reason why anyone would want to kill Miss Marshall?'

'Kill her? No, of course not. She's a schoolteacher. Why would anyone want to kill her? How did it happen?'

DC Jarvis closed his notebook and put it away. He looked Craig in the eye and studied him.

'We believe that she disturbed a burglar at some point between nine o'clock last night and six o'clock this morning. She was stabbed, Mr Dunlop. She died at the scene.'

'Oh my God.'

'I'm very sorry,' said DC Jarvis. 'Thank you for your help.'

The King's Prerogative

He rose from his chair, and PC McMillan opened the door to the hall.

'One final thing, before we go. Can you tell us what your movements were last evening?'

'Yes.' Craig furrowed his brow. He was finding it hard to keep from thinking about Claire, dead. 'I finished work about five forty-five and went straight to the library. I stayed there till closing time, which would be about eight o'clock, then I came back here, made some dinner and watched some TV. I went to bed about eleven.'

'Did you speak to anyone after you came home?'

'Yes, my father rang about nine-thirty.'

'Thanks again Mr Dunlop. If anything comes to mind you think might be useful, you will let us know?'

'I will.'

The policemen left and Craig shut the door. He went back into the living room and slumped in his chair. Claire, dead? Murdered? How was it possible? Things like that didn't happen in Stranraer. He picked up the phone and dialled his parents' number. The phone gave three rings and his father answered. Craig spoke to him briefly then his mother came on. She couldn't believe how awful it was. Helen was in pieces. Was he okay? He assured her that he was, and she hung up. Then Craig just sat in the chair, looking at the blank television in the corner.

***

Ninety miles away in Glasgow, a man lay on the bed in his hotel room, waiting. He looked at his watch, sat up, reached for the telephone and dialled a number. After a few seconds it rang at the other end and was answered.

'Hello.'

'It's Blake.'

'Did you tie off the loose end?'

'Yes.'

'Did you find the letter?'

'Yes.'

'I hear something in your voice. What is it?'

'It was a copy.'

Pause.

'You don't have the original?'

'No.'

'Then we still have a loose end.'

Pause.

'Yes,' admitted Blake.

'Was it necessary to kill the woman *before* she could tell you where the original was?'

Blake tightened his jaw.

'I had no choice.'

'Go back to Stranraer. Find out if anyone else is involved and who she might have talked to. Keep me updated. I don't need to remind you of the consequences. And Blake, try not to stumble into the police investigation.'

The line went dead. Blake swore. He detested those phone calls. He went to the bathroom and washed his face and combed his fingers through his hair. He hated this part of the job. He hated the long periods of inactivity followed by the spells of blind panic on the part of his bosses that invariably led to him having to do the dirty work.

Blake's thoughts turned to his wife and his son and daughter. How much of a relief would it be to turn his back on all this and resign. He half smiled ruefully. Resignation in his line of work wasn't an option. They didn't offer retirement packages for faithful service. Not in the normal sense.

He looked at the mirror. He felt old. He looked old. Older than a forty-two-year-old should look. He sighed. Time to get back to work, he told the reflection.

Chapter 7

Friday 11th March, 1983

It felt like the whole town had been in a state of shock since the murder of one of Stranraer Academy's most popular teachers. Craig and Helen sent a card to Claire's parents, as did Peter and Marion. It felt painfully inadequate but they could think of nothing else to do. News coverage of the murder had been in all the papers which must have been even more heart-breaking for Claire's family, thought Craig. The funeral notice in the Free Press that week requested that no flowers be sent. Instead, friends of Claire were invited to donate to the charity of their choice. Which was exactly what Claire would have wanted, he reflected. He couldn't imagine the sense of loss and anguish her parents were going through. The funeral couldn't be arranged until the Procurator Fiscal's inquiry into her death was completed, and the delay only seemed to increase the sense of numbness friends, family, colleagues and pupils felt. Helen had been in a state of shock since the news broke. She hadn't slept or eaten much. Craig wished he could help her – somehow, anyhow – but he didn't know what to do. In the end he just sat with her and they talked about Claire and he listened to the stories Helen recalled from when they were growing up.

The day of the funeral arrived. For the second time that year Craig put on his dark suit and his black tie. His father drove them the short distance to the High Kirk. They made their way into the church and sat near the back. Beside the altar, Claire's coffin was supported on a low trestle. It was festooned with Spring flowers, all yellows and whites and purples. The rows of pews filled up until the church couldn't hold any more people, and a man in a black suit closed the door. The vestry door opened, and Claire's family emerged with the minister. They took their seat on the front pews, and the minister stood in front of the coffin. Craig could see Claire's mother sob uncontrollably as her husband put his arm round her shoulder. The service was brief. The minister offered prayers of comfort to the family and he read out some words prepared by Claire's parents. Craig realised that the prospect of saying those words in person must have been too painful for Claire's father, and for the first time since it happened, Craig wept.

After the service, the Dunlops joined the cortege and drove the mile to the town's cemetery. It was located on a hill overlooking the town and the long horseshoe of Loch Ryan beyond. On a clear day you could see north up to the Ailsa Craig and on a really clear day you could see as far as Arran. Craig couldn't think of a more beautiful spot. They kept a respectful distance from the graveside as Claire's family stood round the coffin. The minister said a few words and the coffin was then lowered into the ground. The family were led away, back to the funeral cars which moved off slowly, out of the cemetery and back towards the town.

As Craig turned to walk back to their car, he nodded to a few people he knew. Some were friends of Helen, and she stopped to give them brief hugs. As he waited for Helen to catch up, he noticed a man standing perhaps twenty yards away, scanning the sizeable group of friends and acquaintances who had made their way to the cemetery to pay their respects. There was something incongruous about his presence there, like he didn't belong. He wore a beige raincoat over a grey suit, though Craig didn't think that was the reason for the incongruity. As people began to drift away, the man turned and walked in a semi-circle along the path towards the main gate. As he passed level with the thinning crowd, he turned and looked again at Craig's group before walking on. That's it, thought Craig. Who wears suede Chelsea boots at a funeral?

***

Blake walked to his car, lit a cigarette and waited until the last of the mourners had left the cemetery before driving back to his hotel. He took off his coat and jacket and sat on top of the bed. He thought about phoning the office again but decided against it. There was nothing new to report, there would be no fresh instructions to receive and he wasn't in the mood for more sarcastic criticism. He lit another cigarette and watched the smoke as it spiralled upwards. It was almost certain that he was wasting his time. He was only ever brought in when an alarm rang and this particular alarm had lain dormant for years until it rang two weeks ago. He'd been charged with tracking the source and quietly silencing it. He'd tracked the letter to the teacher but the teacher only had a copy. She'd made the mistake of trying to run and now unfortunately she was dead. In his head he tried to argue the case that the original letter no longer existed. The teacher's copy was all there was. But he knew that wasn't the case. The boffins had done tests and were able to tell that the ink on the Photostat copy was fresh, probably no more than ten to twenty days old. Not ten to twenty months old. Certainly not ten to twenty years old. And they could tell that it was a copy of an original document, not a copy of a copy. The conclusion was inescapable. The original was copied recently, which prompted the urgent questions: where is it, why has it surfaced now, how many copies have been made, and how widely have they been circulated? And most importantly: where was Irving?

Blake had a sudden thought. He put out his cigarette. He stood up and walked over to the wardrobe, opened it, reached up and took down an attaché case from the top shelf. He placed it on the bed and opened it. He sifted through various maps, tickets and folders inside until he found the letter. He sat down and read it. He turned it over and once again studied the writing on the back:

BI
S Uni
LHB
141 SJRd
G4 0LT
041 220 3311

CD2462

He'd already compared it with notes he'd found in the teacher's house. It was definitely her handwriting. The first part was obvious enough, Irving's office address and phone number. The second part was written like a doodle, it had been traced in pen over and over, circled and underlined. What was CD2462? A serial number? It wasn't in the correct format for a driving licence or a passport or a post code. A phone number? Not enough digits. A receipt number? Receipt for what? A combination to a safe? A code for an ATM card? A date? The 2nd of April 1962? There must have been something he'd missed.

Five hours later he was still lying on his bed. He realised he must have fallen asleep. He reached for a cigarette but the packet was empty. He decided to go for a walk. In the time it took him to walk round the block he'd decided that he wasn't going to find out anything more by hanging around in Stranraer that he didn't already know. Plus, the police were conducting a murder enquiry, which in itself wasn't a great problem for him but he didn't want suspicious eyes looking in his direction if he could avoid it. It was time to make himself scarce. He'd head back to Glasgow and pick up the trail again there. He'd do one more check first. He looked at his watch. A quarter to ten. He'd give it a couple of hours then go back to the teacher's house.

***

The back door opened easily enough. Blake stepped inside and shut the door. He clicked on his pencil torch and looked round the kitchen. He could see where the police had been, dusting for prints and checking for clues to the identity of the killer. The window that Blake had broken was boarded up. He couldn't be sure if the police would be able to work out that it had been broken after the teacher died, not before, but it didn't matter. The important thing was that for now they seemed to believe that was how the burglar got in. Blake checked the drawers and cupboards again. He went through the other rooms and checked every paper, book and magazine he found. Every shelf, cabinet and box, anything that might conceal a letter. He'd already checked them once but he had to be thorough. He came out into the hall. There was a telephone on a small stand and a Yellow Pages below it. He thumbed through the Yellow Pages but there was nothing hidden inside. He shone his torch around the walls and the floor. The beam fell on a handful of envelopes and a free newspaper on the carpet by the front door. Blake picked up the post and took it through to the kitchen where he opened it. Two were utility bills, one was a newsletter from the teachers' union and the last envelope contained a bank statement. A thought struck him. He opened the kitchen drawers again. In the second one down he found the chequebook he'd seen earlier. He took it out and opened the blue plastic cover, then thumbed through the cheque stubs. Typical teacher, thought Blake. Each one carefully notated with the date, payee and amount. But there were no unusual payees, no indications that she'd travelled anywhere recently. All the cheques were either written to supermarkets or to the electricity board or BT. As he went to close the chequebook he noticed that the inside of the plastic cover had a built-in sleeve that was conveniently provided for pay-in receipts and the like. It bore the outline of something that had been placed in there some time ago, which had left an indentation. Blake pushed his fingers inside and produced a metal key.

He turned it over in his hand as he examined it. Well well, the teacher had a safe deposit box, he thought. He opened the chequebook again and noted the address of her branch. It was on Bridge Street, right here in Stranraer.

Chapter 8

Monday 14th March, 1983.

It was an effort for Craig to get up with the alarm when it went off so he hit the snooze button and dozed for another ten minutes before hitting the shower. He normally liked to get to work before half past eight but this morning it was nearly nine o'clock when he put the key in the main door and let himself in. The office was already in full swing with the tellers counting the contents of night safe wallets, the machine room girls processing the inward clearing items and the ledger team opening the mail.

'Morning Craig.'

'Morning guys. Good weekend?'

'Same old, same old.' John McNiven looked as if he was going to reciprocate the question but thought better of it and instead continued opening envelopes and sorting correspondence into piles.

'Anything exciting in the post today?' asked Craig.

'The new rates standing orders are still coming in thick and fast,' replied John, pointing at a small hill of brown pre-printed forms on the desk.

'Wonderful. I don't mind cracking on with those to be honest. I could do with keeping busy but not having to think too hard today,' volunteered Craig.

'Be my guest.'

At nine-thirty on the dot Mr Hamilton, the bank messenger, opened the doors and the first customers began filtering in. Craig was aware of someone approaching the ledgers counter and John greeting them. After a few seconds something about their conversation flicked a switch in Craig's subconscious ear and he tuned into it. He caught the thread of the discussion even though the glass bandit screen prevented him from hearing what the customer was saying.

'I'm sorry sir, that's in breach of bank policy.'

Pause.

'I appreciate that, but you're not the account holder.'

Pause.

'I understand. However it still doesn't change bank policy. We would need to see a court order.

Pause.

'By all means. May I see a warrant card or some identification?'

Craig heard the metal partition slide back and forward.

'Would you excuse me for just a minute, Detective Sergeant.'

Craig shifted in his chair to get a view of the customer. He thought he'd seen him before but couldn't be sure. John McNiven left the counter and walked through the back office to the row of interview rooms and manager's offices at the far end of the branch. He knocked on one, waited for a couple of seconds then disappeared inside.

Blake stood at the counter, waiting. He disliked having to use the warrant card but sometimes it was necessary. When seeking to enlist the cooperation of the local yokels, having Scotland Yard credentials normally ensured the desired effect. What was occupying his thoughts right at this instant however was the other young bank officer seated at the desk behind the counter. He'd placed him immediately. For two reasons: one, his police training meant that he rarely forgot a face; and two, the local people familiar to him more or less amounted to those who attended the funeral on Friday.

Just then, a door to his left opened and the young man he'd spoken to emerged and walked up the office.

'If you'd follow me please, the manager will see you.'

Blake followed him through to one of the rooms off a small passageway.

'Detective Sergeant Wilson, I'm Donald Grant.' Although the fifty-seven-year-old bank manager was significantly shorter than Blake, he was used to being in control in formal situations, particularly in his own office. He offered his hand and Blake shook it. 'Please, take a seat. Thank you, John.'

The young man closed the door behind him as he went out. Donald Grant handed back the warrant card in the name of Detective Sergeant George Wilson.

'Now, I understand you were asking about one of our safe custody boxes?'

'That's correct Mr… em… Grant. It's a box we believe belonged to one of your customers, Miss Claire Marshall.'

'Yes indeed. Tragic incident, just dreadful. Shocking to think that something like that could happen at all, never mind happen in a town like this. Forgive me for asking, but what interest does the Metropolitan Police have in Miss Marshall's death?'

'It was a fortuitous accident,' said Blake, 'If you'll pardon the expression. I've been on a fishing holiday and I saw the news about Miss Marshall's murder. The fishing wasn't particularly successful so I called my boss and asked if I could make myself useful while I was here. As you might guess, the local CID is under considerable pressure to make an arrest.'

'Yes I can imagine. I'm sure they must be grateful to have someone with your expertise assisting the investigation. Well Detective Sergeant, I have to tell you that strictly speaking it is against bank policy to release the contents of a safe custody box without a warrant from the local Sheriff Court.'

'I fully understand that, Mr Grant, but as you'll appreciate, we are following dozens of leads and time is against us.

I was hoping we could count on your cooperation under the circumstances.'

Donald Grant thought for a moment. He'd been as shocked as everyone else by the news of Claire's death and, like most people, what had left the deepest impression on him was the feeling of personal vulnerability and helplessness. He thought for a long moment then seemed to come to a decision. Perhaps he wasn't completely helpless in the face of this horrible crime after all.

'I can exercise an element of discretion. I can't let you remove any items under safe custody, but I am willing to let you inspect them if that would serve your needs just as well. Under supervision by us of course.'

'Of course. That would be fine, Mr Grant, thank you. I'm not expecting to find anything pertinent to the crime but it would eliminate one line of enquiry.'

'Good. Would you excuse me for one moment?' Mr Grant rose from behind his desk and left the room. He returned less than five minutes later accompanied by another man carrying a metal box about the size of a home video recorder.

'Detective Sergeant Wilson, this is Mr Campbell.'

The two men exchanged greetings and Campbell placed the box on the desk. Blake took the key from his pocket and unlocked the box after some jiggling with the lock. He transferred the contents to the desk, and sifted through the items one by one, putting each one back into the box after he'd examined it. They comprised three insurance policies, some share certificates, a small jewellery case containing a string of pearls, and the title deeds to Claire Marshall's house in Bayview Crescent. Blake concealed his disappointment. He placed all the items back in the box, then reached inside his jacket and produced the letter. He made sure the correct side was facing upwards before handing it to Donald Grant.

'Do these numbers have any significance to you? Could they be an account number perhaps?'

'CD2462. No, I'm afraid not,' said Donald Grant. 'It's far

The King's Prerogative

too small for an account number and our account numbers aren't alphanumeric.' He turned the paper over but before he could read the letter, Blake took it back and showed the numbers to Campbell.

'Do you have any idea what these numbers might mean?'

Campbell studied the figures and then stared at the ceiling as though searching for inspiration. A thought came to him and he stretched over the desk and picked up the telephone receiver.

'May I?'

Donald Grant nodded.

Campbell dialled a number then after a few seconds looked smugly pleased with himself. 'It's a phone number,' he announced. 'A local phone number. It's ringing.' He pointed to the heavy pen strokes on the paper. 'The figures are doodled over, see?' It's the kind of thing some people do when they're on hold.'

Blake blinked. 'A phone number?'

'Yes, of course, it's so obvious now I see it,' said Donald Grant, 'The Stranraer telephone exchange is quite small, all the local numbers only have four digits. We're not in Edinburgh or London I'm afraid.' He looked amused at the fact that his Assistant Accountant had outsmarted the big city detective.

Blake inwardly cursed himself. How could he have been so negligent?

Campbell's eyebrows lifted slightly as he put the phone down. 'It went to an Ansafone. The strangest coincidence though… it's Craig's number.'

'Who's Craig?' asked Blake.

'Craig Dunlop. He's one of our bank officers,' said Campbell.

CD. Craig Dunlop.

'Is he in the office today? May I speak to him?'

'Certainly,' said Donald Grant. 'Mr Campbell, would you ask Craig to join us?'

Craig must have looked at the door to the manager's office about twenty times in the last five minutes. John had rushed back to share the gossip that a policeman from London had asked to see Claire's safe custody box. Craig was sweating but he wasn't sure why. What did the police want? He saw the Assistant Accountant come out and walk through the office.

'Craig?'

Craig swallowed. 'Yes, Mr. Campbell?'

'Would you go and see Mr. Grant?'

'What's up?'

'He'll explain it all.'

'Is it to do with Claire Marshall?'

'He'll explain it all.'

Craig knocked and entered, and was about to close the door behind him when Campbell followed him in. Donald Grant was sitting at his desk and the policeman was leaning against the window sill looking at Craig intently. Campbell shut the door and stood in the corner with his arms folded.

'Craig, this is Detective Sergeant Wilson. He has some questions he'd like to ask you.'

Craig noticed that as he spoke Mr. Grant was slightly pinker than usual. He evidently must have felt awkward about the conversation that was about to take place. Craig looked at the detective. For some reason he thought he recognised the policeman from somewhere, but he couldn't remember where. Then he noticed his brown suede Chelsea boots and things fell into place. Craig knew he was the stranger he'd seen at Claire's funeral. He suddenly felt the room become cold.

'Have a seat Mr Dunlop,' said Blake.

Craig sat. 'What's this about?' His mind began to race. Had the police been following him? Was he under suspicion? He looked at Mr Grant and Mr Campbell as if to seek their support. Familiar faces who could steady his nerves. They weren't smiling. Their expressions did nothing to ease the mounting discomfort Craig could feel rising in him.

Blake's voice brought Craig's attention back on him. 'What can you tell me about this letter?' he asked. He handed over the letter and studied Craig's reaction as he read its contents. Blake noted the look of recognition on the young man's face.

'Why are you asking me?' Craig asked defensively.

'Because your telephone number is on the back, Mr Dunlop', said Blake in a tone that Craig didn't much care for.

Craig resented the implication that he had something to answer for. It wasn't his fault that Claire was dead. He felt his cheeks go red with indignation. A brief burst of adrenaline rushed to his head, only for it to abruptly about-turn and settle like concrete in his gut. It wasn't indignation he felt, but an attack of conscience. At that moment he realized that for the past two weeks he'd tried to convince himself that the burglary had nothing to do with the letter he was holding in his hand. But now the police had made the connection and a stomach-churning sense of guilt suddenly crushed in on him.

He took a long breath.

'Claire and I were looking into the story behind the letter.'

'You both were?' asked Blake.

Craig thought it was a curiously worded question. What did this policeman already know?

'Yes.'

Craig studied Blake for a moment, then looked back at the letter. 'Do you think this is what the burglar was looking for? I mean…'

Blake stopped him short. 'Just a second, Mr Dunlop.' He had to consider his next move carefully and he needed an exit strategy. What he didn't need was Dunlop spilling his guts in front of witnesses. This had to be settled somewhere quiet. And if the bank teller didn't cooperate initially, Blake knew he'd get what he needed from him eventually. It would be a day or two before Dunlop would be posted missing. That would give him more than enough time, Blake reasoned.

'I'd like you to come with me so that we can conduct a formal interview at the station.'

The concrete in the pit of Craig's stomach turned over. He looked at Mr Grant and Mr Campbell. 'I haven't done anything wrong.'

Donald Grant had been fidgeting throughout the conversation and clearly felt he should contribute something at this point. 'Craig, I'm sure there's no suggestion that you've done anything wrong. DS Wilson is only trying to establish the facts surrounding Miss Marshall's em...' he hesitated, not able to bring himself to say the M word.'...death. If you know anything at all you must tell the police.'

Blake unfolded his arms. 'Your assistance could be a great help to us, Mr Dunlop. Are you willing to make a statement?'

Craig's shoulders sagged. He realised it would be pointless not to comply.

'Certainly.'

Blake took the letter from Craig, folded it and put it back in his jacket.

Craig could feel the eyes of everyone in the office staring at him as he accompanied Blake out of the front door of the bank. Blake took out a car key from his pocket and indicated that they should walk round the building to the car park at the rear. He unlocked a car that was parked in one of the twelve spaces reserved for customers. It was a black Fiat 131 Sport, almost new. As Blake got in the driver's side and stretched across to release the passenger lock, Craig felt a strange compulsion to escape.

He could make a run for it.

Craig realised it was just the flight or fight impulse kicking in. He closed his eyes and fought hard against it. It would be okay, he told himself. He'd be glad of the opportunity to tell his story to the police.

He opened the car door and got in. Blake started the engine, reversed neatly out of the parking space and set off.

Chapter 9

Craig looked out of his passenger window and couldn't stop the thoughts he'd suppressed over the past two weeks from coming to the surface. Why was the burglar in Claire's house? Was he looking to steal cash, jewellery, the telly? Or – Craig screwed up his eyes as his worst fear resurfaced – maybe the burglar had somehow found out about the letter and decided it would be worth money to the papers? Oh, why did Claire have to disturb him? Why the hell couldn't she just have slept through the robbery? He wished more than anything right then that he'd never found the letter. Claire might still be alive if he hadn't got her involved in his stupid research.

Another wave of guilt swept over him and he turned to the policeman. 'You don't think I had anything to do with Claire's murder, do you?'

Blake couldn't contain the small laugh that escaped his lips. 'Let's just say you could have information crucial to our investigation.'

Craig turned away again, and looked out of the window. As he took in the surrounding buildings he realised they weren't going to the police station, but were headed in the opposite direction.

'Where are we going?'

'Not far.'

The Fiat headed south towards the outskirts of Stranraer. Craig shifted uncomfortably in his seat. This felt wrong. There was nothing south of Stranraer. The peninsula extended sixteen miles to the Mull of Galloway, the most southerly point in Scotland. And it was only about four or five miles wide at its broadest point – where the hell were they going?

'Where exactly are we heading?'

'I have to pick up a colleague first. It's just a slight detour.'

'Where?'

They passed a road sign that said 'Stoneykirk 5, Sandhead 8, Portpatrick 7'. Blake seemed to remember seeing a pamphlet in his hotel room extolling the virtues of the charming fishing village and holiday resort seven miles from Stranraer.

'Portpatrick.'

Craig frowned. Something else had been bothering him since the discussion in Donald Grant's office. He looked at Blake.

'How did you get hold of it?'

Blake kept his eyes on the road. He chose his next words carefully. 'The Hess letter? It was in Miss Marshall's safe custody box.'

He turned to look at Craig, scanning his face for any telltale signs. Yes, there it was. This guy was no poker player, thought Blake. Dunlop knew exactly what the letter was. Blake smiled inwardly. Soon he would know everything this bank teller knew and he would be a step closer to tying up this loose end.

Craig turned away from the driver and looked out of his window. The policeman had called it *the Hess letter*. So, the police knew that the letter belonged to Hess. Okay, thought Craig, maybe it wasn't valueless after all. But the policeman had just blatantly lied. Claire hadn't put the letter into safe custody, there was no need to, it was just a copy. Why did this DS Wilson lie about that? What was happening?

He replayed the events of the last few minutes in his head. If the police had already found the letter in Claire's house, why were they subsequently going through her safe custody box? And if the letter was what the burglary was about, why hadn't the burglar taken it when he broke in? Craig couldn't make the pieces of the puzzle fit together, but he had a creeping feeling that this was bad. Bad for him. He was being framed, or fitted up, or whatever the phrase was. The police needed an early arrest. His fingerprints were probably all over Claire's flat. He didn't have the strongest alibi for the night Claire died, he knew that.

Craig's mind gathered speed as it spun faster. There must be more to it. Do the police think Claire was killed because of the letter itself? But why? What was in it that was so important? And why wasn't he being taken straight to the police station? Where *was* he being taken? There was nothing south of Stranraer, the area was one large cul-de-sac. Hold on. There was West Freugh. RAF West Freugh was a Ministry of Defence base a few miles away. That must be where he was being taken, thought Craig. But wait, why would they do that? Why couldn't they interview him, or charge him even, in Stranraer? He was being taken somewhere by aeroplane. Why? Where? This was wrong. This felt very wrong.

The flight or fight impulse returned, and this time Craig couldn't stop it. A sense of panic rose in his throat. Blind, primitive panic. Something inside his head screamed at Craig to get out of the car. Now. He saw that a queue of cars and lorries in front of them was slowing down for a temporary traffic light. Roadworks. The council spending its budget before the financial year end. Blake slowed the car to a crawl as they came up to the car ahead. Craig weighed the odds against the car having automatic passenger locks. He presumed that police cars would have them in the back seats but probably not in the front. He tugged at the door handle and leant against the door with his shoulder. It opened. He pushed the door wide and slid out of the passenger seat in one fluid movement. Without looking to see what the policeman was doing he sprinted away from the car, back in the direction they had come from. The following twenty seconds passed in slow motion, or seemed that way because Craig's brain was in overdrive. He had to get out of the policeman's line of sight as soon as he could. The first turning was on the right, down an access road that led along the side of some small factories and industrial buildings. He didn't dare slow down to look back as he took the corner, but was relieved to notice that another car was slowing for the red light. Hopefully it would stop close enough to the Fiat to prevent the policeman from reversing and going after him.

Chapter 10

Blake made a grab for Dunlop a split second too late as he realised he was making a break for it. He jammed the car into reverse and looked out of the rear window. Another car had pulled up behind and stopped two feet away from the Fiat's bumper. His car wasn't going anywhere fast. Blake jumped out of the driver's door and half ran, half vaulted round the bonnet and started running after the younger, fitter man, who by then was turning a corner and disappearing from sight. He cursed as he sprinted for the same spot, thirty yards away. He got to the corner and used a lamp post to spin himself ninety degrees into the side road, then pulled up as he saw an empty pavement stretching in front of him. A row of small industrial units lined the road for maybe three hundred yards. No sign of Dunlop. Blake ran to the next corner and looked both ways, left and right. The street was empty apart from a few cars and vans parked by the kerb. He ran to the first industrial unit and checked round the back. More parked cars, maybe ten in all. He ran along the front row of cars and looked between them. He didn't see any crouched figures. Blake went back round to the front of the unit and surveyed the block. He was in a small estate, containing perhaps twenty small business units. Dunlop could be anywhere. Plus, he had local knowledge and it was likely that he knew the rat runs to get from one side of town to the other.

Blake decided to regroup and rethink. He jogged back to his car, by now sitting on its own in the middle of the road. Another car blasted its horn as it negotiated its way round the stationary Fiat. Blake got in, performed a three-point turn amid more horn blasts, and turned into the industrial estate. He drove around the small grid of roads, stopping at each opening to peer at the car parks and loading bays. He pulled up at an older brick-built office, with a couple of vans parked behind it, and could see that there was a pedestrian path beyond it that led north, back in the direction of the town centre. Blake came to a decision. He put the Fiat into gear and sped off, turned two corners and found himself back at the main road again.

Blake was convinced that this Dunlop knew all about the letter, and its significance. He had his man. Or soon would have his man. Meanwhile he had a phone call to make and he decided that he should make it sooner rather than later. Phone call… a thought struck him. About a hundred yards ahead there was a café with a metal 'open' sign outside on the pavement. He pulled in, two wheels on the pavement and two wheels still on the road. He jumped out and entered the café. It looked like its clientele were mainly housewives meeting up for a coffee and older people taking advantage of the breakfast special. A wireless was playing 'The Look of Love' by ABC at a discreet volume.

Blake went up to the counter and asked the assistant if they had a pay phone.

'Over there.' She pointed to a phone in a corner to the left of the counter. It was wall-mounted, with a Perspex bubble canopy above it to provide an element of privacy. Blake saw that there was a local telephone directory on a shelf below the phone. He pulled it out. It was thin by normal telephone directory standards. Blake knew it would be. He'd used a similar phone book to trace the teacher's address nearly two weeks earlier. He opened it at the Ds, skipped the pages till he got to Du. Duffs, Duffields, Duffys... next page: Duncans, Dunlevys, Dunlops. Good, there were only about a couple of dozen Dunlops. He reached into his inside pocket and pulled out the photostat. He looked at the phone number that the recently deceased Claire Marshall had jotted down. It took Blake all of ten seconds to find the matching phone book entry. He scribbled the address down, then went back to the assistant, who was giving change to a young customer.

'How do I get to Dalrymple Street?' The assistant didn't much care for this interruption and gave him a 'charming – and you're not even going to buy anything, are you?' look.

After a pause she said, 'Go right at the roundabout at the end of the street, follow the road to the end, first left, first right and that's you on Dalrymple Street.' Blake nodded his understanding and dived back out the door. He jumped in the car and bounced the Fiat back into the traffic.

The roundabout was only a couple of hundred yards along the road. There were four exits. He made a decision, and chose what looked to be the busier of the two right-hand exits. He followed the road to the end and at the T junction turned left. Almost immediately he saw the right turn, and on the gable end of the building in front a sign said Dalrymple Street. He gunned the big engine up the residential street. A large van was ahead of him, heading south, and Blake realised that he'd seen another two with identical livery earlier, parked behind the red brick office. He smiled. Dunlop's house was close to the industrial estate. 'Gotcha', he murmured. He saw the house he was looking for on the left. It looked like it was originally one house that had been split into two flats. Numbers 75 and 75a. He pulled up about fifty yards past it, got out of the car and walked back. He rapped the door knocker to No. 75a and waited. Ten, twenty seconds. No answer. He didn't expect one. He looked around. It was unfortunate that the door opened straight onto the street, with no garden to obscure the view from passers-by.

Blake fumbled with the Yale lock, making it look like he was fiddling with keys.

'Hello?'.

Blake immediately put his hand back in his coat pocket and turned to face the questioner. He saw a small woman, maybe in her seventies, wheeling a shopping bag behind her.

'There's no one in, son. The postman's just left a delivery with me'.

'Oh. Okay, thanks.' He cursed his luck at being interrupted and turned to go back to his car.

'But if you're looking for Craig, I just saw him going into his parents' house'.

Blake stopped and turned round again. 'Really? Yes I was meant to meet him earlier but I'm running late. Could you tell me which house it is?'.

'Number 122, up the road on the other side.'

'Thanks, you're a life saver'. Blake turned to go back to his car with a smile on his face as he relished the irony of his last comment. Small towns had their advantages after all.

Chapter 11

It had taken Craig no more than a minute to find a temporary hiding place in the industrial estate, out of sight of the queue of cars at the road works. He crouched behind one of the Galloway Beef Co. vans parked behind the brick office building. Partly to catch his breath, but mainly to let his brain catch up with what had just happened. More pressingly, he had to decide what to do next. In the sheer panic of running from DS Wilson, adrenaline had taken over and it was as if he'd followed it to where he now hid, panting and sweating. He could feel his pulse pumping in his ears, he could almost hear it. He looked around but from where he was positioned he could see no sign of Wilson. His breathing slowed down as the seconds passed. But now that his heart rate had returned to something like normal, the enormity of the last few minutes opened up to him. They say that people who fall off buildings or out of aeroplanes don't scream or panic because their brains shut down and block out the reality of imminent death. Craig felt as though he was spinning, spiralling towards the ground like the figure in a poster he'd seen for Hitchcock's *Vertigo*.

At that moment he was snapped back into the present by the sight of Wilson's car coming up the street towards him. Craig skittered on his hands and feet like a crab, round the side of the van, out of sight from the approaching car. For some reason he thought it best to lean against the back wheel, just in case Wilson should decide to get out of the car, lie down on the ground and look underneath the van for the legs of anyone hiding on the far side. He held his breath. He heard the car get closer, slow down and stop. The two-litre engine growled rhythmically for a few seconds as it idled, then cleared its throat loudly and sped off, changing tone as Wilson moved up through the gears. Craig heard the car turn a corner and the growl grew quieter until all Craig could hear was the sound of a machine chattering from somewhere inside the red brick office. Craig breathed out. He closed his eyes and tried to clear his mind of the noise in his head. He knew he had to decide what to do, what his next step needed to be. Why had he run? That would only make him look guilty. But his survival instinct told him he'd done the right thing. And now he was here, sitting on this tarmac, and he knew he had to make a decision. He opened his eyes, and he saw the path he used most days to walk the dog. He made a decision. He knew there was one person he wanted to turn to more than any other. Fiona. Easier said than done, he knew that, but as soon as her name popped into his head, he knew it was the right thing to do.

He carefully looked round the back of the van at the street. No movement. He got to his feet and ran across the tarmac square that served as the car park for employees of the Galloway Beef Co, and kept up the pace all the way along the pedestrian pathway. After less than a quarter of a mile, the pathway opened up into a country lane which was bordered on each side by small hedgerows. The lane skirted the southern edge of Stranraer and was a regular haunt of the local dog walkers and joggers. Craig followed the lane for about half a mile then turned left and came to the back entrance of the local cottage hospital. Dalrymple Street was just the other side of the hospital grounds. The noise of a car engine behind him made him jump, but to Craig's relief it was only a small Royal Mail van turning into the hospital. Craig watched the van as it went past him and drove up to the main door of the hospital. A man got out and disappeared inside.

Craig continued past the main door, past the windows of the medical and surgical wards and joined Dalrymple Street.

He hurriedly crossed the street and walked the few yards to number 122. He went round the gable end of the house into the back garden and tried the back door. Good, it was open, which meant that his mother was home. Craig stepped into the kitchen and heard the Hoover upstairs. The dog was curled up in his basket giving the impression of being asleep but eagerly jumped up and presented his face to Craig. Craig scratched its chin and ears as usual. 'Good boy.' Guinness then resumed his duties by curling up in his basket once more. Craig went through into the hall and called out. 'Mum?' No response, and the noise of the Hoover continued to fill the house. He went into the small dining room off the hall and rifled through the top drawer of a rosewood sideboard. When he'd been round for dinner the previous evening he left his grandfather's wallet there because his father wanted to show it to an old friend. Craig found the wallet and put it in his inside suit pocket. As he closed the drawer he saw his passport. He picked it up and double-checked that it was still in date even though he knew it still had three years left on it. He slipped it into his jacket too. The Hoover upstairs stopped and Craig went back out into the hall and bounded up the staircase, taking the steps two at a time. His mother peered at him from the landing. 'Oh it's you Craig! I got such a fright when I heard the noise, I thought we were being burgled'. Her choice of phrase sent a chill through Craig's veins. 'Is everything okay? Are you feeling ill?'.

'No, mum, I'm fine. Listen, I need to ask you a huge favour. I don't have time to explain right now but I promise I will, soon. I need to take some time off work, probably just a few days, and I need to go now'.

'What's happened?'

'Nothing. Well, I mean, I'm not sure.' He could see worry starting to etch itself on his mother's face.

'What?! Craig, you're not making sense. What's this all about? Are you in trouble at the bank?'

'Kind of. No. I don't know. I know this sounds crazy but if anyone calls here looking for me please for God's sake say you haven't seen or heard from me at all today. It's important.'

'What have you done, son? Wait, I'll phone your father, he needs to hear what you've got to say. He'll be able to help, he knows your manager'.

'Mum, no!!' Craig couldn't disguise the frustration in his voice. His mother stopped dead in her tracks and stared back at him, confused and scared. Her eyes started to fill with tears. 'Mum, I'm sorry, I didn't mean to shout at you. Listen, you have to trust me'. He took her by the shoulders. 'I haven't done anything, I swear on my life. But I think I'm in trouble and I have to try to sort it out. I don't have much time. They're bound to come looking for me here sooner rather than later so I need to go. I need to find someone.'

'Go where? Who's looking for you? What trouble?'

'It's better that you don't know for now'.

'Craig, I'm your mother.'

Craig thought for a second. 'A man might come looking for me. He's about my height, early to mid-40s-looking, fair hair, and speaks with an English accent.'

'Who is he?'

'He's a policeman. Plain clothes. Metropolitan Police. His name's Detective Sergeant Wilson. He's been looking into Claire's murder. Whatever you do, don't let him into the house'.

'Claire's murder? What has that got to do with you?'

'Mum, please! I just need some space and time to try to figure everything out. I had nothing to do with Claire's death but someone thinks I know more than I do. I think it's got something to do with that letter I found in Grandad's wallet. I need to find the lecturer we sent the letter to and get him to talk to the police.'

Marion Dunlop looked at her son for a couple of seconds

then drew herself up to her full five feet five inches. Her eyes recovered the steely resolve of a west of Scotland matriarch who was used to defending her kith and kin.

'Don't you worry, I'll know what to say to anyone who comes round looking for you'.

'There's one other thing Mum. I'm going to have to borrow some money. Just till I can cash a cheque'.

'You're in luck. I was at the post office yesterday'.

Marion hurried through to the kitchen, opened a drawer in the worktop and pulled out an envelope that contained a Post Office book and a small wad of banknotes. Without a word, she handed the notes to Craig, but held on to his hand a little longer than she normally would have. Craig gave her a hug, rubbing her back as he did so.

'Thanks Mum, I probably don't tell you this very often. But you're the best. I'll give you a ring in the next couple of days, but don't worry. I'll sort this out'.

And with that he headed towards the hallway, only to freeze where he stood at the familiar signature squeak of the front gate opening. This was the best early warning system the Dunlops could have asked for. Within a second of hearing the noise, the dog had jumped out and ran past Craig into the hall. Guinness leapt up at the front door and began barking with the ferocity you would expect of an animal his size. He performed this routine every time a stranger came to the door, and Craig used to wonder what canine sixth sense enabled the dog to distinguish between the front gate squeak made by a family member's entrance as opposed to that made by unknown visitors.

Through the frosted glass on the upper half of the front door, Craig could see the dark outline of a figure getting closer. '

'I'll get it. Go, go!' said Marion, shooing Craig away with a tea towel she'd just picked up to use on the dog. She marched into the hall, closing the kitchen door behind her to block any kind of view that the visitor might get from their side of the frosted glass. Craig also knew that it would prevent a tell-tale through draught when the front and back doors were both open at the same time. He silently exited the way he had come in, skirted the back lawn, scaled the small wall at the back of the garden and landed softly on the other side. From there he made his way round the side of the neighbouring house and emerged onto the street parallel to Dalrymple Street. He crossed the street and disappeared into the housing estate beyond.

Chapter 12

The doorbell rang. Marion Dunlop flicked her tea towel at the Doberman as it continued to bark at the visitor's arrival. She had to aim several smacks at the dog's nose before it made space for her to open the door. 'Guinness, down. Down!' Normally she would take it through to another room, but on this occasion she was happy for it to push at her legs in an attempt to tackle the stranger. She grabbed its collar with one hand and opened the door with the other. It opened six inches then jarred to a stop on the security chain. 'Yes, can I help you?'.

'Mrs Dunlop?'.

'Yes.'

'DS Wilson.' Blake flashed his warrant card through the small gap. 'Would it be possible to come in for a moment?'

'You couldn't have picked a worse moment to be honest, would it be possible to come back later?' Marion Dunlop realised how weak that sounded and tried to shore up the paper-thin excuse as best she could. 'It's not convenient for me at the moment as you can see, and I'm just getting ready to go out, I'm already late for an appointment'. Oh for God's sake Marion, she thought, you're just making it worse, you couldn't have made it more obvious that you're hiding something if you tried. Why don't you just tell him you're hiding your son and be done with it. She knew she couldn't lie to save her life and hoped that this stranger would think that her flustered appearance was due to the persistent pulling of the dog against her grip.

'It's important. I'm looking for your son, Craig. It's in connection with Claire Marshall's death'.

Marion saw half a chance to wriggle out of the hole she'd dug for herself. 'Oh I know, that was just awful. But I'm sorry, Craig's at work at the moment, and he doesn't actually live here any more. It's a mistake most people make. He lives down the road at number 75a. But he's already spoken to the police about poor Claire so I don't think he can add any more. But as I say, he's at his work – Royal Bank on Bridge Street. Sorry, I'm going to have to go. Guinness! Get down!'

Blake weighed up his options. He could of course insist she take the Hound of the Baskervilles into another room and shut it in, allowing him to gain entry and flush Dunlop out. If he was still there at all. If Dunlop had any intelligence he would have known this would be the first, or rather, the second place Blake would look for him and would therefore have made himself scarce, pronto. He must have gone to his parents' house for a reason. To seek help? Perhaps. But would Dunlop expect to be protected from the police by his parents? Doubtful. And there was no way Dunlop could have known that the warrant card he was using didn't belong to him, but to the *real* DS Wilson. No. He had obviously asked his mother to buy him time. Which meant that this could get messy. Was it worth forcing her to reveal his whereabouts? He considered it then discarded that option. Too messy, given that Blake had been given directions here by the old neighbour, who'd be able to give his description to the local plod. Far too messy. Besides, it was likely that Dunlop had already got what he came for – money probably, a car perhaps – and was gone.

'Do you or your son have a car?' There hadn't been one in the driveway but he'd noticed there was a garage beside the house.

Marion looked puzzled for a second but was slightly relieved at this turn in the conversation and took it as a sign that the stranger had abandoned his attempt to get into the house. 'Em no, Craig doesn't have a car but my husband does. He took it to work this morning. Why?'

'What's the make and model?'

'It's a Triumph 2000, white'.

'Registration?'

'TOS 245N'

'And where does your husband work?'

'At the council offices on Lewis Street, but he doesn't know anything about Claire's death either, I'm afraid.'

'You've been very helpful, thank you. And when you see your son could you ask him to contact the police station as soon as possible'.

'I will'.

Blake guessed there was little chance of that happening so his cover was safe enough for the moment. He turned on his heel and went back out the gate. With that, Marion Dunlop closed the door again and went into the living room, out of sight. She breathed out, and listened for the sound of Wilson's footsteps returning, or the gate squeaking again. They didn't. She held the tea towel to her mouth and burst into silent tears.

Blake got back in the Fiat and drove off. He performed a U-turn and headed back in the direction of the town centre. He made two left turns and drove slowly along the street looking at the gaps between the neat rows of bungalows. He tried to gauge the depth and size of the gardens that backed onto the houses on Dalrymple Street. He paused for a moment, then drove off again. At the end of the street a roundabout gave him the option of heading back down Dalrymple Street or on towards the industrial estate and the southern outskirts of town. He chose Dalrymple Street, and slowly drove past number 122 and then carried on past 75a. No sign. He pulled in, consulted a street map in the glove compartment, located Lewis Street, and pulled away again. Five minutes later, he found the council offices easily enough, and parked the car on the kerb a few yards from the building. From there he could see the front entrance and a side entrance. He'd be able to see anyone going in or coming out. He could also see a row of seven cars parked adjacent to the building. The third car from the left was a white Triumph 2000 Mark 2, registration number TOS 245N. He lit a cigarette, wound down the window and rested his elbow on the open door sill. It was a small town. Sooner or later Dunlop would have to show himself. Meantime he could plan what he needed to do next.

Chapter 13

Craig kept to the back streets as he hurried through the housing estate. Despite the panic he felt, or perhaps because of the panic he felt, he knew he couldn't stay put. He realised that he was trapped in a small town, small in area and small in the sense that he knew half the people in it, and they knew the other half. If he tried to go into hiding with family or a friend, the way the jungle drums operated it would take all of two hours for word to get round. As soon as it became known that Craig Dunlop was wanted by the police in connection with his friend's murder folk would have a field day. He ruled out a hotel or B&B too. Most of the hoteliers had an account at the bank and he was known to many of them by sight. Craig might consider himself to be a likeable young professional but he couldn't imagine that a respectable local businessman or woman would be willing to harbour a fugitive from the law.

No, he knew that he had to get out of Stranraer. He had to get to Glasgow. Get to Fiona. She'd be able to help. And he could be anonymous there. But getting there was going to be difficult thanks to the geography of this part of the world. The biggest problem was the fact that to all intents and purposes Stranraer was an island. Situated at the bottleneck of a peninsula, the only routes out by road or rail were to the north or east. Positioned in the very southwestern corner of Scotland, the Rhins of Galloway were as remote as some of the Highlands. It was fifty miles to Ayr in the north, and seventy-five miles to Dumfries in the east. It was a standing joke among Craig and his friends that since the old art deco Regal closed its doors almost ten years ago, the closest cinema was in Belfast. He knew he had three options: by road via the A77 north or A75 east, or by train north. Craig decided that the railway station would be the first place the police would stake out. Besides, the trains were infrequent and if he didn't time it right he could end up conspicuously hanging around on the platform, just waiting to be picked up by the police. Even if he made it on to a train it would be a simple enough task for the police to arrange for a colleague to be waiting for him in Ayr or Glasgow. The same went for the bus station, Craig ruled that out too. No, he'd have to find another way.

After fifteen minutes' brisk walk, stopping at every junction to look for any sign of the black Fiat, he had worked his way down to the corner of Sun Street and Lewis Street. His father would be livid at the imposition but Craig knew that he'd let him borrow the car. He turned into Lewis Street and stopped dead. A hundred yards ahead, parked at the end of a row of cars, was the black Fiat. Two men were walking abreast towards Craig, chatting as they made their way in his direction. Just before they passed him, Craig pretended that he'd forgotten something and turned round to walk back the way he had come. The men obscured the view from the parked Fiat until they reached the corner. Then Craig turned back up Sun Street. After a few steps he ran as fast as he could up the steep hill, as far as the next corner. He turned right and ducked into a path that led down a flight of stone steps. He got to the bottom before he stopped running.

He'd ended up on the shoreline of Loch Ryan, in what locals called the Clayhole, or Cly-hole as it was usually pronounced. Panting heavily, he caught his breath. Wilson's car had been parked facing away from Craig, so with luck the worst that happened was the policeman would have caught a glimpse of him in his rear-view mirror. Craig swore. No chance of getting to borrow his father's car. The choices available to him were reducing in number rapidly and Craig could feel the panic once again rising in his throat. His face felt clammy from sweat, a cold, cloying, cadaverous dampness that clung to his skin. He was conscious of a feeling that his world had suddenly tilted on its axis and everything was different. The streets that had been familiar to him his whole life now seemed strange and foreboding, as if the everyday colour around him had darkened as the result of some kind of solar eclipse.

He shook his head to try to clear it of the feeling of dislocation. Why was this happening? How had it happened? Craig felt an overwhelming desire to turn the clock back and make everything go away. The letter, Claire's death, the police, and most of all, this awful sickening feeling in his stomach. He could feel everything ebbing away from him, his home, his career. How could he explain this away at the bank? Innocent people don't run from the police.

He caught himself in mid-thought. That was the whole point, he *was* innocent. He hadn't done anything. Anger slowly rose within him. The sick feeling in his gut began to turn into a burning resentment. Concentrate, dammit, he thought. He looked along the shoreline. In front of him there was a small park that led to a boating lake. It was easy enough to follow the footpath round the park and lake, then hug the railings along the old fishing harbour that eventually led to the main ferry terminal. Craig set off in that direction, round the park, the lake, the old harbour, and after less than a mile he came across the final hurdle to cross before he got to the ferry terminal.

Across the road was the local police station. It was a small, low rise 1960s building. It could have been a library if it hadn't been for the array of large radio antennae on the flat roof. It was set back from the road slightly, within a small enclosed car park surrounded by a low wall. A turquoise and white Ford Escort panda car emerged from the opening to the car park, indicating left. Across the street Craig made sure he walked steadily, eyes ahead but aware of the panda car in his peripheral vision. He imagined that the driver and passenger were watching him as he walked. He expected to see the blue light on the car's roof start to flash, with accompanying siren. He expected the car to shoot out of the police station, lurch across the road, turn right and pull in to the kerb ahead of him. He expected the doors to fly open and the policemen to run up to him and grab him and bundle him in the back. But none of that happened. Instead, the panda waited for a couple of cars to pass, then moved off, heading into the centre of town. Craig felt a delayed surge of adrenalin course through him. He came to the approach to the ferry terminal. Beyond the expanse of light grey tarmac, Craig could see the pier, which was broad enough to also serve as the railway station. Passengers arriving into the station had only a few yards to walk to board the ferry to Larne.

Craig looked beyond the railway station and out into the loch. A ship was approaching. As it sailed closer its bow opened upward as if it was about to take a bite out of the end of the pier. Craig allowed himself a half smile. When he decided to come this way, he'd known there were a number of variables that could either work to his advantage or to his disadvantage. The first was that the police would have been alerted to his escape and he could be recognised as he walked past the police station. His luck had been in there. The second was that at this time of day, either no ferry would be in port, or the *Antrim Princess* would be in, or the *Dalriada* would be in. The *Antrim Princess* chiefly carried foot passengers and cars, with only a comparatively small number of lorries crossing on her at a time. The *Dalriada* carried more big lorries. Craig could see that it was the *Dalriada* coming in. Perfect, he thought. He watched as the Sealink ferry drew smoothly alongside the jetty and the mooring ropes were made secure. He made his way along the pavement, still on the other side of the security fence from the area that marked out the approach to the ferry port itself. He could see the usual security staff talking to some drivers waiting to board, inspecting lorry cabs and trailers. Both ends of the ferry journey were subject to routine security checks for the obvious reason that Larne was only a short journey up the coast from Belfast. Craig came to the junction that served as the exit point for vehicles heading for routes leading out of Stranraer. In his experience he found the ferry terminal building, just beyond the junction, the best place to pick up a lift from one of the drivers. He'd done it before, on the odd occasion when he'd been completely skint before pay day. The lorries could only head north to Glasgow and the central belt, or east towards Dumfries and England, so it was a pretty reliable way of getting to where you wanted to go. He went into the ferry terminal, which in truth was little more than a dilapidated café and waiting area. He bought a coffee which seemed hardly worthy of the name, and sat down at a table away from the window. There were half a dozen other people sitting around, waiting on the announcement that the next ferry was boarding.

After a few minutes, a couple of men came in, one after the other. One went to the gents and the other went up to the counter to order something from the sparse menu handwritten on a blackboard on the wall. He paid, collected a cup of tea and a roll with something, selected a table and sat down. The other man came out of the gents and went out the way he came. Craig waited until the roll was eaten and the tea almost drunk before getting up and going over to the man's table. He kept a respectful distance, but leaned forward to make sure he didn't have to speak too loudly.

'Excuse me mate, you wouldn't happen to be heading to Glasgow by any chance?'

'Looking for a lift?' the man replied. He was from down south, maybe Yorkshire, thought Craig. The man looked Craig up and down. 'Sorry pal, I'm heading to Folkestone.'

'No bother, thanks anyway.' Craig sat down again.

After fifteen minutes and three failed attempts, Craig's nerve was beginning to crack. Every time the door opened he expected to see the police come in to search the ferry terminal, find him, and take him away in handcuffs. He was on the verge of giving up and making another run for it, maybe he could thumb a lift on the road. Too risky, he decided. He knew he couldn't stand it much longer, just waiting there to be caught.

He decided to wait for five more minutes and then he'd make a move. He might have more luck if he managed to creep into the lorry park and speak to the drivers there. But that would attract suspicion, he thought. He got up and went to the toilet. He washed his face and told himself to calm down. Okay, time to go, he thought. He dried his face and hands.

As he left the gents, he finally struck it lucky. A driver was paying for a drink at the counter and was correcting the waitress when she called him Irish. He was from Ulster, he'd said, smiling at her. Craig waited for the man to sit down and then went up to speak to him. As it turned out he had come from Lisburn and was headed to Bellshill outside Glasgow. Was that any good to him? Sure was, said Craig. The driver noticed Craig's lounge suit and the absence of a bag or holdall or rucksack and looked at him, not so much suspicion in his expression as conspiratorial brotherhood. 'Oh aye, been caught on the hop have ye?'

'Eh, yeah, kind of,' said Craig, trying to inject a note of 'what can you do' humour into his tone.

'Football or female?'

'Sorry?'

'Are you going up for the football or are you seeing a wee lassie?'

Craig realised what he meant, and remembered that Rangers were playing a rescheduled cup match that night at Ibrox. He was suddenly grateful for the polarising nature of football in the west of Scotland. The gravitational force of the two Glasgow giants extended way beyond the boundaries of the city, and pulled in a fan base from all along the west coast and into Northern Ireland. And because support was sharply delineated along hard sectarian lines, it didn't take Sherlock Holmes to work out that this Ulsterman was of the red, white and blue persuasion.

Craig relaxed and smiled. 'Haha, yeah, well it's a bit of both actually, a mate's got hold of a ticket for me, so I'm skiving off work and I was hoping to crash at a wee pal's afterwards.'

'Ya jammy beggar! Come on, you can fill me in on the details on the way, I've got to get moving.' The driver swallowed the rest of his tea and got up to go.

Chapter 14

'When's the next train to Glasgow?'

'Three twenty-five, on the dot.'

Blake looked at his watch. Ten past twelve. He'd missed the previous train by twenty-five minutes, or to be accurate he'd missed being there to see who'd got on it. He'd already been to the bus station but found no sign of Dunlop hanging around. In retrospect the train had been a better bet. By Blake's reckoning the slippery bastard had had plenty of time to make the 11:45. Which would get him into Glasgow before half past two. No time to waste. He exited the station, got back into his car and gunned it back down the broad pier, out past the ferry terminal and down the short stretch of road to his hotel. He asked reception to make up his bill and went up to his room to pack. Then he sat on the bed and made a phone call.

'What progress?' asked the voice on the other end of the telephone.

'It was worth pursuing the safe deposit angle. There's a local bank teller who's been working with the teacher. He knows what the letter is.'

'Have you taken care of him?'

'No. He bolted after I questioned him.'

There was a pause on the other end of the line.

'How soon will you reacquire him?'

'I know where he's headed,' said Blake. 'Has there been any indication of where Irving is?'

There was a pause. 'Not yet,' came the reply. 'He's gone to ground.'

The King's Prerogative

'Then the teller is our best chance. I think he will lead us to him.'

'I hope you're right. What's the teller's name?'

'Dunlop. Craig Dunlop.'

'Don't let me keep you. And Blake... no more loose ends. Get me that letter.'

'Yes, sir.'

'And when you catch up with Irving do dispose of him cleanly. I do not want anything being traced back to this office.'

With that, the line went dead. Blake replaced the receiver. It was easy for them, he thought. In their plush swivelling leather and chrome chairs. Events on the ground are seldom neat and tidy. He picked up his overnight bag and the room key and went out into the hall. Five minutes later he was back in his car and on his way along the A77 towards the outskirts of town. A sign said Girvan 29, Ayr 51, Glasgow 90. Blake looked at his watch. Twelve forty-five. He should make Glasgow by two-fifteen.

Chapter 15

'See ye next time, gie the teddies a cheer fae me.'

'Aye, I will. You never know, Davie Cooper might even have one of his good games. Thanks again.' Craig climbed down from the cab, swung the door shut and gave it two raps with his knuckles. The brakes hissed at him and the gears strained against the weight in the back as the lorry rolled forward and got back under way. He'd told the driver he'd arranged to meet his mate with the football ticket in town, so the driver dropped him at Eglinton Toll before swinging east to avoid the city centre traffic. From there it was a brisk fifteen-minute walk up Eglinton Street until Craig came to Bridge Street subway station. He bought a ticket and as he went through the barrier and down the steps to the platform, the familiar smell of the Clockwork Orange filled his nostrils and immediately transported him back to the time when he used to spend his weekends here. The trip back and forward to Hillhead, the nights out, the bleary mornings. He experienced a pang of regret as he realised that those days should have lasted longer than they did. The gigs at Tiffany's or the Barrowlands. The parties, the all-nighters at the Grosvenor cinema. He was shaken from his thoughts by the arrival of the orange underground train.

Donald Grant looked at the wall clock one more time, then picked up the telephone receiver on his desk. He consulted the address finder sitting next to it, moving a sliding tab to the letter 'P' before pressing a small square button. The plastic cover flipped up to reveal a list of handwritten names and phone numbers. He selected one, dialled the number, and waited for the clicks and burrs of the automated telephone exchange to complete their metallic search before rewarding him with the sound of a number ringing at the other end.

'Stranraer Police Station,' said a polite Scottish voice.

'Oh hello, I wonder if I could speak with Detective Sergeant Wilson please.'

There was a short pause at the other end.

'I'm sorry sir, there's no one of that name here.'

'Oh, you mean he's not in the station at the moment?'

'No sir, I mean there's no officer of that name attached to this station.'

'There must be some mistake. He was here in my office this morning investigating the death of Claire Marshall.'

'And you are?'

'Donald Grant, manager at the Royal Bank on Bridge Street.'

'Okay Mr Grant, would you hold one moment please? Perhaps you should speak to the officer in charge.'

'Yes, perhaps I should.'

Twenty minutes later two uniformed officers and one officer in plain clothes were shown into Donald Grant's office. The plain clothes officer introduced himself as Detective Inspector Bruce Cowie, temporarily attached to the Stranraer constabulary from Dumfries. He was the officer in charge of the investigation into Claire Marshall's murder. Donald Grant invited them to sit, and then described how Wilson had arrived that morning, opened the safe custody box and then asked Craig Dunlop some questions. One of the policemen took copious notes in a small notebook as he talked. DI Cowie paused a moment, taking time to choose his first question.

'Did this DS Wilson show you any identification?'

'Yes, he showed me his warrant card.'

'And it was a Metropolitan Police warrant card?'
'Yes.'
'Have you seen one of those before?'
'No.'
'Hmmm. Did he say where he obtained the key to Miss Marshall's safe custody box?'
'No, he didn't. I assumed it was among the effects in your possession belonging to Miss Marshall, and of course we would wish to give the police every assistance under the circumstances.'

'I understand,' said DI Cowie. 'The thing is, there is no DS Wilson attached to this investigation. In fact there is no one outside of Dumfries and Galloway Constabulary working on this case, far less a detective from Scotland Yard.'

Donald Grant looked nonplussed. Cowie continued.

'Didn't you think it was odd that someone from the Met was investigating a local crime?'

'He told me that he was holidaying in the area and as this was his area of expertise, he had offered his services to the local CID.'

Cowie arched an eyebrow. 'Very conscientious of him, I'm sure.' He sighed. 'What did this DS Wilson look like?'

'He looked in his early forties, about my height – five foot ten – short fair hair. Spoke with a London or home counties accent. That's about as much as I can say.'

Bruce Cowie nodded his head as he absorbed this information.

'Could I speak to Mr Dunlop?'

'That's the thing, he left with this DS Wilson and he hasn't come back.'

DI Cowie's expression changed.

'They left together?'

'Yes.'

Cowie and the other police officers exchanged looks. The detective took a moment to gather his thoughts, before leaning forward in his seat.

'You see Mr Grant, I checked before I left the station and there are two DS Wilsons in the Met. One is a very talented young lady called Yvonne, destined for higher things. I spoke to the other one on the phone. He's a fifty-seven-year-old forensics specialist who speaks with a broad Liverpool accent. He's in London right now, and says he hasn't been north of Newcastle in his life.'

Chapter 16

Craig emerged into the sunlight after getting off the subway train at Hillhead station. He looked up and down Byres Road before turning left and heading towards Ashton Lane and his favourite café in the whole world, The Grosvenor. Inside was noisy and busy with students ordering food and drinks and chatting with each other and generally going about their normal lives in the normal manner. It gave Craig a comforting sense of familiarity to stand at the counter and look at the menu and wait for a table to become free and to slide in and take up residence there again. He looked at his watch. A quarter to four. A grey-haired woman who looked to Craig as wide as she was short came up to his table, took out a cloth from a pocket in her pink nylon tabard, gave his table a wipe and asked him what he fancied. Craig ordered a coffee and a cheeseburger and the waitress disappeared behind the counter again. The coffee and burger duly arrived and Craig spent the next thirty minutes making it last as long as he could, while checking out every face that came into the café.

Two girls about nineteen bounced in, looked around, saw that there were no tables free and asked if they could share Craig's. No problem he replied, and they sat down and ordered hot chocolate and became engrossed in their own conversation. Craig tried to calculate how long he'd have to wait and realised that he could be there a long time. There was no guarantee that Fiona would come in to the café at all. In the rare silences during the ride in the lorry, he'd pondered over how it would be when he saw Fiona again. He hadn't seen her or spoken to her for so long. He wasn't even sure if she stayed in the same flat any longer. Eventually he decided that it would be a chance in a hundred that she would stop in at the café and his plan of engineering a casual 'fancy seeing you here' meeting was clutching at straws to say the least. He'd have to go to her door and he wasn't looking forward to that one iota. He knew he had no choice though and he'd put it off long enough.

Craig paid his bill and walked back out into the spring air. It had turned cooler. Evening was approaching, and Craig turned up his jacket collar. He realised that he was still wearing his work suit. It seemed so long since he'd put it on that morning. He crossed Byres Road and took Ruthven Lane up to Victoria Crescent Place. He arrived at Fiona's door and rang the buzzer for flat four. No answer. Craig rang it again, this time for a second longer. Still no reply. He stepped back onto the pavement and looked up at the window. No signs of life. He looked around. There was a small park opposite so he walked over to it, found a bench that gave him a good view of the flats opposite and settled in to wait.

Nearly two hours later it was pitch dark and Craig was beginning to think that he had wasted his time. He was weighing up his options when he recognised a blonde girl walking past the row of flats towards number four. Her hair was shorter and he didn't recognise the red duffle coat she was wearing but his heart skipped a beat as he realised it was his ex-girlfriend. She skipped up the stone steps to the door of the flat. He called her name.

'Fiona?'

She turned round and stared at Craig.

'Oh my God! Craig? How are you? What are you doing here?' She rushed back down the steps and gave him a hug. Then she regained her composure, stepped back and slapped him hard on the face.

'Ouch! I liked the first greeting better,' said Craig, unable to keep the smile off his face despite it smarting like blazes. 'It's so good to see you.'

It *was* good to see her, he realised. He'd forgotten how beautiful Fi was. Five foot seven, slim, blonde, cornflower blue eyes. She had the kind of look that people called classic or timeless. Like Louise Brooks or Grace Kelly or Audrey Hepburn. And smart. Fiona Rankin was intelligent. Both book smart and sharp as a tack. She'd sailed through her Highers and sailed into Glasgow University. She was in the 3rd year of her law degree and was consistently top of her class. Craig had adored her. And then he blew it. His friends told him he'd blown it, his family told him he'd blown it and worst of all, Fiona confirmed it from her own lips.

'It's good to see you too,' said Fiona at last. 'But you're a fucking arse and don't think for one second that I've forgiven you.' She was building up a head of steam and Craig wasn't ready to receive the onslaught right now.

'Fiona, I'm in trouble and I need your help. I've got nowhere else to go.'

Fiona stopped in mid flow and suddenly realised that his appearance here wasn't about her.

'Craig, what's happened?'

'I've been freezing my arse off waiting for you to come home, do you mind if we get a heat first?'

'God yeah, of course. Come on.'

They went inside and walked up the staircase till they came to flat number 4. Fiona unlocked the door and she showed Craig into the living room. She switched on the electric fire and went into the kitchen to put the kettle on. Craig sat on the hearth rug and warmed his hands and face on the heat radiating from the three bars. Fiona came back in with two mugs of coffee and handed one to Craig. 'Still milk and one sugar?'

'Yes, thanks.' He took a sip and for the first time since that morning he felt safe and warm and able to relax. Even though he knew it was only a temporary feeling, he was grateful for the respite and he told Fiona so.

'Have you warmed up a bit?'

'Yes, thanks. I feel almost human.'

'What's this all about?'

Craig told the whole story, from his grandfather's funeral right through to that afternoon, and waiting for her in The Grosvenor café. Fiona listened intently, only interrupting to clarify her understanding here and there. It took Craig a full hour to finish and when he came to the end he felt grateful to Fiona for the second time that evening. Getting it all out made him feel better and it felt good talking to Fiona again. For a long minute Fiona said nothing. She'd been sitting on the sofa with her hands resting on her knee, and now she placed her hands over her nose and mouth as if she was about to sneeze. Craig recognised the look – she was thinking hard. Finally he couldn't bear the silence any longer.

'What do you think I should do?'

Fiona put her hands back on her knee. 'I don't know what you should do about the police right now, but one thing's for sure, you can't outrun them for ever. You know that.'

'I know.'

'Leaving that aside, I think there's three things you have to do. Tomorrow, you'll get in touch with Brian Irving at Strathclyde University. If your thinking is right and this all has something to do with the letter then you need to get him involved. But right now you'll phone your parents and tell them you're okay.'

Craig nodded. 'You're right. What's the third thing?'

'You'll eat something.' With that she stood up, then bent down, kissed Craig on the cheek and walked through to the kitchen. She shouted through from the other room. 'Phone your mum, you know where the phone is.'

Craig took a seat on the sofa and picked up the phone that was sitting on a small table next to the arm. He noticed a large notepad that the phone had been sitting on. Written on the notepad was a list divided into two columns, one labelled Fiona and the other labelled Chris, with the duration of phone calls jotted under each name. Craig's heart sank. Who was Chris? Just a flatmate or was it a boyfriend? It shouldn't have come as a surprise that Fiona might be seeing someone or even living with someone. The old feelings of jealousy began to seep into his head. Stop it, he thought, stop it right now. He didn't have the time for this, nor did he have the right to feel jealous. He shook the thoughts from his head and dialled his parents' number.

Fifteen minutes later Fiona came back through from the kitchen carrying two empty plates and a large bowl of pasta in some kind of tomato sauce. She placed them on the small dining table, then went back to the kitchen to fetch some cutlery and two glasses of water for them.

'Sorry it's just water, I wasn't expecting guests,' said Fiona.

'Don't be daft, this is great, really.' They sat at the table and Craig squeezed her hand. 'Thanks Fiona, I don't know what I'd have done today without you.'

Fiona smiled her smile at him. 'You haven't told me that for a long time.' She punched his arm again, only lightly this time. 'Eat. And tell me what your mum and dad said.'

Craig told Fiona about his phone call home. Firstly, he'd told his dad that he was okay and staying over at a friend's. He didn't want to say he was at Fiona's because that would have triggered a whole other conversation he didn't want to get into. He asked what had been happening in Stranraer and his father told Craig that a policeman had called that morning, and a further two policemen visited at lunch time. His mother hadn't been able to tell them where Craig was. But then they had returned around six pm and told his parents that Craig had been missing since roughly ten o'clock and they were anxious to find him. His parents had no choice but to tell them that Craig had been in touch earlier in the day but that he was alright. The policemen admonished them and instructed them to telephone the local police station as soon as Craig got in touch again. His father pleaded with Craig to contact the police. Whatever had happened, they could sort it out. Craig told his father that he planned to contact someone who could help sort it all out the following morning and then he would go to the police. His father sounded relieved. Craig spoke briefly with his mother who also begged him to contact the police. Craig promised her too then rung off.

'Your dad is right,' said Fiona. 'You should go to the police. It's not fair on your mum and dad. You know it'll only look worse for you in the long run. It looks bad enough as it is. You escaped police custody for heaven's sake.'

'I wasn't in police custody, I wasn't under arrest,' said Craig. 'And I ran because something's not right, Fi. That detective, Wilson, lied to me about how he got the letter and every single thing he said or did was suspicious. He was at Claire's funeral. He had Claire's copy of the letter, he knew that the letter was connected to Hess, he had her safe custody key, and then he drove *away* from the police station when he wanted me to make a statement. This whole thing stinks. Wilson as much as confirmed that Claire's murder was connected to the letter, and by extension that means the police must suspect me. Why else was he so keen to talk to me? And where was he taking me? It could only have been the airfield at West Freugh. Then where? What else am I supposed to think other than they're convinced I killed Claire? They haven't found the real murderer so they're desperate to pin it on someone. They'd only have my word that I didn't do it, and the only person who can corroborate my story and get me out of this mess is Brian Irving. I have to speak to him.'

'Craig, listen to yourself, that's paranoia.'

'Is it? I'm telling you, I got the distinct feeling that I'm being fitted up for this. Even my boss looked at me as if I'd done it.' He stared at his hands. 'I just need another day.'

Fiona looked at her watch. It said nine-thirty. She looked back at him. 'You look dead beat.'

Craig nodded and made to stand up. 'You're right, I am. I should go and find somewhere…'

'You can sleep on the couch tonight. I'll get you a duvet.'

Craig was relieved that he wasn't being kicked out. 'Thank you, Fi. I keep saying that tonight don't I? I promise I'll be gone first thing.'

'Shut up. You know I'd always help you if I could.' She went through into the hall to get a spare duvet from the airing cupboard and she took a spare pillow from her bed. By the time she went back through to the living room, Craig was already fast asleep on the sofa. She put the duvet over him and switched off the light on her way to bed.

Chapter 17

Tuesday 15th March, 1983

Craig woke to the sound of curtains being opened. He experienced that feeling where he expected to see his own bedroom and was then confused for a few seconds while his brain tried to work out where he was.

'Morning!'

He turned towards the familiar voice and his brain finally caught up with itself. He snapped awake.

'Hi. What time is it?'

'A quarter past eight. Did you sleep okay?'

'I must have. I don't remember going to sleep.'

'You've got a busy day today. Go and have a shower and I'll make us some tea and toast.' She threw a sweater at him. 'There's a towel in the bathroom, and you can wear this.'

Craig caught the sweater and held it out to look at it. It was grey, crew neck, far too big for Fiona.

'This is mine,' he said.

'I know, you left it here last time you visited.' Fiona arched an eyebrow and tightened her lips at him as if to say 'And let's not revisit what happened that night'. She breezed into the kitchen and Craig could hear her getting in to full morning mode, radio switched on, tap running, drawers opening, switches clicking. He got off the couch and made his way through to the bathroom.

Ten minutes later he was showered and dressed. He made a mental note to buy himself some fresh underwear today. He looked like he'd slept in his suit trousers (which he had), but at least he was ready to face the world. When he put on the sweater he was pleasantly surprised to smell Fiona's perfume. She'd been wearing it recently. He kidded himself on that it might be a sign but he shunted the thought to the back of his head. He walked through to the living room where Fiona was already sitting at the table with a pot of tea and a small mound of buttered toast. Craig sat down and poured a cup.

'What time do you need to get off to uni?'

'I don't have a lecture till eleven o'clock. I thought it would be an idea to try to get hold of Doctor Irving early. I've already looked up the number.' She slid a piece of paper across to him with a telephone number written on it.

'Thanks,' said Craig. He took a sip of tea then moved to the couch, picked up the phone and dialled the number. Fiona watched him as he waited a few seconds then spoke into the receiver.

'Oh, hello. I wonder if you could put me through to the department of political science, please?'

Pause.

'Yes, I think that must be it. Thanks.'

Pause.

'Hi, could I speak to Doctor Irving please?'

Pause.

'Craig Dunlop. I spoke with Doctor Irving a couple of weeks ago. He was looking into something for me.'

Long pause.

'Really? Do you know where he is?'

Pause.

'And no one's heard from him at all?'

Another long pause.

'Of course.' Craig looked at the telephone dial. 'It's 276 5963. Thank you.'

He put down the receiver and looked at Fiona. 'He's disappeared. He took some time off and they were expecting him back at work yesterday but he hasn't shown up.'

'What?'

Craig was deep in thought. He was counting back the days since Claire last spoke to him. 'No one's heard from him for over two weeks, nearly three. Claire heard from him on the 18th of February to say he'd received the letter, then apparently he took a fortnight's annual leave from the 28th. He was due back yesterday but didn't turn up.'

'Well that settles it, you have to go to the police now.'

'Hold on. I'm thinking.'

'What is there to think about?'

'Give me a minute.'

Fiona sighed, muttered under her breath, took her mug of tea through to the kitchen, made some banging noises then walked through the living room and into the hall. Craig could hear more banging noises coming from her bedroom. Then they suddenly stopped. She appeared at the doorway to the living room.

'I've got an idea. I know someone who might be able to help.'

Craig looked up in surprise. 'Who?'

'I know someone who used to be a journalist and now works for a publisher in Edinburgh. Specialises in historical non-fiction. I thought that she might be able to help, or still have contacts at the paper who could help. It can't do any harm to contact her, what do you think?'

Craig couldn't hide a smile. 'You mean you thought she might be able to talk some sense into me?'

Fiona smiled back at him. 'Well, that too.'

Fiona was born and raised in Edinburgh and her parents still lived there. They were both successful professionals, a solicitor and a doctor, which explained where Fiona got her brains. She checked the time on her watch then picked up the telephone and phoned her mum's office.

'Hi, could I speak to Mrs Rankin please if she's in yet? It's her daughter here. Thanks.'

The secretary put the call through and Valerie Rankin's voice was bright and cheerful when she picked up.

'Hi darling, this is an unexpected pleasure, how are you? Everything okay?'

'Hi Mum, yeah I'm fine ta, how's things?'

'All the better for hearing from you. What's up?'

'I'm looking for a wee favour. Do you still have Lynn Simon's number? I said I'd put a friend in touch with her.'

'Yes of course I do, give me a second.' Fiona heard the sound of rustling, then the receiver being picked up from a desk.

'Here it is, got a pen?'

'Yep.'

'031 225 1212.'

'Got it. Thanks Mum.'

'You're welcome. Give her my best when you speak to her and remind her that it's her turn for lunch. Speaking of which, will we have the pleasure of your company soon?'

'Maybe in a couple of weekends' time, Mum. Chris and I have got stuff on this weekend. But say hi to Dad for me and give him my love.'

'I certainly will, darling. Ring soon, love you.'

'Love you too, Mum. Bye.'

She looked up at Craig and saw his hangdog look.

'What?'

'Nothing.' But he couldn't help himself. 'Have you been seeing Chris long?'

Fiona snorted. 'What if I have?'

'No reason. Sorry, it's none of my business.'

'You're damn right it's not. Anyway, shut up, I've got to make another call.'

Lynn Simon walked along the cobbles that formed Edinburgh's narrow Hill Street. Her car was in the garage because it had been making some unusual and disconcerting noises, and then suddenly it died at the weekend. A truck came and took it away and the garage wasn't sure when Lynn would see it again. So it was back to the good old maroon and cream Lothian Regional Transport buses, which to be honest wasn't such a hardship for her. She had worked at Hamilton Dunbar for five years now, after leaving *The Scotsman* where she'd worked, woman and girl, for fifteen years. Lynn fell into her new career as a literary agent almost by accident. A features writer for the paper, she'd also written a couple of books about Scottish history and it was through that connection that she'd been approached by the agency to join them. They'd convinced her that making the leap would give her more time to write, plus the 'what's in it for them' was that they'd benefit from her journalistic ability to sort the wheat from the chaff. But they admitted that the main reason for wanting to have her on board was the clout her name would bring them. They wanted to attract more non-fiction business and Lynn Simon would help to do that. And so it proved. It had been a mutually satisfying five years and Lynn loved her job. She actually felt five years younger, not older, and at forty-seven she still attracted admiring glances in the street. She was wearing a smart blue skirt suit and her shoulder length auburn hair was in a high pony tail. Her winter mane, as she liked to call it, was auburn, although in the summer months she usually went a shade or two blonder. Today in her suit and her heels and with the merest hint of makeup she could pass for ten years younger.

'Morning, Julia.'

'Morning, Lynn. Coffee?'

'You read my mind. Thank you.'

Lynn picked up some papers from the receptionist's desk and climbed the few stairs to the main landing where the offices were. Hamilton Dunbar was based in a long Georgian terrace that was typically Edinburgh New Town. The history of the city being such, the area to the north of the famous castle was called the New Town even though it was conceived and built over two hundred years previously. The New Town had a solidity and a grandeur that suited firms of solicitors and banks and consulates, and it suited Hamilton Dunbar too. Lynn shared an office with her young assistant, David Halliday, who came on board as a YOPer eighteen months ago and whose enthusiasm and attitude had impressed them so much they kept him on.

David was already at his desk looking through some mail when Lynn came in.

'Good morning, Davie.'

'Morning, boss.'

'How was your date last night?'

'It's the last time I let my pal set me up on a blind date. She was a total munter.'

'Charming. I'm sure she speaks very highly of you too.'

David laughed as he stood up and waited for Lynn to take her seat, before laying a manuscript on her desk.

'This came in for you this morning, it's the one you've been expecting.'

'Brilliant. Is there a covering letter?'

David handed her a letter. 'He says there's no hurry but it would be good to get your thoughts at your earliest convenience et cetera, et cetera.'

'Excellent. Thanks Davie.'

At that, the receptionist came in with Lynn's coffee, and left after giving David a wink. Lynn read the letter and then turned to the manuscript. It was the latest book from Edward Hart-Davis, one of the authors who had been attracted to Hamilton Dunbar by Lynn's good offices. For the past two years he'd been writing what he considered to be the definitive work about England at the time of the Black Death and if it was as good as his previous titles it would be another feather in Hamilton Dunbar's cap.

'I know how much you love a good book full of mayhem, pestilence, intrigue and death,' said David as she began to read.

The King's Prerogative

'Can't beat it, Davie, you should try it.'

The phone rang on David's desk and he answered it.

'It's for you Lynn, a Fiona Rankin. She says it's urgent or I'd have taken a message.' He pushed a button and the phone on Lynn's desk rang.

'Hi Fiona, it's Lynn. Long time, no speak.'

'Hi Lynn, thanks for taking my call, I know you're busy.'

'What can I do for you?'

'Have you got five minutes to spare? I've got a bit of a story to tell you, and I was hoping you could offer some advice.'

'Fire away.'

Fiona kept the story brief and to the point. She told Lynn about Craig and the letter and about the approach to Doctor Irving, and Claire's death and how suspicion was now falling on Craig, and finally that Doctor Irving hadn't returned to work and no one knew where he was.

Lynn had been expecting Fiona to ask about the best place to take her parents for a nice meal, or if she could recommend a place to stay in London, or maybe even to help her track down a rare book. This conversation was unexpected to say the least and Lynn struggled to grasp everything Fiona was telling her.

'Fiona, hang on. So you're saying that your friend found a letter that belonged to Rudolf Hess, approached a Doctor Irving to help authenticate it, and this Doctor Irving is now missing? And meanwhile, a friend of his was killed?'

'Yes.'

Lynn was struggling to grasp what Fiona was asking her. 'I'm sorry, Fiona, I'm not sure what I can do. If the two things are connected at all, it sounds like a police matter to me.'

'I know, Lynn. But Craig has hit a brick wall and he's scared to go to the police. He just wants to find Doctor Irving so he can back up Craig's story. And that's when I thought of you because of your connections.'

'My connections are all in the newspaper or publishing

business, as you know.' Through the earpiece Lynn could hear Fiona whisper briefly to someone else in the background. 'Is your friend with you just now?'

'Yes he is.'

'Can I speak to him for a second?'

'Hold on.'

Fiona passed the receiver to Craig.

'Hello Mrs Simon? It's Craig Dunlop here.'

'Hello. I'm afraid to say I'm not sure how I can help you. I'm very sorry about your friend, but if this person you approached is missing then that's also a matter for the police. If you want my advice I would let them deal with it and offer them whatever help you can.'

Craig realised that he'd allowed his hopes to build and now he couldn't disguise the disappointment from creeping into his voice. 'I understand that. And I will go to the police, thank you for your time.' He handed the phone back to Fiona.

'Hi Lynn.'

'Hi, listen I'm sorry Fiona. Under other circumstances it would be fascinating to get involved, but to be honest the best thing your friend can do is let the police handle it.'

'I know, thanks anyway. Oh, my mum says hi and says it's your turn for lunch.'

Lynn laughed. 'I can take a hint. Okay, I'll give her a ring. Nice speaking to you and sorry again.'

'No problem, thanks Lynn. Bye.'

Lynn was about to hang up when a bell rang in her head and she stopped her hand in mid-air.

'Hello? Fiona?'

'Yes?'

'Could I have another quick word with your friend?'

Craig took the receiver.

'Hello?'

'Which university is it?'

'Pardon?'

The King's Prerogative

'Where this Doctor Irving works?'

'Strathclyde.'

Lynn racked her brain. Scotland was a fairly small pond in the academic world and she had rubbed shoulders with a fair number of Scottish university professors in her time. Irving. Irving. Irving. After a long moment a name came to her.

'Was it Brian Irving you spoke to?'

'Yes it was.'

'I think I know him. I'm sure we met at an industry dinner once.' Lynn thought for a moment, her journalistic cogs turning.

'Does he have your letter?'

'Yes.'

'And you sent him the letter before your friend died?'

'Yes, it was Claire who sent it to him.'

'And how long was it between him receiving the letter and Claire's death?'

'Just under a fortnight.'

'How was your friend killed?'

'The police say she disturbed a burglar who then stabbed her.'

'She was murdered? I assumed from what Fiona said that it was some kind of accident. Where was this?'

'In Stranraer.'

Another bell rang in Lynn's head. She'd read about it in the papers.

'The murder that was in the news recently?'

'Yes.'

Lynn's old journalist's radar was pinging like a pinball machine but as hard as she tried she just couldn't make the connection she needed to.

'I need you to help me here Craig. I've written about the Hess affair in the past, a long time ago when I was on the paper, but I'm a bit rusty to say the least.'

Craig was thinking hard too. Was this a waste of time

or could Lynn Simon actually help? He began thinking out loud.

'You're a publisher?'

'A literary agent.'

'So you know authors and publishers?'

'Yes.'

'And your specialism is historical non-fiction?'

'That's right,' said Lynn.

Craig followed his own train of thought. 'Did Brian Irving also write books?'

'Yes, one or two I believe.'

'And his specialism was?'

Lynn couldn't recall, or decided that she didn't know.

'I don't know. History perhaps. Maybe politics.'

Craig rubbed his forehead with his free hand. 'Brian told me that he was going to do some more research. Where would the overlap be between politics and historical non-fiction? If you were going to research Rudolf Hess where would you go?'

Lynn followed his reasoning but nothing came to her. She looked down. The manuscript was still on her desk. Her eyes widened.

'I don't know, but I know a man who might.'

'Who?'

'Another author.' The journalist in her took over. She looked at the clock on the office wall, then consulted her desk diary even though she knew it was empty till one-thirty. 'Where are you at the moment?'

'Glasgow.'

'Can you get through to Edinburgh this morning?'

'Well, yes.'

'Okay, can you come to my office? Eleven Hill Street. Hamilton Dunbar is the name of the agency.'

'Of course, I'll get there as soon as I can. Thank you so much Mrs Simon.'

'Don't thank me yet. The chances are this could probably be a dead end but we can see where it takes us.'

'That's funny.'
'What is?'
'That's almost exactly what Brian Irving said to me a month ago. I should see you in a couple of hours or so.'

Craig hung up. He couldn't help himself and threw his arms round Fiona in a bear hug.
'What's that for?'
'For being clever as well as beautiful.' Their eyes held each other's gaze for a second too long. Fiona looked away and stood up.
'Come on then.'
'What?'
'Well I assume from your conversation that you're going through to meet Lynn. You'll need someone to introduce you.'
'No I won't.'
'Well you'll need someone to frog march you down to the police station afterwards. Your mum would never forgive me if I didn't.' She padded through to the hall. 'And we'll stop off at Boots to get you a toothbrush before you meet Lynn. Your breath's honking.'

***

Two miles away Blake answered a telephone.
'Hello, Detective Wilson?'
'Speaking.'
'It's Lorraine Johnston from Strathclyde University. You asked me to give you a ring if anyone should contact the office looking for Doctor Irving?'
'Yes, thank you for calling. Has someone asked for him?'
'Yes, a Craig Dunlop called a few minutes ago. He said that Doctor Irving was doing something for him.'
'Is that all?'
'Yes.'

'Did he leave an address or say where he was?'

'No, but he left a phone number in case Doctor Irving got in touch. It's a Glasgow number, 276 5963.'

'Thank you Miss Johnston. And please call me again if this Craig Dunlop or anyone else contacts you.'

Blake replaced the receiver, picked up his car keys and went out into the grey Glasgow drizzle.

Chapter 18

It was just after nine o'clock when Craig and Fiona crossed a bustling Byres Road heading for the subway station. Their first stop was a chemist where Craig bought himself a toothbrush and toothpaste. When they reached Hillhead subway station, they descended the steps and arrived at a crowded platform. They'd missed the bulk of the morning rush hour but the platform was still busy. They only had to wait for a couple of minutes before the train arrived. The beauty of the Glasgow underground was that it ran in one circular loop, with the trains travelling either clockwise on what was known as the Outer Circle, or anti-clockwise on the Inner Circle. This was a handy arrangement if you were new to the city or were a bit worse for wear from the night before. As long as you stood at the correct platform you were guaranteed to get on the right train, and even if you caught the train heading in the opposite direction you'd eventually get to your destination, albeit later than intended. As it was, Craig and Fiona boarded the Outer Circle train and four stops later they emerged at Buchanan Street and two minutes after that they were in the queue at the ticket office at Queen Street railway station.

Fiona dug around in her bag for her young person's railcard and Craig realised that he didn't have his with him so he had to pay full fare. He paid for both tickets and they went out on to the concourse.

'We've just missed a train so the next one's in twenty-five minutes, do you fancy some breakfast?' asked Craig, and Fiona looked at him like he was a half-wit.

'You've had breakfast.'

'Eh, no, I've had half a slice of toast and two sips of tea.' So Craig bought himself a bacon cheeseburger from a fast food stall called Casey Jones. He was always amused by the name, due to the fact that any time he'd frequented it in the past he'd usually been a-steamin' and a-rollin'. He felt very different this morning. He bought two coffees and gave one to Fiona, and they headed to the platform. The train was already sitting there so they got on and found a free table.

'You seem to be in a good mood this morning,' said Fiona.

Craig did feel a lot better and it dawned on him that the main reason was that he was spending time with Fiona again. 'I suppose I am,' he said.

Fiona reached over and touched his hand. 'It sounds as if you've had a tough couple of weeks.'

Craig nodded. Since Claire's murder he felt that he'd been carrying a burden by himself. Maybe the build-up of pressure was the reason he'd reacted the way he had when the policeman brought things to a head. Who knows. But this morning he felt a sense of relief because Fiona had taken a share of the load from his shoulders, and now they were on their way to meet someone else who might be able to help. Even if it didn't lead to them finding Brian Irving, Craig felt that he wasn't on his own any longer and in a strange way that would make it easier when the time came to face the police.

Outside on the platform a guard blew a whistle and the train moved off. It would take just shy of an hour to get through to Edinburgh so they settled in for the journey.

'Do you go home much these days?' asked Craig.

'Usually once or twice a month,' said Fiona. 'Mainly to see my mum and dad and Robert.' Robert was her younger brother. She studied him for a long moment. 'How's it been for you in Stranraer?' She immediately realised it was an insensitive choice of words and she flushed slightly. 'Sorry, sweetheart, I mean before all this happened.'

Craig's stomach flipped slightly at the mention of the pet name she used. He couldn't look her in the eye. 'It's been fine, well, okay.'

A heavy silence hung between them for a while. Craig eventually broke the tension.

'As we're on our way to Edinburgh, I have to ask – are you still putting salt and sauce on your chips?' They both smiled. The question was in reference to the great divide in Scottish society. The default condiments used by Glasgow fish and chip shops were salt and vinegar. Travel forty miles to Edinburgh in the east however and the same supper would be smothered in salt and brown sauce. After several years of visiting football grounds across central Scotland, Craig discovered that the tipping point of this continental divide was Linlithgow, where, if you didn't declare a preference, they put all three on your chips.

'Oh, I'm still an Edinburgh girl at heart,' smiled Fiona.

The train rattled on, stopping at Falkirk High and Polmont stations. Craig could see the aluminium crown of St Michael's church as they approached Linlithgow, and just behind it, the ruined palace. They hadn't spoken for a few minutes and the silence between them became heavy once again. Craig searched for something else to say.

'How do you know Lynn Simon?' he asked eventually.

'She's been a friend of my mum's since their schooldays,' replied Fiona. 'They used to go on holiday together when they were both in their twenties, backpacking through France and Spain on a shoestring budget. Lynn even fell in love with a French guy. In Nice. She was all set to stay there and they were going to grow vines and make wine.'

'What happened?'

'She wanted a career, so she moved back to Scotland.'

'Shame.'

'Not at all. Nicolas, that's his name, followed her back, and they got married. Simon is actually *See-mong* but it's easier for her to use the anglicised pronunciation for work.'

'She sounds like quite a formidable lady.'
'She is. I suppose you don't become successful in a career like journalism if you're a shrinking violet.'

The train was approaching the suburbs of Edinburgh. As Craig stared out of the window they passed a square brick building with *Jenner's Depository* written on it in large white letters, they then skirted Murrayfield Stadium before the train slowed down through some marshalling yards and drew into Haymarket station. A slow five minutes later and they were walking along the platform at Waverley. Craig realised that he hadn't been in Edinburgh for a long time and he thought back to the weekends he'd enjoyed here with Fiona, and the week long training courses he'd attended at the staff college in the south side of the city.

They climbed the Waverley Steps onto Princes Street, with the impressive old North British Hotel on their right and the equally impressive Scott Monument on their left. It felt several degrees colder on Princes Street than it did on Byres Road and Craig buttoned his jacket against the stiff breeze that whistled round the corner of the large sandstone hotel. They crossed the busy shopping street, dodging a maroon and cream double decker bus that was advertising the new Robert de Niro film, *The King of Comedy*. Hill Street ran parallel to the main New Town thoroughfares of Princes Street and George Street, and Craig and Fiona reached the offices of Hamilton Dunbar on foot without too much trouble. The receptionist showed them straight up to Lynn Simon's office where Lynn greeted Fiona with a kiss, Fiona introduced Craig, and Lynn introduced them both to David Halliday. Lynn invited them to sit round a small table in one corner of the office and she waited for Craig to speak. Craig took out the wallet and opened it on the table. He reached inside, pulled out the photocopy and turned it round so that it faced Lynn.

'This is the letter I told you about on the phone. Brian Irving has the original.'

Fiona read the letter, and pursed her lips as she breathed out in a quiet whistle. 'I can see why this might have caught Doctor Irving's attention.'

'He was far from convinced initially, and because it's all gone quiet I don't know if he's convinced at all.'

'You know what the implications of this letter are?'

'I think so. The main implication is that Hess's flight was arranged in advance. The letter might have been part of a sting operation by the British intelligence services. On the other hand, there might actually have been people here who wanted Britain to make peace with Germany.'

'And do you know which angle Brian Irving was approaching it from?'

'Well first and foremost he wanted to try to find out if the letter was genuine.'

'Hmmmmm, quite,' mused Lynn. 'If it was me, I know which would be the more straightforward path to explore.'

'What would that be?' asked Craig.

'My first port of call would be MI5.'

'Really? You can do that?'

'Why not? They're not ex-directory. The trick would be to find a way in, through the right contact. Otherwise they'd be likely to deny all knowledge and stonewall your enquiry.'

'Do you know the right contact? You said you might know a man who could help.'

'I'll come back to that, but first I want to understand more about your discussion with Brian.' She retraced the steps in her mind. 'In principle I think it would be easier to try to get confirmation that there was an MI5 or MI6 operation. There should be records in existence even if they're still under wraps. It's unlikely you'd be able to see any records but you might get confirmation from the civil service that there was an operation of some kind at the time. Is that an angle that Brian would have followed do you think?'

'Brian didn't seem to think there was a sting operation, mainly because Britain hushed up the whole affair afterwards.'

'That's a fair point.' said Lynn. 'How much do you know about the night that Hess landed?'

'A fair amount, not least because of what my grandfather told me.'

'And did your grandfather tell you about the curious anomalies in procedure that night?'

'Anomalies?'

Lynn retrieved a box file from her desk. 'I wrote an article a few years back for *The Scotsman*. It was shortly after the Duke of Hamilton died, so the article was a retrospective about his life and the lasting impact on him of the Hess affair. I've spent the last couple of hours refreshing my memory.'

She opened the file and handed Craig a newspaper article that took up almost the whole of a broadsheet page. Craig read it and handed it to Fiona who did the same. When she finished she handed the article back and Lynn folded it and put it back into the box file.

Lynn restarted the conversation. 'Weird isn't it? The Duke of Hamilton was in charge of Scotland's air defences at the time, and yet the RAF didn't make a huge effort to intercept Hess's plane even though it had been picked up on radar and identified as German. But it's the breaches in regulations that are the most astonishing.'

'Definitely,' agreed Craig. 'I hadn't appreciated that as a captured airman, Hess, or Horn as he called himself, should have been interrogated by the local RAF intelligence officer as soon as he landed, as a matter of standard procedure. But both he and his commanding officer decided to wait until *the next morning* before getting involved. The pilot could have had vital information about that night's intended bombing raids.'

'And who was that RAF intelligence man's commanding officer?' asked Lynn, rhetorically. 'It was the Duke of Hamilton. You could view it as a serious breach of operational procedure, or you could view it as deliberate negligence.'

'Very strange when you put it together with the fact that Hess specifically asked to be taken to the Duke,' said Craig.

Lynn tapped the table with a fingernail. 'But there was an even more blatant breach of security about that night,' she said. 'And it makes me think that Hess *was* expected.'

Chapter 19

'It's not in my article,' Lynn continued, 'although I did make a note about it at the time. On the night Hess arrived, more than one radar station on the east coast had identified the plane as a Messerschmitt 110.'

'And the RAF didn't manage to shoot it down,' said Fiona.

'That in itself wasn't so unusual, to be honest. It was a single plane after all. Flying fast in pitch darkness.'

'What then?'

'How many crew normally flew in a Messerschmitt 110?'

Craig suddenly realised where Lynn was heading. 'Two. They seated two.'

'Correct. But there was no search for a second airman.'

'Why not?' asked Fiona.

'Because Hess told his captors that he was alone,' said Lynn.

'And they believed him?' asked Fiona.

'It would appear so. It seems incredible that there was no search for a second parachutist. The officers at the scene were happy to take Hauptmann Alfred Horn's word that he was alone and unarmed. Even though you might expect a captured pilot to say that, to give his comrade the best chance of escape.'

'Bloody hell,' said Craig. 'Why has that never occurred to me before? A second airman could have posed a serious threat to security, but there was no obvious search conducted and no mention of a body in the wreckage.'

'But they wouldn't search for anyone else if they knew Hess was coming alone,' said David.

The King's Prerogative

'Whoever "they" were,' said Craig.

A silence hovered over the table. David was the first to break it.

'I realise I'm coming to this late, but didn't Britain and Germany both say that Hess was mad? Maybe we're overthinking this and it really is as simple as that. There was no peace initiative and there was no intelligence operation to entice Hess over to Britain.'

Craig and Lynn looked at David and then gave each other a look that said 'Will you tell him or will I?' Craig took the initiative. He was glad of the chance to test out his thinking and see if it might coincide with Lynn's. He turned to David. 'When there had been no word from Hess after a couple of days, the Germans assumed that he had been captured. It was Hitler who broke the news to the world. He gave a broadcast on German radio telling the nation that Hess was suffering from a mental disorder and was having hallucinations. Hitler announced that Hess had set off on a flight from Augsburg in Bavaria, had not returned and it was assumed he'd jumped out of his plane or had met with an accident.'

'It was Hitler who broke the news, not the British?'

'That's right.'

'Was that not a bit strange? Wouldn't it have been extremely embarrassing for Hitler?'

'It was the lesser of two evils. When it became apparent that the plan had failed, Hitler had to maintain plausible deniability. He had to keep Stalin off the scent.'

'The scent of what?' asked David.

'Hitler was playing a game of misdirection. He was planning an attack on the Soviet Union but wanted to make it look like he was still planning an invasion of Britain.'

'But he *was* planning an invasion of Britain,' said David. 'Wasn't it called Operation Sea Lion?'

Craig shook his head. 'No he wasn't. He wanted it to *look* like he was. I've read everything I can get my hands on. He never committed anything like the resources needed to launch an attack on Britain. In fact, he didn't actually want a war with Britain at all. Even during the battle for France, Hitler gave Britain every chance to walk away.'

'What?'

'You've heard about the miracle of Dunkirk?

'Yes.'

'Well in truth the fact that thousands of British soldiers managed to escape from under the Germans' noses wasn't all that much of a miracle. The only reason it was allowed to happen was because Hitler gave direct orders for all German forces to hold their position for three days. The orders were even sent uncoded and were picked up by the British. Hitler's generals were astounded.'

'Why would he do that?'

'He was certain that Britain would want to make peace and he viewed the escape of the British Expeditionary Force as a gesture that would allow the UK to have "peace with honour".'

'That's crazy.'

'It might seem crazy in retrospect but think about it from Hitler's perspective at the time. After the Munich Agreement Hitler was sure that Britain didn't want war. He didn't think Britain would stand up for Poland, and was surprised when Chamberlain did declare war. But if you look at events afterwards, Britain did next to nothing when Poland was attacked. The Phoney War lasted the best part of nine months. All the evidence in front of him encouraged Hitler to think that Britain's heart wasn't in a war. He was convinced that all Britain was looking for was a means of securing peace without losing face.'

'He got that one seriously wrong,' said David.

'He did. And there was one main reason why he miscalculated Britain's mood.'

'Which was?'

'Chamberlain was no longer Prime Minister. Churchill

became Prime Minister on the 10th of May 1940. Dunkirk happened a fortnight later.'

David thought for a few seconds. 'But why would Hitler want peace with Britain? He'd already flattened half of Europe by that time.'

'Because in Hitler's vision of a new world order he saw the British Empire as a necessary counterpoint to the spread of communism. It's in *Mein Kampf*. It was always his intention to push eastwards into Russia.'

'But Germany and the Soviet Union were allies at the start of the war.'

'Yes, but that was only a necessary expediency on the part of the Soviet Union to buy time. In the year leading up to the invasion of Poland, Stalin was worried that Britain and France were trying to provoke a German–Soviet war. You have to remember that at the time both the British and French governments believed that a strong Germany would actually be desirable because it would provide a buffer against Soviet expansion. Stalin had offered Britain and France a defence pact in early 1939 but they were both lukewarm about it to say the least. So Stalin took matters into his own hands and signed the non-aggression pact with Germany to buy his country time to prepare for the war he was sure would happen. It was always Hitler's intention to attack the Soviets.'

David let this sink in. 'So, Hitler wanted peace with Britain so that he could focus on Russia?'

'That's right,' said Craig. 'But his intentions had to be ultra-secret so that Stalin wouldn't suspect. And that's why he disowned Hess's mission. He had to make it look like he was still facing westward. Any hint that he was putting out peace feelers to Britain would have alerted Stalin to danger. So from that point of view, Operation Sea Lion was a complete success, as a diversionary tactic. Even when Hitler deployed his Panzer divisions to the east in the run up to his attack, the cover story was that they were being moved out of range of RAF bombers, and Stalin believed it. When the invasion finally came it achieved complete surprise.'

'There was an additional reason why Hitler might have tried to convince the world that Hess had taken leave of his senses,' said Lynn. 'Under the terms of the Geneva Convention, if it was accepted that Hess was mad the British would have been compelled to repatriate him.'

'Which could explain why the British preferred to hush the whole affair up,' said Fiona. 'So they could keep him prisoner without too many questions being asked. But can I ask something?'

'Of course,' said Lynn.

'Hess may have been lured here, or he may have come up with the idea alone. In either case, isn't it likely that Hitler was telling the truth? I see the need for him to keep Stalin in the dark about a possible invasion, I get that. But maybe Hess *did* take leave of his senses. Maybe he *was* a lone maverick trying to do the right thing by his Fuhrer and his country by taking Britain out of the war. He was deluded, but he was acting alone and there was no master plan behind it.'

'In a nutshell, that's been the official line for forty years,' said Lynn.

'I've read everything I could lay my hands on over the past few weeks,' said Craig. 'And I'm convinced that Hess made his flight in full possession of his faculties and with Hitler's blessing.'

Now it was Lynn who provided the challenge. 'What makes you say that? Apart from the timing of it regarding the invasion of Russia?' Craig couldn't tell if she asked this to test how much he knew or to prove that he was an idiot, but he took a deep breath and held out his fingers, ready to count them. He touched his thumb.

'Okay. One: there's a common belief that Hess was Hitler's poodle, a puppet who'd slavishly and blindly do anything for him. In public he was the model Nazi, declaring unswerving devotion to his Fuhrer. In private however, he was one of the few who actively challenged Hitler over policy, and it's on record that he *argued* with Hitler.'

Fiona raised an eyebrow. 'I can't imagine anyone would have argued with Hitler.'

'He was the only one of the inner circle who did,' said Craig. 'Or the only one who did and survived to tell the tale. For example, they had a huge row over Dunkirk because Hess thought the generals were right and Hitler's tactic was wrong. But he'd earned the right to argue with him because he'd been through thick and thin with Hitler over a period of twenty years, been in prison with him, and effectively co-wrote *Mein Kampf*. He was anything but unintelligent or politically naïve, and he was no "yes man".'

'Okay, I grant you that might have been the case in the twenties and thirties,' said Lynn. 'But was the point not that he had been side-lined in 1941 and he pulled the stunt to get back into favour with his beloved Fuhrer?'

'That's a myth too,' said Craig. He tapped his index finger to indicate that he was coming to his second point. 'The received wisdom is that Hess felt alienated because when war broke out he didn't have a job to do. He was deputy head of the party, only a figurehead according to the legend that's been propagated since the war. From what I've read, nothing could be further from the truth. Hitler used him as his right-hand man, his sounding board, the one man he could trust implicitly. More than one neutral writer who observed them at close quarters referred to Hess as Hitler's alter ego. Originally it was Hitler who was Hess's protégé, not the other way round.'

'What?' asked Fiona with more than a hint of scepticism in her voice.

'I know, it sounds strange, but it's true. For example, before he met important foreign dignitaries, Hitler used to consult Hess about how he should approach the meeting and took his advice on how to act. They were very much a partnership.' Craig warmed to the topic and felt he was on a roll. 'Hess also had some interesting responsibilities over and above his role as "minister without portfolio". Apart from in effect being the head of the Nazi party, he was head of technical development. Which was the department responsible for developing the German atomic bomb. And he was also in charge of the Auslandorganisation, or AO. In other words, the German foreign intelligence-gathering network.'

'Interesting,' said David. 'That sounds like a handy position to be in if you're hatching a plan to make a peace offer to the UK.'

'Exactly,' said Craig.

'You're saying that Hess and Hitler hatched the plan together?' asked Lynn.

'There's a lot of circumstantial evidence that points to it, yes. You could be forgiven for overlooking individual pieces of the jigsaw, but when you put them all together after the event it creates an interesting picture.'

'Such as?'

'Well, when Hess was training to make his flight, his tutor was none other than Hitler's personal pilot. You can't tell me that Hitler didn't know about that, or it was allowed to happen without Hitler's approval. And in the build up to the flight, Hitler's diary reveals some interesting things. If Hess had been persona non grata, or at least side-lined, I don't think Hitler would have asked him to give the annual May Day speech to the German people just days before his flight. Hitler was supposed to have given the speech personally. He'd given the speech every year since coming to power in 1933, but he changed his mind in May 1941 and asked Hess to do it. It's almost like he was reminding the German people of Hess's importance. And the two men had a private meeting before Hess left Berlin for the last time, which lasted for five hours. Five hours. What did they discuss?'

'The flight?' asked Fiona.

'I can't think what else would occupy them for that long.'

Craig touched the middle finger of his left hand, indicating the third point he wanted to make. 'But thirdly, and probably most importantly, it is inconceivable that Hess would have abandoned his wife and young son to Hitler's wrath. It was well known that Hitler's policy was collective liability for any act of treachery. They even had a word for it – *Sippenhaft* – all family and friends of a traitor were punished as part of the retribution. Interestingly, not only were his family not punished, they were allowed to stay in the family home and Hitler personally ensured Hess's wife Ilse received a generous pension as the dependant of Luftwaffe Hauptmann Alfred Horn! Hess's aides also escaped any punishment even though they admitted helping with preparations. Even Willi Messerschmitt, the head of the aircraft company, was only given a token questioning even though he knew that Hess's preparations pointed to a long-distance solo flight. The truth is, the myth of Hess as lone crackpot was created in retrospect because it suited the purposes of those who wanted to conceal his true mission. I think it's very interesting that after Hess's capture, Hitler made Martin Bormann Head of the Nazi Party, but he stopped short of making him Deputy Fuhrer. It was as if no one else could take Hess's place.'

The other three looked at Craig.

'Wow,' said Fiona. 'I don't know what's scarier, the fact that you know so much about it or that you haven't taken a breath for the last five minutes.'

'Sorry, all this stuff has been swimming around inside my head for the last few weeks and it's had nowhere to go.'

Lynn looked at him. 'You've done your homework, Craig, I'll give you that. I'm not convinced that the jigsaw pieces fit together quite as you describe, but I tend to agree there's a bigger story here.'

Craig couldn't hide the smile from creeping across his mouth. 'Thanks Mrs Simon. Thank you for at least hearing me out. I wasn't sure if I was losing my marbles or if I was just getting paranoid.'

'You still need to go to the police. The fact that you ran away makes you look very guilty, even if you did it for the best of reasons. And for heaven's sake, my name's Lynn.'

Craig's smile faded. 'You're right Lynn. But I do feel better for having this chat. You mentioned...'

The sound of the telephone on David's desk interrupted Craig before he could continue. David pushed himself away from the table, the casters on his chair rolling him across to his desk a few feet away. He picked up the receiver.

'Hello, Lynn Simon's office.'

Pause.

'Yes, Mr Hart-Davis, she's here. Can you hold for one second please?' He put his hand over the mouthpiece and offered the receiver to Lynn, who perched on the edge of David's desk before taking it from him.

'Hello, Edward? Thank you for returning my call so quickly.'

'The message you left on my machine sounded urgent. Did you get my manuscript?'

'Yes, Edward, thank you, it arrived this morning and I've already started reading it. I'm looking forward to getting to grips with it. But I wanted to pick your brain on something unrelated.'

'By all means my dear, how can I help?'

'I have a friend who's doing some research on clandestine intelligence operations carried out during the war. He's reached the point where he's looking for additional corroboration of his facts.' She winked at Craig, who smiled back. 'I remembered your book on the origins of the Cold War and I wondered if you had any contacts that might provide a route into that world. I thought an introduction from you would open doors that might otherwise remain firmly shut. If that's not an imposition, of course.'

Edward Hart-Davis chuckled. Lynn liked the seventy-six-year-old author because amongst other things they shared the same martini-dry sense of humour. She had made the lengthy and frequently tiresome process of bringing out a book easy and painless for him. He'd known her for nearly five years and counted her as a friend. Which meant he could tell when she was up to something.

'I think you've found a particularly juicy bone to chew on, Mrs Simon. I recognise the signs.'

'Why Edward, whatever can you mean?' Her words said one thing but the tone of her voice said another thing altogether. It said, 'You know that and I know that, but don't ask me anything else because I'm not ready to tell you the answer quite yet.'

Edward chuckled again. 'Well I do know someone, he's one of my old Cambridge clique. But I'm not going to put you in touch with him if you're going to cause trouble. He's a friend and I'd like to keep it that way.'

It was Lynn's turn to laugh. 'Brownie's honour, Edward. I'll be on my best behaviour.'

'Good girl. Well, you'll have to give me a few details and I'll pass your number on to him, how would that be?'

'That would be very good of you, kind sir.'

Lynn gave Edward the briefest synopsis. She didn't mention Craig but instead she told Edward that it was Brian Irving who was conducting the research. She thought a little white lie would simplify matters so said that she was Brian's agent and he had found some secret documentation dating from 1941 that he wanted to authenticate. Hence his desire to foster a contact in the Home Office or MI5.

'And this document relates to?' asked Edward.

Lynn covered the mouthpiece and looked at Craig. 'Can I tell him it's about Hess?'

Craig nodded.

'It's to do with Rudolf Hess's flight to Scotland.'

'Really?' said Edward. 'I think that should get his attention. How urgently do you need a response?'

'That's the thing. As soon as possible.'

'I'll get in touch with him today.'

'Thank you so much Edward. I really appreciate it. Speak to you soon.'

Lynn put the phone down and re-joined the others at the meeting table.

'That sounded positive,' said Fiona.

'Yes it was, Edward is a good man to know. He's been to most corners of the world and he knows just about everyone.' She looked at the clock on the wall. It was nearly twelve-thirty. 'What are your plans now?'

Craig looked at Fiona. 'Well I suppose we could go to lunch and then I'll pay a visit to the nearest police station.'

Lynn's face had a mischievous look.

'What?' asked Fiona.

'Well it would be a shame if we didn't give Edward a chance to phone us back with some news.'

'But you said…?'

'I know what I said, but the police will still be there tomorrow after all. On *The Scotsman* I had my fair share of run-ins with Edinburgh's finest, so I wouldn't just walk in and announce myself if I were you. Tell you what, let's give Edward a few hours, and if we hit a brick wall, I'll take you to police headquarters. I think I still know one or two of them in there.'

Craig looked at Fiona again. She shrugged her shoulders. 'What the hell. Let's go and get some lunch.'

Chapter 20

Detective Inspector Bruce Cowie vented his spleen at the officers in the room. They had gathered for the morning case briefing and his junior DC had provided the latest update that they had taken nearly a 120 statements from people who knew Claire Marshall and spoken to twice that number of friends, colleagues and neighbours.

'Do you consider that progress?' Bruce Cowie's glare was enough to make the DC study his feet in silence. 'It's not good enough, people!'

The fourteen-man team – well the twelve man and two woman team – all stared at their feet.

It was nearly two weeks since the murder and Bruce Cowie had made only negligible progress with the investigation. The police had been exhaustive in tracing every known housebreaker, convicted or otherwise, every drug addict, every violent criminal who matched the M.O. within a hundred-mile radius including Northern Ireland and northern England. Those that weren't in prison were interviewed. Even those who were in prison were spoken to, on the chance that they knew something. Alibis were checked, every tentative line of enquiry followed through. A few leads looked promising initially but came to a loose end when it became clear that the potential suspects couldn't be in two places at once. The police were still no closer to finding the murderer.

One loose end in particular was troubling Cowie.

'Where are we with finding Craig Dunlop?'

DC Jarvis spoke up. 'Nothing since we visited his parents again yesterday. He didn't buy a train ticket and we showed his passport photo to the bus drivers who worked yesterday and none of them remember seeing him.'

'If he didn't take a bus or a train, did he take a boat?'

Another policeman looked up. 'He didn't board a ferry yesterday either, sir.'

'Well if he didn't leave town by ferry, bus or train then either he left by car or he's still in Stranraer. Have we spoken to all his friends and family?'

'Yes sir. The last person to see him was his mother at around ten-thirty am yesterday.'

'Is it possible that he fabricated the story he told his mother about this man masquerading as DS Wilson? Or that she lied to us?'

'I think she told us the truth, sir. When I spoke to his parents last night they were both worried. They weren't faking.'

'I want this other man traced. Anyone who goes to the length of getting hold of a warrant card is up to no good, but I want to know what he *is* up to. Either he's aiding and abetting Dunlop or he wants to stop Dunlop from talking to us. What have you found out?'

'Just the description the bank manager and staff gave us,' said his detective sergeant, DS Derek Campbell.

'And do we know how he got hold of the real DS Wilson's warrant card?'

'DS Wilson told us that he mislaid his warrant card in the changing rooms at his local swimming pool about two months ago.'

'Did he report it as lost or stolen?'

'Of course.'

'Conclusions?'

'He was followed. This man stole it.'

Bruce Cowie didn't like the way the investigation seemed to be slipping out of his control.

'Right. Go back over every statement we've taken. Look

for any connection to a man fitting this fake DS Wilson's description. Next, I want Dunlop's parents and sister brought in for questioning. Find out everything they know. And I want every shop, café, pub, bed and breakfast and public toilet in this town visited, and everyone in them shown a picture of Craig Dunlop. And I want the results today.'

He dismissed his team and they hurried out of the room, all except DS Campbell, who waited for the door to close. Bruce Cowie stood at the large bulletin board in the briefing room, studying the pieces of paper and photographs that represented the few facts definitively known about Claire Marshall's murder, and the even fewer leads.

'The guys are working flat out, sir,' said the detective sergeant. 'We just need a touch of luck.'

Bruce Cowie said nothing, and DS Campbell opened the door and closed it behind him.

A minute later the door opened again and Derek Campbell stepped back in.

'Sir, I think you should see this.' He handed Cowie a slip of paper with handwritten notes on it.

'Where's Jarvis?'

DS Campbell summoned the junior DC, who duly arrived.

'Here I am, sir.'

'This just came in this morning?'

'Five minutes ago, sir.'

'Come with me. You too, Derek.'

The North West Castle Hotel in Stranraer was built in the 1820s and was originally home to a famous Arctic explorer. As a hotel it was in the fortunate position of being popular throughout the year. In the summer months it was full of holidaymakers who used it either as a base for touring in that part of Scotland, or as a stopping-off point for a trip to Ireland. Off season it was a Mecca for curlers who combined a relaxing mini-break with a few games on the hotel's own indoor ice rink. Most weekends there was a function of some description taking place, usually a wedding. And then there was the constant stream of golfers who came to this corner of Scotland to enjoy good food and good whisky as well as to play a few rounds.

On this particular Tuesday the hotel was about half full, with roughly thirty of the rooms occupied. The duty manager saw the policemen walk up the steps as they approached the main door. He had been expecting them and had already made his office ready in preparation for their visit.

'Good morning officers,' he said, extending a hand in greeting. 'I'm Andrew Strachan, duty manager.'

Bruce Cowie showed Strachan his warrant card and introduced the others.

'Pleased to meet you, would you come this way?' Strachan led them behind the reception desk into a small room where there was a desk with a chair behind it and four chairs set out in front of it. A tea trolley was stationed to one side with some refreshments that looked freshly made. A young woman sat on one of the four chairs in front of the desk. When the others arrived, she stood up and faced the policemen. She looked to be in her early twenties, with a round pink face that made her look embarrassed but was probably just the result of years spent in the fresh country air.

'Gentlemen, let me introduce Lorna, one of our receptionists.'

Bruce Cowie introduced himself and shook Lorna's hand. The duty manager invited them all to be seated.

'Can I offer you a tea or a coffee?' asked Strachan.

'No, thank you.' DI Cowie turned his chair so it faced Lorna's straight on. The other policemen followed suit.

'Lorna, first of all I'd like to thank you for contacting us this morning, you've been a great help already. But I'd like to ask you a few questions if you don't mind.'

'Well, it was Mr Strachan who contacted you, but I said to him about the car.'

Andrew Strachan stepped in. 'Yes, that's right. One of your young officers was here yesterday afternoon and told us that you were keen to speak to two men who might have been guests in one of the local hotels. He provided a description of the men and a car they were using. When Lorna came in to start her shift this morning, she knew that one of our guests matched the description.'

DI Cowie gave the man a smile that didn't quite reach the eyes. Strachan stopped talking.

Bruce Cowie turned back to the receptionist.

'Lorna, we know one of the men was called Craig Dunlop.' He opened a thin document folder and produced Craig's passport photograph for Lorna to look at.

'I know Craig,' said Lorna. 'He hasn't been here.'

'How do you know him?'

'A friend of a friend. I sometimes see him at the same parties or in the pub.'

'I see. So you'd definitely recognise him if you saw him.'

'Definitely.'

'And what about this other man?'

'Well it was more the car I recognised. From the description Mr Strachan told me about. He said you were looking for a man in a black two door Fiat 131 saloon.'

'Yes, it was seen leaving the Royal Bank on Bridge Street just after ten o'clock yesterday morning. And you're sure the man who had that car stayed here?'

'Definitely.'

'Do you have his hotel registration details?'

Strachan handed over a small card about six by eight inches in size. Bruce Cowie read the details:

Name: Michael Green
Address: c/o Vulcan Holdings, Limehouse, London E14.
Car Registration: AYS 560Y
Booked 7 Nights: Thurs 10th – Thurs 17th March 1983
Checked out Monday 14th March. The previous day, noted Cowie.

'Michael Green.'

'Yes,' said Lorna.

'Did you speak to him?'

'Yes, I made up his bill for him when he checked out.' Andrew Strachan handed over the hotel's copy of the bill.

'What did he look like?'

'Just as the description said. A bit under six foot, medium build, fair hair, spoke with a London accent.'

'No distinguishing marks?'

'No.'

Bruce Cowie read the bill. Four nights' stay, and Green had checked out earlier than planned.

'There's an item here for phone calls made. Do you have a record of them?'

'Just the dates and the cost, he dialled direct from his room and the system doesn't record the numbers.'

'Pity.'

'When you spoke to him, Lorna, how did he seem? How did he come across to you?'

'Well he was always polite to me. Didn't say much usually. But on that last day when he asked for his bill to be made up, he was bordering on rude. He said he was in a hurry and he needed his bill straight away.'

'I see. How did he pay?'

'Cash.'

'Mmmm hmmm. And you're definitely certain that his car was a black Fiat two-door?'

'Mr Cowie, I know my cars. It's my hobby. My brother has an original Lancia Beta Montecarlo. I helped him restore it from the wheels up. And this guest's car was a black Fiat 131 Supermirafiori Sport two door saloon. The four-door versions are quite popular, you see a few of them around the town. The two-door ones look the same apart from the sports headlights. But I've only ever seen two of those in Stranraer, this guest's one and another one. And that other one is owned by my friend's dad, and it's red.'

Bruce Cowie couldn't conceal a smile from breaking over his face. 'Thank you again Lorna, you've been a great help. DC Jarvis here will take a statement from you, just to make sure we've got a record of everything you've told us.'

Andrew Strachan shifted in his seat. 'Em, there's something else, DI Cowie.'

'Yes?'

'We keep our guests' cards for eighteen months, we like to keep track of any special requirements they have for their next visit.'

'Yes?'

'Michael Green was here before, recently in fact.' He gave the policeman a second hotel card. No car registration number was noted, but the card told Cowie that Green had stayed at the hotel two weeks earlier. He'd stayed for a couple of nights and checked out on Wednesday 2nd March. The day Claire Marshall's body was found.

Five minutes later DI Cowie and DS Campbell were on their way back to the station. They both immediately recognised AYS as a Glasgow registration number, so it looked like the investigation was going to shift focus to Glasgow and London, assuming the address Green had given wasn't bogus.

'Right, Derek, get Records in Dumfries to do a cross-check on the name Michael Green, and ask Maureen to get on the blower to every constabulary in Scotland and the north of England with a description of the car. Contact the DVLA and find out who it's registered to. As soon as the details come through, contact Strathclyde and get them to move on it urgently. I'm going to speak to Scotland Yard about this Vulcan Holdings of Limehouse.'

Bruce Cowie strode back into the police station and called the rest of his team together.

Chapter 21

Craig and Fiona were finishing their lunch in a nice pub in the West End, just along from the Caledonian Hotel. Craig was in no hurry to move, no doubt because his body had to divert resources to tackle the steak pie and veg he'd just consumed.

'You made short work of that,' said Fiona.

'I was starving. Must be nervous energy.'

He put his knife and fork together on his plate just as a waitress came to clear them away.

'Thank you for arranging this morning and coming through with me,' he said to Fiona. A thought came to him, and he looked at his watch. It was just before two o'clock. The pub was starting to empty as office workers drifted back to work. 'What about your classes?'

'Oh, don't worry about those, I was glad of the excuse to miss today's lectures if I'm honest. What did you make of Lynn?'

'She's a smart cookie,' said Craig. 'And I get the feeling I wouldn't want to get on the wrong side of her.'

'No, that wouldn't be the best idea in the world. But you handled yourself well in there. I mean, considering how you must be feeling and everything,' said Fiona.

Craig finished the last mouthful of his drink. 'You're being nice. But thank you.'

'No, I mean it. She's got a reputation for being a bit hard-nosed, and you managed to impress her. I could tell.'

'Well I'm grateful that she decided to contact her author

The King's Prerogative

friend. I hope he can put me in touch with someone who can help unravel this mess.' He looked at Fiona. 'Can I tell you something? I need to do this, Fi. I need to find Brian Irving. I have to make sense of it all. I need to do it for Claire.'

'You need to do this for yourself, Craig.' She stared at him closely. 'You aren't responsible for Claire's death.'

'I am.'

'No, you're not.' She leaned forward and put her elbows on the table. 'Stop putting it on your shoulders. Listen, it was just one of those awful, tragic things. You can't take the blame. You won't take the blame. I won't let you. So snap out of it, now.'

Craig visibly flinched. Fiona reached across the table and took his hand.

'This thing isn't your fault. Be honest with me. Be honest with yourself. This is about proving your own self-worth. You forget, I know you better than you know yourself. Everybody loves you. Your mum and dad, Helen, your friends, me.' She paused for a split second, then carried on. 'But you hate yourself, Craig. You do. That's why we split up. You put me on a pedestal and you never ever thought you were good enough. But you were. You always were. You are. But you don't see it.' She squeezed his hand as tightly as she could. 'So, buster, you're going to find Brian Irving, you're going to sort this out, you're going to get yourself cleared by the police, and then you'll grovel to your boss and do a Rudolf Hess.'

'A what?'

'You'll say to him that you had a temporary brainstorm and that's why you panicked and fled, but you're okay now and his star employee is back, fighting fit and ready to climb back on that career ladder.'

Craig couldn't help but grin at her, sitting there across the table, all feisty and just the way she was the first time he set eyes on her.

'Yes, boss.'

She smiled.

'Can I tell you something?'

'Of course.'

'I do still love you,' she said. Just as quickly, the smile faded from her lips. The words had slipped out and she hadn't meant them to. Fiona looked down at her hands as she struggled to suppress a painful emotion. She kicked herself for letting her guard down even if it was only for an instant. 'You hurt me so badly,' she said quietly, half to herself.

Craig couldn't find the right words to use in response. In the end he could only manage, 'I know, I'm sorry.' He was going to go on to say something about wishing he could turn the clock back but when he played the words over in his mind he realised they were painfully inadequate. So they sat in silence.

Fiona exhaled and looked up at him. 'I don't know if I can go back to that place again, Craig. Where I could get hurt again.'

'I know.' It was all Craig could think of to say. He could taste salt in his mouth as he willed himself not to get emotional. He breathed out, and it felt like he'd been holding his breath for a long, long time. For over a year in fact.

'Fi?'

'What?'

'I can't tell you how sorry I am for everything.'

Fiona searched his face, her eyes deep and penetrating. 'Yes,' she decided. 'I think you are.'

Craig couldn't hold his curiosity back any longer. He had to know the answer to the question that had been bothering him since the day before. 'What about Chris?'

Fiona blinked. 'What about Chris?'

'If you still have feelings for me, what about your feelings for him?'

Fiona paused long enough to allow her composure to recover.

'You're an idiot, you do know that don't you?'

'What?'

'Chris is my flatmate, not my boyfriend. I haven't seen anyone since you.'

'Oh.'

Fiona took out a paper hankie and blew her nose.

'There's one thing though.'

'What?'

'I need to take you shopping. You look like a bag of shit. You're paying.'

After two hours at the shops Craig felt he was losing the will to live and was ready to turn himself in to the police. Needless to say it had been a while since he'd been shopping with Fiona and it seemed that she'd been saving up that particular brand of female torture for him. They avoided the chain stores on Princes Street and George Street and walked into the Old Town via Cockburn Street, stopping off at cut price denim shops, second hand retro stores and a shoe shop that seemed to sell every kind of work shoe known to man. He was now equipped from head to toe with new tee-shirts, a tartan lumberjack shirt, boxer shorts, socks, Wrangler jeans, a black zip-up Harrington jacket and a new pair of oxblood Dr Marten shoes. Craig was pretty sure he could have performed the same rigmarole in half the time, but it was done now and he had to admit he was pleased with his purchases. He used a changing room to put on his new outfit and he stuffed his work suit and shoes into the biggest of his carrier bags alongside his spare tee shirts and underwear. He went back out into the main shop, where Fiona was waiting for him.

'What do you think?'

Fiona adjusted the lapel of his jacket and stepped back to look him over from head to toe.

'You'll do.' She stood on her tip toes and gave him a kiss on his cheek. 'Come on, we'll stop off and get you some shaving things on the way back to Lynn's office. Hopefully she'll have heard something.'

Lynn hadn't heard back from Edward Hart-Davis, and it was obvious when they saw her that she was too busy to stop and chat, so Fiona said they were going home to her parents' and maybe Lynn could check in with them later. Lynn said she'd definitely do that, and apologised for being rushed off her feet.

When they were back out on the street, Craig turned to Fiona.

'So we're going to your mum and dad's?'

'Well, yes, I had to think of somewhere Lynn could contact us.'

'We could have gone back to Glasgow.'

'Don't be silly, it'll be fine.'

'Aye, right,' said Craig, demonstrating once again that Scots is the only language where two positives can make a negative.

They caught a number 11 bus from Princes Street and half an hour later they reached Fiona's parents' house. They lived in the south side of Edinburgh in the quietly well-to-do neighbourhood of Church Hill. Another strange World War Two coincidence, thought Craig, not that he was aware of any connection between the man and the place. He used to like visiting Fiona's house because her mum and dad always made him feel part of the family and they used to sit round the dinner table and drink bottles of wine that Craig hadn't heard of before, and talk for hours about anything and everything. He also liked visiting because their house was less than five minutes' walk from the fabulous Dominion Cinema. They'd seen the premiere of *Gregory's Girl* there a couple of years before on one of their first proper dates and they'd usually make a point of going to see a film whenever they were in that neck of the woods.

But that was all before Craig had split up with Fiona and he wasn't looking forward to the reception he was about to receive.

The King's Prerogative

The house itself was an early Victorian sandstone semi-detached villa that looked like it had roots as deep as the old sycamore tree in its front garden. Fiona tried the front door handle but the door wouldn't budge. Lights were on behind the fanlight over the door so Fiona knew someone was in. She rang the bell and a few seconds later her brother Robert opened the door.

'Hi. Mum and Dad aren't in yet.'

'Is that it?' asked Fiona. 'No "Hello sis, how are you, I haven't seen you in ages"?'

'Funny. Next time, use your key.' Fiona's lanky nineteen-year-old brother disappeared up a broad staircase.

'I see he's still as chatty, then,' said Craig.

Fiona laughed. 'Yeah, he still hasn't got over Ian Curtis's suicide, but I suppose it's only been three years.'

'Someone should tell him that if New Order can get over it then there's every chance he'll make a full recovery too.'

Fiona led the way into the large kitchen at the back of the house, and invited Craig to have a seat. In the middle of the room, dominating the space was a huge kitchen table that looked like it could have been fashioned from timber retrieved from HMS *Victory*. Craig selected a chair that faced the business end of the kitchen and sat down. Fiona filled a kettle and placed it on a massive range and turned on the gas under it.

'Tea or coffee?'

'Tea, please,' said Craig. He looked around. It seemed a long time since he'd sat at that table and yet at the same time it felt like just last week. Everything was so familiar to him. Only the wall calendar and the notes on the fridge had changed. 'I'm not looking forward to this,' he said.

'Don't be silly, it'll be fine.'

'Hmmmm,' was the best answer Craig could come up with.

They drank their tea and made small-talk for twenty minutes, then Fiona forced Craig to ring his parents again. Craig dutifully rang them and immediately wished he hadn't. By now they were beside themselves with worry. Not only that, but he learned that they'd spent four hours at the police station being interviewed.

'What did you tell them?' asked Craig.

'Everything we knew,' said his father. 'What else could we do?'

Craig felt a pang of guilt as large as a medicine ball pressing in on his chest. 'I'm so sorry, Dad.'

'Where are you, son? Are you okay?' Craig could tell from his father's voice that he wasn't looking for information to pass on to the police. Peter Dunlop asked the question purely because he was concerned for his son's safety.

'I'm okay Dad, really. I'm in Edinburgh. I only need a couple more days then I'll go to the police myself and I'll get this all cleared up. I've met with a lady from a literary agency in Edinburgh, she's been helping me to track down Brian Irving. I'm sure he'll be able to help if only I can get hold of him. Listen, I need to go, but I'll phone again soon. Give my love to Mum and Helen. Bye.' He hung up the phone and gave Fiona the update from Stranraer. She came over and hugged him. It was all she could think of to do right at that moment.

Just before six o'clock they heard a key in the front door's Yale lock, and the clip-clop of high heels approaching. A face appeared round the door and saw Fiona.

'Hi darling, I didn't expect to see you!'.

'Hi Mum.' Fiona bounced over and gave her mum a kiss and a hug.

Valerie Rankin was the image of her daughter, fast-forwarded twenty-five years. Slim, blonde, with her hair in a business-like long bob, and just one or two lines beginning to show around her eyes and mouth where she smiled. The lines disappeared when she saw Craig.

'Oh. Hello, Craig.' She looked at her daughter then back at the visitor.

Craig stood up involuntarily. 'Hello Mrs Rankin, you're looking well.'

She stared at him for a couple of seconds. 'Still the charmer, I see.' She looked at him for a couple of seconds more, then remembered her manners and walked over and gave him a hug. 'How are you? How are your mum and dad?'

'Fine, fine, they're doing well thanks.'

Fiona came over to the table and sat down, and Craig took his seat again.

'We came through to see Lynn this morning,' said Fiona.

'Did you? Let me get my shoes and jacket off and you can fill me in.'

An hour later the three of them were busy preparing dinner. Craig put Valerie's initial reaction to seeing him down to surprise, because since then she'd been warm and chatty with him. When she left the room to get changed out of her work things, Fiona suggested to Craig that they leave out the part about him being a fugitive from the law, what with her mum being a solicitor. So they told her about Craig's grandad and the letter and about Brian Irving and finally, about Lynn and her phone call with her author client.

'It all sounds fascinating,' said Valerie, 'do you have the letter with you? No, on second thoughts, let's wait till Denis gets home. We'll have some dinner and then you can show us, if you like.'

'By all means,' said Craig. He was beginning to feel like showing the letter to people was his party trick, but he admitted to himself that it felt good to be back in that house again and he didn't mind singing for his supper one little bit.

A few minutes later Denis Rankin got home and Craig had another surge of anxiety, but again it was short-lived. Denis Rankin was a big, powerful man, six foot three and he looked every inch the ex-rugby player he was. When he shook Craig's hand, Craig remembered that his was the firmest handshake he'd ever experienced. Dinner was grilled lamb cutlets with lemon juice and fresh rosemary, and a simple salad. It was delicious, and as usual Craig was amazed at how Valerie could create something so tasty that was simplicity itself. They demolished a bottle and a half of red wine between them. Robert stuck to Irn-Bru much to his sister's amusement.

'Dessert is just some biscuits and cheese, with some fruit, if that's okay?' said Valerie.

'Of course, Mum,' said Fiona. Valerie brought the biscuits and cheese out onto the table for everyone to help themselves.

'Right Craig, let's see this letter,' said Denis. 'I have to say I'm hooked before I even lay eyes on it.'

Craig's jacket was outside hanging up in the hall so he fetched the wallet from the inside pocket and brought it back through to his hosts. Just as he'd done that morning in Lynn's office, he performed the ritual of opening the wallet, taking out the letter and showing it round the table. Denis, Valerie and Robert all read the letter in turn. Robert then excused himself and disappeared back up the stair, having stayed just long enough to be polite. The four remaining diners chatted animatedly about what it could mean and about holding history in their hands and how amazing it was that it had been hidden in the wallet all these years. Valerie picked up and looked at the wallet, feeling its soft, worn leather. 'We use wallets to this day that are very similar,' she said.

'Do you? In your law firm?' asked Craig.

'Yes, for those fancy clients with lots of money,' she said with a grin. She ran a finger over the gold initials *AH* on the corner of one of the outside panels.

'AH?'

'Yes,' said Craig. 'I don't think Hess would have gone to the lengths of getting the fictitious Alfred Horn's initials engraved on it, but you never know. He was supposed to have been very meticulous so it wouldn't surprise me if he had.'

'Adolf Hitler, maybe?' asked Valerie.

'Who knows, I did think of that too. I somehow doubt it,

though. When I was reading up on all this stuff I found out that Hess was very close to a man called Albrecht Haushofer. He was the son of Hess's professor, Karl Haushofer, when Hess was a young student at Munich University. Albrecht Haushofer was an interesting man. He spent a great amount of time in Britain prior to the war and was well respected here. He was a close friend of the Duke of Hamilton and believe it or not, he was a guest at the coronation of King George VI in 1937.'

'Really?' said Denis.

'Absolutely. I think he was the "middle man" if you like, between Hess and the British. Hess had Karl and Albrecht Haushofer's visiting cards with him when he landed in Scotland.'

'Fascinating,' said Denis. 'Do you think...'

'Sorry to interrupt,' said Valerie. They all turned to look at her. She was still holding the wallet in both hands, but now she was kneading the left-hand panel, which formed the front of the wallet when folded closed. She began pressing all around the inside of the panel with her thumbs.

'You do know there's something inside this lining?' She announced it rather than asked it.

'What?' said Craig, his eyes glued to her hands as she felt round the edges of the leather.

'Feel it for yourself, look.' Valerie handed the wallet over, and guided his hands to the edges as she had done, where the leather met the silk lining.

'Feel that?'

'Isn't that just a bit of padding?' said Craig.

'The other panel doesn't have padding, or did you take it out with the letter when you found it?' asked Valerie.

'No, there wasn't any,' said Craig, confused. He began to feel round the right-hand panel, the one that had the torn lining where he had found the letter, for comparison. There was definitely a difference in thickness. Slight, but pronounced nonetheless.

'You could be right,' he said. He looked up at Fiona. 'Have you got a sharp knife?'

'Better than that,' she said. She disappeared out of the room and came back a minute later with a small sewing box. She placed it on the table, opened it, took out a small pair of scissors and gave them to Craig. Craig carefully snipped at one of the bottom corners, cutting all along the bottom. He lifted the lining and put his hand inside. He looked up at Valerie. 'You're right Mrs R, there's something here.' He pulled out a folded piece of paper. It was quite thick, more like parchment. He checked that there was nothing else hidden inside the lining, then he moved the wallet to one side, and unfolded the paper. It had two folds into the middle, and when laid flat it revealed itself to be a foolscap size letter. The letter contained a few typewritten lines and a handwritten set of initials:

15th April 1941

Erik Nyberg,
Consulate of Sweden,
185 St Vincent Street,
Glasgow,
Scotland

Dear Mr Nyberg,

Please provide the bearer of this letter with sealed package number DR41/074 on production of his credentials.

Yours sincerely,

AH

Craig read and re-read the letter, then sat back in stunned silence. He looked at Fiona, who picked up the letter, read it, then gave it to her father, who also read it and handed it to his wife.

Craig spoke at last. 'I'm glad you're all here as witnesses to this. You saw where that came from. I didn't just make it up.' He said it as if he was trying to convince himself of the fact that this moment was real and he wasn't imagining it.

'We did,' said Fiona. 'Incredible.'

'*AH* again, did you notice?' said Denis. 'Even though they're only initials I'd have thought it would be fairly straightforward to compare that handwriting with known examples of Haushofer's or, well…'

'Hitler's handwriting,' said Craig.

'Yes. It feels funny holding a piece of paper that might have been held by Hitler himself.' Valerie shuddered and gave the letter back to Craig.

'Why would Hess have a second letter hidden in the wallet? Why is it addressed to the Swedish Consulate in Glasgow?'

'Well, we've got something to tell Lynn now,' said Fiona. She went to grab the phone sitting on the kitchen's window sill, when the doorbell rang. Denis went to answer it, and reappeared a moment later closely followed by Lynn Simon.

'Lynn!' exclaimed Valerie, rushing over to give her friend a kiss, 'Fiona was just about to ring you, Craig's got something to show you.'

'Well I've got some good news for you,' said Lynn. 'Will I go first?'

Chapter 22

In one sense DI Bruce Cowie felt like they'd made progress in the last few hours. He'd interviewed Peter, Marion and Helen Dunlop at the station. Separately of course. They'd told him about the connection between Craig Dunlop and Claire Marshall. One of the local restaurateurs said that Dunlop and Claire Marshall had been deep in conversation on his premises a few weeks ago and seemed to be discussing a document of some kind. The bank manager had said that this DS Wilson had a letter that he confronted Dunlop with. Dunlop himself had told DC Jarvis that he had been doing some 'research' with Miss Marshall. And at last they had identified the bogus DS Wilson as a Michael Green, and were following up a firm lead based on the car he was driving. More significantly, the hotel records placed him in Stranraer at the time of the murder.

On the other hand Bruce Cowie couldn't escape the feeling that he was chasing shadows. He couldn't understand what it was about this letter that provided a link between the murder and Michael Green, and Michael Green and Craig Dunlop. Peter Dunlop had described the letter and the circumstances of how it had come to be in Craig Dunlop's possession. It was an old letter dating from during the war that allegedly was in the possession of Rudolf Hess. DI Cowie had made some initial enquiries and the letter might have some intrinsic value to a collector of such historical paraphernalia. Similar letters and memos from the period which bore the signature of someone famous had sold for a few pounds, maybe a couple of hundred in some cases. Certainly not enough to kill someone over. Was it a red herring? What connection was he missing?

DI Cowie's enquiry into Vulcan Holdings had also drawn a blank. It was a fictitious company. Why had this Green made so much of an effort to conceal his identity, to the point of stealing a Metropolitan Police warrant card, bluffing his way into the local bank, and asking to see Claire Marshall's safe custody box?

There was one thing above all else that vexed Bruce Cowie. How did Green get hold of the safe custody key? The police had checked with Claire Marshall's parents, they didn't have it and they hadn't been approached by anyone suspicious either before or after the murder. No, Green must have got it from the house, or from Craig Dunlop himself. Maybe it had been an elaborate set-up. Dunlop would probably have aroused suspicion if he'd tried to access the box on his own. DI Cowie knew that they were kept under what's known as dual control. No one member of bank staff can access them alone. He would have needed an accomplice, perhaps masquerading as a policeman, to open the box. But why? The bank manager had shown them the box, and there was nothing out of the ordinary amongst the contents. No, there must have been another reason. Who was this Green? He wasn't local. Why was he in Stranraer? Was he blackmailing Dunlop? Blackmailing him about what? Did he know something incriminating about how or why Claire Marshall died?

There was a knock on the door and DC Jarvis came in without waiting for a response.

'Boss, we've traced the car through the DVLA. It's registered to Avis car hire.'

'Get them on the phone.'

'I already have. Wait till you hear this. The car was rented to a guy called Frank Blake. That was the name on his driving licence. He rented it from their office at Glasgow airport the same day he checked into the North West Castle. He used a credit card in the name of Frank Blake, and provided a driving licence in the same name. The address on the driving licence is 117 West India Dock Road, Limehouse, London E14.

'Good work, Gordon. So this Frank Blake and Michael Green are one and the same?'

'Looks like it boss. I've been on to the local cop shop and they're checking on the address now.'

'Good man. Let me know as soon as they get back to you.'

Bruce Cowie came to a decision. Both the men he wanted to trace had now been missing for over twenty-four hours. It was time to put the newspapers to work.

Chapter 23

'I got a phone call just as I was packing up to leave the office,' Lynn began. 'It was from a friend of Edward's, the friend he told me about this morning.'

They all sat round the table again, and Lynn took off her coat and scarf. Valerie fetched a glass from a kitchen cabinet and poured some wine for her friend.

'Thanks, Val.' Lynn took a sip and put the glass down. 'His name is Clive Prior, and he's the professor of European history at Emmanuel College, Cambridge. He said he was excited to get Edward's call explaining my request, and he was keen to speak to me as soon as possible. So much so, that he wants me to go down to see him.'

'Really?' asked Craig. 'That's brilliant news. Did he say what made him so keen?'

'Well, that was where the conversation got really interesting. I told him what I told Edward, that Doctor Irving was one of my authors et cetera, et cetera. That's when he told me that Brian had already contacted him to ask about the letter.'

Craig couldn't contain himself. 'Brian contacted him? When? How?'

Lynn looked at him. 'I assume that's a Scottish "how" that's actually a "why"?'

'Sorry, yes, I meant why?'

'He said that Brian contacted him about three weeks ago, at the end of February. He phoned him because as I understand it Professor Prior is an acknowledged authority on the world wars. I did think his name rang a bell when he introduced himself. I found him quite modest on the phone, rather charming actually. Anyway, Brian must have decided he was the man who could help him authenticate the letter. Professor Prior said he was – quote – "quite taken in" by the story that Brian told him on the phone. They arranged to meet in person a couple of days later but Brian didn't turn up, and he's heard nothing since.'

'Nothing?' said Craig.

'No word from him after that phone call. Professor Prior waited in all afternoon, but Brian didn't show up and he didn't call back to give a reason. The professor assumed that he'd received a better offer but did think it was quite rude of him not to at least get in touch. So when Edward Hart-Davis rang him today he got the scent back in his nostrils again, as he put it. He's very keen to see the letter.'

'I should speak to him,' said Craig. He quickly decided that having a Cambridge professor in his corner would do no harm at all. And on a practical level if Professor Prior was one of the last people to speak to Brian Irving then it must surely be helpful.

'We can ring him again in the morning,' said Lynn. 'I'll have to bring you into the conversation and break it to him that the letter belongs to you, but I'm sure he won't mind our little subterfuge. Now, what did you want to show me?'

Lynn was just as taken aback as the others had been when she read the new letter.

'This was hidden in the wallet too?'

'Yes, in the front panel this time. I'm kicking myself that I didn't notice it before now.' But when Craig thought about it, he realised why he hadn't found the letter earlier. When the wallet was stuffed with the old cigarette cards it was impossible to tell that either one of the panels held a secret in their lining, never mind both of them. And he'd been in such a panic when he spilled coffee on the wallet all those weeks ago that he'd been too distracted to notice anything strange about the front panel.

Lynn studied the letter. 'Have you had any thoughts on what this could be about?'

Craig scratched the stubble on his chin. 'All I can think of is that either it was a package intended for Hess as some kind of collateral, or it was a package that was sent in advance by Hess as part of his plan.'

'Why though?'

'I don't know. But I intend to find out. Mr R, can I borrow your phone for a minute?'

'Help yourself,' said Denis.

Craig took the letter back from Lynn and walked over to the telephone, picked up the receiver and pushed three buttons; 1, then 9, then 2. After a few seconds a woman's voice answered.

'Good evening, directory enquiries, which town please?'

'Hello, could you give me a number for the Consulate of Sweden in Glasgow, please?' There was a small pad of paper and a pen on the window sill. Craig picked up the pen and poised himself to write.

There was a brief pause on the other end. 'That's 041 204 4041. Would you like me to connect you?'

Craig wrote down the number. 'Yes please. Oh, excuse me, before you do, could you confirm that address?'

'Yes sir, it's 185 St Vincent Street. One second please.' The woman's voice was replaced by electro-mechanical burps and chirps followed by the familiar double ring tone as the number connected. It rang for a few seconds then an automated message clicked in. It told Craig that the Consulate was closed for the day and confirmed what the office hours were, then gave him another number to ring in case of emergencies. Craig hung up.

'Well the Swedish Consulate is still in St Vincent Street. I didn't even know there was a Swedish Consulate in Glasgow. They're closed for the evening, open again at ten am.'

Fiona looked at him. 'What are you going to do?'

'I'm going back through to Glasgow. I need to find out

what this package is all about and I'm hoping the Consulate will tell me.'

'Why don't you just ring them in the morning?' asked Fiona.

'Because I want to show them the letter. They'd probably laugh if I just phoned them. Think about it – "Excuse me, do you have a package from 1941 in your possession?" No, I'm going to have to speak to them in person.'

Lynn looked thoughtful. 'It says you have to present certain credentials.'

'I'll play that by ear,' said Craig. He folded the letter and put it back in the wallet. 'Mrs R, thank you so much for dinner, it was lovely. And it was really nice to see you both again.'

Valerie grabbed him by his wrist. 'Excuse me, where are you going?'

Craig was touched by the gesture. 'I'll get back through to Glasgow tonight and I'll be on their doorstep at ten o'clock.'

'You'll do no such thing,' corrected Valerie. 'You'll stay here tonight and you can go through in the morning when you're feeling fresh. No arguments.'

Craig couldn't help but smile. 'Thank you, it's very kind.'

'Rubbish,' said Denis. 'It'll give us more of a chance to talk.'

And talk they did. Denis opened another bottle of wine and they chewed over the letter and talked about Clive Prior and speculated about what could have happened to Brian Irving. Craig decided to tell them everything. He filled in the details about getting Brian Irving on board, and about Claire's murder, his subsequent brush with DS Wilson and how he came to be at Fiona's flat the night before. The mood changed. The excitement of earlier in the evening evaporated and the enormity of the situation pressed in on them all. They fell quiet.

Valerie at last broke the silence. 'What makes you so sure that Claire's murder is connected to the letter?'

'I'm not certain that there is a connection at all', said Craig, 'but the police wanted to interview me about it, that's for sure.'

'What will you do, Craig?' asked Denis.

'I was going to ask you what you think I should do, Mrs R,' said Craig, 'seeing as you're a solicitor.'

Valerie thought for a long moment. 'Well, I'm not a criminal lawyer, as you know. But I'd have to advise you to go to the police before *they* catch up with *you*.'

'But I know I haven't done anything wrong,' he said, almost to himself.

'That's as maybe. But the fact remains you were asked to help police with their enquiries and you, well…'

'Ran away.' Craig finished Valerie's sentence for her.

Lynn decided it was time to move the conversation on. 'Do you know what? Bugger it. So what if you ran off, you obviously had your reasons. And if you hadn't, now you wouldn't have a potential ally in Professor Prior. So for what it's worth I think you should follow this as far as it takes you, for better or worse.'

'So do I,' said Fiona.

'Me too, Craig,' said Denis.

They all looked at Valerie.

'What?'

'Come on, Val,' said Lynn. 'Aren't you the slightest bit intrigued about where this could lead?'

Valerie took a large sip of her wine. 'I just want it known that I gave Craig my professional advice. But yes, I have to confess this is all very interesting.' She smiled at Lynn, and in that instant Craig could see where Fiona got her magnetism from.

Lynn laughed. 'Good girl, that's the Val I know and love.' She turned to Craig. 'Right then Mr Dunlop, you're in charge, what next?'

Craig leaned back in his chair and pursed his lips. He leaned forward once more and put his elbows on the table.

'I think I should see what I can find out at the Swedish Consulate first thing, and then when we contact Professor Prior we'll have something else to ask him about.'

'Agreed,' said Lynn. 'I'll make a space in my diary from say, three o'clock? You should be back by then, and we can call Clive Prior from my office.'

'Sounds like a plan,' said Craig.

'Sounds like a good plan,' added Fiona. 'I'll come along with you.'

'You've got uni,' said Craig.

'No I don't,' said Fiona. 'Not tomorrow. No lectures till Thursday, and I'm up to date with my essays. Besides, you'll need someone to keep you out of trouble.'

It was nearly ten o'clock when Lynn bid them all goodnight. Valerie left the others in the kitchen and went upstairs to look out a couple of fresh towels for Craig and to turn up the radiator in the guest bedroom. Fiona put the kettle on and put the empty wine bottles in the bin.

'Three and a half bottles on a school night,' said Denis. 'I'll feel it in the morning.' He filled a glass with water from the tap and bid them both goodnight.

'Cuppa?' asked Fiona, when it was just the two of them left in the kitchen.

'No thanks, Fi.' Craig looked at her as she busied herself with mugs and milk and tea bags. 'Thank you for today. For everything.' She turned round to face him. 'It's been my pleasure.' They heard footsteps coming down the stair, and Fiona hurried back to her tea making while Craig tidied up the wine glasses.

Valerie came back into the kitchen. 'That's your room ready Craig, do you remember the one? Top of the stair, straight ahead, next to the bathroom.'

'I do, thank you,' said Craig. 'I'll say goodnight then.'

'Goodnight, Craig, nice to see you again.'

''Night,' chimed Fiona. 'I'll give you a knock about seven.'

The King's Prerogative

'Great, thanks. See you in the morning.' Craig paused in the hall long enough to pick up his shopping bags and then climbed the carpeted staircase. He found the bedroom alright, picked up a towel from the small pile Valerie had left on his bed, and went through to the bathroom to brush his teeth. Five minutes later he was undressed, in bed and had switched the bedside lamp off. He lay looking up at the darkness, reflecting on the day's events and imagining what the following day might bring. He was asleep three minutes later.

Downstairs in the kitchen Fiona and Valerie were drinking their tea at the table.

'So?' asked Valerie.

'So what?' countered Fiona.

'Has Craig told you that he wants you back?'

'Mum!' Fiona tutted and took a sip of her hot tea.

'It was so obvious tonight that he still adores you. He could hardly take his eyes off you all the way through dinner.'

'Do you think so?'

'Definitely.' Valerie reached out and held her daughter's hand. 'Just be careful. You know how upset you were after you two split up.'

'I know mum. And I will be careful. Thanks.' Fiona put her cup in the sink, kissed her mum on the cheek, said goodnight and headed up the stairs to her room.

Chapter 24

Wednesday 16th March, 1983

Craig woke up and for the second morning in a row it took him a few seconds to get his bearings. He stretched over and looked at his watch on the bedside table. It told him that it was five past seven. Just then there was a gentle tap on the door.

'Hi,' Craig said.

'Can I come in?'

'Of course.'

Fiona opened the door and peered in. Craig caught a glimpse of red tartan pyjamas and wondered how she could manage to look so fabulous at silly o'clock in the morning, straight from her kip. 'Good morning, how did you sleep?'

'I slept great, thanks, like a log,' said Craig. 'I've just woken up this second.' He came to the conclusion that he'd quite happily be woken up like this every morning.

'The bathroom's free, help yourself. Just come down when you're ready.'

Fifty minutes later Craig and Fiona were ready to leave the house. Valerie convinced Craig to leave his suit with her, she'd pop it into the dry cleaners on her way to work. Craig thanked her for the hundredth time and Valerie told him to think nothing of it and shooed the two of them out the door.

'Have you got everything?' asked Fiona.

'Think so,' said Craig. He had his grandad's wallet as well

his own, and he'd emptied his suit pockets of his house keys, passport and the small Dictaphone he used at work. 'It might come in handy,' he told Fiona. She looked at him quizzically. 'It just makes an unnecessary bulge in your jacket pocket,' she admonished.

'Yeah, cos it's really important that I make a sartorial impression today,' retorted Craig. Fiona called him an arse and punched him on the arm.

They decided to walk round to the bus stop rather than wait for a lift from Denis or Valerie. The sun was bright and low in the sky as they stepped out into the cold air. The morning rush hour had started and the driver of a passing Morris Marina had his visor down to protect his eyes as he drove eastwards. There was a small queue by the time they reached the bus shelter which they took to be a good sign, and sure enough the number 11 trundled along a couple of minutes later.

By the time they got to Waverley the station was going like a fair with people arriving for work. Craig and Fiona made their way through to the ticket office then fought their way on to the platform, boarded their train and found a seat easily enough.

They spent the journey through to Glasgow rehearsing what they were going to say when they got there. They were just about happy with their plan by the time the train arrived at the Queen Street terminus, fifteen minutes late due to a signal failure outside Glasgow. They allowed themselves to be swept along with the tide of students, shoppers and office workers disgorging onto the open space of George Square, then they turned right onto St Vincent Place. Craig looked at his watch. It was just before ten to ten, good timing. They headed up St Vincent Street for half a dozen blocks. From there, across the street, they saw the Consulate. From the outside it could have been an office or a city centre medical practice if it hadn't been for the large blue flag with the distinctive yellow cross hanging above the main doorway.

Craig realised that the solicitors' office he'd visited with his dad a couple of months back was only a couple of blocks away.

They stopped across the street from the Consulate. 'Ready?' asked Craig.

'As I'll ever be,' said Fiona. They crossed the road, climbed the few steps up to the building and stepped inside. A nearby church chimed the hour.

Inside, the Swedish Consulate could indeed just as easily have been a city centre medical practice. There was an anteroom off a tiled and rather spartan main hallway. Above the door was a sign that said 'enquiries' in English and also in what Craig assumed to be Swedish. They entered the ante room and were faced by a smiling young man sitting behind a white desk. Craig looked around the room. The walls were painted in a two-tone colour scheme, divided by a thin dado rail at head height, with the lower half pale blue and the upper half, and the ceiling, white. Along the walls were some travel posters urging visitors to come to Sweden, where the locals looked impossibly healthy and happy. Metal chairs with blue fabric seats were lined up along three of the walls, presumably provided for people while they waited for something to be processed by the Consulate staff. Craig and Fiona were the first ones to arrive this morning. The place was empty.

'Can I help you?'

Fiona stepped forward. 'Yes, please. I've come to collect this, if I may.' She handed over the letter. 'It is rather old, I should say.'

The young man looked at the letter for longer than they would have expected him to. 'It certainly is old. I'm not entirely sure what this relates to. Can I ask your name, please?'

'Of course, it's Fiona Rankin.'

'Please, take a seat, Miss Rankin. Would you excuse me for one moment?' He got up from behind the desk and went out of the door Craig and Fiona had just come in. They sat down under a poster extolling the virtues of the Swedish lakes. After a good five minutes, Fiona leaned into Craig.

'Where do you think he's gone?'

'I don't know,' said Craig. 'Why are you whispering?'

'Why are you whispering?' asked Fiona.

'Because you are.'

The door opened and the young man returned, followed by a tall man in his mid-to-late forties. He had short blond hair in a rather severe side parting that gave his face an angular look. He strode into the room, offering his outstretched hand to Fiona.

'Miss Rankin? I'm Carl Persson, the consul here. Sorry to keep you waiting. I'm very pleased to meet you.' They shook hands, then Fiona introduced Craig.

'This is my boyfriend, Craig Dunlop.' Craig shook hands with the consul, rather pleased at his promotion to the status of boyfriend, even if it was only for show.

'Pleased to meet you, Mr Persson.'

'Won't you come this way, I'll take you to my office, we'll be more comfortable there.'

He showed them out into the main hall then up a flight of stairs to a landing with five doors leading off it. Craig could hear the familiar tip-tapping of fingernails on typewriters behind one of the doors, and Carl Persson showed them through another of the doors into a bright, spacious office, decorated in the same colour scheme as the ante room downstairs but with the added warmth of a deep mustard-coloured carpet. There was a desk beside the window but the consul led them to a couple of low couches facing each other over a glass coffee table. He invited Craig and Fiona to sit on one and he hitched up the knees of his trousers and sat on the other.

'Henrik, could you bring us some coffee, please? Is coffee alright with you?' Fiona nodded. 'Thanks Henrik,' said Persson, and the young man exited.

'Now then, I have to tell you that this is a very unusual request. We here in the Consulate didn't think that the package would ever be claimed.'

'You have the package here?' blurted Craig and then immediately kicked himself. Fiona shot him a scathing look that said 'stick to the script', then turned back to the consul.

'You still have the package here in the Consulate?'

'Yes indeed. I have had the privilege of being the consul in your beautiful city for only three years, but some of my staff have worked in the Consulate for twenty years and more. The package has become something of a…' the consul searched for the correct word, 'a fixture here, and there has been a – how can I say – a mystique built up around it.' Craig noticed that he spoke in that careful manner used by people for whom English wasn't their native tongue.

'Is that so?' said Fiona.

'Yes indeed. So I hope you'll indulge my curiosity in asking you some questions about it.'

'By all means, not that I know much about it,' laughed Fiona. Craig was impressed, she was warming to the task beautifully and playing her role to perfection so far.

The door opened and a young woman brought in a tray with three cups, a coffee pot and milk and sugar. She set it down on the table, smiled at Fiona then left.

'Milk and sugar?' asked Persson as he poured the hot coffee into the cups.

'Yes, please,' they said in unison. Persson completed the task and handed them a cup each.

Henrik knocked on the door and entered. He walked over to the desk and placed a large book on it.

'Thank you, Henrik,' said Persson. Henrik smiled, nodded and left the room. Persson looked at Fiona.

'Firstly, Miss Rankin, may I ask how you came to be in possession of this letter?' He placed the letter on the coffee table in a manner that made Craig feel like all that was missing was Persson adding the words 'Exhibit A' to the end of his sentence. He pushed the thought from his mind and sipped his coffee.

Fiona put her cup down, crossed her legs and fished around in her handbag. Craig noticed that Persson let his eyes stray to Fiona's legs for a microsecond. Under her coat she'd worn a smart skirt and sweater combination for the occasion, with black stockings and her smartest black heels. Good choice, thought Craig.

Fiona found Craig's wallet in her bag and handed it to Persson. On the way through from Edinburgh, Craig had emptied it of the cigarette cards, the old press cuttings and the photocopied letter of safe conduct, so that now it was empty. Persson looked at it, opened it with mild interest, and closed it again.

'It's actually a bit of a sad story,' began Fiona. 'I'm a quarter Swedish, on my mother's side, you see.'

'Congratulations,' said Persson, smiling. 'I thought you had the look of a Swede about you. I do hope that's not the sad part of the story.'

'Thank you.' She flashed him one of her smiles. 'My grandfather on my mum's side is... or should I say, was, a man called Alfred Horn, who lived in Sweden as a young man and moved here after the war. He married a Scottish girl, settled here and had a family. Well, he died not so long ago, and this wallet with the letter inside was found with his effects. It was in my grandfather's attic, lost among some other household papers.'

Persson nodded in understanding and sympathy. 'I'm sorry for your loss, Miss Rankin. As a Swedish national living in Scotland, we would have been informed of his passing, I'm sure.'

Craig's senses switched to full alert. They'd hoped to avoid any complications. On the train he decided that their plan would involve sticking as close to the truth as possible, but for Fiona to use her charm and her plausibly Scandinavian looks to concoct a story based around her family, rather than his. He also decided they would use the name Alfred Horn and gamble on the fact that the package might have been sent using that name, in which case the Consulate could have a corresponding record in their files that they would cross-check. Or at the very least, presenting the old leather wallet with the initials *AH* engraved on it might make it easier to sell the story. Now the gamble looked like it would unravel and he wished he'd decided to be the one doing the talking. If the Consulate checked for the death of an Alfred Horn and couldn't find one, their story would be blown.

'Well, I don't know if you would have been advised,' said Fiona. 'When my grandmother died a few years back, my grandad Alfred moved back to Sweden. He still had a brother and a sister there you see.'

'Ah yes, I understand.'

'I didn't get much of a chance to see him in the last few years, which is such a shame because he's not here any more.' Fiona began to tear up and the tip of her nose turned red. Craig dug in his pocket and produced a handkerchief for her. She blew her nose quietly, and composed herself again. 'Thank you, Craig. Mr Persson, I'd be so grateful for anything you can do to help.'

'Of course, of course. Please don't upset yourself. If I might explain, most of the work we do here concerns promoting trade links between Scotland and Sweden. We perform a number of services for Swedish companies who have links to customers and partners here. At any one time we hold many trading documents and import/export files on behalf of clients. We hold the documents for as long as necessary. Most are released after a particular piece of business is completed, usually after a few weeks or months. But our rules are quite simple. We hold documents in safe keeping until we're asked to release them as per the instructions given to us by clients. Although it is very unusual to have anything in our keeping for such a long time, we are not actually required to dispose of such documents until fifty years have passed. May I ask, what kind of business was your grandfather in?'

'I think he was a timber merchant in his younger days, but I'm not certain,' said Fiona.

'Ah yes, well that might explain it,' said Persson. 'During the Second World War Sweden was neutral of course but we continued to trade with the UK, and also with Germany it has to be said. Perhaps your grandfather's package was in relation to a shipment of timber which was sunk by a U-boat or a mine. Regrettably such things happened all too often during the war. In such circumstances, we would probably have either released the associated paperwork on request or contacted our client after a period of time had elapsed. In the case of your grandfather's package, it would seem there was no contact address and so the package remained with us indefinitely.'

Craig marvelled at Fiona's improvised performance, and the information it had produced so far. He sensed that the conversation was approaching the crucial moment. Right on cue, Fiona asked the key question.

'Would it be possible for me to see the package?' she asked.

'There are one or two formalities to observe before we can get to that point, I'm afraid,' said Persson. He lifted himself from the couch and walked to his desk where he consulted the ledger that Henrik had brought in earlier. 'This is where the details of the package were recorded back in 1941,' he explained. He flicked forward a few pages and traced a finger down a page. 'Ah, yes. DR41/074. Here we are.' He lifted the ledger from the desk and brought it over to the coffee table. 'It says I have to ask you for two things, Miss Rankin. Firstly, are you the bearer of the letter? Clearly you are. Secondly, can you identify yourself?'

'Pardon?'

'Do you have proof of identity?'

'I should have.' She opened her bag again and rooted around in it. She produced her driving licence and handed it to Persson. Craig breathed out, thankful that they hadn't been too clever. On the train they discussed giving Fiona a pseudonym for the occasion, but Fiona decided that they'd have enough to concentrate on without having to keep using a false name.

'Thank you. All I am required to do according to the client instructions is to record your details in the ledger… like… so.' He copied down Fiona's name and address into the ledger and handed back the driving licence. 'Now, if you'll excuse me for one moment?' Persson left with the ledger, and Craig and Fiona were left alone again.

'Do you think we've done it?' whispered Fiona.

'Shhhh,' said Craig. 'You know what walls have.'

'Ice cream?'

'Funny girl.' He squeezed her hand. 'You're amazing,' he whispered.

'I know.' She smiled at him and once more he was lost for words.

Persson came back in with what looked like a small canvas bag about the size of a sofa cushion, slightly longer than it was wide. There were no distinguishing marks on it apart from a label on which was written the ledger code and the date 15/4/41.

'Here we are. I do apologise for the dust, Marta did the best she could with a damp cloth, but it is over forty years old.' Persson gave a small laugh then handed the package over to Fiona. 'I did a little checking a moment ago, and the ledger code was applied to the package by our Foreign Office in Stockholm back in 1941. That's where it originated.'

'That would make sense, that's where my grandad was from,' said Fiona.

Carl Persson clasped his hands and looked like a man who was as keen to know what was inside as they were.

Fiona read his intention. 'Oh, I'm sorry Mr Persson, I promised my mum that we'd open it together when I get home. I hope you understand.'

The King's Prerogative

'Oh please forgive me, Miss Rankin, of course I completely understand. He was your mum's father, after all. No apology is necessary. Please, let me show you out.'

He walked Craig and Fiona down the stairs and opened the main door for them. 'You must come back and let us know if there is anything exciting in the package, although I have to be honest and ask you not to build up your hopes too much. It is probably a shipping manifest or a contract for some timber your grandfather was sending for the war effort.'

'Oh I will, Mr Persson, and thank you for all your help, and for the coffee.'

Persson then handed Fiona the letter. 'Don't forget this.'

'Oh. Yes, thank you again. Goodbye.'

They all shook hands.

Carl Persson watched as they crossed St Vincent Street and made their way in the direction of George Square.

Chapter 25

Craig and Fiona walked down the street, deliberately not hurrying and trying to resist the temptation to look back. Craig expected to feel a hand on his shoulder any second, their scam exposed by the Consulate staff. After five minutes Craig finally accepted that they weren't being chased or followed and that they'd got away with their little performance. Or rather, Fiona had.

'That was the most incredible adlibbing I've ever seen.'

'I know, I was good wasn't I?' said Fiona, grinning from ear to ear.

'You almost had *me* in tears when you talked about your poor Swedish grandad.'

'Why thank you.' Fiona gave a small curtsey. 'What now?'

'Now, I buy you a coffee and a massive piece of cake and we find out what's in this.'

They turned a corner onto Queen Street and walked a few yards to a little café with a sign saying *City Bakeries* above the window. It was narrow but extended some way back beyond a long counter, where the room opened up into the café proper. There were a dozen tables, most of them unoccupied. Craig thought it was ideal, they couldn't be seen from the window and the corner table they selected was reasonably secluded from prying eyes. A waitress came over and took their order. Fiona asked what cakes they had and decided on a strawberry tart, and they ordered two coffees.

Craig studied the package. It was a canvas bag, made from a material not dissimilar to sail cloth, like those large kit bags you sometimes see servicemen carry on their shoulders. The mouth of the bag had been folded over and sealed with a pliable metal band. Where the two ends of the band met there was a clasp. Craig couldn't decide if it would be easier to hack his way through the clasp, the metal band or the canvas itself. In any event, he came to the conclusion he wasn't going to be hacking into anything until he could find something more industrial than a butter knife to use.

'I need to get a pair of pliers or wire-cutters for this.'

'There's a tool box at my flat,' said Fiona. 'Why don't we stop off there, then we'll have more privacy too.'

'Good idea.'

***

Blake left the Glasgow drizzle and took the M8 to Edinburgh. After driving around the New Town looking for a suitable parking space, he found one on Frederick Street. He walked down Hill Street until he came to Hamilton Dunbar. He stopped, looked around, and walked through the main door and up to the reception. The receptionist, Julia, saw him approach and looked Blake up and down. With his unfashionable raincoat, wide shirt collar and even wider tie, he didn't look like one of the usual publishing types. They wouldn't be seen dead in that get up.

'Can I help you?'

'Yes, I hope so. I'm Detective Sergeant Wilson. Metropolitan Police.' Blake showed her his warrant card. 'I'm looking for a Mr Craig Dunlop. I have reason to believe he paid your office a visit either yesterday or the day before. Would that be correct?'

Julia wasn't sure what to say, but in the split second she had to make up her mind, she decided that this policeman obviously knew that Craig had been there so it was pointless denying it. 'Yes, Mr Dunlop was here to meet one of our literary agents, Mrs Simon.'

'May I speak with her?'

'One moment please.' Julia picked up a telephone and dialled Lynn's internal extension. 'Hi Lynn, I've a Detective Sergeant Wilson here asking to see you.'

Upstairs at her desk, Lynn didn't reply. She froze, unable to think of the right words to say. Or any words to say.

'Lynn? Lynn, can you hear me okay?'

'Eh... yes, yes Julia, I can hear you.' She looked around her office as if looking for an escape route. There was nothing she could do. 'Em, could you show Detective Wilson up to my office please.' Her brain recovered from the shock and clicked into gear. 'Oh Julia, could you take your time?'

Lynn hung up then dialled another internal extension number. It rang once, twice, three times. 'Come on, come on.' A voice answered. It was one of the other literary agents, Neil Paterson.

'Hello?'

'Hi Neil, it's Lynn. Could you do me a favour?'

'Surely.'

'Could you come to my office in five minutes and remind me that I'm late for a meeting?'

'What?'

'Could you just do that? I'll explain later, but it's really important. In five minutes exactly.'

'Okay.'

'Thanks.' She hung up and looked across at David Halliday. 'Davie, no time to explain, but don't you dare leave this office for the next few minutes.'

'What?'

'And I need you to act normally. Craig Dunlop's policeman is here.'

'The police?'

'Yes, don't say a word. Nothing. Not a word about Craig

or our meeting, or...' The door opened, and Julia entered, followed by Blake.

'Lynn, this is Detective Sergeant Wilson.'

Lynn stepped forward briskly and offered her hand. 'Lynn Simon, pleased to meet you.' They shook hands. 'And this is my assistant, David Halliday.' David and Blake shook hands. Julia left them and returned to her desk. Lynn deliberately didn't invite Blake to take a seat, so the three of them remained standing. Lynn looked at her watch. 'Forgive me, but I'm on my way to a meeting. Is there something I can help you with?'

Blake took in his surroundings and studied Lynn and David carefully. He made a point of taking out a notebook and flipping it open to a blank page, ready to take down what she had to say. You might think you're going somewhere, thought Blake, but not till I'm good and ready.

'Yes, I'm investigating the disappearance of a university lecturer. A Doctor Brian Irving of Strathclyde University. Do you know him?' He examined her face. Either she didn't know Irving or she was a good poker player, he thought.

'Irving, did you say? No, I don't think I know the name.' Lynn decided to play her own little game. 'Has he published any work that I might have heard of?'

Blake paused a beat, which gave Lynn the answer she was looking for. 'I don't have that information,' he said. He produced a four by five inch photograph from his inside pocket and gave it to Lynn to look at. 'Could you look at this photograph and tell me if you recognise him?'

'This is Doctor Irving?' asked Fiona. She knew it was the man she'd remembered meeting some time ago, but she gambled that Blake wouldn't know that their paths had crossed.

'Yes,' replied Blake. 'Do you know him?'

'I'm afraid not.'

'And you haven't seen him recently?'

'No, I can't say I have.'

Blake took back the photo and gave it to David, who also confirmed that he didn't know the man.

'I understand that Craig Dunlop visited you yesterday. Can I ask what you discussed?'

Lynn held his gaze, but Blake noticed that David shifted uncomfortably at the mention of Craig's name.

'Yes, he did.' She tried to buy some time while her mind frantically tried to produce a plausible cover story. 'What has that got to do with Doctor Irving?'

'Please answer the question.' Blake's eyes flitted between Lynn and David, searching for a weakness.

'He's an old friend of the family, and he just popped by to say hello in passing.'

'An old friend of your family?'

'That's right.'

'Then you know his parents, Alan and Jenifer?'

'Yes, I've known them for, oh, must be ten years or more,' said Lynn.

Just then, the door opened and Neil Paterson popped his head round. 'Sorry to intrude, Lynn. You know that the reps from Armstrongs are waiting for us in the conference room?'

Blake turned to look at the intruder, as Lynn acknowledged that her presence was needed elsewhere.

'I'm very sorry, Detective Sergeant, I'm already late for a meeting. I wish I could be of more help, but as I say I don't know Doctor Irving. I don't know what his connection is to Craig, but I'm sure Craig can tell you that for himself.' She decided to take another calculated risk. 'I can give you his home address if that would be helpful.'

Blake thought for a moment. 'No, that won't be necessary, Mrs Simon. I don't want to keep you from your meeting, but perhaps I could ask your assistant some more questions?'

'Oh, I'm very sorry, David's needed at the meeting too. Maybe I could ring you when I'm free?'

Blake wrote a telephone number in his notebook and ripped out the page, giving it to Lynn.

'Please do, I can be contacted at this number.'

Lynn walked Blake back down the staircase and out the

main door. She waited till he'd walked fifty yards down Hill Street, then she closed the door and leaned against it.

Neil Paterson stood at the foot of the stair. 'What have you got yourself into now?' he asked.

'God only knows,' said Lynn.

Blake found a telephone box and dialled a long-distance number. The other end rang twice, and a man's voice answered.

'Hello?'

'It's Blake. I've confirmed that the literary agent did meet with Dunlop. What's interesting is that she lied to me. She claimed to know his family, but didn't know their names. I want to know why she's lying, so I'm going to stay here for the moment.'

'Very good. Before long she'll lead us to both Dunlop and Irving. Keep me updated.'

The line went dead.

Chapter 26

Craig and Fiona arrived at the main door of Fiona's flat. Fiona rummaged about in her bag for her Yale key, opened the lock to let them in and shut the door behind them. Once in the hall, she stopped dead.

'What's wrong?' asked Craig, seeing the look of fear on her face.

'Something's not right,' she said, looking around the hall.

Craig couldn't see anything that might explain her sudden anxiety. 'What is it?'

'I always close all the doors before I leave. They're open.'

'Doesn't Chris have a key?'

'Yes, but Chris is away in Ireland all week, on a field trip.' She went into the living room. The bookshelves were empty, and the collections of books and VHS videotapes that used to be stacked on them were strewn across the floor. The tapes had been taken out of their boxes and randomly thrown into a loose pile on the carpet. The seat cushions from the sofa and chairs were also on the floor, as were the contents of two small wooden storage units. 'Oh good God!' Fiona put her hand to her mouth in shock.

'Stay in here,' said Craig. He checked the other rooms. There were two bedrooms, a bathroom and a kitchen, and each room had been similarly ransacked. Craig re-joined Fiona in the living room. 'Whoever was here has gone.'

Fiona replaced the seat cushions and looked for the phone, which she found on the carpet near the window. The receiver was off the hook and she had to press the studs on the cradle a few times to get a dialling tone. Craig looked around. The TV and video recorder were still there, as was the stereo unit. A thought came to him. 'How quickly could you tell what's missing?' he asked.

'I'll check in a moment, after I call the landlord and the police.'

'Hold on.'

'It's okay Craig, you can go to the Grosvenor Café for an hour until they're done, I won't let them find you.'

Craig took the receiver from Fiona, put it back on the cradle and placed the telephone back on its table. 'Listen to me for just a second, Fi.'

'Craig, I need to report this.'

Craig held her by both hands and led her to the sofa. 'Fi, sit down for a moment.' They sat down, and Craig could still see the fear in Fiona's face. 'I need you to check to see what's missing, if anything. Did you keep any money here? Chequebooks, bank cards, jewellery?'

Fiona took her hands away from his and swept her hair back over an ear, trying to compose herself as she looked round.

'My chequebook and guarantee card are in my handbag. I don't have any money here. Oh no, that's wrong, Chris and I have a food kitty in the kitchen, there's usually a few quid in it for bread and milk et cetera.'

They went through to the kitchen and Fiona checked an old tea tin on top of the fridge. She opened the lid and pulled out three pound notes and some change. 'That looks about right,' she said. She suddenly turned round and went back into the hall, then into another room to the right of the kitchen. 'It just dawned on me that Chris keeps some money beside the bed usually, for the rent.' The bedding was on the floor as were the contents of the small wardrobe behind the door. Fiona went over to the bedside table. It was missing its drawer, because the drawer was now upside down on the bare mattress. She picked it up and put it back where it belonged.

She sifted through a handful of items that had been dumped onto the bed, a small watch, some paper handkerchiefs, bits and pieces of make-up and a small white envelope, unsealed but with the flap tucked in. Fiona opened it and pulled out a handful of cash. She checked through the notes. 'A hundred and forty pounds. That's what the rent costs. It's all here.'

She rushed out of the room and into her own bedroom. Her jewellery box was sitting on her dressing table, beside cans of hairspray and tubes of make-up, half empty bottles of perfume and a collection of glass, pottery and ceramic owls lined up in a row. She picked up the box. 'The lock's been forced,' she told Craig. She opened the lid and ran a finger over the items inside; three gold rings, some bracelets, two necklaces, a strip of passport-sized photographs of Fiona and another girl, taken in a photo booth. She came across a small velvet pouch which she opened, tipping the contents into her palm. Craig could see the pair of diamond earrings her parents had given her for her twenty-first birthday. They'd cost an absolute fortune at the time, he remembered.

'It's all here,' she said again. 'They've burst the lock but didn't take anything. I don't understand it.'

'They didn't take the telly or the video. Or your hi-fi.'

'Neither they have,' agreed Fiona, puzzlement replacing the look of fear across her eyes. 'Who would have done this but not taken anything?'

'They were looking for something.'

'What?'

Craig took the wallet from his jacket pocket. 'This.'

Fiona looked at the wallet as if she was seeing it for the first time. 'You think so?'

'Yes. And I'll tell you why. Claire's house was burgled too. But the police couldn't confirm if anything had been taken from there either.' He took Fiona out into the hall again and opened the front door. He showed her the lock and the door frame. 'Look. No sign of damage, and you opened the door with your key when we came in.'

Fiona's puzzled expression deepened. 'I don't understand.' She wrapped her arms round herself, hugging her own slim frame.

'Whoever broke in was a professional. They picked the lock.' He rubbed the top of Fiona's arm. 'I think you should stay at your mum and dad's for a few nights.'

'Shouldn't we phone the police?'

'I think it would be a waste of time.'

'Why do you say that?'

'Because despite the mess, there's no damage, nothing's been taken, and I'd bet any money the police wouldn't find any fingerprints.'

Fiona looked at him and the penny dropped. 'Do you think that the same person who did this also burgled Claire's house?'

Craig didn't want to make Fiona any more scared than she already was. 'I'm not saying that, but whoever did this knew what he was doing.' An icy hand gripped Craig's chest as he came to the realisation that the burglar had also known what he was doing when he broke Claire's kitchen window. It must have been a smokescreen to throw the local police off the track and make them think it was an opportunist's crime. To divert them away from the fact that he had broken in with one purpose in mind – to find the letter.

'We should go now,' said Craig.

'But the mess.'

'Forget it.'

'But Chris will come back and find it. We should leave a note at least.'

'Okay, leave a note. Tell him not to stay here until he speaks to you.'

'Chris is a she. Christine.'

'Oh.'

Under other circumstances Craig would have been delighted to hear the news that Chris was a female, but right now he wanted to be out of the flat as soon as humanly possible. He went through to the living room, and hurriedly stacked some books and tapes back on the shelves until he found the telephone note pad and paper hidden among the mess on the floor. He brought it through for Fiona. She scrawled a note, and using a length of Sellotape retrieved from the kitchen, pinned it to the outside of her flatmate's bedroom door. Craig read it, then ripped it off. 'You can't tell her where you are or leave a phone number. Tell her to go to her parents and you'll call her there.'

'Her parents live in Doncaster.'

Craig thought for a second. 'Okay, tell her to go to the police.'

'What?'

'When are you expecting her back?'

'Sunday.'

'I'll have gone to the police myself by then. Probably. In any event, it'll be the safest thing for her to do. Say you're okay, you'll explain later, and tell her to stay at a pal's till you get a chance to speak to her.'

'She'll be worried.'

'What's the first thing she'll do when she sees your note?'

Fiona pondered for a moment. 'She'll phone my mum and dad looking for me.'

'Ideal. Just don't write asking her to do that.'

'Why not?'

'Because if whoever broke in didn't find what they were looking for, they'll either come back here, or try to find out where you could be. Have you got anything here with your home address in Edinburgh written on it?'

'I don't think so. All my mail goes home and the mail that comes here is for the landlord.'

'Okay. Good.'

Fiona rewrote the note on a fresh piece of paper and stuck it to the door, then they picked up their belongings and the canvas bag and left the flat.

Half an hour later they were back at Queen Street station.

The King's Prerogative

The elation they'd felt when they left the Swedish Consulate was now a distant memory. Craig's overwhelming sense of guilt had returned with a vengeance. Firstly he'd roped Claire into this mess, then his parents and sister, now Fiona. And God knows what had happened to Brian Irving. There was another feeling that cut through his guilt however. Craig was angry. Furious. It wasn't merely the injustice of it that riled him, it was the fact that someone thought they had a right to break into Claire's house, and now Fiona's flat. When he'd heard about Claire's murder he was shocked to the core, but now that shock had turned into a cold, burning rage. Claire had been defenceless, but she'd challenged the intruder nevertheless. The papers said the killer hadn't broken into the house with the intention of killing her, because she'd been stabbed with one of her own kitchen knives. Craig wished he had been there; if he had, then maybe Claire would still be alive.

Fiona roused him from his train of thought. 'We're much earlier than we said we'd be, it's only just gone twelve. What do you want to do before we see Lynn?'

'I'll give her a call and see if she's free,' said Craig. He made his way to the bank of payphones, dialled 192 and got Hamilton Dunbar's number. He hung up and redialled the office number, and asked to speak to Lynn.

'Hello, Lynn Simon speaking.'

'Hi Lynn, it's Craig.'

'Oh Craig, thank God you phoned.'

'What's happened?'

'Your policeman, Detective Sergeant Wilson, was here.'

'What?'

'Detective Sergeant Wilson was here in my office this morning, asking questions about you and Brian Irving.'

'How's that possible?' Craig mentally retraced his steps since Monday. He was almost certain he hadn't made any slip-ups.

'Did you tell anyone where you were going?' asked Lynn.

'No. Wait a minute. Yes, my parents, on the phone. I told them I was meeting you. Not by name, but I said I was meeting an Edinburgh literary agent.'

'That must be it, they must have told the police.'

'Shite. God, I'm sorry Lynn. What happened?'

'It's okay, I fended him off. But I wouldn't come to the office again if I were you. Where are you now?'

'We're back at Queen Street. Lynn, we went to Fiona's flat in Hillhead. She's been burgled. But there were no signs of a forced entry and nothing was taken.'

'What? Bloody hell. Do you think they were after you?'

'It's hard to escape that conclusion. But the really strange thing is, I didn't tell anyone I was going to Fiona's, not even my parents.'

'It's not beyond the realms of possibility that the police know about your past and present partners in crime, Craig.'

'Maybe not, but I don't think the police count breaking and entering as part of routine procedure.' A troubled thought crossed his mind, and he was almost reluctant to voice it. 'Not unless the police themselves have got something to hide.'

'Like what?'

'I don't know. But my options seem to be narrowing.'

'You mean they've narrowed down to Clive Prior?'

'Yes.'

'Do you want me to phone him?'

'Yes. Can you tell him I want to come and see him?'

'You want to see him? Why don't we just phone him?'

'Because a phone call won't give me what I want.' What Craig actually meant was that he'd already had his fingers burned by an academic once and he wasn't going to take any chances a second time. He'd spoken to Brian Irving on the phone and he'd subsequently disappeared with Craig's document. He wasn't going to take the risk again even though he knew he needed Clive Prior's help. 'Anyway, I think he'll want to make the time to see me.'

The King's Prerogative

'Why so?'

'We picked up the package from the Consulate.'

'Really? So it was there?'

'It sure was. We haven't opened it yet. Events sort of overtook us.'

'Okay. I'll tell Professor Prior that you want to meet him.'

'Thanks. If Brian Irving thought he was a good man to speak to then I'm sure it'll be time well spent.'

'Leave it with me. Where will you go now?'

'We'll head to Fiona's mum and dad's.'

'Okay, I'll get finished up here as quickly as I can and I'll meet you there.'

'Good. See you later.'

Craig hung up and re-joined Fiona who had been checking on the Edinburgh train. He quickly brought her up to date with Lynn's news, and they were about to make their way to the platform when a thought occurred to Craig.

'Have you got ten pence?'

Fiona ferreted around in her bag and produced a purse from which she retrieved two ten pence pieces. Craig took them and went back to the payphones. He dialled the number again and was put through to Lynn.

'Hi Craig, did you forget something?'

'Yes. Could you do me a favour? When you come to Denis and Valerie's house, could you take a roundabout route?'

'What?'

'Please. Just indulge me. Take a couple of buses or a taxi in the wrong direction, or make it look like you're taking a train.'

'You think the police would follow me?'

'They found you once.'

Lynn thought about it.

'Okay. And you should buy some tickets to Helensburgh.'

'You're joking.'

'What's sauce for the goose.'

'Point taken.'

Craig hung up and wondered how he'd explain this to Fiona without making it look like he'd gone completely paranoid. He clutched the canvas bag all the tighter as he made his way back to her.

Chapter 27

There was no one home when Craig and Fiona arrived back at the house in Church Hill, so Fiona used her key to let them in. They took off their jackets, hung them up, and went through to the kitchen. Craig could see Fiona visibly relax as she put the kettle on, clearly relieved to be back in the protective womb of her parents' house once again. He wanted to put his arms around her and give her a hug. Instead he just said, 'You were great today, really great.'

'Oh I don't think so.'

'Yes you were. Firstly in the Consulate, then in the flat. Talented and brave in the same day. Add blowing bubbles and we could sell tickets.'

She snorted daintily, as if trying to stop herself from laughing but not quite managing to. 'Cheeky.'

The sound of the doorbell interrupted them, and they both jumped at the unexpected intrusion. Fiona stuck her head through the kitchen doorway and peered down the hall. Craig had closed the storm door on their way in so she couldn't see who it was. 'Could you get it, Craig? Please. I'm still a bit jittery from before.'

'Of course.' He slipped past her and walked down the hall. As he opened the door, Craig felt a jangle of nerves too. He opened the door a few inches and was relieved to see Lynn standing there.

'Only me,' she said, but there was no mirth in her voice. 'I'm frozen stiff, can I come in?'

Craig apologised and opened the door wide. Lynn stepped

inside and Craig shut the storm door behind her. They went through to the kitchen and Lynn took off her raincoat and jacket.

'A bus and two taxis I took to get here,' she said. 'I've been standing on the corner for ten minutes, then I saw you arrive.'

'Coffee? Tea?' asked Fiona.

'Tea, please.' She squeezed Fiona's arm on her way past. 'How are you? You must have had an awful shock.'

'I did. I'm glad Craig was there.'

'Was there much mess?'

'That's the thing, there was no damage as such, just things shoved on the floor mainly.'

'It's as if they were looking for something in particular. They were methodical in their messiness, if you know what I mean,' said Craig.

'And nothing was taken?' asked Lynn.

'Not a thing. Not even my diamond earrings, although they broke the lock on my jewellery box to get into it,' said Fiona.

Lynn and Craig exchanged looks, and Craig knew that Lynn was thinking the same as him.

'I think they were looking for the wallet, or the letter,' said Lynn.

'Anything else wouldn't make sense,' agreed Craig.

'Except now there are two letters,' Lynn added. Her eyes strayed to the bag Craig had placed on the kitchen table. 'And a package, by the look of things.'

'Will we?' asked Fiona.

'Got any wire-cutters?' said Craig.

They sat around the table and Craig clipped at the metal strip that sealed the bag. It wasn't too different from the metal bands used to seal note remittances at the bank. The soft metal snapped easily enough under the torque of the secateurs Fiona had fetched from the greenhouse in the garden. Craig pulled the metal through a series of eyelets in the canvas bag, unfolded the bag and laid it flat. He reached inside and pulled out a black leather pouch, perhaps eighteen inches long by twelve inches wide, with a brass zip along one long edge, secured by a small locking clasp mechanism, like the ones you'd find on a briefcase.

'It's a document pouch,' said Lynn. 'And whatever's inside looks quite thick.'

Craig held the pouch loosely and moved his hands up and down, as if guessing its weight. 'Not too heavy.' He examined the fastening. 'I'll have to break the lock. Does your dad have pliers anywhere?'

Fiona left the kitchen and returned two minutes later with a metal toolbox. Craig opened out both sides of the box and dug around the bottom, pulling out a pair of heavy pliers and a thick screwdriver. He set to work on the lock and decided after a couple of minutes that it would be easier to break the metal tag attached to the zip rather than the actual fastening itself. After several twists and thumps, the tag gave way. Craig unzipped the pouch, reached inside and pulled out a neat clutch of papers, tied together with a piece of red ribbon. On the front page, printed across the top half of the paper, was a stylised coat of arms. It was of a large black eagle, with wings outstretched, holding in its claws a laurel wreath. Inside the wreath was a symbol. A thick, black crooked cross, turned forty-five degrees from the vertical.

'Well, I think it's safe to say this isn't a shipping manifest for Swedish timber,' said Craig.

Fiona and Lynn pulled their chairs round so they could sit on either side of Craig as he untied the ribbon and turned over the first page.

The document was addressed to His Majesty King George VI of the United Kingdom of Great Britain, Northern Ireland and the Dominions of the British Empire.

Craig caught his breath. He continued to read in silence,

turning the pages slowly as he got to the bottom of each one. The entire document was forty-two pages long, neatly typed in English, and signed on the last sheet by Deputy Reichsführer Rudolf Hess himself, on behalf of the German people. Craig experienced a peculiar feeling of disembodiment, as if he was watching himself from the other side of the room. He slowly came to terms with the fact that what he was holding in his hands was nothing less than a detailed peace proposal from Germany to Britain.

Dated 10th April 1941, it began with a preamble, outlining the importance of Hess's mission and stressing the genetic, hereditary, ideological and social links between the Nordic races of Britain and Germany, and the respect that the German people had for their British kin. It expressed deep regret for the current hostilities and assured the British people that it was never the intention of Germany to pursue a war against Britain and its empire. It then stated the main reason for the peace offer – the threat to European stability posed by the continued growth of Soviet Communism. Hitler wanted to focus his war effort in the east. It went on to explain why this would be best for Britain in the long term. Notwithstanding the fact that Britain was losing the war in April 1941, the document emphasised the risk attached to the growing economic and military dependence Britain had on the United States of America. Germany predicted that the crippling debt Britain was amassing would cause the break-up of the empire and ensure that the UK would be in a permanently weakened position and a subservient junior partner in its relationship with the Americans.

The document then laid out the German vision for the future. It was in both Britain and Germany's best interests, it said, to forge a pan-European alliance. Germany would be dominant in continental Europe, trading in harmony with a strong and prosperous British Empire. The alternative, it explained, would be further bloodshed, continued privations as a result of the successful U-boat campaign and an inevitable weakening of both proud nations, to the benefit of the USA and the Soviet Union. It noted that President Roosevelt was on record as declaring that British global imperialism was as reprehensible to the US as German continental imperialism. It was in American business interests that Britain and Germany fight each other to exhaustion. A British–German alliance however would provide a strong European powerhouse against the rising influence of communism in the east and American capitalism in the west.

Craig paused as he reached the end of this opening preamble, which stretched to a full eighteen pages. 'Can you believe this?' he asked of no one in particular.

'Incredible,' said Lynn as she pored over the pages Craig had already turned over. 'This is utterly incredible. Every sentence reeks of the self-confidence of a Germany at the height of its success in 1941. Masters of Europe and all it surveyed. The sheer arrogance of the logic is astounding.'

'But isn't it creepy that it foresaw the disintegration of the British Empire after the Second World War,' said Fiona. 'And our growing dependence on America since.'

'Hitler knew that Churchill was half American and naturally leaned towards Roosevelt,' mused Craig. 'Hitler didn't want America in the war. This is a pitch for creating a United States of Europe with Britain and Germany providing the main power bloc.'

He turned the next page. 'Oh my God,' he breathed as he began to read. 'Here are the peace terms. The actual peace terms.' The three of them read on, conscious that they were the first people in over forty years to hold this piece of history in their hands.

They continued reading for several minutes, only the ticking kitchen clock reminding them that time hadn't in fact stood still. The peace terms took up the remainder of the document, describing Germany's offer in specific detail. Each point was explained and rationalised, intended to persuade as well as to define and delineate. It started by confirming that Germany would cease all hostilities in the west if Britain agreed to a number of terms. Firstly, she would be required immediately to end all hostile actions by the Royal Navy and the RAF against Germany and German dependencies overseas. A reduction in the size of the British navy, army and air force would be imposed, commensurate with its peacetime needs to provide security across its global territories.

Britain would adopt an attitude of 'benevolent neutrality' towards Germany as it conducted its plans for eastern Europe. The document proposed a twenty-five-year alliance between Britain and Germany that would secure peace, foster mutual prosperity and ensure the continued existence of the British Empire.

In return, Germany would undertake a number of actions in good faith as part of the peace accord. It would evacuate all of France except for the regions of Alsace, Lorraine and the industrial centre in the north-east of the country. It would also withdraw from the Netherlands, Belgium, Norway and Denmark but retain control over Luxembourg, which it saw as a German state. Germany would in addition withdraw from Yugoslavia and Greece and would use its good offices to effect an agreement between Britain and Italy to settle the Mediterranean conflict. No belligerent or neutral country would seek or be entitled to reparations from any other nation.

Turning to the struggle against communism, the document stated that Germany would commit to taking receipt of the full output of British war production, thus preventing the British economy from sinking into another depression. Germany would take sole responsibility for defeating the evil of Bolshevism, thereby convincing a doubtful world of its benevolent intention to save humanity. It was not necessary to provide military details of how that would be accomplished as that was a matter for Germany alone.

The proposal went on to describe several other actions that would be performed following the cessation of hostilities, including plans for plebiscites in the occupied countries and population exchanges for displaced people across western Europe and the Balkans.

Craig then came to a strange clause in the document. It declared that, as part of the intended population realignment in Europe, Britain would be required to allow free passage to German ships sailing through the Mediterranean and the Suez Canal. The German vision for a new Europe required the transportation of all Jews from Germany and occupied territories to Madagascar. The island off the east coast of Africa would become a new Jewish state. The document explained that this was also to Britain's advantage because it would resolve the problem of a prospective Jewish settlement in British-occupied Palestine.

Craig finally got to the end of the document and looked at the signature at the foot of the last page. It occurred to him that everything that had happened, everything he'd done in the last few days, was suddenly focused right there. It crystallised on the ink in that signature, on that page, on that table, in that kitchen. It felt to him like the eye of a hurricane, and he knew that he had to find a way to navigate through the storm to the other side.

He looked at Lynn, then at Fiona. 'It's all true,' Craig finally said. 'All of it.' He realised that what began with the letter of safe conduct had now led him to the proof that there *had* been a peace offer after all. It was obvious that it had been thought out carefully, and despite the crooked logic it contained, it was coherent and meticulous and above all, it seemed *authentic*. It had lain in the Swedish Consulate since 1941, Craig had seen the proof of that with his own eyes.

Right there and then, Craig knew why Claire had been killed. The authorities must know that the peace offer existed. Hess would have explained the offer to his captors all those years ago when he first arrived. The government must have known how explosive the details would be if they ever got out. What if it came out that they had the chance to save thousands, if not millions of lives by shortening the war by four years? That must have been why it was hushed up at the time.

Even now, after all these years, it would create a sensation. The government would have some difficult questions to answer. Craig realised that they'd do anything to prevent the details from getting out. Hess had withheld the location of the printed copy of the proposal for reasons known only to him. Maybe for the same reason he gave the hidden letters to his grandad, to protect the people involved at the British end. Now Craig knew why the police wanted to speak to him about the letter. They wanted to silence him and prevent the possibility of those details leaking out. Craig thought hard. He needed to think harder. He needed help, now more than ever.

He turned to Lynn. 'Did you speak to Clive Prior?'

'Yes. He wants to meet you. He'll definitely want to meet you now,' said Lynn as her eyes pointed to the document on the table.

'Did he say when he was free?'

'He'll make time for us as soon as we can get there.'

'I need to go to Cambridge tomorrow.' He backtracked a step. 'Wait a minute, as soon as *we* can get there?'

'I'm going too.' She turned to Fiona. 'Fiona, do you want to come too?'

'Too right I do.'

Craig held up his hands, as if trying to stop a juggernaut suddenly bearing down on him. 'Hold on, hold on. I can't ask you to give up any more time on this. You're a busy lady, and Fi, you've got uni. Lynn, you've been more help than I could ever thank you for, and you've got me in to see a Cambridge professor who might be able to sort out this mess.'

'No chance,' said Lynn. 'I'm protecting my investment.'
'What investment?'
'I'm assuming when this story breaks, you'll want a publisher not to mention someone who can help you tell the story?'
'Do you honestly think this will be allowed to see the light of day?'
'They said that about Watergate too.'
'Well, I hadn't…'
'Good. That's settled. I'm coming too.'
Craig was struck dumb temporarily. After a moment he admitted to himself that he'd be glad of Lynn's company not to mention her expertise in dealing with academic types like Clive Prior.
'I don't know what to say.'
'Say nothing.'

Chapter 28

Thursday 17th March, 1983

Craig and Fiona took a bus heading out of town, then jumped on a number 11 heading back in, got off at Tollcross and hailed a taxi to take them to Waverley station. Craig had only just managed to convince Fiona that it wasn't his paranoia getting the better of him. Now that he knew that Wilson was in Edinburgh he thought it was an essential precaution to take. He had to avoid the police until he got the chance to get Clive Prior on board. With a Cambridge professor and a well-respected literary agent in his corner he'd feel much more secure when the time came to hand himself in.

The night before, Craig and Fiona reached a compromise about the trip. Fiona would go to her uni lecture and afterwards do some research at the library. She insisted that she wanted to do *something*, even if it was going through the records of the time to try to piece together more of the background picture. Craig and Lynn would meet Professor Prior.

It was chilly on the station concourse as they waited for Lynn to appear. 'It's freezing this morning,' said Craig, stamping his feet and rubbing his hands. He turned the collar up on his jacket to conjure the psychological illusion of warmth. Fiona had lent him an Adidas holdall for the journey, and now he wished he'd packed a scarf and gloves along with his things. Fiona saw Lynn making her way towards them, and she didn't look happy. In fact, she looked extremely worried. Fiona tugged Craig's arm, and he turned to see what had caught her attention.

'Morning Lynn, everything okay?'

'Not exactly.' She grabbed him by the arm and pulled him towards a quiet corner away from most of the morning hustle and bustle. When she was sure that they couldn't be overheard, she produced a copy of that morning's *Scotsman* and opened it to the home news items on page four. She folded the broadsheet in half, then in half again to make it easier to handle, and gave it to Craig. He recognised the photograph above the news article. It was his own passport photo.

'Jesus.'

The headline read:

Police seek men in Stranraer murder case

He read on:

Police investigating the brutal murder of Stranraer teacher Claire Marshall on 2nd March are keen to trace a local man, Craig Dunlop (25). Detective Inspector Bruce Cowie who is heading the investigation told reporters yesterday that they are looking for Dunlop, who has been missing from his Stranraer home since Monday. He confirmed that police are also searching for a second man, Frank Blake (42) who is described as of medium build with short light brown hair. DI Cowie urged the public not to approach these men but to contact the police incident room on 0776 2688 if either is sighted.

'This is all I need,' sighed Craig. He was surprised to discover that he felt no sense of panic, simply irritation. 'I can't let the police catch up with me yet.'

'Well it could be worse,' said Lynn. 'I phoned the city desk this morning. My old chum Eric Jobson told me that they put the story on page four because the police haven't actually come out and said that you're a suspect, but it seems they're getting desperate and you're one of the few strong leads they have. Anyway, it's a lousy picture so with luck no one will recognise you.'

'Thanks.'

'You know what I mean. Here, wear this till we get on the train.' Lynn produced a baseball cap from the small rucksack she was carrying and gave it to Craig. 'It'll help to hide your face.' Craig put it on and felt no better, in fact he felt like the cap drew attention to him, probably because he wasn't in the habit of wearing one. He looked around and realised that none of the dozens of commuters within twenty yards of him was paying him the slightest interest. Lynn continued. 'The other good thing is that the article is only in the Scottish papers for now, so with luck no one will recognise you in Cambridge.'

Their London train was due to leave in fifteen minutes so Craig and Lynn said their goodbyes to Fiona and made their way to platform 2 to wait for it to arrive.

'Who's Frank Blake?' asked Lynn when they got to the platform.

'I have no idea,' said Craig. The name hadn't rung a bell when he read the newspaper article, and despite having racked his brains for the last few minutes he couldn't think of anyone he knew called Frank Blake. 'Maybe they think he has some information, or maybe the police found something in Claire's house with his name on it and they want to eliminate him from the enquiry.'

'Maybe.' Lynn wasn't convinced by either of those possibilities, but she saw that Craig had other things on his mind so she didn't press the point.

A tannoy announcement told them that their train was arriving, and a small crowd of passengers jostled for position on the platform as the train entered the station and slowed to a stop. Craig and Lynn managed to get a table to themselves and settled in for the journey. The train would take them to Peterborough where they'd change for a connection to Cambridge. Craig looked at his watch. 8:50. They should get to Cambridge before three o'clock. Lynn decided it would be better for Craig to stay put rather than wander around the train, so she went to the buffet car to get some coffees. She returned a few minutes later with the drinks and a couple of small packets of shortbread.

'One pound twenty for two coffees and two biscuits,' she said. 'Daylight robbery.'

They took a few sips of their drink and made some small talk. Craig asked if her husband was okay with her suddenly travelling to Cambridge.

'Yes, it's all good. Nicolas was fine with my change of plans for today, he's kind of used to it with my line of work.'

They took another few sips of their coffee, then Craig brought the conversation back round to the document. He looked round to see if anyone was within earshot. In the seat across the aisle, a young man was plugged into a Sony Walkman that was loud enough for Craig to hear the *tsk tsk tsk tsk* of the drumbeat from where he was sitting.

Craig looked out of the window at the passing countryside, then back at Lynn. 'Have you had any more thoughts since last night about the document we found?'

Lynn gave a slight shrug. 'The dust hasn't settled on that one yet.' She looked at him. 'You look like you didn't get much sleep last night, no need to ask if you've had any more thoughts on it.'

'I keep thinking about what would have happened if Britain had accepted those terms.'

'That's dangerous thinking,' said Lynn.

'Why do you say that?'

'That would involve a complete rewrite of history.'

'I know,' said Craig. 'That's what kept me awake.'

He looked out of the window again for a long minute.

'The world might be a different place today,' he said.

'Craig.'

'What?'

Lynn looked at him with concern written on her face. 'You have to stop taking everything on your shoulders.'

'I'm not.'

'What was keeping you awake then?'

'It scares me how attractive the offer looked and how its view of the future was uncannily accurate. How dependent we now are on America, and how in debt we are to them. And look at the growth of communism. Look at the Warsaw Pact, and the Berlin Wall. What's happened in western Europe is that Germany and France have become the power bloc, not Germany and Britain. Ironic.'

'What do you think about the collapse of the British Empire?' asked Lynn.

He thought for a moment before replying. 'Don't get me wrong,' he said, 'I think it was inevitable and of course it's only right and proper that countries that used to be British territories run their own affairs. The Commonwealth feels like a much better institution than the empire was.'

'It wasn't such a bad thing that Britain lost its empire then?'

'Totally. But I'm thinking about all those people who died fighting between 1941 and 1945.'

'To defeat Nazism. That has to be worth it.'

'You're right. Of course Nazism had to be defeated. God, you could get tied up in knots just getting your head around it,' said Craig. He realised he was very tired. The last three days were catching up with him. Was it only three days since he was last at his desk in the bank? He dragged his thoughts back to the present, or to be accurate, back to that forty-year-old document. 'Lynn, what did you make of the part that talked about Madagascar?'

'That bit disturbed me I have to confess,' replied Lynn. She locked her fingers together, making a steeple with her index fingers and pressing them to her lips, deep in thought.

'I thought so too,' said Craig.

Lynn at last voiced what she was thinking. 'Do you know about the Wannsee Conference?'

'Yes,' replied Craig.

Nothing more needed to be said. They both knew the significance. At a conference of senior Nazi officials held in the Berlin suburb of Wannsee in January 1942, approval was given to build the extermination camps in eastern Europe. That meeting was a full eight months *after* the failure of Hess's peace mission. Eight months after the Madagascar plan was included in the peace proposal.

Lynn and Craig stared out of the train window.

Chapter 29

They changed trains at Peterborough as planned and arrived in Cambridge at 2:45pm. They walked through the ticket barrier on to the main station area and studied the information signs to get their bearings. The signs told them that the toilets and left luggage lockers were to the left and buses and taxis were to the right. Craig insisted that they put the holdall into left luggage.

'Call me paranoid if you like, but what if the first thing Clive Prior does is call the police?'

'You're paranoid,' Lynn confirmed.

'I'm in the papers, that's what I am.'

'He won't do that, he told Edward Hart-Davis that he'd be happy to help us.'

'That was before I was a fugitive from justice.'

'Aren't you being a bit dramatic?'

'Perhaps, but I'd rather play it my way for now. It'll be easy enough to come back and get the document later.'

'Okay, but you're paying for the extra taxi fares.'

'Extra taxi fares? I forked out the best part of forty quid for two return tickets to Cambridge.'

They laughed. 'Consider that an investment, matey,' said Lynn. 'Come on, let's go.'

It wasn't a long walk to Emmanuel College from the station. Craig remarked on how much the green spaces and the old buildings reminded him of Edinburgh. There were fewer cars and more bicycles than in the Scottish capital, but they agreed there was a similar feel to the two old university

The King's Prerogative

cities. They arrived at the college and walked through a cloistered entrance into the wide grassy front court. The old college surrounded them on all four sides and looked every inch the venerable seat of learning it had been since 1584. Small groups of students were making their way one way or the other around the quadrant.

'Can I help you?'

Craig and Lynn turned in the direction of the voice. A small man in his fifties was striding towards them. He was in shirt sleeves which were rolled up to the elbow, and his tie hung loosely around his neck, the end tucked into his shirt front. He looked like he'd been shifting something heavy, or perhaps he was just out of shape.

'Yes, we're here to see Professor Prior,' said Craig.

'Professor Prior, of European History?' queried the man.

'That's right.'

'Is he expecting you?'

'Yes, we spoke to him on the phone yesterday.' Craig decided he might get away with a half-lie.

The man looked at his watch.

'Just a minute, please.' The man disappeared into a room built into a corner of the quadrant and emerged a full minute later. 'Professor Prior should be in his study at this time of day. Follow me, please.'

He started off along the cloistered path, walking quickly. Craig and Lynn had to speed up to keep pace. They walked along two sides of the front court and through a further two courtyards until they approached an imposing old sandstone building, covered in ivy. The man led them through a large door, along a wooden hallway and up two flights of stairs until they arrived at a door which had the name Prof. C.D. Prior inscribed on a small wooden plate. The man knocked and waited for the instruction 'Come!' before entering. He took two steps into a large study, or perhaps it was a small library, Craig couldn't be sure.

'Two visitors for you, professor.'

A rather small man was standing on a stool at the far end of the study, in the act of replacing a book into a bookcase that took up the entire length and breadth of one wall. He stepped down from the stool, looked round and took off a pair of reading glasses. He looked to be in his seventies, with a wiry frame, thinning grey hair and pale deeply-wrinkled skin that suggested that he'd smoked all his life. He wore a tight-fitting grey herringbone jacket over a green sweater which in turn was stretched over a checked shirt, buttoned at the collar. A plain brown tie, tied impeccably in a half Windsor knot, completed the ensemble. Craig noticed that the man's shoes were old Hush Puppies that, like him, seemed to have seen better days.

The man stepped forward and offered his hand to Lynn.

'Thank you Pugh. Mrs Simon I presume? We spoke on the telephone. I am Clive Prior. So nice of you to make the journey from Edinburgh to see me.' They shook hands. Pugh closed the door behind him as he returned to his duties. If Professor Prior had been surprised at their unexpected arrival, he managed to conceal it with charm and good grace. He turned his head to look at Craig, his eyes searching Craig's face.

Craig stretched out his hand. 'Professor Prior, my name is Craig Dunlop, I hope you'll forgive us for landing on you unannounced like this.'

'Delighted, dear boy, delighted.' They shook hands and the professor invited them to take a seat on two chairs on the near side of a large mahogany desk.

'May I offer you some refreshment?'

'No thank you, Professor,' said Lynn. 'We hope we're not disturbing you, but we wanted to meet with you urgently. We've come straight from the railway station.'

'Indeed?' The professor arched an eyebrow and looked between Lynn and Craig. He walked behind his desk and sat down. 'Edward Hart-Davis spoke very highly of you, Mrs Simon, so I was only too happy to offer my help, such as it is.

He told me that it concerns a letter dating from the war, is that correct? I believe it might be the same letter that Doctor Irving told me about it when we spoke on the telephone.' His eyes settled on Craig, inviting him to speak.

Craig took the wallet from his jacket and handed it to the professor. 'Yes sir, this wallet belonged to my grandfather. He died recently and so the wallet came to me, as a keepsake, if you like.'

'Your grandfather?'

'Yes, my grandfather was the farmer who first came upon Hess when he landed by parachute.'

'You don't say? Fascinating. Fascinating. And it was in his possession all these years?'

'Yes. It was only when it came to me that I found the letter hidden in the lining.'

'Is that so? Fascinating.'

Clive Prior turned the wallet over in his hands, feeling its texture. 'May I?'

'Please do.'

He opened the wallet and took out the two letters tucked inside. He put his reading glasses back on, unfolded the first letter and read it carefully.

'This appears to be a photostatic copy of an original document,' he said, looking up at Craig over the top of his glasses. 'I assume you also have the original?'

'I did, but I sent it to Doctor Irving. He wanted to examine it, and I asked him if he could authenticate it. You mentioned that Doctor Irving contacted you?'

'Yes, yes, he did. A few weeks ago now. He seemed quite excited when he telephoned and I found his excitement contagious. We arranged to meet, but he didn't appear I regret to say. It was very strange.'

'He didn't call again?'

'No.'

'And he didn't give you an indication of how far he'd taken his research?'

'I'm afraid not. I was looking forward to him telling me at our meeting.'

'What would be your assessment of that letter?'

The professor coughed and took a handkerchief from his breast pocket to wipe his mouth before speaking. 'It is very interesting I have to say, and is entirely consistent with my knowledge of the operation at the time.'

'The operation?'

'Yes, the operation run by the British intelligence service. Frightfully clever people.' The professor turned his attention to the second letter. 'What is this?'

'It would be easier to explain after you've looked at it,' said Craig.

Clive Prior unfolded the second letter and read it. Craig was sure he saw a look of surprise flit across the professor's face for an instant. His gaze didn't move from the paper for more than half a minute. When he finally looked up, Clive Prior's expression was unreadable. His eyes however rooted Craig to the spot.

'This was in the wallet too?'

'Yes, but we only found it the other evening.'

'Do you know what it refers to?'

'Yes. I visited the Swedish Consulate yesterday and they still had the package after all these years.'

'Did you see it?'

'Yes, I was given it.'

Clive Prior's eyes sparkled. 'What was in the package?'

'It was a peace offer from Hess, addressed to the King.' Craig saw the Adam's apple in Professor Prior's throat dip slightly. The professor leaned forward. 'Do you have it with you? I'd very much like to see it.'

'I don't have it with me at the moment, but it is here in Cambridge.'

Clive Prior stretched over and poured a glass of water from a jug on the desk. 'Fascinating, most fascinating.' He took a sip and put the glass down. 'I can help translate it for you, it would be my pleasure. I have passable German.'

Craig and Lynn exchanged looks. 'It was written in English, Professor,' said Craig.

'It was? Even better. I assume you've read it? I expect it contains a lot about Germany allowing Britain to keep its empire in return for us turning a blind eye to the Germans invading Russia?'

Craig and Lynn looked at each other again, surprised that the professor had hit the nail on the head.

'That's exactly what it says,' confirmed Lynn. 'How did you know?'

'Hess's interviews in captivity were recorded, and that is essentially the thrust of what he told his interrogators at the time. Of course, we had no intention of acting on what he said.'

Craig couldn't suppress a feeling of disappointment. 'Forgive me Professor, but reading the document might give you a different perspective. The offer is incredibly detailed and it left me with the impression that it was a genuine proposal to take Britain out of the war.' He looked at Lynn who nodded her agreement.

'Oh my dear boy, I'm sure it did,' said the professor. 'I don't mean to belittle your discovery at all, far from it. But it was all a ruse. I don't know how much you know about that era, but during the time that Britain stood alone, there was a huge chess game going on between the intelligence services of Britain and Germany.'

He waited for Lynn and Craig to take this in before continuing once again. 'You see, Germany wanted to take Britain out of the war, for reasons I'm sure you know of, and the British secret service was happy to lead them on. It was a no-lose situation for us, as our American cousins might say. Either we'd be able to demonstrate to Stalin that Hitler was deceiving him, undermining the German–Soviet pact, or we could string the Germans along long enough for them to gain confidence to attack Russia, and bring them into the war on our side. Which, of course, is what happened.'

'So I understand you fully, Professor,' said Craig. 'you're saying that this *was* an intelligence sting? Hess was lured here in order to precipitate Operation Barbarossa?'

'Absolutely, my dear chap. So you see, it's no surprise that this peace offer of yours looks impressive, because as far as the Germans were concerned, it was genuine.'

Craig couldn't help but feel downcast although he didn't know why. He was also confused. He needed to process this.

Lynn spoke up. 'What do you suggest we do, Professor?'

'Well, Mrs Simon, despite all that I've said, I would still very much like to inspect your document. It is bound to be a fascinating artefact. You said you brought it with you?'

'Yes, it's…'

'It's in safekeeping, professor,' interrupted Craig. 'As a potentially important historical document, I thought it wise not to carry it through the streets of Cambridge. Not until we had a chance to speak with you.'

'Yes, I see.' The professor picked up a pipe from a small rack on his desk and proceeded to fill it from a tobacco pouch retrieved from his jacket pocket. For a long minute no one spoke as the old man concentrated on his task. He was clearly thinking. Finally he looked at Craig over the bowl of the pipe as he lit it, blowing thick clouds of smoke into the air. 'Perhaps Edward Hart-Davis mentioned to you that I still have one or two contacts in the Home Office. You know Cambridge, recruiting ground for all kinds of rum types in the old days.' He winked at Lynn conspiratorially. 'I'd be happy to make some calls on your behalf and let's see if we can't find someone who can provide some clarity for you.'

'That would be very kind of you, Professor,' said Craig.

'Meantime, may I offer you some beds for the night? I live not too far from the college, and I have plenty of room. My wife would be glad of the company, if I'm honest. I can make my phone calls and hopefully by this evening or tomorrow we'll have some answers.'

Craig jumped in before Lynn could open her mouth.

'That's very kind of you Professor, but we've already made other arrangements for this evening.' He subtly kicked Lynn's foot. 'Lynn's taking the opportunity to catch up with some friends. I hope you won't think us rude.'

'Oh not at all,' said the professor. Craig could tell that the old man was offended in spite of his manners. He rose from his seat and handed the wallet back to Craig. The two men shook hands.

'Thank you very much, Professor. Shall we ring you at some point tomorrow?'

'By all means, please do. I have lectures until midday but I'm free for most of the afternoon. Let me give you the best number to reach me on.' The old man scribbled a number on a slip of paper and gave it to Craig before showing them to the door. 'Hopefully I'll have some news for you by the next time we speak. And you won't forget that document, will you?'

'Of course. Speak to you tomorrow.'

The professor showed them to the door and gave them a small wave before going back into his study.

Lynn waited until they reached the street beyond the college courtyard before grabbing Craig's arm. 'What was that all about?' she asked. 'I thought you'd jump at the chance to spend more time with Professor Prior. What was all that 'Lynn's got other arrangements' stuff about?'

'Yes, sorry about that. It was the first thing that came into my head. I didn't want to impose on the professor.'

'Impose?' Lynn looked at him scathingly. 'Craig, just because Brian Irving disappeared with your letter doesn't mean that Clive Prior intends to disappear with your peace document.'

Craig looked around him. Maybe he was being paranoid after all. 'Okay, you're right, maybe I overreacted.'

'I think you did, just a bit.' Lynn stopped and a look of sudden realisation swept over her face. 'Oh I get it,' she said.

'What?'

'You want to phone your girlfriend tonight and didn't want to be constrained by etiquette while in Professor Prior's house.' Lynn was pleased at her little joke and found it hard to wipe the smirk from her face.

Craig blushed. 'That's rubbish.'

Lynn saw that she had touched a nerve. 'Oh no it's not.'

'Yes it is, Lynn. This is more important than my personal feelings. And in case no one told you, Fi is not my girlfriend.'

'Well are you going to tell me the real reason?'

Craig felt a bit sheepish. 'I can't. I don't know why.' He didn't enjoy locking horns with Lynn. Apart from being in debt to her, he had quickly grown to respect her and he disliked the feeling that in her eyes he'd just blotted his copybook. The truth was that something about the conversation with Professor Prior troubled him. He couldn't put his finger on it, but the hairs on the back of his neck told him that he couldn't yet put his trust in the old man.

Lynn pursed her lips, then shrugged her shoulders. 'No real harm done I don't suppose, but Craig, remember that you want Clive Prior's advice so you need to keep in his good books.'

'Yes, I suppose so. Sorry Lynn, I suppose the last few days have made me a bit on edge.'

'Understandable.'

But Craig couldn't shake the feeling that rather than making things clearer, their meeting with Professor Prior had muddied the waters further. 'There *was* something a bit odd about our discussion with the professor. Don't you think so?'

'He was a bit dittery but apart from that he was charming,' said Lynn. 'I liked him. He seemed like he genuinely wants to help.'

'Yes, I know. But still.'

'What?'

Craig couldn't decide if his mind was playing tricks on

him or not. His encounter with Blake had perhaps made him feel more wary. 'Did it strike you as a bit strange that the professor's words and figures differed?'

'What does that mean?'

'Sorry, it's a banking analogy. It's when we look to see if a cheque's been made out properly. What I mean is that the professor was quick to dismiss the peace offer on the one hand, but on the other hand he's very keen to see the document for himself.'

'I didn't read anything into that,' said Lynn. 'I think he wanted to set your expectations at a realistic level.'

'Hmmm maybe. I saw his reaction to that second letter, though. I think he was genuinely surprised.'

They continued walking in silence, each deep in thought.

After a few minutes they reached the centre of town and came to the tourist information office. Lynn offered to go in and organise a couple of hotel rooms for the night. Craig walked around the block to kill some time and found himself outside a music shop. He'd always fancied himself as a bit of a guitarist. He stopped to look in the window and admire the collection of electric and acoustic guitars lined up. A thought suddenly came to him, and he went inside. He asked the man behind the counter if he sold sheet music.

'Of course,' said the man, and he showed Craig to a section in the back of the shop. 'What are you looking for?'

'Some old instrumental pieces, really whatever takes my interest. The older the better.'

'Piano? Strings? Woodwind? Brass?'

'Piano or strings. Or brass.'

The assistant pulled a face that said 'I've got a right one here' but he looked out a stack of sheets, sifting them into piles. Craig noticed some old jazz scores that seemed to date from the 1920s and 30s, and began looking through them.

'How much for all of these?' Craig picked up more than a dozen pieces of sheet music.

'All of them?'

'Yes.'

The man looked through the scores and sorted them into two small piles. 'These ten sheets are £2 each and I can let you have the other six for £1.50 each.'

Craig mused. 'What if I give you twenty-five for the lot?'

The assistant pursed his lips and looked at the old jazz music. Craig could tell he was weighing up the odds of whether or not another mug would be so keen to hand over so much cash for some long-forgotten ragtime tunes.

'Deal,' the assistant finally said.

They concluded their business and Craig left the shop with the music sheets safely in his inside jacket pocket. By the time he got back to the tourist information office Lynn had finished her own business and was waiting outside.

'Where were you?'

'Just round the block.'

'I've got us in to a small two-star hotel near the station.'

'Good,' said Craig. 'We can stop off at the left luggage lockers on the way.'

Chapter 30

Fiona's lecture ended at one pm and she jumped on a bus into town a few minutes later. As it stopped and started along Great Western Road she gazed out of the window and wondered what Craig and Lynn were doing. Still on the train, no doubt. She realised that she hadn't thought this much about Craig for a long time. Despite her better judgement she realised she enjoyed it. She liked the fact that he had come to her when he needed help, and she also liked seeing this new side to Craig, with the bit between his teeth. She snapped back to the present when she saw that the bus was coming up to Charing Cross. A short walk later and Fiona reached the Mitchell Library. She always looked forward to seeing the old Edwardian Baroque building with its colonnades and its domed roof. To her, the library was as iconic a Scottish landmark as Edinburgh Castle or the Forth Bridge.

She went inside and found the reference section. That'd be where she'd find the old newspapers from the period, she assumed. She went up to a desk to speak to one of the assistants, who gave her a card to fill out. Fiona decided that she'd check the *Glasgow Herald* for the whole of May and June 1941, and then for the period covering the Nuremberg war trials after the war. According to Craig that would cover Hess's arrival and his next and only public appearance.

Once she'd filled it in, Fiona took her card up to the desk and handed it to the assistant. He disappeared for a few minutes. When she returned Fiona was surprised not to see any newspapers.

'Here you are,' he said. 'We recently put most of our older papers on to microfiche. Have you used it before?'

'I can't say I have,' admitted Fiona.

'No problem, it's all fairly straightforward. I'll show you. This way.' She followed the assistant as he walked through to a spacious room that formed the library's main reading hall. He walked along a long line of tables, most of them occupied by people reading large books or writing notes. He came to a long table that had a row of what looked like TV monitors lined up facing the same number of chairs. He flicked a switch and spent a minute showing Fiona how to use the viewer.

'You just place the fiche here and move this control. You can scan back and forward to the place you want. This knob here adjusts the focus.'

'Got it, thanks.'

The assistant left her to it and Fiona settled down to her task. She pulled a pad and pen from her bag and began jotting down notes.

Three hours later Fiona finally put her pen down and rubbed her wrist. She must have looked through the best part of 200 newspapers and her eyes were as tired as her writing hand. She had learned a great deal about Hess from the articles written at the time, and a great deal that was puzzling to her. Plenty to tell Craig about in any case. She looked at her watch and decided it was time to make the train journey back through to Edinburgh. She switched off the machine and took the fiche back to the desk. The assistant from earlier had been replaced by an older woman, who took the pieces of plastic from Fiona and looked at the serial numbers on the sleeve. She found the corresponding ring binders and filed them away, initialling the index card on each. 'That's a coincidence,' she said.

The King's Prerogative

'What is?'

'Each one of these fiche were taken out on the same day nearly three weeks ago. Were you here before, looking at the same papers?'

'No, I wasn't,' said Fiona. 'That is weird.' She thanked the assistant and made her way out of the front door, buttoning up her duffel coat. She crossed the road and walked down Bath Street. She thought about those microfiche all the way between the library and the station. By the time she bought her ticket at Queen Street she reached a conclusion: she'd just spent the afternoon following in Brian Irving's footsteps.

After dinner that evening, Fiona filled her parents in on her day's research. They listened with interest, happy that their daughter was back with them for the weekend. Shortly after 8:30, the telephone rang and Fiona jumped up to answer it after the first ring.

'Hello?'

'Hi Fi, it's Craig. How're things?'

'Oh hi! Fine, everything's fine thanks. I had a good afternoon in the library, I've just been telling Mum and Dad all about it. First things first: how did you and Lynn get on with Professor Prior?'

Craig sighed. 'Hmmm, it went okay. He offered to help by contacting one of his Cambridge crowd who's in the civil service.'

'It sounds as if there's a "but" coming?'

'Kind of. Lynn thinks I'm either paranoid or I'm expecting too much from him. Perhaps she's right. Maybe I'm a bit disappointed that he didn't seem as excited as I was when I discovered the letters.'

'What did he say when he read the peace offer?'

'Em...'

'What?'

'I didn't take it with me. I put it into left luggage. I didn't want a repeat of the Brian Irving fiasco. I wanted to meet him before deciding if he actually was the man to help me.'

'Oh Craig! For heaven's sake.'

'I know, I know. I'm taking it with me tomorrow when we go back to see him.'

'What was he like?'

'He seemed nice to be fair. He had a big enough study in the middle of the college so he's obviously well respected. He was very charming and polite. We'll see what tomorrow brings. Anyway, tell me how you got on at the library.'

Fiona reached for her bag and dug out her notes. 'Does the phone there take incoming calls? I can phone you back if you like?'

'I don't think it does take incoming calls, I'm on the pay phone in a small hotel not far from the station in Cambridge. But I've got plenty of change, enough for about ten minutes, anyway.'

Fiona told him what she'd found from the papers she read on microfiche.

'I discovered some interesting details about Hess's flight. The papers said that initially there was some doubt about Hess's destination, but that it was later confirmed that he'd planned to land at Dungavel House. You know, the home of the Duke of Hamilton. Apparently there was a grass landing strip attached to the house that would have been suitable for a plane like Hess's. It seems that Hess had planned to stay for no more than two days and fly back to Germany. He didn't even have a change of clothes with him. Craig? Are you still there?'

'Yeah, I'm listening. Carry on.'

'Well, I found a strange coincidence about the night that Hess landed. If you remember, the Blitz had been going on from September of 1940 right through the winter and into the spring of 1941.'

'Yes, that sounds about right.'

'Okay. So, on the night of the 10th of May 1941, the night Hess landed, Hitler inflicted the largest bomber raid to date on London. The Luftwaffe ceased bombing raids on the UK immediately after that raid. Don't you think that's strange?'

Craig hadn't registered the connection between those two events before. 'God yeah, that seems to be too much of a coincidence now you mention it.'

'Well that's not all that was strange. I then went on to look at the *Glasgow Herald*'s coverage of the Nuremberg Trials. Not only was it the first time that Hess had been seen *in public* since the night he landed, but it was the first time he had been seen *at all* in the whole of that time. No photographs of him had been taken, or at least released, during his time in captivity. It was reported that he looked a shadow of his former self at the trial. The strange thing however is that at the trial, he didn't recognise people he'd known closely for years, including Karl Haushofer and Hermann Goering, and he denied knowledge of things that he had been responsible for. What did the British do to him for those four years to make him act like that?'

'It could have been a tactical ploy though,' said Craig. 'His defence was based on amnesia. I remember reading that he also refused to see his wife, and he refused to put his signature to anything, claiming that the allies were trying to trick him. Maybe he was trying to suggest that he had truly lost his mind in the hope that he'd escape the gallows.'

'Or maybe he did lose his mind,' said Fiona.

Fiona was about to go into more detail when the phone line interrupted them with a series of urgent high-pitched beeps.

'Damn, there go the pips, I'm out of cash, hold on.' Craig fished in his pocket and found three 2p pieces which he quickly put in the phone's coin slot. 'I've only got 6p so I just wanted to say thanks before I go.'

'It's okay. Quick, listen. I think Brian Irving looked at the same papers as me, three weeks ago.'

'Really? That means we...' but the pips cut him off then the phone line went dead. 'Must be on the same track,' he finished.

Fiona put the phone down and put her notepad back in

her bag. 'They better have separate bedrooms,' she thought. Then she realised how that would sound if she were to say it out loud and she laughed to herself.

'What are you laughing at?' asked Valerie.

'That's for me to know and you to find out,' replied Fiona.

'I hate when you've got that look on your face,' said her mum.

Fiona smiled and gave her a hug.

Chapter 31

Friday 18th March, 1983

Craig knocked on Lynn's door just before 8:30 and they went down to breakfast together. The small breakfast room had six tables and fellow breakfasters were sitting at two of them eating bacon, sausage and eggs. A young waitress showed them to a table and took their order, then disappeared through a swing door and reappeared two minutes later carrying a pot of tea and a pot of coffee for their table. Craig and Lynn talked about what they should do that morning and agreed that Craig should lie low at the hotel just in case his photograph had made the English papers. Lynn suggested that in that case they should arrange to stay for one more night so that the hotel owners wouldn't look for them to vacate by check-out time.

'It's very good of you to pay for our digs, Lynn. I'll pay you back as soon as this is all cleared up,' said Craig.

'Oh don't mention it,' said Lynn with a dismissive wave of her hand. 'Anyway, it's an interesting break from routine, and it'll do no harm for me to add a Cambridge professor to my list of contacts.'

The waitress brought Craig his sausage, bacon and eggs and Lynn her scrambled egg on toast, and they ate in silence. After finishing their drinks they went back to their rooms. Fifteen minutes later Lynn knocked on Craig's door and told him that she was going out but she'd be back by eleven o'clock. She intended to look in on the Cambridge University Press seeing as she was in the neighbourhood.

Craig spent the morning reading the peace offer and preparing his newly purchased music sheets. He hoped they would turn out to be a waste of money but he justified the expense to himself – better to have them and not need them than to need them and not have them.

When Lynn had not appeared back by 11:40 Craig began to get worried. He put his things into his Adidas holdall, picked up his jacket and went out onto the landing. He locked his door and turned round to see Lynn coming up the stair.

'Thank God,' said Craig, 'I thought something had happened.'

'You *are* jumpy today! Sorry, I just got chatting with the folk at C.U.P. and, well, let's just say if nothing else happens today my trip has been worth it.' Lynn saw the look on Craig's face and immediately regretted her choice of words.

'Oh Craig, I didn't mean it like that. Think positively, Professor Prior will come good today, I'm certain of it.'

She took her bedroom key out and unlocked her door.

'I'm just going to freshen up for a minute, you wait for me downstairs. Take this.' She produced a British Telecom phone card and handed it to Craig.

'I thought it would save all that ferreting around for cash you usually do.'

Craig smiled. 'Thanks Lynn, yes it will.'

Lynn went into her room and Craig went downstairs to sit in the hotel's lounge/television room. It was the same size as the breakfast room, decorated with the same emulsioned-over Anaglypta wallpaper. There was no one else in the room and the television wasn't on. Craig picked up a copy of the local newspaper from a low wooden coffee table and scanned the pages for any familiar names or pictures. Thankfully a murder story from north of the border hadn't made it to this part of England, or if it had, it was old news by then. In a curious way, Craig felt sad about that, about the idea of Claire being old news. Yesterday's news wrapping today's fish and chips.

The King's Prerogative

Lynn joined him and he snapped out of his thoughts. 'All set?' she asked. Craig saw that she'd applied fresh makeup and had done something with her hair. She'd put on a crisp white shirt with her jeans and even with the brown leather jacket she wore yesterday, Craig decided that she looked very professional. Maybe he should invest in some better gear too, he thought. One day perhaps, but not today.

'Yep, all set. Shall we go?' He picked up his bag and they set off, instinctively heading in the direction of the railway station and its banks of telephone kiosks. Lynn had made a good decision with the phone card because when they arrived at the station all the pay phones were occupied apart from two which didn't take cash, just cards. Craig settled into one of the kiosks and took out the scrap of paper with Professor Prior's number on it. He looked at his watch: two minutes to twelve.

Craig dialled the number and it was answered within two rings.

'Hello?'

'Good morning Professor, it's Craig Dunlop.'

'Oh dear boy, good morning, good morning,' replied the professor. 'I was hoping you'd ring nice and early.'

Craig felt a surge of excitement course through his veins. 'That sounds promising, did you have any luck with your phone calls?'

'Yes, yes, I managed to track down the chap I was looking for. I may have mentioned him, he's in the Home Office. Very interested in your story. He's coming down from London to see you, I'm expecting him any time this afternoon.'

'That's excellent news.' Craig looked out at Lynn and gave her a thumbs up sign.

'Can you come to my study?' asked Clive Prior.

'Of course, we'll come along now if that's convenient.'

'Jolly good. And you have the document with you?'

'Yes, I do.'

'Good good. Well I'll get the kettle on, see you and Mrs Simon shortly.'

Craig hung up, took the phone card out of the slot on the telephone unit, and stepped out of the phone box. Lynn walked over to join him. 'Well?'

'Professor Prior wants us to go straight over to see him. There's a Home Office guy coming from London to speak to us. That would suggest that he's taking it seriously. God bless Professor Prior, he must have sold the story well.'

'Great,' said Lynn. She was happy that Craig's reticence from the day before seemed to have evaporated. 'I was going to suggest we walk, but to hell with it, let's get there as quickly as we can.' They made their way to the taxi rank and jumped in the cab at the front of the queue.

Ten minutes later they were walking through the front court at Emmanuel College once again, through the two courtyards behind, along a gravel path and up to the ivy-clad building that seemed to Craig to be much more welcoming today. They walked up the stairs and came to the door of Professor Prior's study. Craig knocked and listened. He heard footsteps across the floor and the door opened.

'Just in time,' said Clive Prior, 'The kettle's boiled. Come in, come in.' He left the door ajar for them as he returned to an oak sideboard where some tea-making accoutrements were lined up. To the right of the sideboard, the large triple window flooded the room with spring sunshine.

Craig and Lynn followed the professor into the study and Lynn closed the door behind them.

'Milk or lemon?'

'Milk, please' said Craig, and Lynn asked for the same.

'Sugar?'

'Yes please,' said Craig.

'Yes please,' said Lynn.

'Please, take a seat.'

His visitors made themselves comfortable and Clive Prior placed two cups of tea in front of them. He took a sip from his own as he took his seat on the other side of the desk.

'Now then, where will we start?' asked the professor, looking at Craig.

'Could you tell us about this friend of yours who's coming to meet us?'

'Yes, yes, of course. Patrick Anson, his name is. Commander Anson actually, ex-Royal Navy. He's an old boy of mine from his time here at Emmanuel. He's high up somewhere in the civil service, all very secret, he hasn't told me exactly what his job is. But a handy man to have on board, he knows practically everyone in Whitehall.' Clive Prior took another sip of tea. 'Anyway, when I told him your story he was extremely interested, and as keen as mustard to see these documents of yours.'

'Did he say what he could do to help?' asked Craig.

'Not exactly, but he said he knew the history surrounding this Hess episode. Or more precisely, he will be fully acquainted with it by the time he arrives in Cambridge. His job grants him access to all sorts of archived information. I'm sure he'll know exactly what to do to, em…' the professor looked a bit embarrassed as he searched for the right phrase.

'To get me off the hook?' offered Craig.

'Precisely. Oh my dear chap, I didn't mean to offend you.'

'Not at all, professor, I'd have been surprised if you weren't already aware of my predicament. May I ask how you know?'

'You've made the paper, I'm afraid.' The professor handed over a copy of that morning's *Times* that had been lying folded on his desk. 'Page six.'

Craig turned to the correct page and found an almost word-for-word copy of the article that had been in the previous day's *Scotsman*. Mercifully there was no photograph this time.

'I had nothing to do with my friend's death, Professor,' said Craig, a little too strenuously, he realised.

'Oh the thought didn't enter my head, dear chap.'

'But I do think the letter I found is connected somehow,' continued Craig. 'That's why I'm keen to have an independent source validate the documents before I go to the police.'

'Yes, yes, I totally understand,' said the professor. He cleared his throat. 'And you said you have the peace document with you?'

'Yes.' Craig opened his bag and brought out the document, bound by its red ribbon. 'Here it is.'

Clive Prior took the bundle from Craig with both hands, and set it down on the desk. He found his reading glasses, put them on, and looked at the front page with its coat of arms of an eagle holding a swastika. He looked up at Craig. 'May I?' he asked, gesturing to the ribbon.

'Please do.'

The professor untied the ribbon and started to read, just as Craig, Lynn and Fiona had done two days earlier. Craig watched his face intently as he turned the pages. The professor's expression seemed to change from wonder to studied concentration as he read. At times Craig thought he saw the old man display the same puzzlement as he himself had experienced. As the professor read on, puzzlement seemed to turn to understanding and as he contemplated the signature at the end, his eyes conveyed a look that may have been satisfaction. At last he met Craig's gaze once again. 'I don't think there's any doubt about it, this is a genuine copy of the original peace offer Hess brought with him.'

'I think it is too,' said Craig. 'Mainly because it lay untouched in a sealed bag for forty years, until the other day.'

Lynn, who had been quiet all this time, spoke up. 'Professor, can you tell us why you're so sure it's genuine? After all, you've only given it a very quick inspection.'

Clive Prior took off his glasses, glanced at the clock on the wall, then fixed Lynn with a look that searched into her eyes. Lynn felt that he was trying to read her as intently as he'd read the document in his hands.

'May I take you into my confidence?'

Lynn looked at Craig before responding. 'Well, yes, Professor, by all means.'

The King's Prerogative

'I mean, what I am about to tell you cannot be revealed outside of this room, far less appear in print at a later date.'

Lynn paused. 'Of course.'

'You see, Mrs Simon, I've seen this document before.'

'What?!' exclaimed Craig and Lynn together.

The professor carefully put the papers together again and retied the ribbon. 'What you have here is a copy of the document Hess had with him when he came to Scotland. I've read it before.' He stood up and walked over to the window and looked out. 'I think you are owed an explanation.' He turned back around to face them, scanning their faces. 'I haven't been entirely candid with you, and I apologise. You see, I worked in the Secret Service during the war. I was one of the team who debriefed Hess. As soon as I saw your document I knew exactly what it was. I had no idea there was a duplicate in existence.'

'Then you know all about the peace mission?' said Lynn.

'Yes, yes, I do. But remember, it was only a peace mission in the eyes of Hess. We lured him here to buy this country some time. We had no intention of negotiating a peace with Hitler.'

'But this is fantastic,' said Craig. 'You can corroborate my story, and with luck Commander Anson can pull a few strings with the police.'

'Well, yes and no, I'm afraid,' said the professor, with an apologetic look on his face. 'Will you excuse me one moment?' He walked to the door and left the room. Craig and Lynn could hear his footsteps fade as they walked down the hall.

Craig furrowed his brow as he furiously tried to make sense of this latest bombshell. After a few seconds he turned to Lynn. 'Quick, keep an eye out at the door for me. Tell me when he comes back.' He picked up the document and untied the ribbon again.

'Craig, what are you doing?' asked Lynn.

'I'll explain later. Please, just check the door.'

Lynn stood up and walked to the door, opening it slightly and looking out. Every so often she glanced back at Craig who was busy putting the document back in his bag.

'Craig, you can't do a runner again! You're going to have to start trusting someone. The professor's trying to help you.'

'I know, Lynn, I know that. Just trust me.'

Lynn heard footsteps approaching. Two sets of footsteps.

'Craig!' she shouted in a whisper. 'He's coming back!' Lynn closed the door and hurried back to her seat.

Chapter 32

The door opened and the professor walked in with a tall, immaculately groomed man who had all the bearing of an ex Royal Navy officer. His hair was still cut in a no-nonsense service style, although perhaps it was half an inch longer than a serving officer's should have been. Clean shaven, with a thin mouth and a long aquiline nose, Craig would have guessed that he was ex-military even if he hadn't been told. He wore a light grey three-piece suit, over a pale pink shirt and a blue tie. His shoes were polished to a deep shine and each was laced up in four straight parallels finishing in a neat double knot. As the man reached out his hand, Craig noticed a cufflink on his shirt sleeve with the initial 'A' on it. Craig wondered if the other cufflink had a letter 'P'.

'Mr Dunlop? I'm Anson. Very pleased to meet you.' Commander Anson then offered his hand to Lynn. 'And Mrs Simon? A pleasure. Professor Prior has already told me so much about you both.' He picked up a straight-backed chair beside the bookcase, and brought it round so that he could sit beside Craig and Lynn.

'May I offer you a cup of tea, Commander?' asked Clive Prior?

'Yes please, Professor, lemon, no sugar.'

The professor poured a cup and handed it to his new guest. Anson put it on the desk in front of him. 'Thank you.' He looked between Craig and Lynn, crossed his legs and flicked an imaginary piece of fluff from the knee of his trousers. He smiled at the two visitors. 'I'm sure the professor has told you that he and I go way back to the days when I studied here. So I was only too pleased to get his call last night, and since then I've been reading up on the whole Hess affair. But before we get into all that, I'd like to hear how you came to be involved in all this.'

Craig told the story for what seemed like the hundredth time. By now he'd honed it to the point where he could cover the main points in less than five minutes. He decided that it made no sense to be anything other than totally open with Commander Anson, so he told him about everything; his grandfather, Claire, Brian Irving, his brush with the police, how he came to meet Lynn, the discovery of the second letter, the trip to the Swedish Consulate, and finally, his and Lynn's trip to Cambridge.

Anson listened carefully and when the story was finished he uncrossed his legs, reached inside his jacket pocket, took out a silver case and removed a cigarette. He offered one to Lynn and Craig, and when they declined, clicked the case shut and put it back in his suit jacket. He took his time lighting the cigarette, and blew a cloud of smoke into the air.

'That's quite some tale,' he said. 'But I have to tell you from the outset that you cannot breathe a word of this to anyone. And the idea of writing about it –' he turned his attention to Lynn, 'is quite out of the question.'

'May we know why?' asked Lynn. She'd been thinking about what the old man had told them earlier, and in her experience when someone tried to fob her off it was usually because they were trying to hide something.

Anson smiled a regretful smile. 'That's an easy question to answer. The whole affair is covered by the Official Secrets Act.'

'But records are normally released after thirty years,' countered Lynn. 'This all happened forty-two years ago.'

'You know your subject, Mrs Simon,' said Anson. 'But you

may also be aware that in certain circumstances records can be kept secret for up to seventy-five years. When it's in the public interest for them to remain so.'

'Why is it in the public interest for these records to be kept secret? The war's been over for a long time,' said Craig.

'Come now Craig, don't be naïve,' said Anson.

A pang of peevishness swept over Craig at the patronising use of his first name, but he swallowed it and maintained his concentration.

'I think I deserve a better explanation than that, Commander. Apart from everything else there's the fact that a murder's been committed. A friend of mine has been killed, and I'd say it's in the public interest to know why.'

Anson held Craig's glare for a long second, then stubbed out his cigarette in the professor's ash tray. He stood up, and looked at Clive Prior, who was still seated behind his desk. Anson gave out a long sigh.

'You're right. You do deserve an explanation. As far as I can gather the police have not established that there is a connection between your documents and Miss Marshall's death.'

'But...'

'Please let me finish. While there's no proof that there's a link between the Hess documents and Miss Marshall's death, I think I can help you explain matters to the police. But firstly let me explain the importance of these documents of yours. Has the professor told you about the Secret Service operation to lure Hess to this country?'

'Yes.'

Anson sat down again, and looked like a man searching for the right words to use. 'There were a great many secret operations carried out during the war, and some of them involved making difficult life or death decisions. This was one of them. In 1941 Britain needed two things. She needed the Soviet Union in the war, and she needed the United States in the war.'

'I know that,' said Craig.

'The Secret Service were handed a gift in September 1940. A man called Albrecht Haushofer... have you heard of him?'

'Yes, he was a friend of Hess's and of the Duke of Hamilton, from before the war.'

'Precisely. Well Haushofer wrote a letter to the Duke of Hamilton, which the Secret Service intercepted, asking if there might be a way for him to meet the duke in a neutral place, for example Portugal.'

'Why?'

'It was an overture to peace talks. This was a significant opportunity for us, but not to make peace, to make the Germans think we wanted to make peace long enough to bring the Soviets into the war, and hopefully the Americans.'

'What did it have to do with the Americans?'

'Nothing directly, but let's say that it was in American interests for the war to continue. Britain making peace with Germany was the last thing they wanted. They had just come out of the Great Depression, and their manufacturing industry was reliant on the armaments and tools being provided to Britain. If the war was to end in 1941, there's every chance that their economy would have sunk back into recession.'

'Do you mean that at the time we were effectively playing everyone against the middle? The Germans, the Russians, and the Americans?'

'Well, that's rather a crude way of putting it, but essentially, yes. You also have to remember that there was a tangible practical benefit to Britain. Hitler ended the Blitz while the peace offer was being considered, or should I say while he was led to believe that the offer was being considered.'

Craig and Lynn sat in silence as they digested what Anson had just told them.

'So you see, these documents of yours could open a huge can of worms for the government if they were to be made public. It would lead to questions, extremely awkward questions. It is one thing to look back at the war with the benefit of our hindsight and for people to make judgements on those in power, but in 1941, when these decisions were made, things looked very different.'

Craig and Lynn exchanged looks. Craig looked at Anson again. 'I can see that.' He looked at his feet. 'I'd like to talk this over with Lynn. It's a lot to take in, and I have to consider what the best thing for me to do is.' The documents were the only bargaining chips he had and he wanted to consider his options before giving them up.

Anson seemed to be able to read his thoughts. 'By all means, you and Mrs Simon should talk things over, and my offer of help still stands. But I have to insist that you leave your documents with me. For safekeeping.'

Craig knew he was cornered. There was nothing else for it. He unzipped his holdall and took out the satchel and handed it to Anson. Anson unzipped the satchel and pulled out the stack of papers wrapped in ribbon. He saw the Nazi crest on the front, nodded to himself, replaced the document and zipped the satchel closed.

'And the other letters?'

Craig pulled out his wallet and opened it, brought out the two letters and handed them to Anson. 'I only have the letter addressed to the Swedish Consulate and a photocopy of the letter of safe conduct.'

'Are there any other copies?'

'Just the one that the police now have, and the original which Brian Irving has.'

'Let me worry about those.'

'May I keep the wallet?' asked Craig, finding it difficult to keep the sarcasm from his voice.

Commander Anson took the wallet from Craig and examined it to make sure it was empty. When he was satisfied that there were no more hidden letters he gave it back to Craig.

'Where are you staying?'

'At the Clarendon Hotel on Tenison Road.'

'I'll get my driver to drop you.'

'No, it's alright thank you,' said Craig, more petulantly than he intended. 'To be honest the fresh air and the walk will do me good.'

Anson smiled. 'Of course. Well, I'll let you both talk things over, and why don't I call on you around five o'clock this afternoon? I'll take you both to dinner. You too, Professor. We'll talk about how we can try to settle matters with the police.'

'That's most kind of you, Commander,' said the professor.

'Thank you,' said Craig. His mouth was dry and the words came out in a croak. He could feel his heartbeat pulsing in his ears.

'Not at all, Craig,' said Anson. 'Hopefully we can get it all sorted out for you quickly.'

'Thank you, Commander Anson,' said Lynn. They shook hands, and the professor showed them to the door and said goodbye.

After they had walked down the stair and out of sight, Commander Anson turned to the professor.

'That seemed to go smoothly enough.'

Chapter 33

As soon as Craig and Lynn got back onto Downing Street, outside the confines of the college, Craig took Lynn by the arm.

'Lynn, I have an apology to give you.'

'What for?'

'I'll tell you back at the hotel, but we don't have long, we need to be quick.'

Lynn stood her ground. 'Craig, for God's sake, what is *wrong* with you? You've been like a cat on hot bricks since we got here. I know this has all been a lot to take in but will you please just calm down?'

Craig realised that she wasn't moving until he explained himself.

'Lynn, did nothing about that conversation seem odd to you?'

'Odd in what way, specifically? Craig, this whole thing is odd. Or is this how you normally spend your time?'

'Odd as in I can smell bullshit. I could smell it off that policeman Wilson and I could smell it off Commander Anson.'

'Oh come on. You just don't trust anybody, that's your big problem.'

'No Lynn, I trust you. And I trust Fiona.'

Lynn looked at him. She looked up at the sky, then relaxed her shoulders and sighed. 'Okay, what is it about Commander Anson that's got your hackles up?'

'His story was wrong.'

'Which part? It seemed logical to me.'

'Well first of all, you could have knocked me down with a feather when the professor told us that he'd seen the original peace offer brought by Hess in 1941.'

'Me too, but it just shows that we've come to the right man. He knows what he's talking about.'

'No Lynn, that's just it. He doesn't.'

'You're making no sense.'

'Hess jumped out of an aeroplane flying at 200 miles an hour. All he had were the clothes he had on, the things in his pockets, and his parachute. His plane crashed and burned to a crisp.'

'So?'

'In which pocket did he have the peace document, then?'

Lynn opened her mouth to speak then shut it again.

'Good God,' she finally mouthed as the realisation struck her. 'He couldn't have had, it would have been too large.'

'Exactly. He might have had it in his plane with him but it would have been destroyed in the crash.'

'But it could have been in some kind of a metal fireproof container that survived the crash.'

'Why would it have been? Hess thought he was going to land at Dungavel. He would have never bargained on baling out of his plane then recovering the peace offer from the wreckage. He arranged to have a copy sent to the Swedish Consulate in advance purely as contingency for any eventuality. Brian Irving said that Hess was a meticulous man. He planned to the last detail.'

'Apart from jumping out of his plane at 200 miles per hour.'

'Quite.' He looked around. 'Listen Lynn, can we get moving, we need to get out of here.' He took her arm and they crossed the street, heading back to their hotel. As they walked, Craig continued talking.

'And as for Commander Anson, I've no doubt that he is who he says he is, but what he said didn't ring true either.'

'Like what?'

'Like, he seemed to know all about Claire's murder on the one hand, but he was quick to disconnect her murder with the documents. And I still say that the whole intelligence sting theory is a cover-up. That smelled like bullshit to me.'

'But Craig, he's in a position to know the truth. Why wouldn't he tell you the facts as they are?'

'He was hiding something Lynn. And did you notice how easily he made himself comfortable in the professor's study?'

'Why wouldn't he?'

'What I'm saying is, it looked to me as if he was used to being there.'

'So, what if he was?'

'He did all he could to emphasise that theirs was a casual relationship from long ago, don and student. It didn't seem that way to me. Words and figures differed. All he wanted was to get his hands on my documents.'

'And now he has.'

'Not exactly.'

'What?'

Craig stopped, opened his holdall and pulled out a ream of old papers.

'Jesus, Craig! That's the peace document! How…. What….?'

'I switched them when the professor went out. As you said, my hackles were up. Call it my natural banker's aversion to risk. I hoped I wouldn't have to use them.'

'What does Commander Anson have?'

'A pile of old music sheets I bought yesterday. I had to fold some to the right size but they were a pretty good fit. I put the cover page from the peace document on top and tied the ribbon round them. I hoped that with only a casual glance Anson wouldn't suspect. The professor had already read the document from cover to cover so I knew he wouldn't look again. I had to gamble that Anson wouldn't untie the ribbon and look through each page.'

'But why music sheets?'

'No reason in particular. I just saw them and they were

roughly the same age as the original document. A ream of new paper would have looked like a ream of new paper, even edge on.'

Lynn looked at him in disbelief. 'And what would you have done if the professor hadn't left the office? How would you have switched the papers then?'

'I would have thought of something. A diversion.'

Lynn looked up to the heavens.

'You know they'll find out soon enough? Good God Craig, what will you do now?'

'I'll take my chances with the police, I have to. But not here, I'd rather face them on home turf.'

'We need to check out of the hotel.'

'I know.'

They got back to the hotel and went into their rooms to pack their things, which took all of three minutes to do. They paid their bill, handed in their keys and were back out onto the street within ten minutes, hurrying the short distance to the railway station. It was too early for the routine business commute but the station was busy with students heading home for the weekend. Small groups of them stood around their bags and rucksacks while others made their way towards the platforms to catch trains. Craig looked at the departures board, hoping to see an imminent departure for Edinburgh, or even Glasgow. Then he remembered that they had changed at Peterborough on the way down and there was little chance that they'd get a direct train to Scotland. He was scanning the boards looking for a Peterborough train when Lynn grabbed his arm.

'Craig, we need to go. NOW!' She pulled his sleeve in the direction of the nearest platform. Craig saw genuine alarm in Lynn's eyes so he followed her without question. A crowd of passengers was going through a gate manned by a lone British Rail official in a dark grey uniform and a small peaked cap. Lynn tagged along with a big group of students who were jostling their way through the gate, and she and Craig reached the platform without being challenged. They boarded a train that was idling at the edge of the platform and walked through the carriages till they found two free seats together. It was only after they sat down that Craig asked a neighbour where the train was heading.

'King's Cross.'

Craig turned to Lynn, who was panting and out of breath. 'Looks like we're going to London,' he said.

A minute later the train's diesel engine growled and it started to move. Lynn eyed the platform as it slowly went past the window.

'What happened?' asked Craig, when Lynn had recovered her composure.

'I saw Anson come into the station with another man.'

'What other man?'

'I didn't recognise him, but they weren't heading for a train. They were looking around them, scanning faces in the crowd. They were looking for us.'

'Christ. Oh Lynn, I'm so sorry I've got you involved in all of this.' Seeing Lynn's panic had reminded him of the sick, paralysing fear he'd experienced when he jumped out of Blake's car. He knew what it felt like and it didn't feel good.

Lynn stared out of the window, not looking at the scenery. Craig said nothing more. What more was there to say? Despite knowing deep down that what he'd done in Clive Prior's study was justified – in his mind anyway – he couldn't help feeling guilty. Maybe he should have come to Cambridge alone.

Lynn finally looked at him. 'Do you know what it is that troubles me the most?'

Craig thought, Oh God here comes another list of my shortcomings, but instead just asked 'What?'

'There was no logical explanation for me feeling scared like that. It's not as if we've broken any laws. I just knew that I was scared and I had to get out of there.'

'I know how that feels, Lynn.' Craig felt relieved that he wasn't the target of a tirade. 'And you're right, we haven't broken any laws. I don't know about you but I'm pissed off with people making me feel like I'm a criminal.'

At last Lynn smiled. 'Thanks Craig.' A fear shared is a fear halved, she thought. 'So, London it is. Then what?'

'Well, I suppose I should check in with my parents, they'll be mortified that I'm in the papers. They won't be able to show their faces in public again.'

A second later they both burst out laughing at the ludicrousness of Craig's comment, and although it was unspoken, they both knew that they needed the safety valve.

They bought their tickets from the inspector on the train which meant that when the train arrived at King's Cross getting through the barriers presented no difficulty. It was a massive station and people were bustling everywhere. No one dawdled, every passenger in the station seemed to be on a mission and knew where they were going. Craig looked at his watch. It was ten to four. Just coming up to the rush hour.

'You go and phone your parents, I'll see if I can get us a hire car,' said Lynn. 'I don't feel like any more trains, do you?'

'It probably makes sense if we have MI5 or whoever Commander Anson works for, on our tail.' Craig gave a nervous laugh and wished he hadn't said that. Lynn didn't seem to mind the faux pas though. Craig quickly changed tack. 'Are you okay to drive back to Edinburgh?'

'God yes, and anyway, I assume you can drive too?'

'Yes.'

'Good, we can split the driving. We should have hired a car in Edinburgh, but hindsight's got twenty-twenty vision I suppose. I'll get you at the café over there when you're done.' She pointed at a large sandwich shop-cum-café on the other side of the concourse and with that, she disappeared through the throng of people exiting the station. Craig found a bank of payphones and waited a couple of minutes until one became free. He took out his phone card, inserted it into the slot, picked up the receiver and dialled his parents' number.

After four rings the phone answered and Craig was surprised to hear his dad's voice. He must have taken time off work.

'Hello 3598?'

'Hello, Dad?'

'Craig! Oh son, thank God you've phoned,' said Peter Dunlop.

'What's happened?'

'What's happened? You're all over the newspapers that's what's happened. Your mum's in a right state.'

'I know, Dad. Listen, I'm sorry.'

'I thought you said you were going to the police?'

'I was. I mean I am. I just had to do something first. I need to ask you something.'

'What is it?'

'Did you tell the police I had gone to see a literary agent in Edinburgh?'

His father was quiet for a moment. 'No Craig, I didn't. Why?'

'Because the police turned up at her office the following day.'

There was another pause at the other end.

'Dad?'

'I'm still here, son. I've got some information to pass on. We've had lots of phone calls since your name was in the paper, as you can imagine.'

'Yes, I know, I'm really sorry Dad, I'll sort it out. I'm going to hand myself into the police as soon as I get back.'

'No, wait a minute. We got a visitor here yesterday looking for you.'

'Oh?'

'Yes. He said his name was Brian Irving.'

Craig thought he had misheard what his father had said. 'Pardon?'

'Brian Irving was here, asking for you.'

Craig found it difficult to connect his brain to his mouth momentarily.

'Craig?'

'Yes Dad, I'm still here. Are you sure it was him?'

'He seemed to know all about what you spoke to him about, if that's what you mean. And he had your grandad's letter on him.'

Craig's mouth suddenly reconnected to his thought process. 'What did he say? Where has he been? Why was he in Stranraer?'

'He saw your name in the paper, and he was here to return the letter. I have it here.'

'Did he say where he's been all this time?'

'He said he's found out a great deal. He needs to speak to you urgently. He left a number for you to call. Hold on.' There was a long pause then Peter Dunlop read out a telephone number, slowly and deliberately. 'It's 0487 3179. Got it?'

'Got it Dad, thanks.' He scribbled the number down on the back of his train ticket. '0487 3179.'

'That's it. And Craig, I bumped into one of your friends from the bank. He said not to worry about that big cash difference. They found it in the teller's book.'

'What?'

'They found the cash difference. It was a clerical error.

'Dad, what are you talking about?'

'I have to go, I hear your mum calling on me. Phone us later, won't you?'

The phone went dead. Craig was left holding his receiver but talking to no one. He looked at it as if he expected the telephone to provide an answer to what had just happened. What was his dad on about? He shook his head, replaced the receiver and took out his card. He thought for a moment, then reversed the operation. He put the card back in and picked up the receiver. He dialled the number he'd written on his train ticket and waited for a response.

The King's Prerogative

'Hello?' An English voice answered, not dissimilar to that of the professor.

'Hello, I'm looking for Brian Irving please?'

'There's no one of that name here.'

'Doctor Brian Irving?'

'You must have the wrong number, this isn't the surgery.'

'No, sorry, you've misunderstood me.' Craig tried a different approach. 'Where is that?'

'What?'

'Where are you speaking from?'

'What are you, an idiot? I'm in my house. Who are you, what do you want?'

'I'm really sorry, what town are you in?'

'Town? Warboys is a village.'

'Warboys?'

'Yes, Warboys, where did you think you were calling? I've had enough of this. Damned nuisance…'

'No sir, wait, please don't hang up. Excuse me, I was given your number, obviously in error. Can you tell me where Warboys is?'

'Where is it? It's in Cambridgeshire, between Cambridge and Peterborough. Good day.' The phone once again went dead, and Craig was even more puzzled than before.

He phoned his parents' number again and again his dad answered.

'Dad, was that number you gave me correct?'

'Yes, it was.'

'But I rang…'

'Craig, it's 0487 3179.' And with that he put the phone down.

Craig retrieved his phone card and walked towards the café at the other side of the station, completely bemused.

Chapter 34

Craig looked around the café to see if he could spot Lynn but there was no sign of her, so instead he found a free table and sat down. A waitress took his order and came back a few minutes later with a coffee and a rather sorry looking cheese and ham sandwich. He was half way through the sandwich when Lynn appeared and sat down opposite him.

'All sorted,' she said. 'I hired a car for the whole week. I thought I might as well do that seeing as my own jalopy is in the garage. I can drop it off at their office in Edinburgh next Friday. It's a Cavalier so you should have enough leg room.' She looked around the café. 'I'm parched, is this waitress service or do you order at the counter?'

It was obvious to Craig that Lynn had gone into organisational mode once again. She attracted the waitress's attention and ordered tea and some quiche Lorraine. She finally asked Craig how things were at home.

'Fine, well, apart from the fact that as expected my parents are having a meltdown. But wait till you hear this. Brian Irving visited my parents yesterday.'

'What?'

'Yes, Brian Irving showed up at my mum and dad's looking for me. He returned the letter and he asked to speak to me.'

'That's brilliant! What did he say when you phoned him?' She saw the look on Craig's face and stopped. 'He must have left a number to reach him on?'

'He did, but when I rang, the person who answered didn't know what I was talking about.'

The King's Prerogative

Lynn raised her eyebrows. 'Are you sure it was the right number?'

'Yes, I phoned my dad back and he confirmed it.'

'That is really weird. What do you want to do now?'

'Lynn, promise you won't shout at me.'

'Why?' She eyed him suspiciously.

'The phone number is in a village in Cambridgeshire. I think we should go and check it out.'

The waitress brought Lynn's pot of tea and her food. Lynn poured a cup before replying.

'Do you mind if I have my tea first?'

Less than forty minutes later they had collected their Vauxhall Cavalier from the car hire office and were on their way. The hardest part of their journey was getting out of London during the rush hour but they eventually found the A10 leading north and before long they passed through Enfield and saw signs for Hertford. Craig and Lynn didn't exchange much in the way of conversation as the first few miles passed. Both of them were wrapped up in their own thoughts. Lynn turned on the radio and tuned it to pick up a station that was broadcasting a tea time news bulletin. There were items about Margaret Thatcher's latest attack on the unions, and an update from the overseas visit by Prince Charles and Princess Diana with nine-month-old Prince William. Next was an item about the latest retail outlook following the recent budget, and finally in sport it was all about Liverpool's march to the title under Bob Paisley who announced he was to retire at the end of the season. Nothing about Craig, he was pleased to note. Lynn turned the radio off and they drove on.

Eventually Craig broke the silence.

'Just let me know when you'd like me to drive.'

'Okay, I will do. I'm fine just now.'

Lynn looked at the dashboard clock. Six-fifteen. It was getting dark outside and she switched on the headlights.

'It looks like we'll have to find a room for the night in Warboys, if they have such a thing as a hotel,' she said.

'I know. Lynn, I'll pay you back every penny, I promise.'

'Oh it's not the money. Tongues will wag you know, I'm a married woman.'

Craig knew better than to dig a hole for himself by saying anything, so he just smiled at her. He liked Lynn Simon. She was smart and funny. He decided that part of the reason he liked her was that she was like an older version of Fiona.

Long minutes went by. They passed a signpost that told them that they were 24 miles from a place called Royston and 42 miles from Cambridge. Craig suddenly jerked upright in his seat.

'That must be it!' He thumped the dashboard and burst out laughing, causing Lynn to lose control of the steering wheel briefly.

'Craig! For God's sake, you nearly gave me a heart attack,' she yelled back at him. 'What are you on about?'

'My dad. He said something cryptic on the phone and at the time I had no idea what he meant.'

'What did he say?'

'When he passed on Brian's phone number he went on to say that the bank had found a cash difference.'

Lynn shot him a look. 'What does that mean?'

'Well I had no idea what he was on about. Why would I be remotely interested in a cash difference at the bank? But I think he was using a code. I think he transposed the numbers.'

'He did *what?*'

'It's a trick you learn when you're a bank teller. I remember telling my dad about it and he thought it was quite clever. He likes curiosities like that. Usually if there's a cash difference either you've screwed up and handed over the wrong cash to somebody, or you've written an entry down wrongly in your cash book. Obviously, you want it to be the second one because that's a simple clerical error that can be corrected quickly.'

'Okay, but I still don't get it.'

'Well one of the first things you learn to look for is whether the difference is divisible by nine. That usually means you've made a mistake writing the figures down.'

'Divisible by *Nine?*'

'Yep. It only clicked with me when I saw that road sign we passed back there. Cambridge was 42 miles away and Royston was 24 miles away. 42 minus 24 is 18. Divisible by nine.'

'So what?'

'Any transposition of two numbers is divisible by nine. Anyway, that doesn't matter. What does matter is that I think my dad was telling me to look at the numbers he gave me and transpose them.'

Lynn tried some simple arithmetic in her head. 'Okay, I get it now. But why would your dad go to such lengths? Why didn't he just tell you the actual number?'

'I'm not certain, but when I asked if he had spoken to the police about me going to see a literary agent in Edinburgh, he said he hadn't. But how else would the police have known to come round and speak to you? We didn't tell anyone else.'

Lynn frowned. 'You don't mean he thinks his phone has been tapped by the police?'

'Maybe he does, or maybe Brian Irving planted the seed in his head that it might be. Maybe he's just a bit paranoid.'

Lynn looked at him strangely and muttered something about chips off old blocks.

Craig picked up a piece of hire company documentation from the door pocket and started scribbling on the white space on the back. He worked out six different possible combinations of the four digits in the Warboys phone number.

'Could you stop at the next place we get to? We may as well try these numbers.'

'Why not. I could do with stretching my legs anyway.' Lynn was still not convinced.

They drove on for a few miles until they reached a village called Puckeridge. She spied a red telephone box on a street corner and pulled in. Craig jumped out of the car, bounded over to the kiosk, opened the heavy door and had dialled the first number before the hinges closed the door behind him. Lynn watched as he tried number after number. Eventually he left the telephone box and walked back to the car.

'No luck?'

'No. Two wrong numbers, a no reply and the others were unobtainable.'

Lynn drove off again. 'Do you think the number that rang out could be Brian Irving's?'

'Who knows.' Craig's excitement had given way to a new feeling of despondency.

Lynn had another thought. 'Did you play around with the local part of the number?'

'Yes.'

'Maybe your dad switched the dialling code too, do you think?'

Craig spun round and looked at Lynn. 'Do you know what, I didn't even think of that, how stupid of me. Of course he could have done that. Why wouldn't he?' He started to scribble numbers again, only this time working with the dialling code. He reasoned that the zero must be in the right place so that gave him four possible variations of the remaining three numbers. Craig gambled that his dad would probably have transposed the same two digits in both the STD code and the local part, so he hoped that would mean he just had four numbers to try.

After a further mile they reached a petrol station and Lynn pulled in. Craig found the public payphone inside the little shop and started dialling the numbers he had written down. The first number was unobtainable but when he dialled the second number it was answered at the third ring.

'Hello, Station Hotel?' It was a female Scottish voice, polite and with a Highland accent.

'Oh hello, I'm looking for a Doctor Brian Irving, is he staying with you?'

After a short pause the girl said, 'He is, sir. If you'll wait one moment please, I'll try his room.'

Craig could hardly contain his excitement. He was put on hold for what seemed like an eternity but was probably only a few seconds.

The soft Highland voice came back. 'I'm sorry sir, there's no reply at the moment. Can I take a message?'

'Yes please. Can you tell him that Craig Dunlop phoned? And could you pass on the message that I'll try him again later tonight or early tomorrow morning?'

'Certainly sir, I'll make sure he gets that message.'

'Thank you very much. Could you tell me your address please?'

'Certainly. It's 54 Princes Street, Thurso.'

'Thurso as in Caithness?'

'That's right, sir.'

'Thanks again. Bye.'

Craig ran back to the car to tell Lynn the news.

'He's in Thurso.'

'Thurso?'

'Yes. The number wasn't 0487 3179. It was 0847 3719. It's a hotel in Thurso.'

'What's he doing there?'

'I don't know, he wasn't in his room so I couldn't speak to him. I said I'd phone again later, or tomorrow.'

'What do you think we should do?' asked Lynn.

'I don't know about you, but I think we should push on to Edinburgh tonight and think about Thurso tomorrow. How does that sound?'

'I think that's a good idea.'

Craig checked the time. Just before seven o'clock. 'I'll

drive for the next stretch if you like. I think we could be in Edinburgh by two o'clock if we're lucky.'

When they stopped for petrol on the motorway north, Craig phoned ahead to say they were on their way back and would it be okay for him to stay over again. Fiona said yes, of course it was. Lynn dropped Craig off at the Rankins' house at 1:50 am.

The rest of the family were asleep so Craig and Fiona took themselves through to the kitchen where Fiona made some hot chocolate while Craig brought her up to date with their time in Cambridge. Fiona added her tuppenceworth on the subject of his second hurried escape from the authorities in less than a week, and asked if she should start calling him Ned Kelly. Craig laughed but pointed out that Lynn eventually agreed with him about Anson and that in fact it was she who had precipitated their speedy departure.

By 2:45 Craig could hardly keep his eyes open, so Fiona showed him to his room.

As she went to her own room she knew that sooner or later she'd have to come to a decision. What was she going to do about Craig Dunlop? The last few days had been a blur. No sooner had Craig reappeared into her life than she found herself swept up in his – what's the word to describe this chain of events, she wondered – this crisis. She hadn't had time to process her own thoughts, never mind ask him about his. She could see that he was scared, though that was only natural in the circumstances. But beyond that he seemed, well, different. Changed. More composed, despite the predicament he was in. She wondered if he'd done some growing up in the last year. She wondered if he was seeing anyone. She realised that she cared about the answer to that question and that's why she didn't ask it. Why had he come to her, of all people? Was it just coincidence, or desperation? Or something more? And how did she feel? He'd hurt her so badly. She'd hated him for what he did. She hated his immaturity.

The King's Prerogative

She hated his insensitivity. She'd been in pieces for weeks after he finished with her. Then she threw herself into her studies and the pain slowly subsided. But her confusion persisted. She couldn't understand what went wrong. But at least she'd got over him. Or so she thought. Then a few days ago he walked back into her life. And she didn't hate him after all. Far from it.

She closed her eyes and tried to get to sleep.

Chapter 35

Saturday 19th March, 1983

Fiona let Craig sleep in till nine o'clock even though he asked to be woken at half seven. When he came down to the kitchen Valerie, Denis and Fiona were sitting around the table reading papers and drinking coffee.

'Morning.'

'Morning, Craig,' said Valerie. Denis was eating a piece of toast so he raised his cup in greeting.

Fiona got up from the table. 'Morning. Sleep okay?'

'Yes thanks. But I overslept.' He was a bit annoyed that Fiona had let him sleep late but he let it go. He was just happy to be back in that kitchen again.

'Well I thought you needed it,' said Fiona. 'Coffee?'

'Oh yes please.' He sat down beside Valerie. 'Thanks for letting me descend on you in the middle of the night.'

'Not at all, it's good to see you. Fiona's been telling us about your trip. It sounds like it didn't work out as planned?'

'You could say that. But one good thing is that in the meantime Brian Irving went to see my parents.'

'Yes, so we gather,' said Denis. 'You must be itching to call him. Feel free to use the phone.'

'Thank you.' Fiona gave him a mug of coffee and he took it over to the telephone. He looked out the piece of paper with the Station Hotel's number and dialled it.

'Good morning, Station Hotel.' It was the soft Highland voice again.

'Good morning, I called yesterday and I think I spoke to you? I'm looking for Doctor Brian Irving.'

'Oh yes, sir. I passed on your message. Give me one moment and I'll try Doctor Irving's room.'

There was a short pause, then Craig heard Brian Irving's familiar voice.

'Hello, Craig?'

'Hello Brian, at last! How are you?'

'Fine, fine. Well, under the circumstances I mean. Sorry I wasn't around when you called yesterday, you got my message then?'

'Yes. Brian, what the hell happened, where have you been all this time?'

'That's a long story.'

'I'm all ears.'

'I'll try to give you the shortened version. First of all, I exhausted my research into Colonel Pilcher, he just seemed to disappear into thin air. So I continued researching into Hess and his flight to Scotland.'

Fiona mouthed the words 'Mitchell Library' and Craig nodded.

'Did you happen to go to the Mitchell Library?'

'Yes, as it happens, why?'

'It was one of our ports of call too. Sorry, I interrupted you. Carry on.'

'I've been all over the country. The main libraries in Glasgow, Edinburgh and London, and every public record office I could find. I pieced together everything I could, and a pattern began to emerge.'

'What pattern?'

'Craig, I think there's been a carefully staged cover-up around the whole Hess affair, stretching back to the war. And I'm almost certain it's still going on today.'

'What?'

'I'll explain everything when we have more time. But then in the middle of my research, something happened. I must have blundered. And that's when I decided I had to lay low. I didn't feel safe.'

'What do you mean?'

'I contacted one of the leading authorities on intelligence activities during the war, and that seemed to set off a chain of events outside of my control.'

'Was it Clive Prior?' asked Craig.

The mention of the professor's name pulled Brian Irving up short. 'How did you know?'

'I went to see him. I saw him yesterday in fact.'

'In Cambridge?' asked Brian.

'Yes. He told me you'd contacted him.'

'How did you make the connection with Clive Prior?'

'A mutual friend of a friend of mine. Another long story.'

'Does he know where you are now?'

'No.'

'Good, keep it that way.'

'Why?'

'I contacted Clive Prior and told him that I was investigating a letter that had been found on Hess's person. I didn't go into the whole story, I merely told him that the letter had come into my possession. That was on the Monday morning. The 1st of March.'

'And you made arrangements to go and meet him?'

'Yes. But I didn't keep the appointment.'

'Why not?'

'My office in Strathclyde University was broken into a few hours later, either on the Monday night or the Tuesday morning.'

'It was? What was taken?'

'All of my notes. The notes I took about Colonel Pilcher and some of the notes I'd researched subsequently.' Brian paused for a second. 'My notes included Claire's contact details.'

Craig had a terrible feeling that he knew where this conversation was heading. 'Claire's phone number?'

'Yes,' said Brian.

'And her address?'

'No, just her name and phone number. But when I read about Claire's murder I couldn't believe it was coincidence. That's when I started putting two and two together. I dare say it would have been a fairly simple job for whoever broke into my office to find out where she lived from the details I wrote down. I feel awful about Claire, beyond words. I had the letter in my briefcase at home. Maybe if I'd left it in my office Claire would still be alive.'

There was a long silence before Brian continued.

'After I saw the news of her murder I thought about it from every angle. It can't be a coincidence that I spoke to Clive Prior in the morning and less than twenty-four hours later my office was burgled. My first impulse was to contact you, to warn you. But I realised that I didn't know your surname, or anything about you other than what you told me about your grandfather.'

As Brian relayed the story, Craig could feel his skin prickling.

'Craig, are you still there?'

'Yes, I'm here.' Craig drew a breath. He wanted to say what was on his mind. It couldn't have been that hard for a university lecturer to track him down, surely. He decided to bite his tongue for the moment to see where the conversation led.

'I thought we got cut off.'

'No I was just deep in thought. Clive Prior introduced us to someone he knew in the intelligence services,' said Craig. 'The professor told me he could help.'

Fiona was listening to Craig's side of the discussion and came over to sit beside him. She saw the worry deepen on his face.

'Who did he introduce you to?' asked Brian.

'A Commander Anson, from the Home Office.'

'I haven't heard of him. How could he help?'

'He told me that he could pull some strings with the police. He seemed to believe me that I had nothing to do with Claire's death.'

Craig knew what his next question needed to be.

'Brian, why didn't you go to the police?'

Now it was Brian's turn to pause.

'Because I think the authorities have been trying to prevent this letter from getting out. I panicked, I didn't know who I could trust. I thought I should keep a low profile until I could find you and we could decide how to handle it together.'

Craig digested this information. Lord knows he could empathise with what Brian was telling him. He wanted to trust Brian. But if the events of the past few days had taught him anything, it was to accept nothing at face value.

'Why did you leave the letter with my parents?'

'Well, first of all, when I saw your name in the papers, that's how I worked out how to get in touch with you. There aren't a lot of Dunlops in the Stranraer phone book. In an ironic kind of way I used the letter as it was originally intended. To prove who I was, in the hope that your parents would pass on my message to you. In the end your father insisted that it was wiser for him to have the letter than for me to keep it. I couldn't refuse. Now it's my turn to ask you – why are the police after you?'

'I panicked too. I felt like I was being fitted up for Claire's murder because the police had no other suspects.'

'It looks like for one reason or another, we're both fugitives.'

'I suppose we are,' replied Craig.

He decided to take Brian into his confidence, at least for now. 'I've got more news to tell you, Brian. My wallet had a second letter hidden in it. And that letter led me to a larger document. I've got a copy of the peace offer Hess brought with him.'

'What?'

'The actual peace offer. There was one after all. It was in Glasgow the whole time, would you believe. In the Swedish Consulate.'

Brian Irving processed this information.

'That makes perfect sense. Hess could have arranged to send it to a convenient pick-up point in Glasgow some time in advance of the flight. The same way Messerschmitt sent fresh drop tanks to Dungavel in preparation for Hess's return flight. Through neutral Sweden.'

'They did?'

'Oh yes. You've no idea what my research has uncovered, I'm looking forward to telling you all about it. But I'm interested in this Commander Anson, who was he?'

'An old student of Professor Prior, apparently. He said he was in the Home Office, but I think he was MI5 or MI6.'

'And you showed him the peace offer?'

'Yes.'

'Pity. I'm assuming he made you hand it over before he let you leave?'

'Yes, well sort of. I made a switch, and they ended up with a bogus set of papers. Which is another reason why I'm not giving myself up just yet. I still have the peace offer with me.'

'You have? That's great news. So you must have had your suspicions about this Anson?'

'Yes, I did. And wait till you hear this. Clive Prior was part of Hess's original debriefing team, back in 1941. He and this other guy, Commander Anson, went out of their way to sell the story that Hess came over as the result of an intelligence sting. They talked about a letter that Albrecht Haushofer wrote to the Duke of Hamilton.'

'Yes, that's what started the process off back then,' confirmed Brian.

'They said that the letter was intercepted and British Intelligence used it to convince Hess to make the flight.'

'But you didn't buy that?' asked Brian.

'No.'

'Why not?'

'Well, just as you and I discussed before, they hardly made capital out of Hess's capture.'

'And how did Professor Prior explain that away?'

'Well it was Anson actually. He said that British Intelligence kept the illusion going that they were considering peace to give Hitler the confidence to attack Russia.'

'You don't believe that?' asked Brian.

'No. It was too contrived,' said Craig. 'If Britain wanted the Soviet Union in the war, when Hess arrived all they had to do was spill the beans to Stalin. That would have been the easiest thing to do, surely? Why risk waiting for Hitler's plan to take effect?'

'I completely agree with you. When you look at the night Hess arrived, if British Intelligence *were* expecting him, they weren't sufficiently organised to pull rank on the local Home Guard and take their prisoner away from them. No, I'm sure the story of an intelligence sting was dreamt up after the event to cover their blushes. Hess had arrived under their noses and they were embarrassed. But arrive he did, and I'm convinced that it was arranged in advance – not by British Intelligence but by people who wanted to take Britain out of the war. I've found out that there *was* a peace group in Britain, and it included some senior people.'

Craig couldn't hide his excitement. Maybe he'd let his paranoia get the better of him earlier, maybe in fact Brian was on his side after all. It looked like the university man had come up with some outstanding findings.

'Brian, that's great work. There's so much that we need to catch up on, and I want you to see the peace offer, it's an incredible document to read. We also need to discuss what to do next. Do you want to meet me in Edinburgh?'

'Is there a chance you could come here?'

'It's a bit tricky to say the least, you've seen the newspapers.'

'I realise that, but I've got things to show you here. It's

important or I wouldn't ask. Without wanting to scare you, the fact that you switched papers on MI6 won't have pleased them one bit. The sooner we can decide what to do the better, and to do that you need to know what I know.'

'Okay I'll try. Let me see what I can sort out and I'll ring you back. Will you be there for an hour or so?'

'Yes, I can stay here.'

'Good, I'll ring back as soon as I can.'

Craig hung up and thanked Denis and Valerie for the use of their phone. He quickly briefed them all on his discussion.

'This puts you back to square one as far as the police is concerned, does it not?' asked Denis.

Craig ran his hand through his hair. 'I suppose so.' He looked up at Fiona's dad. 'It comes down to knowing who I can trust, and apart from you guys and Lynn, I seem to be drawing a blank on that score right now.'

'What about Brian?' asked Fiona.

'I want to trust Brian,' said Craig. 'I really do. But I just don't know. The jury's still out. Why's he so keen for me to go to Thurso? And why didn't he track me down sooner? He knew my grandad's name was Davy McLean, he could have searched through the register of births, marriages and deaths.'

'Did he know your mum's name?' asked Denis.

'No, I don't think I mentioned it.'

'Then he would have had to work through all the David McLeans who got married and had a daughter.'

'But my grandad died in January this year, if he'd started with the most recent and worked back, it wouldn't have taken him long.'

'Did you tell Brian when your grandad died?'

Craig knitted his brow. 'I can't remember. Maybe not.'

'There you go then, for all he knew your grandad could have died back in the sixties or something. I don't know what your definition of a needle in a haystack is but I think that would be close.'

'I suppose so.'

Craig decided to let it drop. He asked if it was okay to use the phone again because he'd like to call Lynn. Valerie told him to go ahead and gave him the number. It was Nicolas who answered. Craig introduced himself, and Nicolas went to fetch Lynn. She sounded tired. Craig told her about his conversation with Brian and asked if she was up for a trip to Thurso.

'I'm really sorry, Craig, I tried ringing a bit earlier but the phone was engaged. Much as I'd like to, I can't. My boss is insisting that he speaks to me on Monday about Edward Hart-Davis's book and I haven't even had the time to read it yet. So I've got a ton of work to do this weekend. I'm so sorry.'

'Is everything okay?'

Lynn sighed, then lowered her voice. 'Well, the other thing is, when I told Nicolas about our brush with our friend Commander Anson, he went into one of his French tantrums. Oh it's fine, he's just being overprotective, and I'm a big girl at the end of the day. But I need to pass on this one. Do give me a ring when you meet with Brian though, I insist.'

'No problem, I will do. Listen, it's okay, I'll sort something out. You've done so much already Lynn, I can't thank you enough. You have a good weekend and I'll be in touch soon.'

Craig put the phone down. Fiona asked him what was wrong and Craig told her.

'You can't risk the train again,' she said.

'Yep, I was thinking the same thing.' He was about to pick up the phone to call Brian Irving back and insist that he make the journey south, when it rang, surprising him. Fiona stretched across him to answer it.

'Hello?'

'Hi, Fiona? It's Lynn here. I've got a suggestion for Craig, can I have a word with him?'

'Sure, Lynn, he's here, hold on.' She handed the receiver to Craig.

'Hi Lynn.'

'Hi Craig, listen, I won't be going anywhere this weekend and I'm sure you won't fancy using the train.'

'Yeah, Fiona's just said that.'

'You can use the hire car if you want.'

'That would be great. Are you sure though?'

'Of course. Come round when you're ready and you can pick it up.' Lynn rang off.

Craig went to get his stuff together with the intention of setting off for Thurso as soon as he picked up the keys of the Cavalier. He was collecting his jacket in the hall when Fiona came out of the kitchen. She picked up a set of car keys from the table next to the front door.

'Mum!' she called through to the kitchen. 'Is it okay if I borrow the car?'

'Help yourself,' came the answer from the kitchen. 'But don't be all day.'

'Thanks mum.' Fiona opened the door and held it for Craig. 'Come on, I'll run you to Lynn's.'

Two minutes later Fiona was at the wheel of her mum's silver Mini Metro, guiding it out of the driveway. Craig adjusted the passenger seat, pushing it as far back as he could to accommodate his six-foot frame.

Craig seemed lost in his own thoughts as they made their way through town towards Lynn's house in Trinity. They drove in silence. The Saturday morning traffic was heavy going into the city centre but once they cleared Princes Street and drove down the steep hill of Dundas Street, their stop-start progress improved and they got through the lights at Goldenacre first time. Fiona slowed as she looked for a parking space that wasn't too far from Lynn's house. As they passed a row of parked cars, something in Craig's peripheral vision caught his attention. As he turned his head to look, a man sitting in one of the parked cars turned his head towards Craig. Blake. He and Craig stared at each other for the full second and a half it took for the Metro to move past the parked Fiat.

'Drive!' shouted Craig.

The sudden shock made Fiona stand on the brake pedal. Craig's forehead nearly hit the windscreen as the wheels locked and the small hatchback rocked forward on its suspension. With no clutch engaged, the engine died. The dashboard lit up with red and orange warning indicators. Craig didn't have time to explain what happened. 'Move over!'. He opened the door and jumped out of the passenger seat just as the door of Blake's Fiat opened ten yards behind them. Craig half ran and half vaulted around the bonnet of the Metro and flung the driver's door open. 'Move over!' he screamed again.

Fiona snapped out of her momentary paralysis, undid her seat belt and slid sideways to her left. Craig got behind the wheel, stepped on the clutch, put the gear stick in first, turned the ignition and pumped the accelerator pedal just as the passenger door opened and Blake reached in to seize Fiona's left arm. Fiona screamed and beat at the intruder's grip with her free hand. The Metro's engine roared into life. Craig released the clutch and grabbed Fiona's right arm to prevent her from being dragged out of the car. The lurch in momentum caused both doors to swing shut. More accurately, Craig's door swung shut, but because it was blocked, Fiona's door bounced off Blake's shoulder. Blake kept pace alongside the car as it began to move. The upper half of Fiona's body was half in and half out of the car, and the only reason she wasn't lying on the road was because Craig was holding on to her. The car's small one litre engine screamed as the revs went into the red. Craig couldn't let go of Fiona's arm to change gear, and as a result the car couldn't pick up speed. An acrid smell from the engine compartment filled his nostrils. In desperation he pressed the clutch down, took his right hand off the steering wheel and stretched it across to move the gear lever into second. The combination of a free steering wheel and the dragging effect of Blake's grip meant that the Metro veered to the left as the higher gear kicked in and the car speeded up. Blake's hip came into sharp contact with an offside wing mirror belonging to a parked Datsun Sunny. With a pained grunt he finally had to let go of Fiona's arm. The Metro bounced off another parked car before Craig regained control of the steering wheel. He changed into third gear and pressed the accelerator to the floor. The Metro sped off and reached a T junction at the end of the road. Craig turned right, straightening the wheel as he moved back up through the gears. He turned right again and headed towards the city centre.

Blake hauled himself to his feet and checked to see if the pain in his hip and arm was serious or not. He thought he'd have bruises in the morning but nothing more. A woman who had been walking her dog on the other side of the street was rooted to the pavement having witnessed the scene unfold in front of her. She stared at Blake in utter disbelief that such a disturbance could happen in her neighbourhood. Her dog was straining at its lead, barking furiously.

'What are you looking at?' growled Blake.

If the woman was scared at witnessing the incident in the first place, she was petrified at being addressed directly. She tugged at her dog, about turned and sped back the way she had come.

Blake ran back to his car and gunned it into life.

Craig felt for the handle under his seat and slid it back to give his legs more room. He looked across at Fiona. Her cheeks were wet with tears but Craig couldn't tell if they were from fear or anger.

'Are you hurt?'

Fiona shook her head.

'Are you okay?'

She looked across at him. 'I don't know. I think so.' She rubbed her arm, as if checking that there was no residual trace of Blake on her sweater. 'Who was that? Why did he attack me?'

'That was that policeman, Wilson. He must have tracked Lynn to her home, but how the hell did he know we were coming?'

'Fucking hell Craig, what are we going to do now?'

Craig shook his head. 'I don't know.' He checked the rear-view mirror. No sign of the Fiat. They came to another T junction and Craig had to stop to let a stream of cars go past. Being one of the main arteries in the north of Edinburgh, it was busy and although Craig inched out, there was no gap in the traffic for him to take advantage of. Suddenly, their necks whiplashed as a loud metallic bang propelled them forward. Craig looked in the mirror and saw Blake's face staring back at him from behind the wheel of the black Fiat. The collision shunted the Metro into the flow of eastbound traffic. Horns blared as cars had to perform emergency stops. Craig put his foot down and shot across the road, turning right and narrowly missing a Sherpa van whose driver mouthed a stream of obscenities through the windscreen.

Craig had no choice but to keep pace with the interminably slow-moving flow of traffic until he reached the first left-hand junction they came to. He hoped it wasn't a cul-de-sac, and was relieved when the narrow street forked right and then joined another road. A rhythmic banging from behind him told Craig that the collision with Blake's car had done some damage to the Metro's rear end.

'Craig, we have to get out of here!' shouted Fiona.

'I know!'

'This road takes us all the way into town.'

Craig knew he couldn't lose the Fiat in a straight line race, especially with the back end hanging off his car. After another hundred yards Craig turned left along a road with a rugby ground on one side and a row of semi-detached houses on the other. Another road on the right took them further into the housing estate, then a left, then a right until Craig finally came to a dead end. He pulled into the driveway of the end house, braked and switched off the engine. The house's small garden was ringed by a box hedge at head height which blocked the view of anyone not directly opposite.

Craig and Fiona held their breath for a long minute, listening.

Chapter 36

Blake cursed. He saw the Metro join the traffic on Ferry Road and edged his Fiat out, holding up traffic as he forced his way on to the westbound carriageway. A double decker bus flashed him and he screeched in front of it. The Metro was now four cars in front and Blake saw it turn left to avoid the traffic lights at Goldenacre. As the small car turned he saw that the rear number plate was hanging at a strange angle and the exhaust pipe was banging off the ground. Good, he won't get far with that, thought Blake.

Blake took the same turn and found himself on a long straight road. He could see several hundred yards ahead, but the Metro was nowhere to be seen. Blake drove past the rugby ground and past an entrance for some botanic gardens. He took the next right and followed the road to the end, took a few turnings, past a private school set back from the road in its own grounds and eventually found himself in a busy shopping street. He pulled over and consulted his Edinburgh street map.

'Where have you gone, Mr Dunlop,' he muttered as his finger traced the route from Trinity.

Craig and Fiona hadn't moved from their seats in the two minutes since they'd pulled up. The front door of the house opened and a man in his early forties came out to find out why a strange car was parked in his driveway. He was dressed in track suit bottoms and a loose-fitting sweatshirt. Craig got out of the car and walked towards him, aware that the other man looked like someone who was about to shout the odds at this invasion of his privacy.

'Hi, I'm sorry about this, we took a wrong turn and we were only going to use your driveway to help turn round. But I seem to have a problem with my exhaust.'

'Well you need to move, I'm just about to leave for the football and you're blocking my drive.'

Fiona got out of the car and the man stopped in mid-rant. Craig wasn't sure if it was because the man took an instant shine to her or because quite frankly Fiona looked a mess. Her eye makeup was smudged with tears and her hair was all over the place.

'Are you okay?' The man stared at Craig suspiciously. Craig wondered if the man thought he might be related to the Yorkshire Ripper or something.

Fiona used a finger to try to minimise the mascara damage under her eyes, and broke into a smile.

'Hi. Not really, my brother's driving us up to the hospital, our mum's been taken ill. We were looking for a shortcut and got a bit lost, then we heard a clunking sound from the car.'

The tactic seemed to work, the man seemed to melt right there in front of her. 'Oh you should have said. Here, let's have a look.' They gathered round the rear of the car and examined the damage. One of the rear lights was broken and the plastic bumper was cracked and loose, but the only significant damage seemed to be that the exhaust pipe had broken free of one of the brackets holding it in place. The man got down on the ground, lay flat and looked under the car. He fiddled a bit with a pipe here and a connection there, then emerged with the satisfied look of a man who knew his way around an exhaust silencer.

'Well the good news is that there's no real damage done, the actual exhaust is still intact. Let me see if I can find something to help you with a running repair for the pipe and the bumper. You'll need to get the light fixed but that's cosmetic.'

The house's driveway led to a single garage with an

up-and-over door which the man opened, squeezing past an orange Opel Manta to a tool cabinet at the far end. He emerged a minute later with a spool of gardening twine and a pair of secateurs. He cut off a good length of twine and wound it around the bumper assembly and the exhaust tail pipe.

'Can you hold this in position for me?'

Craig held the bumper and exhaust in place while the good Samaritan made them secure, tying the whole thing tight and lashing it against the chassis and the towing bar.

'There, that should do it for now.'

'I can't thank you enough,' said Craig, 'that's great.' He shook the man's hand. All the time, he'd been listening to the road, expecting to hear the noise of the Fiat's big two litre engine at any moment.

'Thank you so much,' said Fiona. She bounced over to the man and kissed him on the cheek.

'My pleasure, any time.'

Craig and Fiona reversed out of the driveway and retraced their route. Craig paused at the junction with Inverleith Row.

'What's wrong?' asked Fiona, the sense of alarm returning to her face.

'We have a decision to make. We can't go back to Lynn's. Either we go back to your mum's and think about a plan B, or we make straight for Thurso. What do you think?'

Fiona thought for a moment.

'To hell with it, let's go. I'll phone my mum from Perth and face the music then.'

Craig turned right and headed towards the Forth Road Bridge.

The journey to Thurso was uneventful by comparison. They crossed the Forth, drove up through Fife and stopped at Perth as planned. Fiona phoned Lynn first of all. She was still waiting for Craig to show up, and was stunned to hear

The King's Prerogative

that the policeman who visited her office had staked out her house.

'That gives me the creeps. And it obviously means he didn't totally buy the story I told him the other day,' said Lynn. 'Best you tell Craig to keep a low profile until he gets what he needs from Brian Irving.'

'Well, funnily enough, we're in Perth, heading to Thurso.'

'In your mum's car? Have you told her?'

'Not yet.'

'Good luck with that.'

'I know.'

'Give it ten minutes, I'll speak to her first.'

Craig and Fiona went to get a coffee and when Fiona eventually rang home, Lynn's earlier call had achieved some kind of damage limitation. Valerie was worried, clearly, and furious that they had disappeared with the car. She wanted to blame Craig for getting Fiona mixed up in all this, even though she knew that it would have been her headstrong daughter's own decision. She was on the verge of giving her daughter an ultimatum but stopped herself short. Lynn had reminded her friend of how wild she herself had been in her twenties and told her that if the worst thing Fiona did was take her car for a couple of days then Valerie should count herself lucky.

'Mum, I'm sorry,' said Fiona. 'But don't worry, we'll be okay and we'll bring the car back soon. Well, soonish, promise.' She told her mum that she loved her and she hung up.

'We're both in trouble now,' she told Craig. 'She'll go ballistic when she finds out about the damage to the rear end.'

'You didn't tell her?'

'No, I decided that part could wait. Come on, let's go.'

The A9 running north from Perth took them into Highland countryside and as the miles passed, Craig and Fiona managed to relax slightly. The scenery took Craig by surprise. He was ashamed to say that he hadn't been further north than

Dundee and that was only to go to the football. He hadn't explored Scotland much at all, and he had a weird feeling of being a stranger in his own country. Places like Dunkeld, Pitlochry and Aviemore were known to him by name only despite the fact that they were practically on the doorstep, reachable in only a couple of hours. As they soaked in the scenery Craig and Fiona agreed that the Cairngorms were about as far away from the urban landscapes of Glasgow and Edinburgh as they could get. They continued to chat as the miles ticked by, happy to take their minds off what had happened back in Trinity. They talked about places they'd visited and reminisced about the people they knew and the good times they'd shared. By the time they reached Inverness they vowed to return to the Highlands together one day soon, when all this was over. Craig liked the thought of that.

The landscape north of Inverness became flatter. The newly opened Kessock Bridge took them over the Beauly Firth to the peninsula known as the Black Isle, which was neither black nor an island. After a few more miles they passed Dingwall and looped round to Bonar Bridge before the road turned northeast again towards Wick. Eventually they veered north and arrived in Thurso just after four o'clock.

Craig's first impression of Thurso was how much it reminded him of Stranraer. The northernmost and southernmost towns in Scotland both nestled beside the sea in the midst of low, rolling countryside with headlands to the west and to the east. Craig followed the signs to the railway station, past some expensive-looking houses, across a river and through the busy town centre. He wondered whether the young Thurso residents decided to live and work and get married there, or if they also left for the bigger cities in the Central Belt.

He found the railway station and parked. As they locked up, Craig gave the roof of the Metro a gentle tap in appreciation.

The little Austin had got them where they needed to go and the exhaust was still hanging on in there.

From the name, Craig expected the Station Hotel to be close by and they found it a couple of minutes' walk down the long road from the station itself. It was a fairly small grey granite building with windows on three levels. Its notable feature was a long wooden balcony stretching under the three middle windows on the first floor. The girl Craig had spoken to on the telephone was at reception. He could tell it was her from her voice.

'Hello, can I help you?'

'Hi there,' said Craig, smiling at her. 'We spoke on the phone earlier, I called looking for Doctor Irving.'

The girl looked surprised at the fact that they had come all this way without booking ahead. Craig surmised that they probably didn't get much passing trade.

'We'd like to stay for a night or two, if you've any rooms?'

'Yes, we do, I think.' The receptionist checked a book, tracing a finger across two pages. 'You're in luck. We only have one room left. It's a twin, will that be okay for you?' She looked at Fiona as she said it.

Fiona and Craig exchanged a glance before Fiona answered for both of them. 'That'll be fine, thanks.'

'How long will you be staying?'

'Probably a couple of nights.'

'That's no problem.'

The receptionist invited Craig to complete their registration and she gave him a key.

'It's room 17, on the first floor. Breakfast is seven-thirty till nine-thirty through in the dining room to your left. Do you need a hand with your bags?'

'No thanks, we're fine. Could you tell me which room Doctor Irving is staying in?'

'Would you mind waiting for just one moment, please.'

The girl went through to a small office behind the reception and called up to Brian's room. She returned a minute later.

'Doctor Irving asks if you could call on him when you're ready. He's just along the corridor from you in room 12.'

'Thank you.'

Craig and Fiona took the stairs to the first floor and followed the room numbers to 17, passing room 12 on the way. It was only when they were inside their room that Craig realised that he'd been holding his breath all the way along the corridor. Brian Irving had been the starting point for Craig and finally things were at last coming full circle.

'Are you okay?' asked Fiona.

Craig smiled. 'I'm fine. I'm just a bit nervous, that's all.'

Five minutes later Craig and Fiona knocked on the door of room 12. The door opened and Craig was face to face with Brian Irving.

'Craig?'

'Brian?'

'It's good to meet you finally.'

The two men shook hands, and Brian invited them in. Craig introduced Fiona and Brian asked them to take a seat. They looked round the room but apart from the double bed and a small stool in front of a dressing table there wasn't a lot of choice. Then they noticed the bedroom window was set into a deep recess which had been padded to make it double as a seat big enough for two. Fiona and Craig went over to the window and sat down side by side. Brian sat down on the edge of the bed.

'You got here okay then?' asked Brian.

Craig and Fiona looked at each other. 'Eventually,' said Craig. He told Brian about their run in with Blake.

'He actually ran into the back of your car?'

'Yes.'

'It sounds like they're getting more desperate.'

Craig tried to read Brian's face. He looked like a man who hadn't had much sleep recently, and hadn't shaved in three or four days either.

Brian seemed to know what Craig was thinking. 'I suppose I should apologise for my appearance.' He scratched his chin. 'I've been ploughing a lone furrow recently and haven't been doing much entertaining.'

'What about your wife? Where is she?' asked Fiona.

'I'm not married. Confirmed bachelor, I'm afraid.'

Craig was going to apologise for Fiona's legendary frankness but Brian broke into a smile.

'Quite honestly no one would have me. My manners are deplorable. I haven't even offered you a cup of tea.'

'That would be lovely, thank you,' said Fiona.

Brian busied himself with the tea as he continued talking. 'I'm so glad you're here, I didn't know who else I could involve.'

'Involve?' asked Fiona.

'Yes. I approached Clive Prior and that would appear to have been a mistake. Call me overcautious but I've been loath to take anyone else into my confidence.'

'That sounds familiar,' said Fiona.

'Don't get me wrong, there are loads of research students I could call on for help, but, well, I didn't want to get them caught up in anything. You know.'

'I do,' said Craig.

Brian passed them a cup each and asked them to help themselves to milk and sugar.

Craig felt he had to clear the air. 'Brian, look, I'm really sorry for getting you roped into this. If I had any idea it would turn out the way it has, I would never have started it.'

'Don't apologise. You've done nothing wrong. I'm glad you approached me. This could be a once in a lifetime opportunity, and I'm not stopping now.'

'Once in a lifetime?'

'I think it could be. We have to be on to something massive here. The fact that the police and MI6 – or whoever this Anson works for – are so keen to stop us means this could be as big as… who knows? As big as Watergate.'

Craig made a decision. As Lynn told him only the other day, he had to start trusting someone sometime.

'Funny, that's what Lynn said too,' he said.

'Lynn?'

'Yes, Lynn Simon,' said Fiona. 'She's a friend of my mum's. She used to be a journalist on the *Scotsman*. She's been helping us this week. She says she met you once at a dinner.'

'My memory's clearly not as good as hers I'm afraid.'

'She's been a great help,' added Craig. 'She came with me to see Clive Prior. I trust her too.'

'There's four in our little gang then?' said Brian. 'Quite the conspiracy.' He finished his tea in one go and put his cup down. 'Well, I think we should swap notes and try to put a story together that Lynn can take to the papers. I assume you agree that our best defence is attack and we need to go public?'

Craig smiled. 'My thoughts exactly.'

'Good. Can you show me the peace offer? I can't tell you how much I've been looking forward to seeing it.'

Craig didn't want to admit that as a precaution he'd locked the document in his room before they'd come along the corridor to meet Brian. Instead he said, 'No, please, you go first, bring us up to speed.'

'Okay, of course.'

Brian opened a bedside drawer and pulled out three notebooks, opening all three and laying them flat on the bed. 'These are the notes from my research in Edinburgh and London, with as much as I could remember from the notes that were stolen. It's been a challenge putting it all together. The biggest problem has been the absence of records. So many haven't been released into the public domain. That in itself is revealing in its own way.'

'What's your theory so far?' asked Craig.

'Let me start from the beginning. I looked at as many newspapers and periodicals from the time as I could find, and I backed that up with official records and Hansard publications.'

The King's Prerogative

'The official reports from parliament?' asked Fiona.

'Indeed,' said Brian. 'My starting point was the newspaper reports about Hess, and that allowed me to narrow my search when I went to the public records. The first thing to say is that I'm convinced that there was an organised group of influential figures in Britain who wanted peace. They had different reasons for wanting Britain out of the war. The City of London was worried about the cost of fighting it. Some industrialists were worried that the war would bankrupt Britain completely. Against that backdrop, the Secret Intelligence Service, or MI5 and MI6 as we now know it, was distinctly anti-communist. The head of the SIS, Sir Stewart Menzies, saw Soviet Communism as the main threat. He advocated making peace with Germany so that Germany could focus on the Soviet Union. No matter who won that conflict, both would be weaker as a result, to Britain's advantage.'

'That would back up the theory of an intelligence sting though, surely?'

'No. There's a piece of the jigsaw you're not seeing.'

'What's that?' said Craig.

'Churchill didn't trust Menzies. Before Churchill was prime minister, when he was still First Lord of the Admiralty he strenuously opposed his appointment to the head of the SIS.'

'Couldn't he just get rid of him when he became prime minister, then?'

'It wasn't as simple as that. Firstly, Menzies was well connected. He was close to the king and to most of the cabinet. Remember that at the time, Churchill's position wasn't secure. Plus, Churchill needed to maintain the perception of a united front against Nazism. So, instead, he formed the Special Operations Executive. It was almost the first thing he did after coming into office. The SOE was given special powers direct from Churchill. Their sole purpose was to defeat the Nazis.'

'Wasn't that SIS's purpose too?'

'Of course it was. But their ideologies were completely different. The SOE firmly held the view that Hitler's Reich should be fought to the end. It supported an alliance with the USSR against the Nazis. The SIS on the other hand was nervous about such an alliance. It believed that Stalin was the true enemy and thought that Britain should extract itself from the war and leave Hitler and Stalin to fight each other to a standstill. The two organisations had a simmering feud throughout the war.'

'But what does that have to do with the peace group and Hess's flight?' asked Fiona.

'It's significant because it was the SIS who were involved in the plan to bring Hess to Britain. The SOE were kept in the dark for a very good reason.'

'Why?' asked Craig.

Brian Irving looked up from his notes. 'Part of the plan was to replace Churchill.'

Craig and Fiona stared at Brian.

'What? How could that have been possible?' asked Craig.

'Have you heard of the Royal Prerogative?' Brian replied.

'No.'

'It's an obscure piece of constitutional law and it's no surprise that you haven't heard of it. It's never been invoked. It gives the monarch the right to remove a prime minister from office and replace him with someone of the king or queen's own choosing.'

'Really?'

'Yes. It exists.' Brian referred to his notes. 'The peace group also existed, and by my reckoning it had to include Lord Halifax and Sir Samuel Hoare. One of them would have been the replacement for Churchill. Sir Stewart Menzies was part of it, and it's inconceivable that Lord Beaverbrook wasn't involved, it would have needed his support to oil the necessary wheels. It's also very likely that the Polish government in exile was in on the plan. And finally, of course it had to include the king. Menzies and the Duke of Hamilton had direct access to the king.'

Craig took a minute to absorb this before speaking.

'Brian, when we spoke on the phone back in February, you emphasised that you dealt in facts. How much evidence is there to back this up?'

Brian smiled. 'I have to be honest, most of it is circumstantial. But people have been convicted of murder on circumstantial evidence.' He turned the pages of his notebook. 'The events speak for themselves and those individuals' political views are a matter of record. Your letter of safe conduct exists. But remember when I said that some public records are missing? Retained under the Official Secrets Act?'

'Yes.'

'Whole tranches of the Hess papers are missing from the public record. They haven't been released. There are other seemingly unrelated records, which should be in the public domain, but aren't.'

'Such as?'

Brian Irving flicked through his notes again. 'For example, Sir Samuel Hoare was the British Ambassador to Spain at the time. There was a curious newspaper article in the Vichy press that said that Hoare and Lord Halifax met with Hess and Haushofer in Madrid the month before Hess's flight. Over the weekend of 20–22 April 1941.'

'That can't possibly be true, surely?' said Craig.

'You'd think so wouldn't you? But when I went to corroborate it against the official records, I discovered that all the correspondence between the British Embassy in Madrid and the Foreign Office in London for that weekend is missing. When I asked about it, I was told that those records have been retained under the Official Secrets Act and won't be released for another thirty-five years. And I could go on and on. So many holes. Sometimes when something looks like a duck and quacks like a duck, you have to say it's a duck.'

'You sound convinced,' said Craig.

'I am, or as convinced as I can be without access to the missing records. I'm convinced that Hess's flight was the *final* move in a peace plan, not the first. He had already had correspondence with the British pro-peace group, including a meeting on neutral territory. The spare external fuel tanks sent to Dungavel. That's how organised it all was. The Germans keep excellent records.'

Brian closed his notebooks. 'Craig, I'm telling you. The reason Hess flew to Britain was because he was due to meet the king.'

Chapter 37

Two hours later the three of them were seated around a table in a little Chinese restaurant nearby. Brian had shaved and looked and felt much better. Before they left the hotel, Brian read the peace offer, and they were now discussing it in between steaming mouthfuls of beef with black bean sauce, roast duck with cashew nuts, Singapore noodles and sweet and sour chicken. It was Fiona's idea to order dishes that they could all share and she enjoyed seeing Craig and Brian warm to each other as their conversation batted back and forth.

'I have to say, I've read a great deal about a potential peace offer over the past few weeks but I didn't expect to actually read it with my own eyes,' said Brian, still getting over the shock. 'And although it pains me to say it, you have to admire the efficiency and foresight of the Germans to produce it in English to avoid any misunderstandings that might be caused due to a translation by the British.'

'I've been thinking,' said Craig. 'About what you were saying about the meeting on neutral territory between Haushofer, Hess, Sir Samuel Hoare and Lord Halifax. One thing that struck me as slightly strange about the peace document was how it came to be so, well, *lenient* towards Britain.'

'You mean, considering how weak Britain was at the time?'

'Exactly. It's as if the terms were negotiated.'

'Perhaps they were. In Madrid.'

They chewed that over while they picked over the last of the food.

'I've been thinking about your discussion with Clive Prior,' said Brian. 'I know you had your suspicions about what he told you, but I think maybe he *had* seen the peace offer before.'

'What makes you say that?'

'Well, again, it's all tied up with Churchill and his reaction to the flight. When you look at what he did when Hess arrived and for the weeks and months afterwards, it shows the real genius of the man,' said Brian.

'I have to confess, I haven't really focused on Churchill's actions, it's a bit of a blind spot for me,' said Craig. 'What did he do?'

'Well for me there are three aspects to this. There was how he foiled the "peace plot", if you want to call it that. Then there was how he used the Hess affair to his advantage in terms of conducting the war. And finally – and this is most fascinating – it's how he used Hess to cement his own position as prime minister.'

'We're all ears,' said Fiona.

'Well, like you, I started by looking into what happened on the night that Hess landed. I think we're agreed that he was heading for the airstrip at Dungavel House. Eyewitness accounts said that they saw what could have been landing lights, and then they went out again. That would explain why Hess baled out. He saw the lights, swung round to approach from the west, and by the time he did that, the lights had gone off.'

'Why?' asked Craig.

'There are conflicting views on that. I first of all went down the SOE route, I thought perhaps the air strip was sabotaged by them. There were reports of a fracas in the area on the night of the 10th of May. My own view is that the peace group were rumbled, or something in the plan at this end went awry, and it was the reception committee who switched off the landing lights, as a signal for Hess to abort and head for his alternate destination, Aldergrove outside Belfast. From there he would be taken under cover to the Republic of Ireland. But it was too late, by the time the lights went out Hess had jettisoned his external fuel tanks, so the only thing he could do was bale out.'

'Okay, I see how that might explain why he jumped out of his plane, and the strange behaviour of those on the ground that night.'

'It would. I think the peace group then had to close ranks quickly. The cat was out of the bag as it were, and Hess was in custody. The Home Guard took him to their HQ in Giffnock, and there he was interrogated by a translator. Get this, the translator was a clerk from the Polish Consulate in Glasgow. He spoke to Hess in German for two hours.'

'But Hess could speak perfect English,' said Craig. 'There was no need for them to talk in German.'

'Exactly what I thought too. Which made me investigate this translator, a chap called Roman Battaglia. It turns out that no one called him, no one knew who he was and no one knew where he went after he spoke to Hess. He provided the Home Guard with the briefest of statements and then left.'

'So, what did he talk to him about for two hours?' asked Fiona. 'And who sent him?'

'Good question. No one knows. My theory is that he was sent by the peace group to explain to Hess what had gone wrong, and to tell him to bide his time until a new plan could be thought out. That discussion would have been in German, for obvious reasons. And the visitor had to be someone anonymous, unrecognisable. In the Home Guard's account of that night, it says that Battaglia and Alfred Horn spoke alone. Not that he interrogated him, mind, but that they *spoke*. I find that an interesting choice of words.'

Craig had to agree. Brian put down his chopsticks and a waiter came to clear the table. They ordered some coffee and then Brian picked up his story again.

'So in the panic of that night, I think that the peace group dispatched Battaglia to brief Hess to keep silent, or at least to stick to what must have been a predetermined cover story. We can't tell what they did next, presumably they had to regroup and rethink. Meanwhile, the Duke of Hamilton was summoned to brief Churchill. The Duke had no option but to deny all knowledge of a plot and had to stick to the story that Hess had taken leave of his senses.'

The coffee came, and Craig added milk and sugar to his and stirred it.

'What did Churchill do next?' he asked.

'Churchill was clever. Do you know the first time he made a statement to parliament about Hess's arrival?'

'I do,' said Fiona. 'Not till January 1942.'

'Precisely. I'm impressed, you've done your homework. A whole eight months later. Churchill must have had a pretty good idea who was involved. But I think that instead of using the Defence of the Realm Act to try them as traitors, he used his knowledge of the peace plot like a sword of Damocles over the conspirators. He was effectively saying to them, support me and you can stay in your positions. Step out of line and woe betide you. As it was, he used the episode to strengthen his position. He had his own "night of the long knives" and purged the government of those who opposed his policies.

Craig thought this over. 'Is that why he didn't exploit Hess's capture for propaganda purposes?'

'Exactly,' said Brian. 'It was more useful to keep Hess up his sleeve as it were. Meanwhile, the double whammy was that the longer he dragged proceedings out, the better the chance that Hitler would think the British were mulling over the peace offer.'

Brian leaned forward. Fiona and Craig did the same.

'Which brings me to another strange fact I learned. Did you know that ten days after Hess arrived, a curious thing happened? A German plane landed at an RAF aerodrome and was allowed to take off again, unhindered.'

'What?' chorused Craig and Fiona.

Brian smiled. 'A Luftwaffe aeroplane – to be precise a Dornier 217 – flew from an airfield in Denmark, to Britain. Completely unmolested. It landed at an RAF base near Lincoln where the pilot – a chap named Heinrich Schmitt, handed over a package to a waiting RAF officer. Then he took off again and returned to Denmark.'

Fiona's mouth fell open. 'You're kidding?'

'No, it happened.'

'I'm astounded, but I don't see the connection,' said Craig.

'What if the package handed over by the Luftwaffe officer was the same as the package you picked up from the Swedish Consulate.'

'You mean…?'

'Yes. I think Clive Prior *had* seen the peace offer before. I think Churchill asked for another copy because the original was destroyed in the crash, and it was delivered by this plane. He kept stringing the Germans along.'

Craig rubbed his forehead, trying to take in the implications of what Brian had uncovered. He hadn't even considered the possibility that Churchill orchestrated the events that unfolded following Hess's capture.

'Clever, wasn't it?' said Brian. 'Even though Hess's mission started as an attempt to depose Churchill and take Britain out of the war, Churchill turned it to his advantage like the experienced politician he was. He handed over the operation to the SOE and they ran with it. Hitler invaded the USSR and Britain no longer stood alone.'

'Wow,' said Fiona.

'I'll tell you what blows me away now that I've actually read the peace offer,' said Brian. 'Churchill must have read it at the time. But not only did he not tell parliament about it, he didn't even tell his cabinet about it. He single-handedly suppressed it.'

Fiona looked puzzled. 'But isn't it obvious that he would keep it secret?'

'Maybe. But I do wonder why,' mused Brian. 'Why did he want to keep fighting? Was it in the best interests of Britain? It's easy to look back and think "what if", but as someone who drives an Austin Allegro I can tell you, Britain doesn't seem all that Great to me right now.'

They all stared at their coffees. After a long minute, Craig broke the silence.

'That way madness lies, Brian. Hitler had to be defeated. The only thing we need to do right now is to figure out what we need to do.'

'You're right, Craig. But let me show you one last thing. Tomorrow. Then you'll know everything I know. It might have a bearing on what we do next, but I need to get your take on it.'

'Why?'

'Because I don't know if I've lost the plot.'

'What?' Craig looked nonplussed.

'It'll be easier if I show you. There's a final twist in the tale of Rudolf Hess, and it's only a few miles away. It's why I came to Caithness.'

'I thought you came here because it was remote and you wanted to keep your head down,' said Craig.

'Oh no. There's another reason. Why don't we meet up for breakfast at eight-thirty, and afterwards I'll take you for a run in the car.'

The three of them walked back to the hotel just before eleven o'clock, and Brian bid the others goodnight as he unlocked his door. Once in their own room, Fiona asked if she could use the bathroom first and took her overnight bag in with her. Craig lay down on one of the beds and closed his eyes. He realised that he was very, very tired. Probably a combination of the big meal they'd just eaten and the long drive. And being chased around Edinburgh by the police, he thought. What was that maniac in the car playing at? Craig didn't have the answer, and to be honest he was too tired to do any more thinking. He'd done enough thinking for one day, he decided.

Craig heard the shower stop and a couple of minutes later the door to the bathroom opened. Fiona switched off the bathroom light and stood in the doorway naked, with her wet hair wrapped in a towel. She stood still for a few seconds, looking over at him. Craig's eyes were closed.

'You'd better not be asleep, mister,' she said softly.

Chapter 38

Sunday 20th March, 1983

Breakfast was a hearty bowl of porridge followed by scrambled eggs and bacon.

'You're hungry this morning,' commented Brian as Fiona cleared her plate and reached for a slice of toast.

'Ravenous,' she said, giving Brian one of her smiles while squeezing Craig's knee under the table.

'Where are we off to today?' she asked as she spread a liberal helping of marmalade onto her toast and took a bite.

Brian fished in his jacket pocket and produced an Ordnance Survey map which he opened out in front of him. He located the place he was looking for and turned the map to face Craig and Fiona. They could see that it was a map of the local area, stretching south as far as Brora.

'That's where I want to take you,' he said, pointing to a spot due south of Thurso. Craig leaned in and squinted at the map.

'Where is it?'

'It's a spot called Eagle's Rock.' Brian moved his finger to a point closer to Thurso. 'And that body of water is Loch More. I'll explain its significance later.'

Craig could tell from the way Brian was fidgeting that he was keen to get under way. 'Okay then, let's go. Meet you out front in ten?'

They went back to their respective rooms to pick up their things. Craig decided not to take the peace offer with him, but he didn't like the idea of leaving it in the room either. He left Fiona to lock up and went down to reception. The young receptionist appeared and asked Craig how she could help.

'Do you have a safe here in the hotel?'

'Not as such sir, but I do have a lockable drawer in the office if that will do?'

'And you have the only key?'

'Yes sir, no one else has access.'

Craig thought for a moment then decided to risk it. 'Do you have a large envelope I could pinch from you?'

The receptionist rummaged under the desk and produced a large manila envelope. Craig squeezed the peace offer and his grandad's wallet into the envelope, sealed it and used the desk pen on his side of the reception to sign the top flap. 'Could I pinch some Sellotape too, please?'

The receptionist duly located a roll of tape for Craig. He bit a piece off then stuck the tape over his signature. He repeated the process with the envelope's bottom flap, then turned it over and wrote his name and room number on the front of the envelope before finally handing it over. He thanked the receptionist and watched as she took the envelope through to her small office. He turned to walk back up the stair just as Brian and Fiona came into view.

'All set?' Brian asked.

'Yep. Lead on Macduff.'

They decided to take Brian's car and stopped off at the Mini Metro to allow Fiona to change into a pair of wellingtons kept in the boot. As she climbed in the back, Fiona was about to comment on the fact that only a university lecturer would drive a brown car but thought better of it. Craig took the front passenger seat.

'Don't forget to belt up,' Brian said.

Craig smiled to himself. Being fined £30 for not wearing a seat belt would be the least of his worries if he ran into the police.

The morning sun was climbing in the sky to their left as they drove south, but dark clouds loomed in the distance. Brian provided some local detail as they went.

'Where I'm taking you is a private estate owned by the Dukes of Portland. During the war, the Duke of Portland was chairman of Churchill's Joint Intelligence Committee. That's yet another funny coincidence in itself.'

The road was quiet and they passed few cars as they made their way down the A9.

'It's so flat around here isn't it?' said Fiona as she looked at the featureless moorland on both sides of the road. She spun round to look out of the back window. The horizon ran practically straight in every direction.

'It certainly is,' said Brian as he also looked round. He pointed through the windscreen at some grey hills in the far distance. The first real high ground you come to south of John O' Groats are those hills. They're called the Scarabens. We're heading in that direction.

After about half an hour, the road met the coast and a couple of miles further on they came to a small village clinging to the side of the cliffs. Once through the village, Brian slowed down.

'I'm looking for one of these roads on the right. Ah, here it is.'

They turned into what seemed to be an access road, a single track up a long shallow hill. Their progress was slow, partly because the road was little more than a single set of tyre tracks across the moor, and partly because grazing sheep blocked their path more than once. After a mile or so, the track came to a sudden end when it reached what looked like an abandoned croft.

'From here, it's on foot,' said Brian. He killed the engine and they all got out. Brian pointed west, in the direction the track would have taken if it had continued. 'It's some way further on. About two miles, but the terrain isn't the easiest to negotiate.'

The three zipped up their jackets against the cold wind. As they started walking Craig soon understood what Brian meant. The ground was damp and springy, like walking on a wet, grassy sponge, which made progress slow. The scruffy moorland stretched in front of them as far as they could see. They came to a rise and beyond it Craig could see a small, round loch, not much bigger than a cricket field. A lonely boat house sat at the water's edge, looking as abandoned as the croft had.

'When I was here last I veered right at this point, to keep to the flatter ground,' said Brian. 'But I want to take you this way, so you can bet a better view.' He pointed straight ahead, up a small bracken-covered hill. Craig and Fiona followed Brian as he made the climb. After twenty minutes of slow but steady progress they reached the top and stopped to catch their breath. On the other side of the hill about a quarter of a mile to their left Craig could see a small but fast flowing river. It was swollen by the Spring rainfall coming off the Scarabens, rising immediately beyond. Up close, the hills looked much taller than they seemed from the road. The last of the winter snow still clung to the top of the three peaks, and as Craig looked to the west along the course of the river, the ridge of small mountains reminded him of a defensive wall, like something from Tolkien.

Brian pointed to the river. 'That's Berriedale Water down there. It winds its way down to the North Sea behind us. And if you look on this side of the river, that hill yonder is where we're going.' He pointed to a high point not too far from where they stood. 'That's Eagle's Rock. It's the last significant piece of high ground between here and Thurso. Come on, it's only about a mile as the crow flies, but we have to go down this hill, and walk round the side.'

They pressed on down the hill and across the moor. They were getting tired now, not least because they kept having to backtrack and change course when they came across small burns that were too wide to jump across.

'Who was it that said the shortest distance between two points is a straight line?' asked Fiona.

'Whoever it was never went hillwalking in the Scottish Highlands,' said Craig. By now his shoes were sodden, as were his jeans below the knee.

They began climbing again and Craig stopped looking around him, he just wanted this to be over. He kept his gaze fixed five yards ahead of his feet, looking for the best ground to step on. He almost bumped into Brian, who had stopped. They were nearly at the top of the hill and Brian was pointing at a stone cross that had come into view a hundred yards ahead.

Craig looked around to get his bearings. They'd been walking for nearly two hours and the landscape all around was rugged and barren and inhospitable. He turned a full 360 degrees. There was no sign that any human had ever been there before. He could see no roads, no signposts, no houses, no fences, no electricity pylons. But there in front of them, incongruously, stood a Celtic cross. As they got closer, Craig saw that the cross stood on top of a square plinth. The plinth bore an inscription which read:

> IN MEMORY OF
> AIR CDRE H.R.H. THE DUKE OF KENT
> K.G., K.T., G.C.M.C., G.C.V.O.
> AND HIS COMPANIONS
> WHO LOST THEIR LIVES ON ACTIVE SERVICE
> DURING A FLIGHT TO ICELAND ON A SPECIAL
> MISSION
> THE 25TH OF AUGUST 1942
> "MAY THEY REST IN PEACE"

It took Craig and Fiona a minute or so to catch their breath after the climb.

'The names of the Duke's companions are inscribed on either side, see?' Brian gestured to the sides of the plinth.

Brian sat down and leant against the plinth while the other two walked round it, reading the list of names. 'Okay, you have our attention,' said Craig. 'What's this twist in the tale you have to tell me about?'

Brian reached into his jacket and pulled out one of his notebooks. He opened it at a page marked with a piece of paper, folded small enough to fit inside.

'I stumbled on a couple of things by accident while I was researching old newspapers,' began Brian. 'On one of my visits to the Mitchell Library I asked the assistant if there was an easier way to find relevant newspaper articles. You know, rather than having to plough through paper after paper. He told me they had index fiche, sorted by year, so that sped up my search quite a bit.'

Fiona wished she'd thought of that when she'd been in the library. Meanwhile Craig hoped that this revelation of Brian's was going to get a bit more riveting.

'What was interesting was that when I looked up the index for "aircraft crashes", there was more than one entry. There was Hess's, clearly, but there were others. I checked each of them, mainly out of curiosity.'

Craig couldn't hide his disappointment. 'It was wartime, Brian, planes crashed all the time. Probably.'

'Not as many in Scotland as you'd think. But one caught my eye. This one.' He pointed a thumb at the memorial behind his back. 'The story goes that the king's younger brother, Prince George, the Duke of Kent, was on active service during the war. He was on his way to Iceland to boost the morale of the British servicemen stationed there as well as to meet local Icelandic dignitaries.'

'And his plane crashed, and he and the crew died,' said Craig. He'd gleaned that much from the inscription on the plinth.

'Yes. But call it my naturally suspicious nature, I decided to look into it in more detail, mainly because we're talking about the mysterious death of the king's brother here. There's plenty of conjecture around what happened, which I naturally ignored. But there are some interesting facts surrounding the flight that point to something more than a routine flight to Iceland.'

'Like what?' asked Fiona.

'First of all, the plane that crashed was a Sunderland flying boat, based at Oban. It flew to Invergordon on the Cromarty Firth, where the Duke of Kent met it with his staff. The plane took off just after one o'clock in the afternoon of the 25th August 1942 and an hour later it crashed here, on Eagle's Rock.'

'What's so strange about that?' asked Craig.

'Well, as I said, those flights to Iceland were pretty much routine at the time. Iceland was strategically important in the U-Boat war and flights back and forth were made regularly. It's worth noting that all previous flights had been made by Liberators flying out of Prestwick. It surely would have made more sense for the Duke to go to Prestwick than for a flying boat to meet him 130 miles from Oban, in the completely wrong direction for a flight to Iceland.'

'That may be so, but who's to say there wasn't a good reason to go by flying boat on this occasion?' asked Craig.

'Perhaps. But there's more. The official investigation into the crash said that it was caused by pilot error. The aircraft was on the wrong path and at too low an altitude, it said. For some reason it had deviated from its planned course and hit the rising ground in foggy conditions. But the crew were handpicked. It included the most experienced Sunderland pilot there was, and in total there were four pilots and four navigators on board. It was due to follow the coast up to John O'Groats then turn left towards Iceland. But only sixty miles after taking off from Invergordon, it crashed here.'

'Mechanical failure?'

'The crash investigation said not. And that's another thing. You know how difficult it is to get up here.'

Craig had only just recovered his breath. 'Yes.'

'The RAF removed every last trace of wreckage a matter of days after the crash.'

The King's Prerogative

'Wasn't that routine?'

'Not by a long stretch. Particularly not in as remote an area as this.'

'Why did they do it then?' asked Fiona.

'That's a good question, and it's open to conjecture. Maybe because of the fact that the king's brother was on board, or maybe for other reasons.'

'You don't like conjecture.'

'No I don't. So I'll stick to the facts. The crash enquiry noted that the engine throttles were all open when the plane crashed,' said Brian.

'Meaning what?' asked Craig.

'Meaning that the plane was trying to climb when it ploughed into this hill.'

Craig mulled this over in his head as he stared out over the moorlands below him and the pine forests stretching north.

'What do you think the plane was doing?' he asked.

Brian looked at him. 'I think it was taking off.'

'Taking off?'

'Yes. It makes no sense to say that the pilots and navigators on board all made such a catastrophic error of judgement. I think the plane flew here deliberately. The throttles were wide open. It was taking off. And then you have to consider the timing.'

'The timing?' said Fiona.

'The Sunderland took off at ten past one in the afternoon. Eyewitness reports – or more accurately, earwitness reports – put the crash at approximately two-thirty. A number of locals heard the plane come down. That's eighty minutes in the air. But it should have taken no more than twenty minutes for the plane to reach this spot from Invergordon.'

'Why is there a discrepancy in the timings?' asked Craig.

'I don't think there was a discrepancy.' Brian took out his map. It was already folded so that it showed the Scarabens, and to the north, Loch More. 'I think that the reason they were in a Sunderland from Invergordon is because the plan was for them to land at Loch More, turn round and take off again. That would account for the time delay. And because those planes were slow and sluggish, as it took off it struggled to gain enough height to clear the high ground. I think that also explains why the wreckage was removed.'

'But why did they go to so much effort?' asked Fiona.

'To avoid questions about why the plane was *facing the wrong way* when it crashed,' said Brian. 'You saw how flat the land is to the north of here, well apparently it was not unheard of for pilots flying up the coast to turn inland just past the Scarabens, to cut the corner, so to speak. It saved them from having to fly as far as John O'Groats before making the turn. The official report suggests that the crew misread their instruments, miscalculated their turn and crashed in poor visibility. If that was true, then the plane would surely have been flying west or northwest at the time of impact.' Brian made a gesture with his arm to indicate a line from the sea running parallel with the Scarabens. 'But from the pictures of the wreckage, it's clear that it was on a *northeasterly* course when it crashed.' Brian made a quarter turn and drew an imaginary line in that direction. I think the pilot intended to veer left and follow the path of Berriedale Water to the sea, and tragically, Eagle's Rock was in the way. They turned to port and tried to climb clear, but didn't make it.'

'But if the land is so flat to the north of Loch More, why didn't they take off in that direction, clear of any obstacles?' asked Fiona.

'A very good question. I wrestled with that one, and then the answer came to me when I did some research into that type of aircraft. The Sunderland flying boat needed a lot of water to take off, sometimes up to two miles or more. Loch More is roughly two miles long. They would have needed every yard of water for the take off. And of course, they would have to take off into the wind.'

'So, if the wind was from the south, they'd have to take off facing south, and either climb over the Scarabens or make a turn before they reached them.' said Craig.

'Exactly,' said Brian. He put the map back in his pocket.

The rain eased slightly. Craig ran his hand over his face in a vain attempt to dry it.

'This is all very interesting, and under different circumstances I'm sure it would be fascinating to explore that particular mystery but I don't see what it's got to do with our problem right now.'

Brian's eyes pierced his with a stare that stopped Craig in his tracks.

'Oh but it has everything to do with it. It has everything to do with why some people want to shut us up permanently.'

'What do you mean?'

Brian stood up and pointed to the inscription on the stone.

'This cross wasn't erected by the council or the government or even by the Royal family itself. It's not an official memorial in any way. It was put here by the Duke's bereaved widow. Look around. There are no signs to it, no path, almost as if no one is supposed to know it's here. 'On a special mission' it says on that inscription. I'm convinced that the Sunderland was on a special mission to pick up a passenger and take him to safety.'

'Who?'

'Rudolf Hess.'

Chapter 39

'What?'

Brian looked into the distance. 'The plane landed on Loch More because Rudolf Hess was being kept here in secret. In a lodge nearby.'

Craig shook his head. 'That doesn't make sense. You're saying that Churchill was prepared to release Hess and let him fly out of the country secretly? But something went wrong and the plane crashed without Hess on it?'

'No Craig, what I'm saying is that Hess *was* on the plane when it crashed.'

Craig looked at Brian in disbelief. He didn't know whether to laugh or to cry. He'd decided to trust this man, this respected university lecturer. He'd hoped that he would somehow help to extricate them from the nightmare of the last few weeks. Instead of that, he could only surmise that Doctor Irving had finally cracked under the strain. Craig suddenly felt as alone as he'd ever felt in his entire life. Fiona could see it in his eyes and she reached for his hand and squeezed it in hers.

'I haven't gone crazy,' said Brian. He smiled. 'Although there have been moments, I can assure you.'

Craig shook his head. 'How am I supposed to respond when you come out with something like that, Brian? Hess is in Spandau Prison. He has been there since the end of the war. We've wasted nearly a whole day on a wild goose chase.'

Brian smiled. 'Oh believe me, it gets better.'

He reached into his notebook again, took out the piece of

paper that kept the place and unfolded it. 'This is a Photostat copy of one of the newspaper articles I found. It's from March 1940. I found it quite by accident when I was researching Hess's background.'

He handed it to Craig. The article stretched over two newspaper columns, and was topped with a picture of Rudolf Hess. The headline read *'Pub killer found guilty.'*

Craig re-read the headline then looked at Brian.

'Read on,' said Brian.

Craig read the article.

The man accused of murdering dockyard worker Reginald Corbett was found guilty at the Old Bailey yesterday. Frank Mills, 39, killed Mr Corbett in the Duke of Cumberland pub, Shoreditch, on 12th December last year after the two got into an argument. Mills' defence counsel, Mr Foulkes-Bennett, asked the jury to take into account the fact that Mr Corbett had attacked Mills due to the accused's close resemblance to the Nazi deputy leader Rudolf Hess and that his client was defending himself when the fatal blow was struck. The jury however took only ninety minutes to find Mills guilty of murder. He was taken to Pentonville prison where he will remain until sentencing by Lord Justice Brooks next week.

Craig took in the information but he struggled to make sense of what was there in black and white. He walked a few yards towards the summit of the hill and stopped to stare at the defensive wall of the Scarabens. His mind raced through everything he'd learned about Hess. All the facts, all the dates, all the events.

He turned back to face Brian and Fiona.

'Wait a minute. Hess was kept in a high security camp from the end of May 1941. Mytchett Place in Aldershot. When he was there he complained constantly. He was convinced he was being poisoned and drugged. Then in 1942 he was moved to a new location in Wales. Almost overnight he stopped complaining. He enjoyed walks in the grounds and he even went for drives with his chauffeur. He didn't complain about being poisoned ever again. It's almost as if...'

'As if what?' asked Fiona.

'As if he was a different person,' answered Brian.

'No, no, it's ridiculous,' said Craig.

'Is it though?' asked Brian. 'You just said it. His character completely changed overnight. Look at the picture again. That's Frank Mills. He was only a few years younger than Hess. At Nuremberg people commented that Hess looked different, frailer, more gaunt. But because no photographs were taken of him while he was a prisoner in Britain, nobody could know if that change was gradual or sudden.'

'This is crazy,' said Craig. 'I need to think. I'm going back to the car.'

He set off down the side of the hill, retracing his steps across the dense moorland until he could follow Berriedale Water again. He rounded the little loch with the boat house and finally reached their starting point. It was only when he got to the parked Allegro that he remembered that it was locked, so he took shelter from the wind behind the wall of the croft while he waited for the other two to arrive. It was at times like these that he wished he'd taken up smoking, he thought. The shadow of a large rain cloud swept across the hills and as it moved towards Craig he got the feeling that the Scarabens were closing ranks and hunching up against the cold. He imagined how difficult it would be to fly a lumbering Short Sunderland over those mountains from a standing start only a few miles away.

Brian and Fiona appeared. They were deep in conversation but stopped when they reached the car.

'Hiya,' said Fiona, giving Craig a peck on the lips. 'Are you out of your mood yet?'

'I'm not in a mood,' retorted Craig, a bit more petulantly than he intended.

'Of course you are, but there's no need to be. Brian and I

The King's Prerogative

have been swapping ideas. Will we get into the car before the rain starts again?'

Craig knew that this was Fiona's way of saying 'I need you to be in a moving car you can't jump out of because I'm going to make you listen to me'. He held up his hands in mock surrender.

'Okay, okay.'

Brian unlocked the car and they all climbed in. After a seven-point turn they made their way down the farm track and joined the main road back to Thurso. The rain came on again and Brian switched on the windscreen wipers. They struggled against the downpour so Brian dropped his speed so that he didn't have to peer too far beyond the waterlogged glass.

'Ready?' asked Fiona.

'Ready for what?' asked Craig in return. Two could play this game.

'Ready for the theory we've been chewing over.'

Craig looked at Brian who raised his eyebrows as if to reiterate the question Fiona posed.

Craig sighed. 'Fire away.'

'Brian, tell him about the resurgence of the peace group,' said Fiona.

Brian nodded. 'Okay. By summer 1942, the peace group were ready to try again. Britain's position was still perilous even though America and the Soviet Union had joined us by then. The blitz had stopped, but in the Atlantic we were still losing more ships to U-boats than we could replace. Britain was fighting a losing war against Japan in the Far East, with Singapore, Malaysia and Burma all in Japanese hands. Rommel was making gains in North Africa too. At that point it looked like the Germans would also win in Russia having survived the harsh winter there. Stalingrad was still in the future.' Brian looked at Craig. 'No matter how you looked at it, Britain was still losing the war. Churchill had stalled the peace group up to that point, but the fall of Tobruk in June was a devastating blow to British morale and was probably the catalyst that drove the peace group to play their hand.'

'The timing was right, I get that,' said Craig. 'But when does Loch More come into the story?'

'There's a bit of background I have to explain. Firstly, Frank Mills came to the SOE's attention. He officially died in Pentonville prison in March 1942, but that was a front. You've seen the film *I Was Monty's Double?*"

Craig confirmed that he had. It was an old black and white war film that told the true story of an actor who doubled as General Montgomery to fool the Germans in the lead up to D-Day.

'The SOE were handed a gift with Mills. He was undoubtedly Hess's double. You saw the photo. The SOE even secretly made an exact duplicate of Hess's Luftwaffe uniform for him to wear.'

'Why would they go to such trouble to prepare a doppelganger for Hess?'

'For the same reason as they created a double for Monty. Sleight of hand. But it wasn't to fool the Germans. It was to fool the peace group. And the Poles.'

'The Poles?'

'Yes. The Polish Government in exile was here in Britain. What you have to remember about the Poles is that although they hated the Germans, they feared the Soviets. When Britain signed a twenty-year alliance with the Soviet Union in May 1942, the writing was on the wall for the Poles. The Soviets were pushing for the allies to open a second front in western Europe, which would give Stalin the opportunity to counterattack in the east and roll his forces across Poland and into Germany. The European mainland would be wide open to Soviet domination.'

'Hobson's choice for Poland.'

'Believe me Craig, the Poles wanted to avoid being swallowed up by the Soviet Union as much as they wanted to free themselves of Hitler.'

Fiona piped up from the back seat. 'Tell him about the king's brother.'

Brian smiled. 'Yes Fiona, I was coming to that.' He kept one eye on the road as he turned to Craig. The windscreen wipers continued to fight a losing battle against the cloudburst. 'The Duke of Kent was pivotal in all this. He was in Scotland on the weekend that Hess crashed. He was not only a key link between the peace group and the king, he was part of the reception committee for Hess at Dungavel House. He was also very close with the Poles, so much so that he was offered the Polish throne, would you believe. By summer 1942 the peace group had hatched a plan. Churchill was out of the country in the August, visiting Stalin in Moscow. The peace group could make their move to release Hess with Polish help, and fly him to Sweden as a gesture that they were serious about peace. Talks with Germany would then be conducted with the aim of taking Britain out of the war.'

'I find that very hard to believe,' said Craig.

'Consider this. Churchill received intelligence that the Poles were planning a rescue mission, so he moved Hess from Aldershot to Abergavenny in the June.'

'Why is that strange?'

'It's not strange in itself. But the move was leaked to the press. It was all over the papers. There was a bit of a fanfare about it at the time.'

Craig thought about it. 'Are you saying that was when a switch was done? Mills was publicly installed in Wales while the real Hess was moved to Caithness?'

'Yes,' said Brian. 'The new location in Abergavenny was less secure than Aldershot, which makes no sense whatsoever if they were worried about a rescue attempt.'

Brian peered through the windscreen. 'Here's something else for you. The Sunderland that they used had a typical camouflage pattern, the same as all the other aeroplanes in the squadron. Interestingly, just prior to its final mission, that plane was repainted white.'

Craig wore a puzzled look so Brian elaborated. 'During the war, aircraft flying into or between neutral countries were all painted white, to demonstrate that they were unarmed. If you ask me, that's another reason why they removed the wreckage,' said Brian.

They passed a sign that told them that Thurso was five miles ahead. Craig looked out of the window at the rain and the countryside. He thought about the wording on the memorial on Eagle's Rock. *'...who lost their lives on active service during a flight to Iceland on a special mission.'*

'There's one final strange thing about the crash,' said Brian. 'And it's the strangest thing of all.'

'What?' said Craig.

'The Sunderland took off from Invergordon that day with fifteen people on board; ten crew, their commanding officer, the Duke of Kent and his personal entourage of three. When the plane crashed, among those who rushed to the crash site were local policemen and the local doctor. Later they were joined by an RAF team from Wick who had been in contact with Invergordon to check on the flight and who was on board. Eyewitness accounts said that although some of the bodies were badly burned, all were intact. Later that evening, the Air Ministry confirmed that all the crew had lost their lives. Fifteen bodies were taken off the hillside. The next day, the morning papers reported that all fifteen on board were killed.'

'I sense there's a "but" coming,' said Craig.

'There is. A big but. Almost twenty-four hours later, the tail gunner, Flight Sergeant Andy Jack, turned up at a crofter's cottage two miles away.'

'Alive?'

'Very much so. It would seem that by some miracle he was thrown clear of the crash. He must have been injured and disoriented because he said he wandered around the countryside looking for help. He left the scene before the search parties arrived and didn't show up until early afternoon the following day. Subsequent newspaper reports revised the final body count down to fourteen. The fact remains that they took fifteen bodies off the mountain, not fourteen.'

'How many names are listed on the memorial at Eagle's Rock?' asked Fiona.

'Fourteen,' answered Brian.

'Did the tail gunner confirm what happened?' asked Craig.

'No. He was taken to a local hospital and because he had burns on his face he couldn't make a full statement at the time. He *was* visited the next day by two senior officers who made him sign the Official Secrets Act with his burned hands. And that was that. He said nothing about the crash afterwards. Weirdly, he was not even asked to give evidence at the formal enquiry.'

'That is incredible,' said Craig.

They arrived in Thurso and Brian followed the signs to the railway station and parked close to the hotel. As they hurried along the pavement to avoid the rain, Craig thought of something.

'There's one major flaw in your theory,' said Craig.

'What?' asked Brian.

'Hess is still alive and in West Berlin. Mills was British. Hess is German. It's madness. For one, he wouldn't be able to pass himself off as German let alone pass himself off as Hess.'

'Well, you see, Frank Mills wasn't his real name. He changed it in 1937 before he got married to an English girl. You see, he moved to Britain as a boy with his parents. He was Swiss, from Basel. His real name was Franz Meier and German was his first language. Like so many others at the time, he changed his name to make it sound less Germanic.'

Craig stopped walking and stood still, oblivious to the rain soaking his face and running down his neck. 'You're sure of this, aren't you?' he asked.

The university lecturer looked him straight in the eye. 'It's a matter of public record. It fits, Craig. It all fits. Hess's mission, the peace offer, the Royal Prerogative, the official silence afterwards. And now we've stumbled onto the biggest secret of all. This is why they have to keep it so secret. The authorities can't let it be known that the prisoner in Spandau isn't Hess.'

They entered the hotel and went to Brian's room where they each instinctively took their seat from the day before.

It was Craig who broke the silence again.

'Okay. Let's assume that the Sunderland did pick up someone from Loch More. Isn't it just as likely if not more likely that the person they picked up was Mills? Churchill knew the peace group was planning something and drew them into a trap using Mills as bait.'

'That may have been his plan,' said Brian, 'but remember that Churchill laid the trap for them in Wales. That's why Hess's move from Aldershot was so well publicised. He wanted everyone to think that Hess was in Abergavenny. But it was the peace group who double-bluffed him by finding out about the switch and springing the real Hess from his hiding place in Caithness. It's probable that they received help from an insider, an informer in the SOE who revealed details of the switch and Hess's true location.'

Craig thought about it. 'Okay, but I've thought of another flaw in your theory,' said Craig. 'If the real Hess died as you say, why didn't Churchill quietly dispose of Mills before the end of the war rather than letting him go to trial at Nuremberg?'

'That has me baffled I confess,' said Brian. 'The other thing that baffles me is why would anyone volunteer to accept Hess's fate.'

Brian leafed through his notebook again, as if the answer would present itself if only he turned to the right page. 'If it is true, it would explain why Hess refused to see his wife and son for twenty-four years,' he said. 'Why didn't such a family man ask to see Ilse and Wolf until 1969?'

The King's Prerogative

Neither Craig nor Fiona could offer an appropriate answer to Brian's question.

'Did you know that he's been on his own since 1966?' asked Fiona.

'Yes, that's true,' said Brian. 'Seven men were imprisoned in total. In 1966 his last two fellow inmates – Albert Speer and Baldur von Schirach – were both released, leaving Hess on his own.'

'Why do you think they haven't released him?' Fiona asked. 'Is it because the British are scared?'

'I think it's more to do with the Soviet veto against releasing him,' said Brian. 'Every so often the former Allies discuss it, but each time the Russians veto it.'

'Why?'

'He's a pawn. Spandau is in West Berlin. Each of the four Allied forces takes a turn to guard him a month at a time. So for three months of the year the Soviet Union has a toehold in West Berlin.'

Fiona opened her mouth as if she was going to say something else, then closed it again. Finally she decided to speak.

'Tell Craig about the bullet wound.'

'The bullet wound?' asked Craig.

Brian reached for his notebook again, opened it at the page he was looking for and handed it to Craig. Craig was surprised to see a hand-drawn picture of a man's torso. Or rather, two pictures, showing the front view and the back view. On the front view a large 'X' had been marked in the upper chest midway between the left armpit and the left collar bone. The rear view had a corresponding 'X' drawn between the left shoulder blade and the spine.

'I have a friend who works at the University of Munich,' said Brian. 'I contacted him a few weeks ago to see if he could dig up anything from the German records office. As it turns out, not only were the German records very thorough, they aren't as shrouded in secrecy as the British equivalents. For example, he found documentation describing the preparations for Hess's flight, including the dispatch of spare fuel tanks to Sweden. My friend also found an incredible document in the university archive itself.'

'Oh yes?' said Craig, pricking up his ears at the prospect of actual, physical documentation that might strengthen the story. 'What did he find?'

'A copy of Hess's medical record from his time at the university, after the First World War. It recorded that Hess was wounded twice during his army service. He received shrapnel wounds to his left arm and hand while fighting at Verdun in June 1916. He recovered from those and was posted to Romania, where he suffered a more serious injury.' He pointed to the drawings in his notebook. 'He was shot by a sniper and was hospitalised for four months. But he was lucky. The bullet passed straight through his body without hitting any bones or vital organs.'

'I didn't know that,' said Craig.

Fiona couldn't contain herself. 'Brian and I discussed it while you were away in your huff earlier.' She smiled at him to show that she was merely teasing. 'One of the interesting facts Brian's unearthed was that from the time of Hess's appearance at Nuremberg to now, he's been examined by dozens of doctors. Some of the medical reports go into incredible detail, for example one doctor noted a quarter inch mole on his chest.' She paused for effect. 'Not once in all those examinations were his shrapnel scars or the bullet wound mentioned. Not once. Scars fade over time but they never disappear. Especially not a serious bullet wound which has entry and exit holes.' She beamed at Craig, pleased with her revelation.

Not for the first time that day, Craig was struck dumb. There must be a logical explanation.

Brian drove home the point. 'When I learned about the old war wounds, I explored that particular aspect to see if they were ever mentioned by the British. They weren't. But it turns out that the Americans had their suspicions as early as the Nuremberg trial.

'In what way?' asked Craig.

'Hess was examined by an American psychiatrist at Nuremberg to determine whether he was fit to stand trial. The doctor was approached beforehand by none other than Allen W Dulles, the head of the CIA, who swore him to secrecy before revealing that he had reason to believe that the man he was due to examine was an imposter. Dulles asked him to look for scar tissue above Hess's left lung which would prove his identity.'

'Well that would have settled it once and for all,' said Craig.

'You'd have thought so wouldn't you?'

'What did the doctor find?'

'He wasn't allowed to check. Hess was handcuffed to a British Military Police sergeant who refused to take off the handcuffs to allow Hess to undress, or even unbutton his shirt.'

'But surely they would have been able to examine him afterwards, and countless times since?'

'Of course, but by then, what would have been the point in revealing the deception? In fact, you could argue that the fact that the man was an imposter could have been used as leverage over the British.'

'Leverage for what?' asked Fiona.

'You name it,' said Brian.

A look of realisation swept over Fiona's face.

'Greenham Common, for example,' said Fiona. She had been following news of the women's peace camp since it had been set up in protest at the US deployment of nuclear cruise missiles at the Berkshire base.

'Special relationship right enough,' said Craig sardonically.

Chapter 40

Craig's head was pounding. He had travelled to Thurso in the hope... no, in the belief that finally meeting Brian Irving would provide him with answers. Instead of that, he had provided even more questions. The "huff" that Fiona accused Craig of was simply his way of gaining a modicum of space to think. He was no closer to finding a solution to the urgent problem of how to untangle the mess he was in. He felt the same churning fear clutch at his stomach once again and he had to swallow hard to stop it from enveloping him completely.

He breathed in and released air slowly. He reminded himself that he was now in a stronger place than he was a few days ago. He had Fiona on board, and Lynn too. He'd caught up with Brian Irving. He still had hope that Clive Prior was only trying to do the right thing by bringing Commander Anson and his MI5/MI6 connections into play. At least he had a better idea of who he was up against, and that had to count for something. It looked as if old Professor Prior was involved right at the start of the Hess affair, thought Craig, and who knows, he might still have a role to play.

Craig looked at his watch. Where had the day gone? It was nearly four o'clock. They hadn't eaten since breakfast and he was starving.

'Why don't we go for an early dinner, clear our heads, then work on our plan?' he suggested to the other two.

'Good idea. Why don't we freshen up and you knock on my door in an hour?' said Brian.

'Sounds good,' said Fiona. She stood up and Craig followed her as she made for the door.

'See you in an hour.'

Craig unlocked their door and took off his jacket as he went into the room. He lay down on the bed and put his hands behind his head as he stared at the ceiling.

Fiona sat on the other bed and looked at him.

'Are you okay?'

He turned his head to look at her. 'It's a lot to take in.'

'I know. I have faith in you, do you know that? Look at what you've done this past week.' She came over and lay beside him.

Craig put an arm round her. 'Thanks Fi.' He kissed the top of her head. Her hair smelled good.

'I meant to tell you how much I enjoyed last night.'

Fiona looked up at him. 'Me too.' They kissed.

They lay like that for a while.

Craig broke the silence. 'I've made a decision. We should go back home tomorrow. We've taken this as far as we can on our own. I need the police to start working for me instead of against me.'

Fiona sat up and examined his face, searching for any hint of resignation in his eyes. She couldn't see any. 'What will you say to them?'

'That's what we'll talk about tonight.'

They knocked on Brian's door an hour later and the three of them went back out into the rain. It was Sunday and none of the cafés or restaurants they came across was open, not even the Chinese from the evening before. Rather than wander around getting wetter, they decided to cut their losses and get fish and chips from the first place they found open. They hurried back to the hotel and this time Craig and Fiona hosted Brian in their room. They made short work of the fish suppers then got down to work.

Three hours later, they had the plan worked out, having argued back and forth about what should be in and what should be left out, what would be said, who would say it, and finally about the roles that Craig, Brian, Fiona and Lynn would perform. Brian flicked back and forward through the notes he had taken while they talked.

'Are you sure you're okay with this, Craig?' Brian looked worried.

'What's wrong?' asked Craig. 'We agreed we'd do everything in tandem.'

'Yes, but I wish you'd let me come to the police with you. We can back each other's stories up.'

'Don't worry, I'm counting on you doing that when I need you to. First things first, you and Lynn need to get our story ready for publishing.'

'I know, but you're the one taking all the risk meantime.'

'It's a calculated risk. Anyway, we need to bring this to a head. A few weeks ago I found a letter. Now look what we have.' He looked at Fiona. 'Apart from anything else, I'm fed up running.'

'Well,' said Fiona, squeezing Craig's hand. 'With any luck they'll put you in Barlinnie and not Spandau. Much easier on visiting days.'

Chapter 41

Monday 21st March, 1983

Craig woke. He managed to remove his arm from under Fiona's shoulder without waking her, and stretched over to the bedside table to check his watch. It said 7:15. He slipped out of bed and went for a shave and a shower in the bathroom. By the time he was finished Fiona was awake. He kissed her good morning and while Fiona showered Craig got dressed and pulled his belongings together.

Fiona and Craig knocked on Brian's door at eight-thirty and the three went down to breakfast. There wasn't much conversation at the table. Fiona asked for scrambled eggs while the two men ordered the full breakfast. Craig didn't eat much of it. He was engrossed in his thoughts, mentally rehearsing what would happen when they got back to Edinburgh. He drank his coffee and put his napkin on the plate in front of him. 'I'm done.'

'Me too,' said Fiona.

Brian put his knife and fork down.

'No, Brian, you stay and finish your breakfast,' said Craig. 'I have to go to the bank to get some cash anyway. What time do you want to hit the road?'

Brian looked at his watch. 'Latest checkout time is eleven o'clock, I should have finished tidying up our notes by then. I'll ask reception to make up our bills.'

'Good. See you later.'

Craig and Fiona left Brian in the dining room and went back upstairs.

'Do you need to phone your mum before we leave?' asked Craig.

Fiona twisted her mouth into a crooked half smile and thought for a few seconds. She weighed up the risk against the benefit of getting a head start on finding the right lawyer for Craig.

'Yes you're probably right, I should ring her. I'll phone while you're at the bank. And I'll phone Lynn too.'

'Good. I won't be long.' He picked up his chequebook and guarantee card, put them in his jacket, kissed Fiona and left her to make her phone calls. As Fiona watched him leave she felt good about the decision she'd made about Craig.

It was raining again so Craig zipped up his jacket against the weather as he made his way along the street. For once he didn't mind the rain. It felt good. Better than good. He reflected on the fact that the hotel was on Princes Street, but it wasn't quite as metropolitan as its Edinburgh equivalent. He promised himself that the first chance he got he'd take Fiona out for a proper night on the town. That would be great. They had so much catching up to do.

The bank was a detached stone building which stood directly opposite the junction with Princes Street. As he approached it, he realised that he was too early. The doors were still shut. Craig crossed the wide street and went into a newsagent. He bought a newspaper and took shelter in a shop doorway, flicking through the pages then back through them again, front to back and back to front. Nothing grabbed his attention. No familiar names sprang out at him and no photographs made him jump in recognition.

He looked at his watch. 9:33. He crossed the street once again. The doors of the bank were open and when Craig entered there was already a small queue of customers inside. After a long five minutes it was his turn. He stepped up to the counter. Behind the glass screen a young dark-haired teller said good morning to Craig.

'How can I help you?'

'Good morning. I'd just like to cash a cheque please.'

'Do you have a cheque guarantee card?'

'Yes.' Craig knew that would allow him to cash a cheque for up to £50. Any larger and the teller would have to phone through to the account holding branch to seek approval for the transaction. For obvious reasons Craig wanted to avoid that at all costs.

He wrote out the cheque and handed over his chequebook and card. The teller turned to the last page of his chequebook to stamp the frequency marking page. Multiple stamps on that page would have provided another prompt for the teller to contact Stranraer branch, but Craig knew that the page was clear. As she examined the front of the cheque to make sure it was filled out correctly, Craig felt his heartbeat quicken. Please, please, please don't check your terminal, he thought. It was very likely that his branch had placed an alert on his account and he prayed that the teller wouldn't be tempted to look up his balance. There was no need to, the guarantee card was sufficient to cover the cheque. In theory.

The teller read the name on the cheque and looked up to ask 'How would you like your cash, Mr Dunlop?' but didn't get as far as actually speaking. A look of recognition flashed across her face.

Craig knew that he had never seen the girl before. She looked to be in her late teens or early twenties. He glanced at the metal name plate on the frame of the bandit screen and decided to gamble. 'Don't I know you? Amy, isn't it? He smiled at her, trying to make it seem as genuine as he could.

'Eh, yes, it is,' she said. 'I'm sorry, I thought I recognised you but I'm trying to remember where from.'

'I work in the bank too. I'm sure I saw you on a training course in Edinburgh. When were you there?'

'I did my teller's course last June.'

'That's it. I did my Lending One course at the same time,' he lied. 'I thought I recognised your face. How are you doing?'

'Oh fine, fine.' She looked again at Craig's cheque. 'You're in Stranraer, then?'

'Yes, for my sins.'

'You're a bit off the beaten track aren't you?'

'Visiting relatives. Just for a couple of days.'

'Oh, well I hope you have a nice time. How would you like your cash?'

'Fives and five singles please.'

Craig must have made an impression, or perhaps it was just professional courtesy, because Amy counted out new notes for him and handed them across, along with his chequebook and card.

'There you are, enjoy your stay.'

'Thanks, hope your day goes nice and quick.'

Amy laughed. 'It's Monday, that's a certainty.'

Craig said goodbye and left the bank the way he'd come in. He waited till he had crossed the street before breathing a sigh of relief.

He walked back along Princes Street and was a few yards from the hotel when he felt someone seize his left arm at the bicep and something hard was pressed against his kidney.

'Keep walking, Craig. Nice and easy.'

He jerked his head and shoulders towards the voice but the hand on his arm prevented him from turning round to see the man's face. He recognised the voice immediately though.

'Commander Anson.'

'One and the same. Keep going, let's join Doctor Irving and Miss Rankin.'

The hard object pressed harder into his side and Craig walked into the hotel. Nobody was on reception and no other guests were around. The two men climbed the stairs. Craig's senses had never been more alert. He was aware of the MI6 man's position relative to his own. Two steps behind. Craig put his hand in his jacket pocket. He felt for the Dictaphone he'd taken from his work almost a week earlier. He hoped that Anson's view was obscured as he clicked the recorder on. They reached the first floor landing and when they got to room 12 Anson rapped on the door lightly with one knuckle. It opened and Craig stood face to face with Blake.

'Mr Dunlop. Come in.'

Craig instinctively recoiled, but Anson jabbed him in the back and the two men moved forward and entered the room. Anson closed the door.

Brian, Fiona and Lynn were sitting on the double bed. Craig was shocked to see Lynn, and more shocked to see the state she was in. She had a large purple bruise below her left eye and her bottom lip was cut deep. She was wearing a baggy jumper and jeans, with tennis shoes on her feet. Without makeup and with her hair unkempt, she looked as if she'd been through ten rounds with a boxer. Craig rushed over to her and took both of her hands in his. 'Lynn, oh my God. Are you okay?'

'No, Craig. They've got Nicolas.'

'Good to see you again, Mr Dunlop,' came a voice.

Craig hadn't noticed the old man sitting on the window seat until he spoke. He looked up to see who it was.

'Professor?'

'Yes, I'm afraid so,' said Clive Prior. 'I'm sorry to disappoint you. I believe you know Mr Blake.'

The professor allowed himself the satisfaction of seeing the look of confusion on Craig's face, but only for a moment. His tone of voice changed as he asked his next question.

'Mr Dunlop, where is the document?'

Craig tried to grasp what was happening, but it felt like he was trying to climb a rope that was simultaneously slipping through a pulley. Eventually the rope ran out and he was falling through a vacuum. He looked to Fiona for help, then to Brian. Fiona looked frightened out of her wits, Brian only marginally less so.

'Mr Dunlop, I don't have time for any more charades. You may have thought your theatrics in my office the other day were very amusing, but may I remind you that both Commander Anson and Mr Blake have weapons. Please don't force me to ask them to use them.'

Craig remembered being told long ago that witnesses to bank hold-ups could usually describe the gun in intricate detail but couldn't describe the man holding it. On this occasion the received wisdom was wrong. Craig glared at Blake with a hatred he had never felt before. He took his hands out of his jacket pockets and balled them into fists.

Brian sensed that events were about to spiral out of control and diverted attention to him.

'Why was Mills allowed to stand trial at Nuremberg, Professor?'

Everyone looked at Brian. Clive Prior smiled. He knew what Brian was trying to do.

Craig realised it too, and unballed his fists. He couldn't imagine that the three intruders would let them live, not now they'd played their hand. He hoped against hope that Brian had some kind of a plan in mind.

'I'm impressed, Doctor Irving,' said the professor. 'I surmised that was why you might be in Thurso, although I wasn't sure if you were merely running and hiding. May I ask how you found out about Mr Mills?'

'By pure chance. I came upon the newspaper report of his trial.'

A wry smile swept across the old man's face as he considered the irony. 'If chance will have me king, why, chance may crown me, without my stir.'

He shifted position. 'I don't suppose it can now do any harm for you to know. In answer to your question, Frank Mills stood

The King's Prerogative

trial at Nuremberg through an unfortunate combination of circumstances. By necessity, only a handful of people knew of his existence.' The old man paused as he recalled facts stored away long ago. 'There was Churchill obviously, and the inner circle of the Special Operations Executive. But by the time of the trials, Churchill was no longer PM. He was defeated in the election of July 1945, as you'll know.'

'I can see why that might have been a problem,' said Brian with barely concealed sarcasm.

'Indeed.' The old man seemed to be relishing this brief opportunity to enlighten his fellow academic. 'Mr Churchill no longer had the authority to control the situation. The last throw of the dice therefore was to dispose of Mills. An attempt to kill him by lethal injection was botched, unfortunately. Consequently the security around Hess, or should I say Mills, was strengthened considerably. He was extremely well guarded by people who knew nothing of the deception. And the SOE itself was disbanded soon afterwards, so I personally could get nowhere near him. So Frank Mills was left to his fate. But by that time, Mills had already been well prepared. When the intelligence services discovered that Hess wasn't Hess it was too late, the trial had started and he was under the protection of the court.'

Brian continued to try to buy time. 'Mills prepared? What do you mean? How did you get Mills to play along?'

'It wasn't as difficult as you might think, Doctor Irving. He was already serving a life sentence for murder, so he was a man with very little to lose. He also had a wife and young family, so the promise that they would be well provided for was an attractive spur.'

'For forty years?' asked Fiona, finding her voice despite the panic that gripped her.

Clive Prior turned round and smiled at her. 'Well you see, Miss Rankin, once we had him in our control, we could get to work on him.'

'Get to work on him?'

'We had three years to programme him, as it were. Sodium pentothal was very useful in that regard.'

'The truth drug?' asked Fiona.

'In small doses, yes, it can be used as that. In larger quantities over a longer period, it induces a deeper level of autosuggestion. Three years was more than adequate to programme Mr Mills into actually believing he was Rudolf Hess.'

'You're talking about brainwashing,' said Brian.

'A dreadful Americanism, Doctor Irving. I much prefer the term programming.'

'You programmed him to believe he was Rudolf Hess?'

'Yes. But with the precaution of including amnesia as part of the programming. The rest, as they say, is history.' He allowed himself a brief chuckle at his little bon mot.

'And your job has been to keep a lid on it all these years?' asked Craig.

'Quite so.'

'Who do you work for?'

'Oh, let's just say I'm a conscientious civil servant.'

'It was you who had Claire Marshall killed,' Craig growled.

'I'm afraid that was unfortunate. Mr Blake was overzealous in performing his duties.'

Weeks of guilt, pain, fear and anger welled up in Craig. He stood up and made to lunge for the professor, but Blake anticipated the move and struck him on the side of the jaw with the barrel of his gun. Blake knew there was no contest between bone and metal, and Craig slumped to the ground. His whole skull seemed to reverberate as the room spun around him.

'That was unfortunate, Mr Dunlop,' said the professor. 'Do not try anything of the sort again or Commander Anson will be forced to hurt Miss Rankin.' Anson pulled Fiona to her feet and pressed a small black automatic pistol against her breast to prove the point. Fiona froze to the spot.

'Don't!' yelled Craig, regaining his senses in spite of the searing pain shooting up the side of his face and head.

'Please lower your voice, Mr Dunlop,' said the professor. 'Now, for the second and final time, where is the document?'

'I posted it to myself,' said Craig, reluctantly.

Blake grabbed a pillow from the bed and pushed it against Fiona's face, then jammed his gun deep into the fabric. Fiona's scream was muffled by the pillow pressing against her open mouth.

'I've had enough of your bullshit, Dunlop,' Blake spat. He cocked the hammer of his gun.

'No!' screamed Craig.

'Blake!' Clive Prior called his bulldog to heel. 'You will have your opportunity in due course.' Blake reset the hammer and threw the pillow to the floor. Fiona's face was wet with sweat and tears. She didn't even register that she had wet herself. Lynn comforted her while Fiona sobbed into her friend's shoulder.

'For fuck's sake Craig, tell them!' hissed Lynn. 'They have Nicolas too! It's over. There's no point.'

'Mr Dunlop,' said the professor. 'This has become tiresome. I know too well from personal experience that you would not part with the document. Listen to Mrs Simon. We've checked your room and both vehicles. Now, where is it?'

Craig was about to speak when Anson interrupted. 'I saw him come from the bank a few minutes ago.'

Blake stepped forward, dug his hand into Craig's inside pocket and pulled out his chequebook and card wallet. Craig held his breath, praying that he didn't check his other pockets.

Blake opened the plastic chequebook sleeve and felt inside the flap. Nothing. He checked the plastic card wallet. 'Hold on,' he announced. Inside was a small silver key, similar to the one he found in Claire's house. Blake held it up to Craig's face. 'This is a safe custody key.'

Craig said nothing.

'It's worth checking, professor,' said Blake.

'Last chance, Mr Dunlop,' said Clive Prior.

Craig said nothing.

'Take him to the bank,' said Clive Prior. 'Not you, Blake. Patrick, you take him.' The professor stood face to face with Craig. 'If you're not back in twenty minutes, Miss Rankin will lose an eye.'

Blake produced a knife with a six-inch folding blade.

The professor continued. 'If you come back empty handed, she will lose both eyes.'

Chapter 42

Craig and Anson left the hotel at 10:35. They walked down Princes Street side by side. There was no need for Commander Anson to hold a gun to Craig's back, or to grip his arm. Craig was in no doubt about what would happen if things didn't go according to plan. They entered the bank, and joined the queue of customers waiting to be served. The early morning rush was over and there were only two tellers serving. Anson decided to take a seat at a small table provided for customers to fill out bank slips. His eyes didn't leave Craig's back for a second.

Craig was third in the queue and he tried to calculate whether he would be served by Amy or the other teller on duty. He hoped it would be Amy. A customer went up to the other teller. She was a pensioner who produced a deposit account passbook and proceeded to fill out a pink withdrawal slip while she chatted to the young man behind the counter. Craig was now second in the queue.

A couple of minutes passed and the young woman in front of him approached Amy's telling position. She was wearing a pink nylon tabard over a jumper and jeans. Her dyed red hair was in a spiky pony tail high on the top of her head. Craig guessed she might be from a hairdressers' nearby. The girl handed over a £5 note and chatted to Amy while Amy rummaged in her cash till. Meanwhile the old age pensioner was putting her passbook and her purse back into a cavernous handbag.

Amy pushed a bag of silver coins through the hatch to the

pony tailed woman, who called a loud 'Cheerio' and hurried back out the door. Craig approached the counter and Amy smiled as she saw who her next customer was.

'Amy, hi.' Craig pulled a white pay-in slip from a slot in front of him, turned it over to the blank reverse side and hastily began writing. He hoped against hope that the watching Anson would think that he was filling in a routine request to access his safe custody box, even though the box didn't exist and even if it did, the bank didn't use such a thing as a safe custody access request slip.

He shifted his position very slightly to try to make sure that he blocked Anson's view of the teller, and he passed the slip through the glass. Amy picked it up and looked back at Craig in disbelief. She read the slip again:

Amy, you know me because my photo was in the papers. I am in trouble. I am being watched right now. DON'T REACT. Press your bandit alarm NOW and take me through to an interview room. I will explain there. PLEASE TRUST ME.

***

Clive Prior looked at his watch. 11:03.

'Mr Dunlop is late.'

'It's a Monday morning. The banks will be busy with weekend pay-ins from local businesses,' said Lynn.

'Perhaps.' Clive Prior looked out of the window at the street below. He saw plenty of pedestrians, but none of them was Anson or Craig. He watched the traffic on Princes Street for a couple of minutes.

'What do you want me to do?' asked Blake.

'Nothing yet.' He turned to face the three hostages, perched on the bed. 'You know history, Doctor Irving. A ship's company was always assembled before discipline was meted out to any member of the crew who had committed a misdemeanour. We should wait for your young friend to return so he can witness the punishment.'

The King's Prerogative

Fiona shuddered but she had regained enough composure to look Clive Prior dead in the eye. 'Do you mind if I use the bathroom?'

'By all means. But please don't take too long.'

'Will I go with her?' asked Blake, gesturing to the bathroom door with his gun.

'I don't think that will be necessary, Blake.'

Fiona went into the bathroom, and after a few seconds the others could hear taps running.

Lynn looked up at the professor. 'What do you intend to do with us?'

Clive Prior smiled. 'That depends on you, Mrs Simon. Will you keep your mouth shut?'

Lynn looked at Brian then back at the professor. 'Of course we will. No one needs to get hurt.'

Blake stifled a laugh. He looked at his watch. 11:09.

'This is taking far too long,' he said. A thought occurred to him. 'Come to think of it, I don't see how it could be in a safe custody box. They didn't arrive here until yesterday or Saturday at the earliest, and the banks didn't open till 9:30 this morning.' He raised his gun and pointed it at Brian's forehead. Brian screwed his eyes shut, realising that he had no more time to buy.

There was a knock on the door. It was a simple one, two, three knock from clenched knuckles, not the distinctive one plus two plus one tap favoured by Anson with only the back of his middle knuckle.

Clive Prior motioned to Brian for him to answer. Blake kept the gun pointed at Brian's head. 'Ask who it is and what they want,' he whispered.

'Who... who is it?'

'It's Melanie from reception, Doctor Irving. Just confirming that you'll be checking out this morning?'

Brian looked at the professor. Clive Prior gestured for him to answer.

'Yes thanks, I'll be down in a few minutes.'

'I've made up your bill for you, sir, I'll just leave it with you if I may.'

Everything then seemed to happen at once, but in slow motion. The door handle began to turn, and Blake moved towards it, swinging his gun away from Brian and towards the intruder. His attention was distracted momentarily when the toilet in the bathroom flushed. As his head turned towards the noise, the bedroom door burst open. First through the door was a uniformed policeman, who took two steps into the room before Blake shot him in the chest. A second policeman appeared right behind the first. He pushed his mortally wounded colleague to the side in an effort to reach the gunman, and Craig was third through the door. He launched himself full length at Blake like an inside centre diving for the try line. Blake fired again and a pain unlike anything Craig had experienced before exploded through his chest. It was a blistering, blinding pain that instantaneously robbed him of his breath and caused him to twist in mid-air. His momentum carried him forward and he crashed into Blake's trunk with his right shoulder, knocking him to the ground with Craig on top of him. A second later, two more policemen were on top of Craig.

Chapter 43

Tuesday 22nd March, 1983

'Hello?'
　Pause.
　'Hello, Craig? Can you hear me?'
　Pause.
　Craig couldn't feel anything. He couldn't move anything. Wait. He could sense light through his eyelids. Open them. Open them. Open them, Craig.
　Where was he? He blinked once. There were ceiling tiles. They might be polystyrene ceiling tiles, or maybe not. Where was he?
　A face leaned into his line of sight. The face was blurred. Craig couldn't tell who it was, it might have been a man.
　'Can you hear me, Craig?' The blurry face looked away. 'Nurse. Nurse.'
　Another blurry face leaned in to peer at Craig. Maybe a woman this time.
　'He'll be drowsy. A combination of the anaesthetic, the blood transfusion and the pain relief. Lie still, Mr Dunlop. Don't try to move.'
　Someone fiddled with something in his arm. Craig closed his eyes.

Chapter 44

Wednesday 23rd March, 1983

'Craig, can you hear me?'

Craig opened his eyes. He moved his lips but nothing came out. A straw was put to his mouth and he gratefully sucked in a little cold water. He swallowed and his tongue and throat burned. He took some more and the burning subsided a little. He blinked twice and slowly the world around him started to come into focus.

'Mum?'

'Oh Craig, thank God. Thank God.' Tears streamed down Marion Dunlop's face. She squeezed his hand. 'We've been so worried.'

'Mum?'

'Shh, you need to rest now. We can talk later.'

Chapter 45

Thursday 24th March, 1983

By Thursday Craig was able to sit up, eat a little, and talk for spells before he became too tired. The medical staff made sure that the pain in his chest didn't become unbearable, but the police needed the answers to dozens of questions and so the doctors performed a balancing act, allowing him to be sufficiently alert to be interviewed but stepping in and administering more morphine when the pain became too much.

The door to Craig's hospital room opened and in walked Bruce Cowie, his most frequent visitor, apart from his mum and dad. Cowie's team had spent the past three days gathering evidence and piecing together testimony from people who had come into contact with Craig since the day he hitched a lift out of Stranraer. They'd even tracked down the Rangers-supporting lorry driver who gave him the lift.

'Good morning Craig, how are you feeling today?'

'Morning, DI Cowie. Still sore.'

'Understandable given the size of the hole in your left shoulder. Best not move too much. Are you feeling up to talking for a bit?'

'Okay, they'll probably be back in to top up the drugs soon though.'

Bruce Cowie moved a chair and sat down next to Craig's bedside.

'How's Fiona? Have you spoken to her again?' asked Craig.

'Miss Rankin is fine, Craig. She's going home to Edinburgh with her parents.'

Craig visibly slumped. He'd been told that Fiona had visited the hospital every day since he was admitted, but he hadn't seen her because he'd been drifting in and out of consciousness all the time. He was disappointed beyond words. Hers wasn't the first face he saw when he came round and he so wanted it to be. And now she was going home.

'Are you okay?' asked DI Cowie.

'No,' said Craig.

Later that afternoon the police came back to see Craig. DI Cowie and a uniformed officer entered the room.

'Hello Craig, been awake long?'

'An hour or so.'

'The doctors say you'll be fit enough to move tomorrow. They'll take you through to Glasgow.'

'Okay.'

'I've got one or two questions for you.'

'Okay. Can I ask you something first?'

'Sure, what is it?'

'My parents told me about the policeman that Blake shot in the hotel room. Was he married?'

'Yes, he was.'

'I'm sorry.' He was. Two people had died because of his grandad's wallet. He hadn't pulled the trigger but that didn't make him feel any less guilty. He couldn't think of anything else to say apart from, 'I did tell the police that Blake was armed.'

'You don't have anything to apologise for,' said DI Cowie. 'It was your quick thinking that saved four lives. Five if you include your own. Doctor Irving is convinced that they were planning to kill you all. Having said that, if the bullet that hit you had been another couple of inches further south, we wouldn't be having this conversation.'

DI Cowie produced a cellophane bag with the white bank slip inside it. He held it up and read it.

'Amy, you know me because my photo was in the papers. I am in trouble. I am being watched right now. Don't react. Press your bandit alarm now and take me through to an interview room. I will explain there. Please trust me.'

The detective looked over at Craig. 'That was quick thinking on your part.'

'I was just lucky. I thought she might not to do as I asked. Amy saved five lives, not me.'

'You knew it was a silent alarm. Clever.'

Craig sighed. 'Not really. I guessed it would be the same as the one in Stranraer. No sound in the branch, but the police station is alerted. I've set ours off by accident before. Swarms of police show up within five minutes. It was the only thing I could think of.'

'That was clever with the Dictaphone too.'

'Well, playing the recording to the police saved time,' said Craig. 'I'm grateful that they took me seriously.'

'And you should also be grateful that they went in through the kitchen entrance at the back. Brian and Lynn said that Prior was constantly checking the window facing Princes street. I have a question for you though. How did you know that Commander Anson wouldn't shoot his way out when the police arrived?'

'I didn't know. I had to risk it. A public shootout in a Scottish bank would be the last thing he'd want. Or so I hoped.' Craig suddenly felt the pain in his chest come back with a vengeance. 'I'm sorry, can we talk later, DI Cowie?'

'Of course, I'll look in this evening.'

Craig was given more pain relief and then he drifted off to sleep. When he awoke, he could smell perfume. He recognised the scent.

'Fi?'

'Hi there stranger. Welcome back.' Fiona leant over and kissed him softly. 'It's good to see you. Your mum tells me you were lucky. I couldn't go home without seeing you, how are you feeling?'

'Better for seeing you. How are you?'

Fiona's smile faded. 'Not good. I haven't been able to sleep since it happened.'

'I know.' He knew why. 'I'm sorry.'

Fiona said nothing. She took a handkerchief from a pocket and dabbed her eyes. 'I just don't understand it, Craig. I don't know how you could let them do that to me. I had to see you. I had to ask you. Why?'

Craig thought his heart would burst wide open. He knew he should never have put her in danger. It was unforgiveable. No, it wasn't as simple as that. He was lying to himself. He knew the truth. The plain, awful truth was he'd allowed it to happen. He'd allowed them to point guns at her. To threaten her with disfigurement and worse. He'd protected the peace document when he should have protected her. He'd seen her fear and just when he should have moved heaven and earth to protect her, the one person she should have been able to trust let her down. Again. Craig felt the pain in his chest and grimaced. The pain became unbearable.

All he could think of to say was, 'I'm so sorry.'

'You used me, Craig.'

'No, Fi, don't say that, please.'

'Explain it to me then.'

But Craig couldn't give her the explanation she wanted to hear. His eyes told Fiona all she needed to know. She was right. When the moment of truth came, her safety had been secondary to his needs.

She squeezed his hand. 'I hope you get better soon. Goodbye Craig.' She stood up and left without looking back.

Craig called after her. 'Fiona! Please don't go...'

But she was gone.

At seven o'clock Bruce Cowie returned. He didn't take a seat, standing instead at the foot of the bed. After exchanging small talk for a moment, the policeman fell silent. Craig could see that he wore a strange look on his face.

'What is it?'

'There are some things I haven't told you.'

'Like what?'

'You need to know something. Anson is protected,' said Bruce Cowie.

'What?'

'We can't touch him.'

'But why? He was involved in a conspiracy to murder.'

'That's as may be. MI6 have pulled rank on us. He's being posted overseas with immediate effect. He cooperated fully with us however. Remember I told you that he called off his man, the one holding Nicolas Simon.'

Craig remembered. Then he knitted his eyebrows. 'And Blake?'

'We bartered Anson to get Blake. Blake has been charged with two counts of murder. Footprints we found in Claire's house match his boots. And now we have the tape you recorded. He's being held in custody in Glasgow. Commander Anson was flown to London by his own people.'

'And Clive Prior?'

DI Cowie cleared his throat. 'Em. That's the second piece of news.'

'What?'

'The professor was flown south along with Anson, and released.'

'You're kidding?'

'I'm afraid not. Part of the same deal. But that's not the news I was referring to.' Bruce Cowie gripped the rail at the foot of Craig's bed. 'He was found dead this morning. He hanged himself in his own study.'

Craig felt more fatigued than he'd ever felt in his life. The old professor had evaded the justice due to him after all he'd put them through.

'One last thing,' said Bruce Cowie. 'What was the document they were searching for? The one they mentioned on the tape.'

Craig had been preparing for this question. Now was the moment of truth. He sighed again, deeply. 'It was the original copy of the letter I found in my grandad's wallet. Brian had it, but he'd already returned it to my parents.'

'It wasn't in the bank at all?' asked the detective.

'No. The key I had was for a safe custody box in Stranraer, not in Thurso.'

'That was a huge gamble. Was it worth risking your life and the lives of your friends for an old letter?'

The words stung Craig. That was the question, wasn't it, he thought. Was it worth it? Was any of it worth it?

In the end all he could think of to say was, 'I had to get out of the hotel room to get help.'

'So the document wasn't a peace offer?'

'What peace offer?'

Bruce Cowie looked sceptically at him. 'We'll talk again later, Craig.'

And there it was. Craig was still protecting the document. Despite everything that had happened. Or maybe because of everything that had happened. He thought about Claire and he thought about the policeman who died and he thought about Fiona and his eyes filled with tears.

Craig heard the door open and close as the policemen went out.

A few minutes later the door opened again and Bruce Cowie came back in, accompanied by another man Craig didn't recognise. The man opened a briefcase and pulled out a form.

'Mr Dunlop? I'm from the Home Office. Paterson's the name. I'm afraid I need you to sign a copy of this. DI Cowie will witness your signature.'

'What is it?' asked Craig.

'It's the Official Secrets Act.'

Craig started laughing and winced in pain.

'What's funny, Mr Dunlop?'

'Nothing.'

Craig thought about refusing to sign but realised it was pointless.

'It doesn't matter,' he said.

Chapter 46

Friday 3rd June, 1983

Craig walked into his local. He hadn't been in the Ruddicot for months and he had to admit it felt good to be back. It felt like home, partly because it actually resembled someone's living room. The small bar occupied one corner and the handful of tables were arranged around the padded bench seating that ran around three walls. The whole bar when full could seat no more than twenty-five people.

Kenny and the gang were already there and the pub erupted in cheers when Craig walked in.

'Yeah, yeah, very funny, you lot,' said Craig, laughing. His left arm was still in a sling to support the muscles around his shoulder and he had an intensive course of physiotherapy to look forward to. This was the first week that he'd gone without painkillers since Blake shot him, and to celebrate he had asked Kenny if he fancied a quick drink on Friday night. Kenny had rounded up the troops by the look of things.

'It's good to see you all, thanks for coming out,' said Craig.

'Don't flatter yourself,' said one of his football mates, Jim. 'We've only come out to see Fiona. Where is she?'

'She's on holiday with her parents,' said Craig. He couldn't bring himself to say that she'd been avoiding him these past weeks. They'd only spoken a handful of times on the phone. Her mum suggested that he give her the space and time to get over the ordeal. He had no choice but to go along with Valerie's wishes despite the fact that he ached to see her.

'You mean she passed on the chance of a city break in sunny Stranraer?' said Jim.

'Come on, you might only have one arm but you can still get a round in,' said Kenny.

'It's alright for all of you,' said Craig, 'I'm the only one here who doesn't have a job.' The cheers and boos resounded in equal measure. Everyone laughed, and Craig knew he was going to be ripped mercilessly by his friends all night. Which is exactly what he would have wished for. It was good to relax in the company of old friends again, and to know that they hadn't changed towards him.

It was a good night. Craig moved on to soft drinks after a couple of pints. Three months of being on the wagon had turned him into a lightweight drinker but that was no bad thing, he thought.

Everyone asked him to relate the story of what happened during that week in March, but he had to apologise sincerely and say that he wasn't allowed to say anything. He said it was because the murder case was pending and as a key witness he was *sub judice*. It made life so much easier for him to use that as an excuse rather than admitting the real reason – that he had signed the Official Secrets Act.

He told them how he'd visited the bank, where he'd politely listened to Mr Grant telling him how proud they all were of him; and that he'd been to see Claire's parents. Helen went with him, and although it was a difficult couple of hours Craig felt better for doing it and he got the feeling that they appreciated him making the effort.

'What do you plan to do now you've nearly recovered?' asked Kenny's girlfriend, Susie.

'Well, in the next few weeks I'm going back up to Thurso for a visit. I'm going to see if I can convince Fi to come too, but after what happened I tend to think it'll be the last place she'll want to return to. Anyway, we owe a very nice bank teller a good night out.' He hoped that he'd be able to persuade Fiona to go, despite everything. He'd remind her that they promised each other a return to the Highlands after everything had calmed down. But deep down he knew she wouldn't go. Craig consoled himself with the prospect of returning to pick up the package he'd left at the hotel back in March. When he finally got out of hospital, one of the first things he did was phone the Station Hotel. The manager checked and was able to assure him that his package was still there. Did he want them to forward it? Craig said no thanks, he'd pick it up in person.

'I hear you've got some big news too?' asked Susie.

'Big news?' Craig frowned for a moment before the penny dropped. 'Oh yes, I'm going to university in the autumn.'

'Really? That's great news.' She gave Craig a hug. 'Which uni is it?'

'Edinburgh.'

'Oh, that's brilliant, Craig. What are you going to study?'

Craig took a sip from his drink and put the glass down on the table again.

'European history,' he replied.

THE END

Epilogue

Monday 17th August, 1987

The British military authorities in Berlin announced that Prisoner Number Seven, Rudolf Hess, was dead. He had been found in a small hut in the grounds of Spandau prison with an electric cord round his neck. The post mortem examination concluded that he had hanged himself.

Within six weeks of his death, Spandau Prison was razed to the ground.

The exact circumstances surrounding the death of Prisoner Number Seven remain a mystery.

Source Reference Material

I would not have been able to construct this narrative without the help of several rich sources of reference material. If this story has whetted your appetite to find out more about the mystery of Rudolf Hess's ill-fated flight to Scotland, I would encourage you to seek out the following publications:

Allen, Peter; *The Crown and the Swastika: Hitler, Hess and the Duke of Windsor*. Robert Hale, London, 1983.

Anonymous; *The Inside Story of the Hess Flight*. The American Mercury, May 1943.

Bethune, George; *1942 The Duke of Kent's Crash – A Reconstruction*. Dunbeath Preservation Trust, 2006.

Bird, Eugene; *The Loneliest Man in the World: Rudolf Hess in Spandau*. Sphere, London, 1976.

Douglas-Hamilton, James; *The Truth About Rudolf Hess*. Mainstream, Edinburgh, 1993.

Harris, John & Trow, M.J.; *Hess: the British Conspiracy*. André Deutsch, London, 1999.

Hastings, Max; *All Hell Let Loose: The World At War 1939–1945*. Harper Press, London, 2011.

Hayward, James; *Myths & Legends of the Second World War*. The History Press, London, 2003.

Higham, Charles; *The Secret Life of the Duchess of Windsor*. McGraw-Hill, New York, 1988.

Hitler Adolf; *Mein Kampf*. Hurst & Blackett, London, 1939.

Irving, David; *Hitler's War*. Focal Point, London, 2002.

Levenda, Peter; *Unholy Alliance: A History of Nazi Involvement with the Occult*. Continuum, New York, 1995.

Marr, Andrew; *The Making of Modern Britain*. Macmillan, London, 2009.

Moorhouse, Roger; *Berlin at War*. The Bodley Head, London, 2010.

Nesbit, Roy Conyers & van Acker, Georges; *The Flight of Rudolf Hess: Myths and Reality*. The History Press, London, 2011.

Picknett, Lynn, Prince, Clive and Prior, Stephen; *Double Standards: The Rudolf Hess Cover-up*. Time Warner, London, 2001.

Pile, Jonathan; *Churchill's Secret Enemy*. Amazon

Read, Anthony; *The Devil's Disciples: The Lives and Times of Hitler's Inner Circle*. Pimlico, London, 2004.

The author at Eagle's Rock, Caithness.